U.K. PRAISE

"Ross Raisin was named *Sunday Times* Young Writer of the Year in 2009 following the success of his first novel, *God's Own Country*, which had critics clutching at superlatives. If there's any justice in the world of literary awards, he should now be heading for one of the big ones. Far from joining that teetering pile of disappointing second novels, *Waterline* is stunning—a poignant, shocking, wry, shaming, yet profoundly generous, and cunningly crafted classic in the making. Overselling it? If you're looking for the definitive novel for our times, this is the strongest candidate I've read for ages."
—Mary Crockett, *The Scotsman*

"[A] modern philosophical treatise that drips with dark humor. . . . The mere cadence of the sentences and the meandering storytelling, in a lilting Glaswegian accent, cannot help but carry you away. . . . The dialect throughout is mesmerizing. If Thomas Hardy had wanted to rewrite *Trainspotting* it might have ended up a bit like this."
—Viv Groskop, *The Times*

"*Waterline* announces Raisin as a profound thinker as well as a distinctive voice."
—*Esquire*

"The counterpoint of personal grief and insurmountable social problems are, through Mick's decline, beautifully done. . . . The energy of the book comes from the language, which has the verve of a really good raconteur. . . . Harrowing, and powerfully expressed. . . . Raisin is a novelist of terrific ability and great verve. . . . One day he is going to write a masterpiece."
—Philip Hensher, *The Telegraph*

"The vernacular is only one aspect of the vitality and inventiveness of Raisin's writing. . . . A writer of outstanding talent and it will be fascinating to see what he comes up with next."
—Peter Carty, *The Independent*

"Masterly. . . . There are rare novels that embed themselves in your sensibility so profoundly you can imagine conversations arising between characters that never occurred on the page. . . . Completely comprehensible, yet operatic in its tragedy. At no point do we sense the mechanics of a story: the writing is so subtle and controlled, so liberated from the need for dramatic gestures, that it is hard to single out the individual stations of Mick's collapse. His disintegration is made all the more heartbreaking as the tragedies accumulate. Raisin's creation of Mick is a work of grace: a human being rendered by a triumph of ventriloquism and empathy through a geographically specific Glaswegian working-class voice. The obvious and daunting comparison is with James Kelman: that same austere mastery, sparkling with its own humour, belligerent inner voices constructing a cage of language beyond which the wider society and its oppressions become apparent. . . . Full of compassion and moral imperative."

—Alan Warner, *The Guardian*

"Raisin is shaping up to be one of our most extraordinary writers."

—Catherine Taylor, *The Telegraph*

"Heartbreaking. . . . *Waterline* is harrowing. . . . But it is also lovely and finally redemptive, and Raisin shows a deeper development as a novelist in this book. . . . *Waterline* is a great read, and Mick's story is one you won't forget. With this second novel, Ross Raisin confirms himself as an exciting talent, a unique, gifted, and generous voice, a young writer with a vision broad far beyond his years."

—David Vann, *Financial Times*

"Ross Raisin's debut, *God's Own Country*, was deservedly acclaimed, and *Waterline* is similarly impressive, with Raisin again making vivid, compelling use of the vernacular. . . . It remains to the last supremely empathic, and Raisin's powers of observation, intense."

—Stephanie Cross, *Daily Mail*

"Electric. . . . What impresses about Raisin is the all-encompassing nature of his imaginative empathy, and the way in which he makes the reader complicit in his character's fate."

—Andrew Holgate, *Sunday Times*

PRAISE FOR

Out Backward

"Ross Raisin's story of how a disturbed but basically well-intentioned rural youngster turns into a malevolent sociopath is both chilling in its effect and convincing in its execution."

—J. M. Coetzee

"The lush language in this debut novel has some fine literary ears (Colm Tóibín, Stewart O'Nan, Mary Karr) in awe. . . . Your heart goes out to Sam, creature of the moors. There's an ancient Celtic strain in Raisin's writing, all but unspoken: the idea that monsters are the embodiments of our darkest selves, pushed to the edges of normal life, straining on the outskirts." —*Los Angeles Times*

"*Out Backward* more [than *A Clockwork Orange*] convincingly registers the internal logic of unredeemable delinquency, a dangerous subjectivity that perverts compassion and sees everything as an extension of itself." —*Washington Post Book World*

"Undeniably he's made a new world. . . . Utterly frightening and electrifying." —Joshua Ferris, author of *The Unnamed* and *Then We Came to the End*

"An entirely original voice. . . . Marsdyke, who blends colloquialism with flights of verbal fancy, is like no other character in contemporary fiction." —*Sunday Times* (London)

"From the first sentence, Ross Raisin's deft (and daft) use of language makes the reader swoon. Soon enough, though, you start to feel woozy, as if drunk or under a spell, and by the time you realize exactly what's happening, he and his narrator are holding you close and it's too late to get away. *Out Backward* is equally twisted and brilliant—a lovely, upsetting book."

—Stewart O'Nan, author of *Emily Alone* and *Songs for the Missing*

"*Out Backward* is a helluva read—poetically pitched in the mode of *The Butcher Boy*, and with a plot that you race through. Raisin draws profound moral subtlety and complexity from his sociopath; we're deep in the madman's head, à la Dostoevsky or Kafka. This is a dazzler."

—Mary Karr, author of *Lit*

"First-time novelist Ross Raisin is artfully familiar with classics of the English demotic novel such as Joyce Cary's *The Horse's Mouth* and Anthony Burgess' *A Clockwork Orange*. . . . The plot is familiar, but not the way Raisin deftly uses Yorkshire dialect to create speed and a fictional space that feels new. . . . Here's a writer who uses obscurity to cunning advantage."

—*Los Angeles Times*

"*Out Backward* captures a dark voice with considerable flair and wit and skill. Raisin's control of tone is original, at times playful, a cross between the whimsy and lyricism of *Huckleberry Finn* and the nightmare of *The Butcher Boy*. This is a compelling, disturbing, and often very funny novel."

—Colm Tóibín, author of *Brooklyn* and *The Master*

"A few pages with Sam Marsdyke are unforgettable. Rare are the writers who can create such a funny yet terrifying narrator; the comparison is the murderous Francie Brady in Patrick McCabe's classic *The Butcher Boy*."

—*Financial Times* (London)

"Risk-taking, postmodern, yet defiantly readable. . . . Raisin not only narrates the novel in Marsdyke's voice, but manages to create a world out of the young man's anger and preconceptions. [He] never allows Marsdyke's perspective to shift, or his understanding of himself to change, resulting in a final scene as chilling as any in recent memory."

—*Globe and Mail* (Toronto)

"A masterful debut."

—*The Observer* (London)

"Sam is more than the sum of his language. For all his oddity, and the periodic glint of something jagged and sinister, he holds our attention, even as he slips closer to catastrophe—holds our attention, and our affection, too."

—*New York Observer*

"A beautifully written, utterly absorbing novel by an author destined for great things."

—*The Bookseller* (London)

"The most excitingly original new fiction talent to emerge in Britain since Martin Amis first decided to try his hand at literary satire with *The Rachel Papers*."

—*The Irish Times* (Dublin)

"A wonderfully unique novel—a comic commentary on rural decline and a deeply unsettling character study."

—*The Sunday Telegraph* (London)

ALSO BY ROSS RAISIN

Out Backward
(published in the UK under the title *God's Own Country*)

WATERLINE

Ross Raisin

HARPER PERENNIAL

NEW YORK • LONDON • TORONTO • SYDNEY • NEW DELHI • AUCKLAND

First published in Great Britain in 2010 by Viking, an imprint of Penguin Books.

HarperCollins books may be purchased for educational, business, or sales promotional use. For information please write: Special Markets Department, HarperCollins Publishers, 10 East 53rd Street, New York, NY 10022.

FIRST U.S. EDITION

Library of Congress Cataloging-in-Publication Data is available upon request.

ISBN 978-0-06-210397-0

12 13 14 15 16 /RRD 10 9 8 7 6 5 4 3 2 1

WATERLINE

I

One here, a soft fog of flowers painted on the front.

There's plenty more like that, plus as well the wild flower kinds. Meadows. Bustling hedgerows. A woodland clearing mobbed with bluebells. Hard to imagine there's this many types of card in the supermarket. A churchyard, quiet and peaceful with brown leaves blowing about. A teddy bear. And another here that's for some reason a cat gazing out the window at a sea view.

It's Robbie that wanted to put the cards up. He wasn't much wanting to do it himself, but Robbie had dug the heels in. What else are you going to do with them? Stick them in a drawer? Leave them lying on the counter with the funeral programmes and the electric bills? So now the pair of them are in the corridor, fixing them up to the red ribbon that Robbie's fished out from the Christmas cardboard box. The light dimming in the front door. Dull laughter from the living room, where the rest of them are sat watching the television.

'You know all these people, Da?'

'No really, being honest. There were some the day even, I don't know who they were. A few would've been from the department store. And then the family, course.' He nods at the living room wall. 'I preferred no to ask.'

Robbie is reading inside a card. 'They could've introduced themselves,' he says, closing the card and pegging it with a red plastic Christmas tree. It's normally the wife does this, getting up the greetings cards. This same red ribbon drooping off the pictures about the living room; pinned-up spruce as launch bunting around a ship, dutifully awaiting the chop from whichever of the wee begrudging women of the royalty have been sent up.

There's going to be too many cards will fit in the lobby and corridor. Robbie asks will they get up the rest in the living room when Alan and Lynn are away to their bed. No, he tells him. He isn't having these cards all about the room when Robbie and Craig are sleeping in there. No that it makes a great deal of sense but. When everything else in the room is some kind of reminder. Fact is, if you start taking down all the things in the place that are fingered with memories, then that's the whole house emptied.

Dear Mick,

Words don't say enough. If there's anything we can do, please let us know. All our thoughts are with you the now.

Love from Derek and Jean and all the family

One thing you can be sure, it's the women that have written them. Nay chance any of this coming from the husbands. All our thoughts are with you the now. No that it should be but, no that it should be. It was the same story earlier: the women all hats and hands and kind words while the husbands stood in beside them, cloyed up. He would've been the same but. No denying it. Silent, listening politely while Cathy said everything that was needed. These were men like him, guys he'd worked with, easier with steel sparks showering on top their head and their mate pattering bullshit in their ear. You can't blame them. As natural to them, a funeral, as redundancy. And the response aye the same: straight to the bar, boys.

'I was talking to Claire,' Robbie says. 'You know, was with Maw at the store?'

'I mind her, aye.'

'She was saying how bad they all took it when they heard. Says the place hasn't been the same the last year.' He looks round at the living room door and says in a quieter voice, 'She couldn't understand Lynn's stupid finger food either. Serious, what was all that about?'

'I missed out on it.' He takes a peg from the box and looks up at Robbie. 'They're trying to help, Rob, that's all.'

'Come off it, Da. Mozzarella fucking parcels? In the Empress? Fuck off. There was a whole black bag left afterwards at their end of the table.'

True enough. He'd actually watched Desmond clearing it out

afterwards, when everyone had went. A quick sniff and a nibble of Lynn's various parcels, weighing up the resale possibilities, before dumping them in the bag.

Mick had kept himself in with the main group, huckled together at one end of the spread by the sausage rolls and the cheese sandwiches, Robbie and his wife either side of him like a pair of minders. Craig keeping to himself, away in a corner. Truth be told, he wouldn't've objected trying one of Lynn's mozzarella parcels, but it would have meant going over the other side of the table, where Alan and Lynn were holding court with the rest of Cathy's family. Most of they lot he hadn't even seen since the wedding; so you're talking thirty-five years ago. And that's the ones that came. Some of these he'd probably never clapped eyes on in his life. He'd gave a bye to the idea of going over. Leave that lot to themselves, he thought.

It was only the weans, scootling about the place, who moved between the two groups. And the brother-in-law, of course. Man of the people Alan there, he didn't miss his opportunity to introduce himself. Heartfelt greetings to the ones he knew – quite a few of them from back in the day in the yards – never mind it was him who'd bloody laid them off. Christsake. Smiling away there. No hard feelings, eh? We didn't want to do it but see that was the times, there was no choice.

Mick had made sure to keep his distance. Took himself away for a pee when it looked one moment Alan was coming over to speak to him. When he'd closed the lavvy door behind, he saw that Desmond had gave a proper clean in there. There were toilet rolls stacked in the windowsill, and he'd moved the rotten rolled carpet that used to be outside the window. The blockages cleared from the urinals. A few extra pineapple-soap chunks. Strange how it goes but that was probably the only moment all day when he was close to greeting, when he saw that. He stood there a moment after he'd finished peeing and for a few seconds just, something got hold of him and it was an effort to stop the tears coming on. This pure strong feeling that you could only describe as utter gratefulness toward the guy because he'd cleaned out his toilets.

When he came back out, the brother-in-law had moved away, his big broad shape over on the other side of the room, doing the rounds. He was like a politician. Getting into the group at the bar, shaking hands, making sure everybody knew it was him had paid for it all.

Robbie is looking at him. 'It wasn't on either' – he jerks his head at the wall – 'that speech of his.'

Mick doesn't respond. He pegs up another card, overlapping them as they get near the end of the corridor.

'He barely mentioned you. Craig and me, sure, but anybody could've listened to that and thought you and Maw had never met – that she'd lived her whole life up in the Highlands with the sons of fucking lairds chasing after her. She'd have skelped him, if she'd heard it.'

He goes in the box for one of the last tree pegs. He isn't getting into this the now. No with the guy sat there in the next room. He keeps quiet, and the two of them get on with the job in silence a while.

'Sorry, Da, I don't mean it like that. It's just, mean, he's a bloody blowhard.'

'Robbie.'

'I know, sorry.'

They have done along both sides of the corridor. There is a small stretch just, by the living room door, left to fill.

'I'll put these up in the kitchen somewhere,' Robbie says, holding up his last handful. He walks off, and Mick stands a few seconds looking down the two lines of cards. The sound of the television gets louder, fades away again. There are two cards next to each other, he notices, identical. Foggy flowers in a vase. Intrigued a moment, he steps forward to get a look who they're from.

Pete and Mary; Don and Sheila. He must have opened these cards himself sometime over the last few days, but he hadn't took full notice of the names. Both couples were there the day. There hadn't been much chance to talk but it was good to see them. Familiar faces. The men bloodshot and bald the now but aye familiar. He sees Pete now and then because they stay no that far away still, but Don, he couldn't have seen him in twenty years. Twenty-one, in fact. He can mind fine well actually the last time he saw him: they were in the Empress, the same stools they'd been stuck to for months, fuck this, fuck that, fuck the brother-in-law, fuck Thatcher, fuck the dunny money, bastards. But they'd took their dunny money and by then they'd drunk most of it, and the last he saw of Don he was steamboats and drawling how him and the wife were moving out of the city. They were back the now, they told him. Found themselves a nice done-up flat in a tenement in Drumoyne, where the landlord wasn't quite the robber their last one was.

The wives must have read about Cathy in the *Southside News*. Went to the Co and plumped for the same card. He imagines Mary and Sheila going in for it, putting it on the counter with a paper, pack of fags, Lotto ticket.

He gives Pete and Mary's card a read:

Mick,

We were so very sorry to hear about Cathy. She was such a wee gem. I still mind fine well the launch days and the pair of us dressed up in our finest, and you and Pete three sheets to the wind! Pete is working on the crane at the old John Brown yard at the moment, of all places. I know the last year must have been very hard on you and the family, Mick. If there's anything at all we can do,

All our best,
Pete and Mary

He smiles. She does go on, Mary. He puts the card back up on the ribbon. He's heard about the crane. Turned into a visitor centre. He's seen it lit up pink and red at night a couple of times when he's been over near Clydebank. The last he knew, they were talking about putting a restaurant in the jib and making it revolve. He'd read that in the paper. It was part of a project to represent the industrial heritage of the area. A revolving pink restaurant. You've got to wonder how they dream these things up. And see the view? That's one thing for starters they'll have to change. All very well getting the full panorama but if all you're looking out on is a puddled wasteland every direction – gangs of weans playing football and smoking, pigeons roosting and crapping over the rusted fabrication sheds – it isn't going to make your mozzarella parcels taste much the better, is it?

In the kitchen Robbie has put up the cards on top of the microwave. He takes the last lot out of Mick's hand and arranges them in with the others. Through the wall, next door's baby is wailing. Mick leans against the counter and looks out the window at the back garden, the tubs of flowers that have gone thin and yellow, overgrown.

'Don't feel ye've got to stay, Robbie,' he says.

'We'll stay as long as we can, it's no bother. Anyway, Christ, we've come that far, there's no point us leaving yet.'

'I know that. But Jenna will want to get back soon. It's no right spending too long away when they're that age.'

'He's fine at his grannie's. Knowing Jenna's maw, she's probably teaching him how to make homebrew or go tracking through the bush.' He balances the last card on top of the microwave. 'Anyway, we're not leaving you on your own with the Highlanders.' He is grinning. 'How long do they plan stopping, you know?'

He's about to tell him he isn't sure, they haven't said, but just then the sound of the television comes loudly from the corridor. There are footsteps, which pause a moment, then continue toward the kitchen. Craig comes in the room without speaking or looking at either of them, and opens the fridge. He crouches, looking inside the door, but he obvious can't find what he wants and starts moving aside the packs of sausages on the bottom shelf.

'After a beer, son?'

He doesn't reply. Keeps looking, next shelf up.

'They're in the carrier on the side here, if ye are.'

He gets up, giving a quick look at the cards on the microwave. Then he goes for a can out of the bag over by where Robbie is standing.

'Thanks,' he says, snapping the can open as he leaves the room.

He wakes and looks out the window at the dark. A few wee lights on in a few distant multis. It's awful warm but. He considers a moment getting out of the bed to open a window, and stays a while trying to work up the energy to go do it, but in the end he gives it a miss and stays put where he is. Ye buried the wife today. She died, and ye buried her. Somehow it's no registering. He repeats it to himself a few times, but it's as though the words don't make sense, he can't get understanding them. What he feels instead is the same as he felt the day last week the hospital telephoned to say she'd passed away. Relief, is what it is. It is a relief the funeral's over, that it's went off okay; Craig didn't put the mix in; he doesn't have to talk to Alan about arrangements any more. He doesn't have to imagine her in another bed somewhere while he's lying here. Course there's other things he could be imagining but they're so far off seeming real they're out in fucking hyperspace. He turns over, sticky, heavy and sticky. It was hot the day too. Obvious enough they were all sweaty and tickling in their hats and their suits, but what can you do – it's a funeral.

He kept off saying it earlier, but he's really hoping Robbie and Jenna will stay a while longer before they disappear back to Australia. That he won't be left alone with these more testy elements of the household. Although surely the Highlanders won't be here much longer. There's nothing for them to do now that the funeral is over, and there's nay danger Lynn is wanting to stop around enjoying the luxuries. Craig – that's another story. And not one that he's too keen sharing, that's clear enough. He's here the now because Robbie's told him he has to be here, and probably he'll be away as soon as Robbie's gone. No that Yoker is the other side of the world, but the way he's acting it's fine well possible that it'll be Robbie that's back here again first. He needs to talk with him. Go for a drink. Find out what's going on in that brainbox of his. They both of them need to do that. And if they do, maybe best for his own part swerving the fact he's no greeted once since she died; that all he can think is: it's a relief, and when are all of these lot going to get out of the house.

2

The multis stand solid in a row like a picket line, looking down over the red tenement streets filing toward the Clyde. From up on the seventeenth storey, the view's a beauty. You can see the glimmering glass roof of the Botanical Gardens north of the river. Kelvingrove Park. The Exhibition Centre's silver armadillo. And further on, the skyline of the Campsie Fells, keeping the city in. Joe doesn't much look out at these things though. If he's looking out, it'll be at Ibrox. The ground's a few minutes' walk from the multi just. On match days, he can see the supporters coming in from all around, crowds growing on the pavements outside the pubs, pouring in through the streets.

This morning but he's having a see out the window as the sun comes up. Watching the dismal light peter in through the streets that run straight lines toward the river, bending only where they have to go around the stadium, or broken where they've took out the tenements and no got round to replacing them. By the river, there's the twinkling new apartment blocks at Glasgow Harbour, the dry ski centre, and down the water, the shipyards, what's left of them. Govan, this near side; Scotstoun, across the water. From where he is, he can just make out the top of HMS *Defender*, sat at her berth at Govan. She looks from up here like an Airfix model, with her miniature gun and helicopter pad on the flight deck. That's where Joe is headed, the light nearly up now and him away out the flat, clicking shut the front door to go pick up Suggie.

It is six o'clock. There's never anybody about in the building now except for one queer old ticket he sees on the stair sometimes, who gets up to give his dog a walk. It isn't so bad, this time in the morning. He's tired, but it's fine. The back shift is the one that kills him. He presses the button and the lift doors are straight open. They cleaned it out a week or two ago, so it's no bogging like it was, but it's been wrote on already. CUNT, one wall says, nice and simple. He gets out on the ninth floor and goes toward Suggie's.

He chaps the door. There's a light on underneath. A good sign. He's tired enough himself this time the morning, but he's pure sparkling compared to Suggie. There's times he'll be banging five minutes before there's any answer, and a couple of mornings he's resorted to giving it a wee clang with the fire extinguisher off the wall fixing. The door's looked better, in truth. Today though Suggie opens it on the second knock. He's in his pants still, but he's up.

'Come in, mate.'

Joe follows him in and sits on the settee while Suggie goes in the bedroom to get dressed. The television is on and he looks at it without paying much attention. There's a fair number of empty cans about, on the table, over the floor. Suggie must've had some mates round. No the less, he's dressed quick enough, appearing at the bedroom door in a couple of minutes, red eyes, grinning, his yellow helmet in his hand.

'Right, we off, well?'

Once onto the street the two apprentices get making their way briskly through the crisp cool morning toward the yard. They go over Saturday's match again, a couple of times, but most of the way they walk without talking. The roads are near deserted. A few cars. The old boy from their block, coming back with his dog. They give him a nod.

It wasn't always like this, course. Their fathers and their grandfathers have shown them enough photographs – photographs there's plenty of in the grand crumbling library they are walking past now – how it used to be. These same streets a hundred years ago, sixty, forty even, mobbed with hundreds of workers starting out for the day shift. Tired and quiet, like this pair, getting moving. The noise of boots on the road, the hooter about to sound up the way and signal the start of work. The occasional wife in a tenement window in her nightdress, watching her man off, and him finding his way into his own team, grouping up as they move on – riveters, caulkers, blacksmiths, the welders clear visible in their spotted hats and their leathers, boilermakers, platers – the whole black squad marching on up the road. And at the back, the apprentices, pishing about.

A different story the now. Two lads in blue overalls walking through the empty streets like a pair of convicts who've just survived the end of the world; passing by the primary school, the park, the red-stone tenements, and the terraces of grey pebble-dash houses with their wee patches of front garden.

One of these, the grass growing longer than its neighbours, has a great flash Saab parked bold as day out the front. Inside, Mick is listening to the brother-in-law snoring loudly through the wall. He's put them in the boys' old room, so they will be lying there asleep across the way from each other, the two beds having been pushed years ago as far apart as possible. The sound he's making, Alan must be on this side closest to himself. If there'd been anywhere else to put them, he'd have put them there, but there wasn't, simple as that. So they'll have to put up with it just, staying in a weans' room. Nothing has changed in there since Robbie was eighteen and he moved to Australia – it'd hardly changed in fact for a long time before that – the opposing walls still covered with football stickers and Blu-Tack scabs, a great worn circle of carpet between the two beds, faded from years of board games and fighting.

He turns over, toward the window. The snoring unrelenting. Christsake. The man can't keep quiet even when he's asleep.

Down the stair in the living room, Robbie will be slumbering on the floor with an arm curled around the wife. They are on a pile of stale brown blankets Robbie found from somewhere. No that they two mind. They don't. They're fine. On the other side of the room the older brother lying there in his sleeping bag and his legs poking out from the end of the settee. Thinking his thoughts. Thinking his thoughts and keeping the lot of them to himself.

The truth is, it is good of the Highlanders to have come. They could have drove down for the funeral and then been away back to their lochside and their mighty brick stronghold and that would've been that, never to be seen again. They don't have to be here. It is Alan's choice that they are. That's obvious enough, the way she pin-pricks around the house. The peeved squeezed eyeballs every time she gets inspecting a piece of cutlery or a glass out the cupboard. Go on, well, Lynn, what is it ye think, eh? Because ye're no making it quite clear enough with the subtle facial movements there. Ye think it's a dump, eh? Well go on, then, and get to fuck why don't ye?

The snoring has stopped. For a few minutes, the house is peaceful. A thin shaft of light is through the curtains, falling on the carpet at the bottom of the bed. After a while though, the snoring starts up again, quiet at first, then gaining force. See another way you could look at it: he's retired a long while the now, so an event like this isn't exactly getting in the way of things for them. They can make space for times like this. Births, deaths, the graduation of the miraculous son, no able sadly to make it yesterday because he's over in America, making his millions, how lovely for him.

As well, their summer holiday is by. A trip to France this year, cycling round the vineyards and taking photos of each other in food markets examining the local sausagemeats. He shouldn't be so hard on them. It can't be easy of course for the brother-in-law either, let's no forget, the responsibility he's got to shoulder. The responsibility he's aye got to shoulder.

Mick gets out of bed. It's early still and everyone else will be asleep, but he goes in the bathroom to wash his face, puts on a short-sleeve shirt and trousers, and steps down to the kitchen. He checks in the cupboard to see if there's any bread left, but it's been finished, so he closes the cupboard door and sits down at the table, looking out the window, where a wee disappointed sparrow is hopping about the grass wondering how there's nay food put out for him these days.

So this is grief, well. Sat at the kitchen table with all your joys and your miseries sleeping and snoring about you and you sat there wondering what to do for your breakfast. Maybe it's by, maybe that's it, he's gone through ten months already and the moment when she's dead actually marks the end of it because she's gone now, she's no laid there dying in front of him one day to the next. It's over. He'd greeted back then, alright, when they'd been told. On his own, or the pair of them together sat clutching to each other at this same table. That day the doctor phoned them up and asked could they both please come in to see him. The X-ray results were returned. It wasn't her back. Pleural mesothelioma. A total white-out of her left lung. A year, maybe, at the most. He closes the eyes and tries picturing her, her face, before that, while she looked healthy still. It's a blank but, the brain doesn't want to go there, so he sits with the eyes closed just. A moment of peace. You keep on. What else can you do? You keep on.

Down on the floor by the bin he notices a box of cereal. He picks it up, gets himself a bowl and shakes out the last flakes and the sawdust from the bag inside. The Highlanders are going the messages later, they announced last night, so there will be plenty enough food for them all soon enough, even the wee chap outside, given up and flown off the now. It'll be organic, course, but such is life, eh. Him and the sparrow aren't complaining.

Above his head, somebody is walking about. He puts the box back by the bin and gets the kettle on, returns to his seat at the table. And again, the same thought that keeps coming back: he is alive. He's the picture of bloody health sat at the kitchen table. The floor creaks again above his head. And no just him as well, still alive.

That evening they all sit in the living room with the television on, eating the spaghetti Bolognese that Lynn has made. Everybody agrees it is good and tasty, except for Lynn, who says it should have garlic and it should have tomato purée and it should have whatever else in it. She hadn't thought to get these things when she was in the supermarket. If she'd known there was none in the house she would have bought them. She isn't acting it there; they've bought no end of other unnecessary stuff. Parmesan, wine vinegar, three different kinds of bread. It must have cost a fortune. When they arrived back and got everybody outside helping unload the dozens of carriers from the boot, he and Robbie gave each other a look over the top of the car, the meaning of which was clear enough. How long do they think they're staying? They then proceeded to organize the putting away of the messages, cheerily deciding what was to go where, chucking out whatever dregs or no-good-enoughs were already on the shelves, as if by buying in all this better class of groceries, the kitchen was now theirs to do with as they wished.

The news is on. They sit watching and eating in quiet. It is the fifth night now Robbie and Jenna have brought through the chairs from the kitchen so they can all be in here, and they are in the habit already of keeping to the same seats. Alan and Lynn take the settee and, opposite, Mick sits between Robbie and his wife, the three of them sat close together like a row of naughty schoolweans sent to the headmaster's office. Craig is over in the armchair by the window, the head down, concentrating on his plate.

'It's some place now, the shopping centre at Braehead,' says Alan, setting his empty plate on the carpet in front of him. 'All new stores since we were last down there.'

The three of them look up and agree.

'I suppose it will be,' Mick says. 'I never go.'

'It's a great M&S,' says Lynn. 'Two levels, and a decent café. We stopped in for a sandwich when we'd done. And there's a dry ski slope down there now, I couldn't believe it. You should go over there and take a look, Mick.'

The weather comes on. It has been record temperatures for August, the guy says, and September is going to continue the same. Mick minds the time Cathy went down to the M&S, and what she'd thought about it, coming home with a single carrier of potatoes and mince. She wasn't impressed. It's too bloody expensive, was the verdict.

'You've seen the new apartments at Glasgow Harbour as well, have you?' Robbie says after a while, looking at Lynn.

'Yes. You pointed them out, didn't you, Alan? Very modern. About time they made more use out of all those dead areas along the river.'

'You think?' Robbie says, putting in a mouthful of Bolognese.

'I do,' Jenna breaks in, likely sensing Robbie's mood. 'Better developing than leaving it a wasteland.'

'There you are, then, Da. You should get one. You could have a wee balcony to sit on and look out over the water.'

Jenna gives Robbie a look, which because they are sat so close is right in Mick's face.

'There's no point leaving it to decay like it has been. Those cranes, and the berths all crumbling. It's not safe, for one thing. You're just being a mule, Robbie, you know it.'

He is feeling uncomfortable, these two starting to argue around him. He gets off his seat. Plus he needs to go up and check how much is in his wallet, to give toward the messages. As he leaves, he starts picking up the empty plates from the floor. Jenna is immediately helping him, reaching down for the Highlanders' plates before he has the chance. Maybe it isn't on purpose, but you never know. She's sensitive to things, Jenna; she knows the score.

In the kitchen they stack the plates by the sink. They're about to turn and go out when she presses her hand gently on top of his on the counter.

'You're pretty quiet today, Mick. How are you?'

'Coping on, I suppose.'

She smiles. 'It can't be easy, not when there's' – she raises the eyebrows a little – 'a houseful.'

He feels awkward, their hands touching there like that. Guilty, somehow, daft as it is.

'You shouldn't feel afraid to talk to these boys, you know. Even Craig. He's grieving, that's why he's being like he is.'

He tries to smile. She's a good girl, Jenna. Cathy was aye fond of her. She's down the line, is what it is. Honest. She's like Robbie that way, only less of the argle-bargle tendencies.

'It isnae that simple. He blames me.'

'He shouldn't. He's being selfish.'

'Aye, well. Maybe.' He looks away down the corridor. 'He keeps it inside himself. It was his maw he talked to.'

'Bulldust. You're here. And Robbie. He can talk to you.'

She takes her hand away.

'Come on,' she says, 'let's see how the party's going.'

'Okay. I'll be through in a moment, I'm going the toilet just.'

He goes upstairs to the bedroom. A ten-pound note, plus a bit of smash, it's all he's got on his tail. He can't offer that. If he gets up early again in the morning, maybe, he can nick out to the cash machine before any the rest of them are up. See what's in the account, then give Alan his share when he gets back. He'll tell him later the night that's what he's doing.

It's no exactly cheery, the mood in the living room. They're all sat there in the same positions, the television noisily on in the corner. It's like walking into a hospital waiting room, a bunch of edgy strangers pretending they're interested in the telly adverts – see maybe what he should do is bring in some old magazines for them to have a rummle through, distract themselves with the horoscopes and out-of-date TV listings.

He takes his seat. Looks around the room. Jesus. How long is this going to go on?

Jenna speaks. 'When are you back at the garage, Craig?'

They all turn to look at him. He keeps his eyes on the television.

'Don't know yet. Couple days. Depends how much is booked in.'

'Will you stay here or go back to your flat?'

'Go back. Too far to travel in from here.'

She doesn't push him. That's clear enough all he's going to say on the subject, and the room is silent again as they get back to their television watching. A quiz show. Two families in Englandshire competing one against the other for the incredible cash prize. A bald proud uncle with the spotlight on him now, chosen as the family expert on geography matters. A bit of patter with the show host as the countdown appears in the corner of the screen. Are you feeling confident? he gets asked. He is. It's his favourite category on the *Trivial Pursuits* at Christmas. Wee smiles along the family row.

It is the television that has become the centre of their movements. Up until yesterday it was Cathy. Her bed on the ward, when it had just been Robbie and Jenna here in the house, and then when she went, the arrival of the Highlanders and all the funeral arrangements to be sorted: undertakers, cemetery, wake spread; GP, register office, council. Now that it's all finished though, there's nothing for them to do but stick the TV on. Fact is, if it was to stop working they would be royally fucked. Or go home, maybe. He gives a keek over at Craig. He's sat with the arms folded, no expression, just staring. Don't come near me, is what he's saying. Don't come near me or I'll stiffen ye. He needs to get a moment to speak to him, Jenna is right about that. He'll be away without a word otherwise and then Christ knows what happens after that. Silence, probably.

He has brought it on himself but, he knows it fine well. No like he's made such a big effort to talk to the boy; ever, actually. All they years of sitting in the living room when Craig's come round to visit, leaving him and his maw to have their patter in the kitchen. It adds up sooner than you'd think, all that time. You start no to see that she's the one holding it together, and that without her, what kind of a relationship is there between you? Plus as well the boy as good as thinks that he killed her, which could prove a wee conversational stumbling block.

Alan gets up, asking if anybody is wanting anything from the kitchen. He goes out the room, quietly shutting the door behind him. In a moment – during which the bald uncle gets the spotlight took off him having pure disgraced himself as the family expert on geography matters – Mick follows him. He steps in the lobby just as Lynn is reminding everybody that she had known two of the answers.

Alan is bent inside the fridge. Mick comes in the room and he glances up at him as he pulls out a bottle of wine and sticks it on the counter.

'Would you like a glass, Mick?'

'I'm okay, thanks. No much of a wine drinker.' He stays by the counter, shuffling the great dump of post into more of a tidy pile.

Alan fetches himself a glass from the cupboard, pulls open a drawer for the corkscrew and gets opening his wine. Mick loiters over in the corner. He feels like a bloody houseguest. Alan takes a sip of wine and puts the bottle back in the fridge.

'You get to many Rangers games these days, Mick?'

'No much. Cathy being ill, it's –'

'No, sorry, I don't imagine you have.'

He has another drink of his wine. Mick fingers the envelopes. In truth, it's almost ten years, after Robbie left, since he was going to the games. And as well the season ticket increases. He slots the post in by the mini television. That's another thing will need seeing to before long. Brown envelopes. Some of these are from the same senders. Council. Housing Association. Her name is still on most of them. What happens about that, well? Is it the register office that wires it to all the relevant parties? Your computer tells my computer that such and such is to be wiped from the account. See the way it is with these bastards though, you more likely have to tell them yourself. Ten minutes waiting on the line to tell some poor bored hen in a call centre in East Kilbride that you want to advise a change in circumstances: I'm just ringing up to inform ye that my wife's died. Duly noted, Mr Little, I'll log it in the system for you.

Alan is staring away into the dark outside the window, drinking his wine. Then he turns round to him.

'How's work these days?'

There's a genuine unexpected topic of conversation between the two of them.

'It's a while since I've been driving, actually.'

'When do you think you might go back?'

'Well, I don't know. Soon enough. They said take as long as I want.'

'That's good of them.'

'Well. See they're no too busy.'

He should have said about the money earlier. Quick and simple.

'You know, Mick, you mustn't think that Cathy's family aren't here for you. They are. It's been hard for everybody.'

'I'm sure it has.'

'It's a really tough blow.' He makes it sound like a post office closure. 'You know any time you want to come up and stay at ours you're more than welcome. Have some dinner. Go out on the boat.'

'Right, thanks.'

Alan is stroking the stem of his wine glass. He turns again to look out at the small crap garden.

'Look, all this shopping,' Mick begins. 'Will ye let me give you something for it?'

Alan turns toward him. 'No, Mick, you don't need to.'

'No, I will. I won't have us not paying our way.' He glances up the corridor to the living room door, as though he's been sent to represent the others, the family shop steward.

'I won't take it. It came to a lot, anyway. I wouldn't want you to.'

'Wait here a moment just, will ye?' He leaves Alan fingering his wine glass while he goes from the room.

When he returns, Alan is stood where he was.

'Here.' He holds out the crumpled tenner. 'I'm going the cash machine in the morning, but here's this for now.'

The brother-in-law looks at the note a moment. 'Okay, then, Mick.' With a slow movement, he takes it from him. 'Thank you.'

He puts his glass down on the side and takes his wallet out the trouser pocket. As he flips it open, slipping the note in the back, there's an identity card, the top of his head poking out of one of the slots. A company card. How's he still carrying one of those? He's retired more than five years now. They must have kept him on, well – a consultant or something. An adviser. What I advise you is this: we've no enough orders for new ships and the yard isn't making enough profit, so get out the dunny money packets and lay the buggers off.

He is picking up his glass, and walks by Mick to the door. 'There's beers in the fridge if you want one,' he says over the shoulder.

Mick watches him away, the cards down the corridor flapping in the draught as his great back moves past them.

He stays in the kitchen a while, staring down toward the lobby. Then he opens the fridge and gets out a can. He drinks half of it in a single drain. Puts it down and wipes his lips.

Wanker.

3

It is hot and he can't sleep. The alarm clock across the way getting on for three o'clock. It's been pure stifling like this the last few nights and by now the heat is gathered in the upstairs rooms, no wind to blow it out. Earlier, Robbie and Jenna had went for a bit of air before bed, and came back saying it's near as muggy outside as it is in. Then Craig went out too, on his own, as he'd done the other nights. To the pub; you could smell it on him when he got back in. Mick had waited up after the others were away to their beds, but Craig was later back than usual, and in the end he decided it felt the wrong moment and he gave it a swerve.

He gets up and opens the other window. No difference. He leaves it open anyway and climbs back in the bed. She wouldn't've let him have it open. Breeze or no breeze. She hated a chill that much, grumbling on next to him with the covers pulled up to her chin, cauled tight around her. A soft familiar lump there in the bed. He stares at the alarm clock, waiting for the minute to switch over. This room, it's no like the other rooms. She has a say here still: the mirror with its collection of receipts and holiday competition cuttings wedged in the frame; the clutter of magazines by the wall; the electric heater on the other side of the bed with its broken outer bars.

He gets up again and goes out the room, needing the toilet. Afterwards, he goes down into the kitchen, where he turns the mini television on quiet, sits down at the table. Another quiz show. A young girl hosting it. She's got on this lunatic smile as she picks up the phone, waiting for the caller to guess the blank. The first word is *Iron*. The guy on the line seems pretty sure he's got it. '*Statue*,' he says. The girl turns to look at the giant screen behind her in mock excitement. 'Let's see if it's there . . . No!' She slaps her thigh. 'Not this time, Terry.'

It's fair obvious the people ringing up to do this at half three in the morning are either blootered or they're no the full ticket. The next one, a shrill woman called Christie, could be either way. 'Is it *board*?' she asks. It isn't. 'Unlucky, Christie. Better luck next time.' There is what looks like a flicker of desperation on the girl's face. I hope they pay ye well for this, hen. He turns it off and gets up to go back to bed.

3.54. The alarm clock, that's her as well. She'd got it years ago with his saved-up petrol coupons from the cab. He knocked it on the floor a couple of days ago when he was tidying up the things on her table, and the plug came out. Setting the time and date again proved a complete impossibility – he's never all these years figured out how the thing works – and so for the past two nights the alarm has come on at some point in the early hours. Both times, it took him bloody ages working out which button shuts it up, and then he spent what was left of last night finally fixing it out: time, date, bastard thing. No that he was that put out, in truth. He was awake anyway.

He moves himself over the other side of the bed. He may as well have stayed put in the kitchen. Given a call in to the show. *Iron Age. Iron Lady*. A look of pure relief on the girl that she's no the only sane person up the night. Down there in the kitchen, the living room too, the things are things just, she isn't present in them. Hard to say how that is when it's her that bought most of it but that's how it feels, unlike up here in this room. He's surrounded by her here, but he isn't a part of it himself. It is strange, the other side of the bed. Unknown lumps and bumps of wiring poking up at the mattress. He's got a queer awareness of what it would have felt like for her, on her side. He lies a while longer, staring at the alarm clock, until, at the back of five, he gets out of bed and lays down on the floor next to it, pulling the covers down over him.

There is a toilet roll under the bed. A pair of broken sunglasses. He should give a clean under there, he gets thinking as finally he starts to drift off. Add that to the list.

4

A cemetery worker is busy sweeping along a flagstone path, collecting up the dirt into a wheelbarrow. He has seen the man there by his wife's grave each of the last few days: he comes in the morning and stands there a long time, staring down at the ground. Obvious that he's having a hard time of it, and so he makes sure to keep his distance now as he gets about clearing the path and tidying the area around a plot he's to measure and mark later the morning.

He has seen the rest of the family here as well. They come all at different times; even before the service, he knows from his manager that there'd been some difficulties with the arrangements. A guy that it seems is the brother of the deceased comes with his wife, and they stay a short time rearranging the flowers; the son with the queer accent, he gets here after lunch and stays holding his partner's hand; and then the older son comes after the others have gone. He's always the one that stays the longest. Yesterday, he was sat on the grass next to the grave almost the whole afternoon, getting a book out at one point and just staying there reading.

He pushes the wheelbarrow off down the lawn to the store room, where he puts it away with the broom and the shovel. He fills a bucket with water and takes a stiff brush, a pair of black rubber gloves and a container of solvent from a shelf, then he goes out of the store and down toward the road. The cemetery wall has been defaced again – K.A.H., it reads, sprayed in large black lettering over the concrete – and he kneels down on the pavement to get scrubbing at it with the thick creamy solvent. From where he is, he can just about see the grey head of the man, grieving beside his wife's grave. Poor guy. There had been kind of an awkward atmosphere after the service, and it's a fair guess the family relationship's no the best. Always politics somewhere. He was in the yards, this one, according to his manager. That whole length of path is lined with the names of yardmen, copped their whack before their time.

A whole shop floor under that lawn, he'd heard the registrar say a while back, and it would be true enough, except that so many of them are the wives and weans. He keeps on scouring the wall a few more minutes – it doesn't get rid of it, but it's the best he can do, the solvent and then the sun beating down on it between now and when it gets painted over at the end of the summer. When he's done, he picks up the bucket and container and walks back through the cemetery, passing the man, who is stood now by the black iron palings on the other side of the grave, gazing down.

Mick is reading the tags on the flower bouquets. There's a new big bunch from the Highlanders that they must have got in the Marks and Spencer. A smaller one from Pete and Mary. He puts the tags back as they were, and gets ready to leave. The first few times he's come here, he's stayed almost an hour, looking down at the mound of not yet sunken earth. He tries to imagine her. It's no easy but. Each time, he ends up standing there just, trying to feel that she's there, trying to see her face, but it's no happening, is the truth – he may as well be stood staring at a car engine for all the closeness he's getting.

Maybe when the headstone is up, it will feel different. Although even that hadn't been without its difficulties. It was him that gave the inscription for it; Alan had paid. The only thing they'd went halves on was the coffin. When they were in the funeral director's, Mick had called for a modest and simple box, saying that it was what she would have wanted, although of course he knew fine well that if she had any say in it she would have gone for the most expensive one in the shop. He turns to leave, looking down at the space next to her as he moves off, lush and well tended, the stalks of the flower bunches resting down over it, like she's saving a seat for him on the bus.

The Highlanders are in the kitchen when he gets back, one of them carefully monitoring the grill and the other holding a saucepan.

'Craig about?' he asks, his head through the doorway. Sausage and beans, it looks like.

'In the bathroom, I think,' says Lynn. 'You ready for some breakfast?'

'Aye, thanks,' he says, eyeing the sausages as she gets turning them over. 'I'll be through in a minute.'

He goes up and waits just inside the bedroom, hoping to catch Craig as he comes past. But when the bathroom door clicks and he makes his move, it is Robbie that is stepping out. They stop there a moment on the stairhead.

'Been the grave?'

'Aye, I'm just back.'

'You okay?'

'I'm fine, Rob, thanks.'

In the kitchen, he and Robbie get themselves a plate of breakfast from the dishes on the table and go through to the living room, where the others are already eating.

Robbie and Jenna have booked their flights, they say. Monday morning. There's a stop-off in Hong Kong, and they could've arranged to stay a night, but they're wanting to get back to the baby. At the mention of this, Lynn gets telling the story of their own trip to India a couple of years ago: how the flight was a nightmare and the locals pack into the trains like pilchards, and there's cows in the road but if you hire a driver he won't even pamp the horn at them. Mick's not much interested in another of Lynn's stories; he's thinking instead how he's going to manage taking Craig aside. His best bet, he knows, is when the house is quieter, that's obvious enough, while the Highlanders are off on one of their visits to the Botanic Gardens or the Tenement House. He'll have to wait just, bide his time. Chin him before he goes visiting the grave.

But the Highlanders have for some reason decided against an excursion. They stay in the house fussing on all morning, and it means the right moment doesn't come; and so by early afternoon, when Robbie and Jenna return from the grave, Craig is out the door. Like the other days, he's away a long while, not getting in until the back of six, when the house is busy and the Highlanders are preparing food again. It isn't until after tea and the evening of television watching, when Craig is about to get up and leave, that he has an opportunity.

Craig is after excusing himself from the room, away to the lobby to put on his jacket. Mick gets off his seat and follows him.

He is by the front door, the jacket on, searching his pockets.

'I might come join ye for a nightcap, if that's alright,' Mick says, reaching for his own brown jacket off the hook. He can feel the eyes looking at him.

'Aye, if ye want.'

They keep on quick along the pavement. The blue light of televisions flickering through windows as they go down the street; heads, lager cans, weans lying on their fronts. Craig is walking at a fair crack. They stay side by side, and he has a job keeping up.

'Ye go the Empress, is it?'

'Usually. It's quiet in there.'

'Aye, well, nothing changes, eh?' He falls back to let Craig pass a lamppost, and hurries on after. 'There many in there ye know?'

'No really. Only Desmond.'

He chuckles. 'See that's what I mean. Nothing changes.'

Desmond. A fine familiar and reassuring figure. Comb-over wrinkling under the gantry lights; the big potato hands lining up whisky tumblers along the drip trays to catch each last drop from the lager taps. He should thank him again for the wake, he gets thinking, as they turn onto the high street. It's busy the night, smokers stood outside the Brazier and a queue out the door of the chip shop. Rangers were away the day but there's still plenty of Bluenoses about the place. The two of them march on through. Keen to get on and be sat down with a drink.

It's not Des behind the bar though. There's a woman he doesn't recognize as he goes up for their drinks and Craig sits down at a table in the corner. The tumblers are there on the drip trays though, so he's about somewhere. Probably in the back, reading his detective novels. Glass of Grouse. Fag plugged in the ashtray. Disturb me at your peril, hen, disturb me at your fucking peril.

She holds the glass under the tap and allows the froth to slurp over the rim, slowly pooling in the tumbler underneath. Mick turns to keek over at Craig, where he is sat by the window staring up at the football highlights. Why is it they're here, again? He's no too sure any more. What was he expecting – a nice wee chat? A pure certainty that isn't going to happen, and yet here they are; he's pushed himself on the boy to come out for a drink but now they're here he knows fine well it can only end in a fight. What choice has he got but? Nay choice. They need to have some kind of a conversation, whatever else happens. It isn't his fault the boy sits there like a cauldron and you can't get near him. Not totally his fault, anyway, no the full share.

He pays for the drinks. As he picks them up off the counter he catches sight, through the bar, of a recognizable shape sat in the parlour, hunched over a Guinness.

'Pat,' he calls through. No response, so Mick puts the pints down a moment to go round and say a quick hello.

'Pat.'

He looks up.

'Mick. How ye getting on?'

'Fine. Keeping a lid on it, ye know.'

Pat looks through to the main bar, past the two lagers sat on the far counter. 'Ye have the family with you, eh?'

'I do. All of them.'

'It was Tuesday, they said.'

'It was, aye.'

Pat nods. 'Ye have my condolences, Mick.'

With that, he turns back to his drink, and the matter is at a close. Condolences dispensed. They say goodbye.

Round the other side, Mick picks up the lagers and regards Pat a moment sipping his Guinness. He's certain a worse state than whenever last he saw him. The nose is badly gone the now, sore and swollen, delicately fractured with blood vessels. What do you expect? The guy's been coming in here for decades. He's in with the bricks. He was sat right there almost thirty years ago when him and Cathy moved back from Australia, his grumbling presence even then moiled into the sight and smell of the place, as crucial a part of it as the framed battleships along the walls or the great dark stain on the ceiling. There was a brief period just, after the smoking ban came in, when he stopped coming. Desmond had told him, the big hands braced on the counter, that he'd no choice but towing the line. He wasn't risking the fine. Pat had simply got up off his stool and walked out. 'That's fine, well. I will take my custom elsewhere.' And he'd went round the bar and left, simple as that, closing the door quietly behind him. That's me, pal. I'm off. Ye have my condolences. He was back within the month though. Climbed onto his seat at the bar and ordered his Guinness as if nothing had ever happened. No word was spoke again about the incident, and you'd never know that Pat gave it another thought except that now, whenever he goes for a smoke outside, he lights up his fag as he's walking through the bar, and takes that first draw while he's still in the lobby, getting open the door.

'Here we are, son.' Mick places the pints on the small table and sits in opposite.

'Cheers.' Craig takes a drink of his lager and looks back up at the television. Mick joins his gaze. Hibs and Aberdeen. No the most compelling TV viewing. The commentator is the main noise in the room, which is pretty empty. A few tables across there is a man silently out with his wife; by the toilets, the occasional whine and clobber of the fruit machine, a young lad going away at it.

'The Rangers game been on yet?' Mick asks.

'No yet. They won though.'

Through the bar, past Pat, there's two old boys on the faded red wall seat that goes around the parlour, pattering away together. He takes a long sup, observing Craig over the top of his glass.

'When did ye last get down?'

'Eh?'

'I say when was it ye last got down?'

'How ye mean? Down where?'

'Ibrox.'

'Oh, right. Years ago. With you, probably.'

'Christ, long time ago, that. Motherwell, was it, two–nil? I can mind that, I think.'

'It was Hearts.'

'Aw, aye, that's right, it was.'

They go quiet again. Get watching the football. The Celtic match comes on and the man and his wife turn to have a look at the screen. They've played at home and he doesn't recognize who they're against, but whoever it is, it looks like Celtic have cuffed them. Is this what he's been doing? he thinks with sudden pity. Sat here watching this keech on his own. Is it that bad he'd rather this than stay in the house? Obviously it is. What can he do about it but?

There's nothing he can say that's going to put everything right, no now, it's too built up, and the boy's obvious no in the mood to listen either so anything he says is just going to dig him up the worse. Being honest, the best thing is for him to get back across town to his flat. Go back to work. See his mates. He's no doing himself any good maundering away here, and the truth is, say what you want about it, but it will be a relief tomorrow when he's gone. There. He admits it. The bastard father, spilling the beans. Celtic's match is still on – three–nil, four–nil, more maybe – but Mick's gaze drops away from the screen and he starts staring at the wall underneath the television mount, at the brown pitted wallpaper like moulding orange peel, and at the pictures hanging unevenly in rows. Ships and footballers, mixed together: the *Bloodhound*, HMS *Valiant*, Davie Meiklejohn, HMS *Indomitable*, Willie Johnston, RMS *Empress of Japan*, Alan 'The Wee Society Man' Morton. Clydebuilt, each every one, crafted and revered all down the water, talked about over people's teatimes, sold off to England. Some of the players probably worked on these ships. They probably did; that's how it was. They would have served their apprenticeships on the yards, black squad, up early for a day's work, and then away for a quick shower and a bite to eat and they'd be down the training pitches. There was one guy he'd went to school with, Andy Loy, was in the juniors at Rangers: a great young player, fast, skilful, but he didn't make the cut. Close, but no quite. He'd stayed on at John Brown's instead, and become the yard's ratcatcher. A terrible job in truth but the daftie bugger had loved it. This wee stinking hut that he'd worked out of – the shelves piled with poisons and explosives and rusted weaponry – but the swarming hordes all about the place never getting any less because Andy wasn't going to risk losing his job so he only ever killed the male ones.

The fruit machine is ringing and a spew of coins clatters into the collect tray. The lad has struck it lucky. You can see by his face how pleased he is, the money falling out from the machine for quite a long while. Good for you, pal. Mick gives him a grin as he comes past on his way to the bar with the coins cupped in his hands, a wee smile from Craig too, glancing down a moment from the television. It's his own face, if anything, not his mother's. They've similar features. It gets more noticeable the older he is. Even a few grey hairs showing already. That'll be another thing he can hold against him.

He stays looking at the boy for a moment before turning back to the wall. Rats. That was one thing that never changed. As a wean, his da would take him into the yard sometimes when a ship was due for its trials, and they'd stand together in a big crowd of boys and yardmen as the ship got fumigated, waiting for the moment when hundreds of rats started pouring down the mooring ropes, and then the popcorn-popping sound as everyone got batting them with their shovels.

Desmond is walking over.

He stands over the table, a great bear blocking out the television.

'Mick. It's good to see you.'

'And yourself, Desmond. How's it going?'

'No bad, aye, no bad. Quiet, like, but what can ye do, eh?' He claps a giant hand onto Craig's shoulder. 'Robbie still here as well, is he?'

'He is. And the Highlanders. They're off the morrow but, any luck.'

'Aye, well, good of them to stay this long, I suppose. Alan been putting the mix in?'

'No, he's been fine, to be fair. Lynn's been cooking for us all, so there's no complaints really. Look, Des, I wanted to say thanks again for the other day. It –'

'Aw, Mick, serious, it's no a problem. Ye're very welcome. And it's no like I'm mobbed with custom, know?' He looks round toward the bar. 'I'm sure Pat coped with himself for a few hours.' He chuckles, taking the hand off Craig's shoulder, and looks down at the table. 'Another drink, boys?'

Craig shakes his head.

'No, we're alright, thanks,' Mick says.

'Okay, well, yous two take care. I'd best go see what state this bar's in.'

His massive arse is moving away to the bar. They look up to the television as the Rangers game comes on. There's an early goal. He doesn't recognize the scorer. Maybe he should try and persuade Craig to stay for another drink. Force something out of him, at least. How's he getting on up in Yoker, for one thing; is the job working out? Apart from the bits and pieces that Robbie's told him, he honestly wouldn't know. Does he have a girlfriend even? The thought of asking him something like that. Excuse me, son, but I was wondering just if ye're seeing anybody the now, and how does she get on with these thundery mood swings of yours? Probably he wouldn't be like that with her though. See she would understand him; she would make time and listen to him.

Desmond is talking to the new barmaid, showing her something at the till. After a moment they move along the bar and he pulls down a couple of whisky bottles from the gantry, unscrews the pourer off the fuller one and starts marrying them together, shaking out the last few drops from the empty. Then back onto the rack. He leaves her to get doing the rest of the bottles while he goes over by the till, carefully patting the comb-over, and observes her. The thought occurs to him then, minding the hand on Craig's shoulder, that possibly Desmond knows more what's going on with him than he does. If this is his hideout, where he comes to get away from the house, from him, he might well have talked a little to Des. Even if no how he's feeling, then maybe at least some of the other stuff, like how's his flat and his job, and is his boss a bastard and all that type of thing.

'I'm off home, Da.'

Craig stands up, pulling his jacket on.

'Okay, son, I'll come with ye.'

It is dark, walking back. The streetlamps are on, and there aren't as many people about as earlier, though there's still a queue in the chip shop. They turn off the high street, through an alleyway, and past a group of bevvied-up young lads playing football in the dim light of a back court. It could have gone worse, he tells himself. They got through it without any explosions, at least. That's something. Give it time, is the best thing. Let him be alone with himself for a while, no having to deal with people in his face the whole day. He's a solitary kind of a person, anyway, so he'll figure himself out if he's left to it. They come past the bus stop at the end of the road and as they get near the house he can see the lights are off downstairs, so Robbie and Jenna must be away to bed.

Even as he opens the front door, it doesn't really hit him that she isn't going to be there. There's no thudding realization whacking him over the head or anything like that, it's more a feeling like she's out, like it's bingo night or something. He goes into the kitchen and gets himself a glass of water while Craig goes up to the bathroom. The Highlanders have tidied away all the cans and the bottles into separate carriers, he notices. He drinks his water and waits until he can hear Craig coming down the stair. They pass in the corridor.

'Night,' Craig says, going into the living room.

'Night, son. See you in the morning.'

He hasn't slept in the bed any of these last nights. All the bedding is now pulled onto the floor, against the wall, with Robbie's old camping mat underneath for him to lie on. He's been sleeping better there. No perfect, but it's better. It still takes a few hours each night, trying to block out the sound of Fred fucking Flintstone through the wall, until he gets drifting off. And when he does, he sleeps in short, deep spurts, waking often, and usually from the most pure vivid dreams. She is there in most of these, even if it's just for a walk-on: crossing the road as he's waiting in a car stopped at the lights, or sat near to him at the bus stop eating a sausage roll. More often though, the dreams are about her, or the two of them together. He had one, she was in the kitchen getting tea ready, some keech on the mini TV in the background, and she's chatting away to herself as he comes in and gets himself a beer out the fridge. Then when she sees him she starts straight away apologizing, saying she's no had time to fix out a proper tea and so it's ham and eggs and he's genuine bemused, laughing, because what's wrong with ham and eggs – that's a great bloody tea.

It is colder the night and he's got the windows closed. Still the odd noise from outside: a front door shutting; a car speeding toward the river. He pulls the covers in close over him, and starts to feel quite snug there on the floor, and maybe it's the beer he drank but it isn't long before he has started gradually, comfortably, to drop off.

He is in the bed and she's lying next to him, facing away, snoring. He can't sleep, it's that loud. The noise increases steadily to a peak, and stops with a jolt; a moment of peace and silence as she lies there breathing heavily, and then it begins again. He props himself up on his elbow and looks over at her. The flesh of her neck bunched against her chin. He gives her a shunt with his elbow and lies quickly down again. Silence. A few moments' respite, and then it gets up again. He gives another nudge and she grunts to a stop. He closes his eyes and pretends he's asleep. She mumbles some nonsense a few seconds and goes quiet. After a while he feels himself starting to fall to sleep, the eyes slowly closing, but then she's at it again. He gives a real shunt this time, and turns quick over onto his other side. There is a chuckle. 'I know what ye're up to. Pack it in, eh.' He kids on he's asleep, but he can't keep it up and soon he's chuckling too.

He turns over toward her, but she's gone – he sees her suddenly over by the wardrobe, getting dressed. 'Come on, you, get a move on. They'll be closing soon.' He gets up and changes and they go down the staircase, but when they get to the bottom they are on the lower deck of a bus, taking a seat at the back over the engine, because she is cold. She keeps chuffing her hands together to warm them up. They are about to get off, and the driver calls to them to come over. When they get to the glass side of the cab he looks in and it is the barmaid from the Empress. She's got all these photos stuck up around the cab. This one of her weans, two wee girls, playing in a paddling pool. She looks annoyed about something. 'Go on, get off, then,' she says, so they do and they step out into the car park of the Co. He fetches a trolley and they go inside, where it's very busy, and hard to move around. He jostles the trolley up an aisle, with the wife in beside him reeling off a list of things they are needing: carrots, tatties, bog roll, flowers. She sends him off to the freezers for a chicken, but when he's got it he can't find her again, the place is too hoaching with shoppers. He tries going down the central aisle to look both sides and he is up and down twice before he sees her – she's at the checkout, sat in a booth. When he gets on the approach he can see that she's wearing a blue shirt and a Co badge with her name on it. He gets unloading the trolley and she passes each of the items over the scanner, her head down. He notices then that she is greeting. 'What is it, hen?' he says, but she doesn't answer, she keeps scanning the shopping. 'It's okay,' and he tries to take her hand as she scans the bog roll. 'We can go now,' he says. He can't see her face but he knows she's smiling, and she stands up to leave the booth, but the door is locked and it won't open. She shakes it, and he gets helping her but it won't budge and he can hear her sobbing again. 'Climb over it, hen. Come on, try, will ye? We can go now, look, I've got all the shopping – I got the tatties, see?'

He's said these last words out loud, he realizes, sitting up from the mat with a plaster-peeling sound. He stays a moment with his arms folded on top of his knees, getting his bearings, looking out the window to get a fix on what is real. The brainbox in a muddle still. He stares out as, slowly, it clears. There's something of a moon the night. You can see it above the dark blocks of the multis. Five or six black shapes with only a few windows lit, and the yellow spines of the stairwell lights – one of them flickering, up near the top.

5

Craig is the first to leave. His bag is packed up and ready by the door when the rest of them have finished their breakfast.

'What time will you start work tomorrow?' Lynn asks him as they gather in the lobby, watching him put on his jacket.

'I'm in early. I'll talk with my boss and see what's what.'

He gives her a stiff hug, and the rest of them line up along the corridor to see him off.

'Don't be a stranger, now,' Alan says to him. The kind of thing you say to people who are strangers.

'Okay,' Craig replies, and it is actually rare comic – the look on his face – it's that obvious he'd rather top himself. Mick looks over at Robbie, wondering if he's thought the same. Robbie's looking pretty serious but. He's next up, and he gives his brother a tight squeeze. There's a look between them that's hard to read. Understanding, maybe. Disagreement.

When it gets his turn it is in the end quite easy. With all the rest of them stood watching there's no question of a wee private chat, so they stick to the formalities just. A brief hold. A pat on the back.

'Come over for your tea sometime soon, eh?'

'Okay, I will.'

And he's away. Off to wait at the bus stop and get moving across town.

The Highlanders are next. A drawn-out carry-on of hugs and promises shortly after *Cash in the Attic*. Poor Lynn hardly able to bring herself to get leaving, she's that torn up about it.

They decide the three of them to go for a walk in the afternoon. The sun's come out again after the cloudy spell of the last couple of days, and they go up the park for a bit of a wander. It's enjoyable. Being able to relax and have a bit of patter finally, and no be wary the whole time of treading on eggshells. It's a shame there's only this day left. Robbie and Jenna's flight goes early in the morning. They've got their taxi to the airport booked already, and Jenna has tidied up their stuff from the living room. For now, walking through the middle of the park, past a fringe of small planted flowers, Jenna is asking him what his plans are for the next couple of days, after they've gone. He'll give a call into work, he says, see when they need him. Get the house cleaned up. Finish off the parmesan. He grins, but the pair of them have got their concerned faces on. Obvious enough what they're thinking: how will he get on, on his own? Will he manage? Will he hit the drink?

'How was it last night, with Craig?' Robbie asks.

'Yeh, it was fine.'

'Really? The two of you get to talk?'

'Aye, well, kind of. Mean, it isnae easy. But there was no bust-up at least. How, has he said anything to you?'

'No. Not much, anyway.' They slow up a moment as a young boy chases across the path after a football. 'See I was just wondering last night if he might talk to you about compensation and that.'

'No, he didnae. He has to you, then?'

'Not directly. I know it's on his mind though. He brought it up the other day, how more cases are being brought, and there's been some big victories and that. There was one last month, apparently, don't know if you saw, a hundred and fifty grand, he says.'

'It's no a victory, Robbie.'

'I know, Christ. That's not how Craig sees it either, you know. He's angry, Da. He's just angry. He needs to blame somebody. And they're as good as anybody, aren't they – the employers, the insurance companies – he's right about that, isn't he?'

They come past a battered play area with a swing and a mangled see-saw. The seat on the swing is come unfixed from the chain on one side, and juts down like a broken bone.

'Da?'

'I don't know, Rob. I don't know what I think.' He looks ahead up the path. 'You agree with him, then? You think we should put in a claim?'

'I'm not sure. It's your decision, Da.' He glances across at Jenna.

'We're obviously not going to be around through it all, so it's not for me to say.'

'Of course it bloody is. She was your maw too. You've as much right as Craig or anybody else.'

Robbie goes quiet as they walk on. He notices, further on, Jenna take his hand as the path widens and they come toward the far side of the park.

'Now's no the time to be thinking about it, anyway,' Mick says after a while. 'Come on.' And they leave the park with the sun still going brightly over the tenements, starting back to the house.

They get a carry-out from the curry shop for their tea, a bit of cargo from the offie. Robbie insists paying for it. Says he's hardly put his hand in his pocket the whole while he's been here. Fine. It's no like you can argue with him anyway. They watch a film after they've eaten – a good one, Australian, as it happens, even though it's just what's on the television. It's about this guy who's a notorious hardcase, robs drug dealers and cuts their toes off kind of thing, but who doesn't let a long stretch in the clink stop him from keeping up with his psychie tendencies: stabbing, torturing, and then writing a book and becoming a celebrity – true story, apparently. Robbie and Jenna tell him the guy's well known over there as a writer and a lunatic. When the film's finished, they stay up and finish the beers. Chatting. No about anything much, just chatting. It's good; he enjoys their company. It is the back of midnight by the time they're done, so when their taxi comes at six the next morning to pick them up, the pair of them are a wee bit groggy-looking as he comes down the stair to say goodbye.

He gets a good long hug off them both.

'Like I said, Da, I'll come over again soon. That's a promise.'

'Ye don't have to promise me, Rob. I know the score. It's okay.'

After the taxi has left he comes back inside and carries upstairs the pile of bedding that Jenna has left neatly folded by the settee. When it's all put away he comes back down and makes himself a cup of tea.

He gets a window open in the living room. Let the place breathe a bit, lessen the aroma of farting sons. Poor Jenna, serious. She for one must be looking forward to being in her own bed again, that's a banker. Getting back to the baby. It's been a long time away for them, new parents that they are, and he's genuine grateful they stayed this long. Robbie might well say that he'll be over again soon but it's a daft promise to make, which is how he wasn't entertaining it, no even for a moment. Maybe if they leave it a while, then next time Damien might be old enough they can bring him too. Get him introduced. It's one of the things he's had a struggle with, Robbie, that his maw never met the baby. He knows that, because Jenna told him. Robbie didn't want to say anything about it himself because he thinks it's too close the knuckle and he doesn't want to make things any the harder for his father. Which is daft, obviously. It's something he wouldn't've minded talking to him about. But that's Robbie: always this sense – whether it's the Highlanders, or it's Craig, or it's the compensation – that he's trying to protect him. Keep things from getting any the worse. That he doesn't completely trust him to cope with things on his own, without him, without Cathy.

He goes into the kitchen and opens a drawer. From under magazines and cookbooks he takes out a card, then goes to sit down at the table and read again the letter that is tucked inside it.

Mick,

I am so sorry for your loss. I wouldn't for a moment tell you I know what you're going through because it's different for all of us, but I know nothing can prepare you for when it happens. And when it does you need to know your friends are there for you, like you and Cathy were for me when John went.

It's not my place to say it Mick but you can't blame yourself. We didn't know in those days. How could we? There wasn't all the studies like there are now. I know it's a difficult situation for you because of Alan being in the management and now's not the time for it either, but if you want I can tell you the people to go to if you're thinking about going down the justice and compensation route. Like I say, I know you probably don't want to think about any of this yet but they knew, Mick. Even back then. They should have done checks. For Christ's sake, John used to come home in his overalls white as a baker and I'd shout at him for getting the dust in my carpets. It's not about the money. It's about justice. If you want to talk then please do give me a call. I'm on the same number. God knows, it might do me good myself. Take your time.

All the best
Alice

After a moment, he slips the letter back inside the card and returns it to the drawer. The idea of it – justice – seems pure absurd. Alice is gone down that route and fair enough, that's her decision, but the thought of it – how many thousands have died and still you've to tear yourself inside out dragging through the courts before any of these bastards will admit for a moment it's their fault. And it's no even him dead. Him that played snowballs with the stuff and came home with it stored in the turn-ups of his trousers. Justice is a word for it maybe, getting the payout, but it doesn't feel sitting here like the right one, no the right one at all.

He goes back through and flicks the tellybox on, settles himself into the cushions, and it isn't long before he is away to sleep.

She is there in his dreams again. They are that real – that's what's hard to get the head round. The two of them are washing and drying up. They're eating chips. They're arguing in the garden. Short dreams that come and go but don't finish, carrying on one to the next but connected somehow, linked up, like a chain of islands each with their different goings on but the same backdrop all around, the same light, the same weather following through the dreams so that if in one of them the wind is blustering at her washing while she hangs it out, in the next she'll be there in the crowd at a ship launch with everybody holding on top of their hats.

The sun is on his face, and he spots the postie turning in through the gate. He gets sat up. The body feels heavy, solid. He listens to the footsteps on the concrete and the clank of the letterbox. He is awake, that's obvious enough, but he has this sense of being detached from things. As if all these goings on around him – the sunshine, Phillip Schofield grinning on the television, the post tummelling onto the mat – they are all part of some other life, one that he can see, but he's not involved in. Mental, really. But that's what it's like. And even though he knows fine well that she isn't going to come down the stair and collect the post – open the door, chat with the postie – he can't shake the feeling that she will; that she is part of this other life, this real one, which he is outside of.

He will need to give work a call later, tell them when he'll be back. They've said he can have as long as he wants, but obviously there's the money to think about, and anyway there's no use really him rotting about the house doing nothing.

He gets up and goes over to look at the photo of Damien on top of the television. He's a cutie, that's for sure. Nay wonder they're keen to get back to him, the wee sausage-fingers. He is grinning away under a massive floppy white sunhat, sat on a rug on a crowded beach, all these brown bodies, baggy shorts, bikinis in the background. His own fat little body though is whiter even than the sand, which you know will be his maw protecting him from the sun, no doubt wary of the wee man's Scottish ancestry. You can see clear enough but that he's an Australian. Even at six months, that's clear enough. It's the eyes, the same as his mother's, big and happy, and no to mention the baggy shorts he's got on already. He's easy-oasy, you can tell. Not like Craig was. Jesus. Craig was never an Australian baby, that's for certain, never mind he was born there. Even as a tiny wean, he was Scottish as thistles, that boy. Greeting or sulking the whole time, and these great red skin rashes he got at even the slightest bit of heat. It was as if he knew already he was a Weegie even before they moved back.

No that the two of them had coped that much the better, being honest. He can mind well enough, even looking at this beautiful beach here, how it had been; how they'd become more unhappy the longer they stayed out there. Port Melbourne. It had seemed like a dream at first, Cathy stood queuing on the dock in her new dress, a whole shop's worth of creams in her handbag. After '72 and then the final ship completion at John Brown's, all the closures and the lay-offs everywhere, here was something to feel hopeful about at last. Free passage. Settling-in allowance. Secure job. Hallefuckinglullah. And it was a decent life too – sixty dollars a week, and no freezing your balls off like on the yards at home – although, that said, it did get sometimes too much the other way, and you'd be there in the plating shed thinking you were going to die of the heat. Stable work but. Strong unions. The wife got a job as a shorthand typist for a shipping firm and for a few years they were happy, they really were. There was the card schools on Fridays and the trips to the beach for the women – a giggling procession of them wrapped up like nuns, they were that feart of the sun. A whole clan of Weegies down there eventually, all staying together within a few streets. The Tartan Terrace. It was bloody true. Didn't last but, didn't last. After Robbie was born, and Cathy pure homesick to get back, biting his ear the whole time to tell him Alan had another job lined up for him, at Govan, where he was a manager the now. The funny thing as well: it probably made it the worse having all they Glaswegians around. That just made her long for the place even more, made it all the more obvious that this wasn't home, however much she tried to re-create it. Plus the heat. They never could quite get used to the heat.

Robbie has managed though. He's adapted much better than they ever did. Strange to think about it now, all the fights they'd had about him moving out there – he was only eighteen, what was he going to do? How was he going to live? – but he's proved them all wrong, that's for sure. He picks up the photograph and puts it on the small table by the settee. Tomorrow, after he's gave work a call, he'll go up the high street and get a wee frame for it. A good plan; that's definitely what he'll do. He is just sitting down again when the sparrow flies right up to the window, perches there, looking in. Here ye are, fat arse. He hops about a moment, and flies off. Poor wee guy, he's been waiting for something to eat round the other side, but he's been forgot about again. A feeling of guilt comes on him, and it's enough to make him get up and go through the kitchen to find the poor bird something to eat.

He empties the last of the bread onto the grass and stays there a moment, waiting for the sparrow. He doesn't come, of course. He's waiting himself, for Mick to clear off back inside, so after a minute Mick turns and gets leaving. He glances over the fence at next door's washing on the line, a baby-sized Rangers kit inamongst the socks and pants. Without even thinking about it he is looking in their garden, and he sees a cot and then the woman next door sat outside her kitchen with her Bristols out. Christ. He ducks down and turns straight around to look the other direction toward the houses on the other side. Fucksake – did she see him? If she did she's going to think he was spying on her, and how's that going to look? The wife's dead less than a fortnight and he's got his tit-goggles on already. He wonders then if in fact she knows about Cathy, if any of the neighbours do. Maybe they don't. But what does that matter – it doesn't – it's no like they spent much time with any of them all these years that they've stayed here. There's no noise of her moving about on the other side of the fence, luckily. He starts walking, slowly, stooped, back into the house.

Bloody hell. Still, you've got to laugh. He opens the fridge, but it's almost empty. Some sausages left though, so he pulls them out and gets a fryer going on the hob. Cathy would knot herself at that story, guaranteed. It's pretty funny, really. The sparrow is there out the window now, and he minds that's the last of the bread, so a sandwich is out the question. When the sausages are ready, he puts them straight onto a plate with a dollop of tommy sauce. He's no that hungry anyway.

He brings the bedding down and sleeps that night on the settee. It's pretty comfortable. More so for him than it would have been for Craig, clearly, himself being a good few inches the shorter. He stays there into the next morning, the sheets pulled over him most of the time because he's getting the occasional shivers, even though the sun is streaming through the gap in the curtains. He lays there and tries willing himself to phone in to work. He should tell them he'll be back by the end of the week. Crazy but he feels genuine nervous about it, even picking up the phone. Like he's a teenager who's met a lassie at the dancing, and he feels all jookery-pokery about ringing her. He minds that first time he called Cathy. Nervous as hell waiting for next door to finish on the line. All they prompts of jokes and conversation ideas written on the back of the *Record*, and his maw eavesdropping through the curtain of their room and kitchen.

'Hello, Muir's Private Hire.'

'Oh, hello, Lynsey? It's Mick Little.'

'Mick, how are ye?'

'Fine. I'm fine. See I'm just calling to say when I'll be back.'

'Aw, right.' There is the noise of the dispatch radio in the background. 'Look, Mick, don't worry about that. It's no problem. We don't need you.'

'No, really, it's nay bother. I can be in Thursday – actually, the morrow, I could come in the morrow.'

A storm of static on the radio and then a voice he doesn't recognize.

'Mick, do ye want to speak to Malc? He's just come in the door.'

'Naw, it's alright.'

'Okay. How are ye anyway? The family are there staying, I heard.'

'Aye.'

'That's good. Must be a comfort eh?'

'It is.'

'Look, Mick, take care of yourself, and take as much time as ye need, alright? We don't need you in, really we don't.'

'Right, okay. I'll see you, well.'

'See you, Mick.'

That's that done, then. His heart is beating quite hard as he puts the phone down and leaves the lobby into the living room. There he is again, the bloody sparrow. He for one knows what Mick's been up to, lazing on the couch, even if nobody else does. Come on well, ye greedy wee bugger, come on.

There's an unopened box of thin toast biscuits in the cupboard, something the Highlanders must've got in. He takes it outside, keeping crouched down, and breaks up the toasts, emptying the whole of one plastic packet onto the grass. He shakes out the crumbs, then he unsnibs the shed lock for one of the fold-out chairs and puts it up against the back of the kitchen. Better sat out here than sweating indoors. He opens another packet and eats a toast. Quite nice. He eats a couple more. There is the sound of a chair scraping on the other side of the fence. A moment later, and there's another. Impossible to know exactly why he does it but he slowly lifts his chair a touch closer, quietly, until he can see a tiny sliver through a crack between the fence slats. Part of her arm is visible. A bit of magazine. It's no that he's being a pervert, that's no it at all, it's – he doesn't know what it is – but he goes in a little closer so the angle widens and there, again, is her breasts. One of them, anyway.

Christsake, man, what are ye doing? But he stays looking, transfixed, with a kind of wonder, no really even aware of himself doing it, as if him and the breast are existing in two different worlds and somehow it's not actually happening.

A breast. It's pure jolted him. When was the last time he'd touched one? Actually touched one, except to sponge underneath? He hasn't thought of sex, he realizes, in a very long while. Not really. Not in a real way. The illness ate away at his own desire for it the same as it ate away at everything else. After a certain point, as she got worse, the need to get her comfortable, to stop her being in pain, it started overpowering all the rest. Even just the physical desire to be touching each other – not just the sexual ways, and let's be honest it's no like they'd been jumping all over each other exactly for quite a long time – but even just needing to be touched, you lose it. You forget. He turns away from the fence. No that it was like that at first though. He'd felt it keenly enough then. The fear of losing all that, their physical needs for each other, as it started becoming visible, even a couple of months in, that the disease was taking hold. She wouldn't let him see her. She started getting changed in the bathroom, and wore his trackie bottoms to bed. When once, near the beginning, he tried to touch her, she had turned away from him, sobbing, and after that he didn't try again for fear of upsetting her.

So that tit in the fence, it's a surprise. He gets up from the chair, looking the other direction – a man two gardens down the way sat with his giant white belly out, drinking a can – and goes back in the house.

There's a jumble of post on the mat. He gives a flick through it. A couple of flyers for a new pizza carry-out; more browns; what looks like a few extra condolence cards. He leaves the lot where it is on the mat and goes back through to the living room. Still this leaden feeling about him, lying in his stomach like a brick. The sausages? No. That was yesterday, and he'd only ate one of them. In fact he should get eating something, and that's maybe it even – the lack of eating anything – because he hasn't ate a full meal since Robbie and Jenna left. He's no hungry but, that's the problem. He'll think about it soon, he resolves, but for now he stays on the settee. Coming inside has made him feel a bit of a chill, so he gathers the covers over him and tries getting warm and comfortable. There's this sense he's got as though he's waiting for something to happen. Everything is dulled, even his hunger. He really is not hungry. Which is a new one. Normally he's a genuine trougher.

He wakes, taking a moment to understand by the light outside and by a dim calculation of the TV schedule what time it is. About six, he guesses. Hungry or not hungry, that means all he's ate in two days is a sausage and a couple of toast biscuits, which is a pure nonsense, clearly.

Fridge: empty, apart from the parmesan. Cupboards: a few bottles of things, a tin of tomatoes and the toast biscuits. He eats all of one packet, chewing drily, and leaves the last couple for emergencies and the sparrow. That'll do as a starter, he decides, looking out at the garden, and the gloaming coming on, the shed door no shut properly. There is the new pizza carry-out, he minds, but straight away gives the idea a bye: he hasn't enough cash on his tail, and as well the thought of going out, of walking on the high street and queuing up in the place with its new bright neons and the brand spanking plastic no yet covered in scratches and stuck with chinex. The effort even of thinking about doing that bears on him like a weight. But just at that moment he has a brainwave. The freezer. He's forgot about it until now and, getting open the door for a look in, it's easy to see how – it being something of a no-go area, the seal covered all around with a huge furry moulding of ice, like frozen moss. Still, there's things in here. There's all kinds of bags and boxes, although you can't see what any of it is because it's all glazed over with a thin dust of ice like a postie's frost, so he puts his hand in and gets brushing it off. Waffles, choc ices, boil-in-the-bag fish in sauce – no thank you very much – peas, the wife's crispy pancakes, which it's more than his life is worth stealing from her –

There is a sudden tug at his stomach, a recoil, like the instant of a fall before the insides catch up. His hands are shaking. A dizzy confused sick sensation and he has to grip the side of the fridge-freezer to steady himself.

Crispy pancakes. Bingo tea.

There are peas gone over the floor, but he stays pressed against the fridge without moving. His stomach is aching, and he feels sick.

And then he is – a dry, coughed-up retch of thin, clinging dribble. Jesus Christ. He didn't see this coming; he'd've been the better going down the new pizza take-out, all things considered, and he starts to chuckle, his forehead juddering against the freezer. See maybe he would've been done in there too, how could you know? They wouldn't have known how to deal with it if he had, that's for sure, looking confused at each other in their smart new caps and uniforms – this wouldn't be in the training.

The box is soft and battered the now, almost a year old. It needs chucking out but as soon as he has the thought he gets the dry boak in his throat again. Bingo tea: crispy pancakes, beans, tinned potatoes, tommy sauce. Her sat eating it and the strange chemically smell of those terrible fucking tatties, then off to the bus and a kiss for him and the boys. Now ye'll no let these two stay up the night, eh? I want them in their beds when I'm back. And always the wee grin between them as she leaves, because she knows well enough there'll be a pair of bahookies scootling up the stair when she comes in. He can see her, clear as anything. Her face, beaming, drunk. Mick, I've bloody gone and won – footering in her bag for the money – I've only bloody gone and won, see, and she pulls it out with a great daft smile like a magician's assistant. His eyeballs feel cold; he closes them. She won two hundred quid once. They spent a few days in Wemyss Bay and bought a mini television for the kitchen. He can't mind her winning that much any other time. Just little wins, tiddlies – ten or twenty pound – and she'd never share it, that money, it was hers, she'd declare with glee, and she'd buy herself tights and Barbara Taylor Bradfords.

He minds abruptly the woman next door; him spying on her through the fence. His stomach starts racing. What was he doing? He feels pure scunnered at himself, and he screws the eyes closed but the thought of it won't let up, the sense, somehow, that she knows.

He realizes then that his forehead is stuck to the freezer.

He tries to pull away but it's joined fast, and the skin stings when he tugs at it. Bollocks, he cries out loud, and draws back again, slowly this time, but no joy, he's too long frozen to it with sweat or tears or however it's happened, it doesn't matter – he's glued on the freezer, is all that counts. Bloody eejit. He is laughing, and it jerks on the skin. Leave him alone two minutes and look what happens.

He tries a new approach, damping a finger with warm spit and rubbing at the join, repeating the action over and over, hoping he might be able to peel away by fractions, but still it doesn't seem to be working, the skin feeling scorched now and him beginning to panic. What a way to go: we found him starved in the kitchen with his head stuck to the fridge-freezer. Suddenly geeing himself up, he places his hands either side and rips himself away. He yelps at the sharp burning sensation. Then, stupidly, as it dies to an achy tingle, he checks if there's any skin left on the ice. There isn't. He shakes his head. What a fucking haddock, serious, and he turns to bathe the head with some warm water from the tap.

Falling, again the sensation of falling. He rests his head, carefully, sideways on the kitchen table but he can't get rid of the falling sensation even when he shuts his eyes, so he just stays there motionless, listening to his belly underneath the table away on a merry dance. He can't see her now. Can't picture her face. The various parts of her are there still when he tries imagining her – the hair, the jimmeny teeth – but he can't pull back and get a sense of her, what she looks like, her face.

Ingredients: cooked chicken (2%), sweetcorn (1%), bacon (1%), coconut fat, smoke flavouring, sodium ascorbate, sodium nitrate . . . Jesus. If it hadn't been the asbestos killed her, it would've been the crispy pancakes. He turns the box over to read the other end, handling it carefully, like an old photograph. Fifteen minutes under the grill, simple as that.

There isn't any tinned tatties, or beans, so he grills up the waffles instead, and arranges them on a plate with the pancakes and a few thumps of tommy sauce. He sits a while looking at it. A familiar smell, and a good one, no like they potatoes. But it's a smell just. And it doesn't make him want to eat it. His stomach is bad still and he knows the second he puts a bite of this down, it'll be coming straight back up. So he sits, staring, toying at it with his fork, pulling open a pancake and pressing out some of the shiny cream gloop. Wondering what in hell he's doing. What, was he going to try and imagine that it's her or something, stupit, fucking stupit, and he feels instantly sick at the thought of what he's doing. He pushes the plate aside and stumbles over to the sink.

6

He cannot sleep properly. Each of the next few nights he wakes in the dark, sweating, the settee hot and clammy against his skin. Staring at the display clock on the video player, waiting for it to be morning. When the dawn does come, and all the familiar shapes in the room start becoming visible, he is up quickly, a restless energy about him. He moves back and forth between the living room and the kitchen, getting the kettle on, both TVs, opening cupboards, then no minding what he's looking for, shutting them again.

By the afternoons, he's tired out. No hungry still either. When it gets dark outside again he forces himself to grill up a waffle, but otherwise he doesn't eat. He stays in front of the television in the living room, not so much looking at the programmes as at the set itself, how familiar it is: the dusty top of the video player; the wee carpet troughs just in front of the broken rollers where it used to stand years ago, before Robbie spilled a Coke bottle over the whole area.

One morning, he gets up off the settee and goes straight upstairs. He strips the walls in the boys' room of the few dog-eared photos stuck above the beds. Then into the bathroom for the framed one above the lavvy; the staircase; the lobby; the photo packets in the kitchen drawer.

He begins piling them in rows on the floor in front of the television, like an audience.

After half an hour, the collection has spread to the settee – a crowd of Cathys laughing and posing, the head always turned a touch the left of the camera. Himself in a lot of them too, stiffly smiling next to her. There are more still with the boys in as he selects through the packets: quite a few from when they were schoolweans, trips to the theme park, the pair of them tired and wet in their macs, or chasing about in their first Rangers kits. One of these, he takes out and puts on the floor with the others. It's of the four of them all together, sat on a bench eating open bags of chips, Craig squeezed in next to Cathy, clung to her like a little demon. He can mind the day still. The first time they'd let the boys on the rides, Robbie biting his ear the whole afternoon for a handful of smash to go on the arcades, and some poor wee lassie boaking up on the rollercoaster, these long tendrils of vomit flying past their faces.

He can't get a fix on her. Even if he stares for minutes at each one, trying to mind what the occasion was, what she'd been saying as the picture was took, it's no use. And anyway, all this, it's just confusing matters, because these photographs cover years, decades, and she looks different from each one to the next. They are all *of* her, clearly – the pretty, smiling teenager, or here with the gelled fringe and blonde bubble perm – but when does the picture stop changing so that he might get a final hold on who she is? Not at the thin, sagging shape that she'd become, no danger. Even if he could pick out an image and say, aye, that's her, that is *her*, it wouldn't fucking be that one.

There aren't any photos of her like that though. The collection stops a few years back, when the camera seized up. The last one is Robbie's wedding. Himself, Cathy and Craig stood in their best, sweating in the sun under this giant tree and looking pure uncomfortable, done up hot and greasy as fish suppers.

It's no doing any good, this. He should leave it by. Plus he needs to get something to eat. The stomach is spitting tacks, and he's got to get something down him. Hard to move but. To get out the room and stop staring at all these pictures laid out on the floor. Each time he thinks he's going to get leaving a new photo will catch his eye and he'll crouch down in front of it trying to remember, trying to be inside it. One here that normally hangs in the lobby near where the coat hooks are. Port Melbourne. Cathy is knelt in her shorts battling on at the garden, her forearms stained up to the elbows in dark, red soil. She never could make anything grow. It was too hot and dry for all the wee shrubs and flowers that she fussed and footered over. In seven years, the only thing he can mind growing in that small, square garden was a single yellow dahlia. The rest the time it was full of balding lilac bushes and brown dead things. She is smiling but, in the photo, ever hopeful. Smooth plump arms. The tan line on her chest as she arches over, going at the ground with a trowel.

Was it already in her then? Dormant. Waiting. How could you know? You couldn't. She looks the picture of health here, that's what anybody would think, and Craig's babby toys are there in one corner of the garden so this is past thirty years ago, but it's possible it was in her even then. Probably it was. They're saying now it can be forty years, the incubation period, hidden away inside the body, inactive, until the moment it decides to crawl out and stiffen you. He peers in closer, even though he knows there is nothing to look for. And even if they had known, even then, would it have been any the better? Would the doctors have been able to stop it? Would they hell. Once it was in, it was in, like Thatcher. The end inevitable, no matter how long and hard the struggle. Better never knowing, is the truth. Better sudden and final.

Stupit, but he studies the other photos, looking for signs, anything. Something they should have spotted at the time. Obviously there's nothing but. Nothing. Only her getting older: smile creases around the eyes; the body a wee helping heavier; grey seams developing in the hair, until for a whole packet it's brown again, and then she lets it have its way and the grey returns.

Enough of this. He needs something to eat.

He goes in the kitchen and keeks warily at the fridge-freezer, and he is about to go toward it, but instead he starts scanning round the shelves and the cupboard tops. He opens a drawer and takes out the cookbooks and then the messy pile of gossip magazines, putting the lot in a pile on the counter. Then he's into the cupboards, taking out a mug, the biscuit tin, a handful of teacloths from another drawer, even a fish magnet from the fridge together with the faded offie coupon underneath. He brings it all through into the living room. He works quickly, too quickly to get thinking about what he's doing and stop himself for being a complete fucking eejit. He goes up the stair to the bathroom. There are things in here too. Her books: she kept the Barbaras in here for some reason he'd never been able to fathom, stacked by the door next to the wash basket, the covers curling over at the corners from damp. He picks up an armful and hurries them down the stair.

As he comes out of the living room again he sees the front door mat and pulls it out from under the post. He stares at it a moment.

Then he puts it in the living room with the rest, and goes back up for her lotions and potions – all of it still there untouched – shower cap, lady razor, her bloody toothbrush even, dried out now as a thistle.

He stands by the television and looks out over what he's done. The settee covered with all this stuff, a wet patch on the arm under the shower cap. Nothing. It looks like a bloody jumble sale.

He needs suddenly to be out of there, out of the house. The heart is going like the clappers and he can feel panic taking a grip of him, this sense that somebody's going to come in any moment and see what he's done.

There is nobody about. Only the sound of his own feet on the pavement, as if the city is emptied from around him. A fine day but. A beauty. The highest windows of the multis glinting in the sun. He carries on along the road and he is going toward the cemetery, simple as that, it's no a decision that he's made, it's just what's happening. When was the last time he spoke to anybody? There's a question. Robbie. No. Lynsey. The thought of it now, talking to somebody – a conversation – he can't imagine it. What would they talk about?

Still but it's good to be out the house. And the sun, a bit of sun on the face, it does you good. He is feeling relaxed. When he gets there he might have a bit of a sit down – there are these benches that he's seen, these old wooden ones that don't exactly look the height of comfort, with three slats for the arse and another three for the back, but so what, who's counting? See if there's one in the sun. A sit down. Maybe a wee snoozle.

It is quiet in the cemetery. The grass has been newly mowed. The smell of it is in the air, and there's shreddings on the path as he walks through past the large older headstones, ruined and leaning like teeth. When he gets to her plot he stands there a while, looking down. The mound has sunk a little, he notices. An odd thing, the peace of it. It's no as if she is here with him, he doesn't believe that – a presence of her beside him – and no that he believes the other either, that she is gone with the Big Man. See if they'd both believed in that, then she's more likely to be in the Bad Fire the now, the way they'd spoke about Him over the years. Anyway about it though, there is genuine a peace here, a slowing down of things, and it is making him calmer. He closes his eyes. Imagines the coffin, lowering slowly into the hole, the steady white-knuckle concentration of the pall bearers guiding it down like cargo. Until that point, there'd been nothing to associate her with this place. They never came here. She's never stood here folding up washing, or eating her tea, or going through him for this that the other that he'd done. Maybe it's because this is the only place she isn't missing from, maybe that's the peace of it.

He sees then the flowers, white ones with egg-yolk centres in a wee pot plant placed where the headstone will be. They are new. The old ones actually have been cleared away, so somebody's obviously come and spruced it up a bit. Craig. It must be. He's been in before work then, or his lunch break – no, he's too far away to get here and back that quick, so it must be after work that he's come, that he's coming. Keeping up his vigil and swerving on the idea of a visit to his da, who's no been the grave himself even once since Craig left last week, as Craig is no doubt aware.

He leaves down the path and out the cemetery, away down the street until he reaches the park. It is quiet here too, nobody about as he goes in through the entrance gate. It's always quiet in here, that's the best thing about it, and how they used to come in from time to time. No the worst park in the world. No the worst. No the best either but, don't kid yourself. All you find in here is the occasional old guy on a bench, or a group of schoolweans having a smoke, or sometimes a scaffer or two smashed up on the superlager, pishing up a tree.

There are plenty of decent-looking flowers in here. They are planted around some of the paths and the trees, and they're no that dry and wilted either, even with the weather like it's been. There is a bed of these nice red ones on the outside of a path that rings a chipped dribbling fountain. Just the job. He follows the path until he gets to the flowers, and he's about to bend down to pick a few when, a short way ahead through the trees, he keeks the parkie, pushing his wheelbarrow of weeds and dirt. Mick carries on along the path. When he comes back round to the same point, the parkie is turned the other way picking something up off the ground, but it's still too much a risk, so he keeps going round. The bastard's probably trying to trick him. Pretending he's fiddling at a plant when in actual fact what he's up to is putting the surveillance on your man here, who to be honest must look like some kind of nutcase, now on his third lap of the fountain. Probably he looks the part too. He's not shaved since the funeral, and also it's fair to say he could maybe do with a wash and a fresh change of clothes but such is life, eh.

The guy is still poking about up the way, so he moves right out of the parkie's line of sight, hiding himself behind a good thick tree. He stays there, waiting, each now and then sticking the head out to check the lay of the land. The parkie's got army shorts on, and a yellow high-vis bib, so it isn't a problem keeping track of him. He waits. Before long the parkie gets moving on, going toward a wee brick outhouse type thing, and Mick takes his chance, stepping out from the tree and quickly across to the fountain.

He kneels down, and starts nipping off the stems of the flowers. The blood is going, he can feel it throbbing in his ears. A grin coming on. Pretty daft, really, the way this has turned out.

'Hey! No, hey, you can't do that!'

He's been clocked. Sounds like an East Europe. He stands up and runs for it.

The guy is still shouting behind him, but Mick doesn't turn round, he makes for the entrance, the stomach cramping and his breath all over the place. Stupit, stupit, pure fucking ridiculous, but all the same there's something of a thrill about having done it and as he gets to the road he holds the flowers aloft, punching them in the air like a baton. He starts laughing. Ye great bloody bampot, serious. He slows to a jog along the pavement and looks round over the palings, where the parkie is standing some distance off, watching him, probably confused at why some headbanger has just nicked his flowers.

He lays the flowers down on the grave, a little way off from the others, and leaves.

When he reaches the turn into his street, he is still breathing quite heavily. In fact that is probably the first exercise he's had in years. Plus as well no having eaten. Nay wonder he's a mess. He is turned into the street and it is quiet, but as he walks on he sees, further up the pavement, one of the drivers from Muir's. Steve. Impossible to know if he's spotted him yet, but there's no turning around the now, it'll be too obvious if he does. Panic starts immediately to tighten through him. He lowers the head and speeds up, staring down at the street, his feet scuffing the tarmac, dog-ends floating beneath the grates of each stank he comes past. The heart is off again, beating wildly – look at the feet, look at the feet – but course that's just going to make him look the more pitiful, isn't it, but so what, so what, if it stops him getting noticed just, stops the possibility of a conversation, of being forced into the world of other people. He should have passed by now. Mick looks up, slowly, angling his head gradually to take in more of the pavement ahead. They've missed each other. He's not been spotted. Relief pours through him, and he glances round to see Steve, a fair way past and crossed onto the other side the road, away with his carriers.

The house. The front door. It opens with a wee stiff shove and there the lobby and the corridor, dark and cool after coming in from the sunshine. The silence of it. Where to put yourself. He comes in and goes through to the kitchen. Gets the kettle going. Mugs clinking out of the cupboard. What a bloody morning. Christsake.

He has made two mugs. No point dwelling on it though. He tips one down the sink and takes hold of the other in both hands, letting it warm through the fingers. Something of a queer smell – probably the milk isn't the freshest. It's fine but, fine, he'll drink it. And then the question again, where to put yourself? What to do now?

What is it that retired folk do with theyselves? All that time they have. Feeding the sparrows, the tellybox on, the park, wee familiar walks down the water, stopping and sitting to chat about this and that. All the patter you can have about characters from the past and how things were before the yards were closed, and what do ye think the now of these high and mighty new flats going up across the way there? The Iron Ladies, as ye used to call them.

There it all is still in the living room. The jumble sale on the settee and the photos still scattered over the floor. It seems even more ridiculous the now than it did before, but he leaves everything where it is and goes to sit in the armchair and finish his tea. He scans out over the photographs, and notices that a couple of them are gone partly under the settee. He gets up and pulls them out. Black and whites, good ones, he'd no paid them much attention earlier. One of them doesn't have Cathy in, he's put it out by mistake: it's himself just, he looks about nine or ten, so it can't be long after his da died, and he's stood in the back court outside him and his maw's tenement, grinning for the camera.

The other one is even better. He can mind it exactly. Twentieth of September, 1967. Launch day of the *QE2*. You don't forget a day like that. He picks up the photo and takes it over to the armchair. Even though it's faded you can still see what a sunny day it was, the yard mobbed with a great crowd, more than 30,000 there. Cathy had fussed on that much when he'd gone to pick her up, getting her clothes right and her flask and her oatcakes ready, that by the time they arrived the yard was that busy it took over half an hour for them to find Pete and Mary. In the photo, the four of them are stood in a line with their arms around each other's shoulders. He can mind even who it was had took it for them: this wee doddery man in a suit with his hair greased down, parted in a side-shed, who'd gave them his walking stick to look after while he fiddled on trying to get understanding the camera buttons. Cathy and Mary, in their bonniest dresses, holding hands. Himself and Pete blootered. Pete is holding the old boy's stick, leaning down on it, and the rest of them laughing at him.

He stares at the picture. He knows the face as well as if he was seventeen still. But it's just a picture. It doesn't tell you who she is. It's just a picture of a young girl on the edge of a photograph, giggling next to her best pal. Mary. He recognizes that face keen enough too. Cathy standing just off to the side, like she always would, no that Mary was any the prettier, nay chance, it was a question of confidence just, that's all it ever was, and Cathy a wee touch the rounder maybe but so what? At the very beginning it was Mary that him and Pete both had their eyes on. And it had dug his insides up at the time when it was Pete lumbered her first at the dancing, and even then that was only because Pete was further on with the refreshments that night.

Cathy knew all this. She'd told the story that many times herself. Still but. Mary had been first choice; see you could joke about it all you like but that was how it had happened. There's no changing it.

Easy to forget with all the time that's passed. For him, anyway, easy for him to forget. But then you start to wonder: does something like that ever genuine go away? Even after the yard folded and the four of them drifted apart – Cathy and him away to Australia, Pete and Mary to one of the New Towns on the outskirts of the city – did she ever think about it?

He and Cathy would only have been seeing each other a couple of months when this photo was took. Probably he was still beeling at Pete. No that you can tell here, the two of them staggering about holding on to each other, fresh from another visit to the friendly old hen in the pinafore apron handing out the specially blended *QE2* whisky. Yous two again, well? Go on, then, give me your cups, ye pair of troublemakers. Near to her, there'd been the bookie taking bets what the name would be: Churchill at three to one, and him and Pete had the John F. Kennedy at five to one, and he can't mind what odds *QE2* had been but certain nobody had guessed it would be that. Except for auld Aberconway, that is, John Brown's chairman, stood up on deck, Princess Margaret in her white wool coat stood in next to him. And then the Queen herself, of course, she knew; even a wee smile from her as she cuts the ribbon and presses the release button, the crowd starting up with the chants when the ship doesn't budge off her blocks. 'We shall not be moved,' they'd sung. Pete shouting out, 'Give her a shove!' and the girls trying to get him to shut his mouth. Then a moment later she starts to shift and there's a great cheer goes up as she slides down into the water and seven hundred tons of drag chain scutter down the slipway after her.

In an instant he is up and grabbing an armful of all this stuff from the settee, bundling it against his chest and away out the room, up the stair.

A shove of the bedroom door and he goes quickly inside, no hanging about as he drops the things onto the bed, the sheets bare and wrinkled, a slant of light hitting where the pillows would be.

He doesn't bother with putting the photos in their proper places, he piles them all together and gets them taken up to the bedroom with the rest, a sweat coming on as he hurries up and down the stair. He can picture Mary well enough. He can see what she looks like – the exact image of her face less than a fortnight ago at the funeral talking to him and giving him her consolations. He can see Mary; but he can't see the wife. In fact he can see just about anybody he puts his mind to apart from her, he can picture Phillip fucking Schofield the better than he can Cathy – the squeezy-arsed grin and the silver hair and the all-of-a-sudden serious hands clasped together leaning forward – there he is, fucking Phillip Schofield.

He collects the cookbooks, magazines, the Barbaras, the lot, all of it dumped into the bedroom, a dribble of sweat running down his temple now as he comes back in the living room for more. All this stuff, he needs shut of it. It's not helping him remember her – no in the right way, it isn't, no the right way at all – it's just reminding him she's dead. And that applies to all of it, the whole fucking lot: tapes, tape player, plant pots, salt cellar, vacuum cleaner, all of it, it can all fucking go.

He stands there, looking around him. Dark outside the window. The room is almost bare: just the settee, the armchair and the television, rooted, in defiance, to their usual positions. He sits down and puts the TV on. The carpet could do with a clean: collections of dust and dirt lined in squares and circles over the floor. The vacuum is away though, buried in the bedroom under a ton of other stuff; and anyway he doesn't care that it's dirty, what does it matter, there's no point being in there even, and he gets up suddenly to go to the kitchen. His mouth is parched. He gets himself a glass of water, drinks it down next to the sink and is about to sit down at the table, only he can't shake this feeling that he needs to keep moving – keep doing something – and if he doesn't he will sit down and never be able to get back up again. Probably sensible, actually. See if he sits and does nothing then that just means he's going to think about it all, and if there's anything he has learnt the day, it's that thinking is an unwise idea; thinking only tires you out, makes you act like a lunatic.

7

'See me over the remote, will ye, hen.'

'Here. Mind there's my programme on soon but.'

'I know.'

He flicks the channel over and hands her back the remote, careful he doesn't overbalance his tray, and carries on eating. It's a good tea. A chilli. She's put something in it, he's no too sure what it is, but it's got a wee bit different of a flavour about it, which he's liking.

'The appointment go okay the day?' he says.

'Fine, aye. The doctor gave her a new prescription. Says it might help her sleep better.'

'Seems to be working, eh?' He smiles, glancing up to the ceiling, and keeps on with his tea. It's quite loud, the TV, he realizes, and he stretches over for the remote to turn it down.

'I saw Mick Little the day, ye know, one of the drivers at Muir's.'

She nods.

'I no tell you his wife died?'

'No, Christ, that's awful.'

'Cancer, I think, mesothelioma.'

'That's awful. Poor man.'

'I know. He looked bad as well, broken, ye know?'

'What do ye expect? His wife died. How ye think he's gonnae look?'

'I know. I know.'

He scrapes up the last forkful of chilli and puts the plate by. She's checking her watch, he notices, no wanting to miss her programme. It's not on for a few minutes yet though, so they keep watching what's on, something with a guy on a boat talking into the camera.

'Ye speak to him?'

'Mick? No. It wasnae the right situation. I was coming back with the messages, I passed him on the street.'

'How ye no speak to him, well?'

'Naw it wasnae the right timing. What am I gonnae say, serious? It's best no intruding. She only died a few weeks ago, I think.'

She finishes eating and puts her tray on the floor.

'He coming back to work?'

'Maybe, I'm no sure. Possibly not actually, what with how quiet things are the now. Might be he's near retirement anyway, I don't know.'

'Ye could give him a knock, maybe, in a few weeks, see if he wants to go for a drink.'

'Maybe, aye.'

'You and Bertie and all them. Give him a while and then call in on him. He'd probably like that, if he's no going back to work.'

'Come on but, what am I going to do, call in at his house? It's no like I know the guy that well. I don't want to go nebbing in on him.'

'Ye've been drinking with him before.'

'Aye, I know, but that's different, that's at work. It wouldnae be normal, chapping his door, ringing him. The guy doesnae want to feel like a fucking charity case, does he?'

'He got family?'

'He's a son, aye, up in Yoker, far as I mind. Guy doesnae want people chapping his door every five minutes does he?'

'I don't know. I don't know the man. It's awfy sad but.'

'It is.'

She picks up the remote and turns the channel, pushing back into her seat as he collects the trays and takes them out the room.

8

The waffles ran out a couple of days ago and he is actually feeling hungry for once. No wanting to leave the house but. No wanting to be in it either, so it's no the ideal situation: moving from one room to the other, unable to settle anywhere until eventually he does sit down at the kitchen table and he stays there for quite a long time, not thinking, waiting just for the hunger to get the better of him and force him out the front door.

There's McDowell's, and that would be the obvious choice, the familiar place, but what he's after is a bit of peace as he's eating his bacon roll and so he goes a bit further down the high street to the other one, the Millennium Star. The same recognizable sounds and smells but: bacon hissing on the fryer, the half-tuned radio, the week's pile of newspapers next to the tea urn. There's a raggedy old ticket near the door, bent over the day's paper. He's probably been in all morning, squinnying at the racing odds. Mick gets himself sat in the corner, away from the old guy and the only other table: three roadworkers silently beasting into chicken dinners with peas and gravy and roast tatties. The girl comes over and he orders himself a roll and a tea. She gives him the once-over before she walks away, but there you go, he's no exactly looking his best, what can you expect?

They're East Europes, these three. Big, quiet baldy crusts – a sure banker there's a whole coachload of them sleeping shifts in a tenement single-end somewhere, and so what, good on them, see if it's no them doing the work then who else is going to do it? These young lads you see loundering about the streets and the schemes complaining there's no work for them? Nay chance. And if all the yards were still standing, you know fine well it would be these boys working on them, building the ships. Hot, hard, dangerous work, no for the lounderers of this world. There'd be no complaint from these but; a bedroom of bogging feet but there goes another paycheque straight on the plane and have you got any more shifts for me, gaffer?

The salty smack of the bacon tastes good. He eats slowly, in stages, making sure it goes down nice and easy. She's still got her eye on him, the waitress, drying cutlery into a tray. Worried he might do a run-out. Maybe he should get out some bits of smash onto the table. She's no half so suspicious of the old ticket by the door but, that's clear enough, the way she's trotting over for a wee patter and a top-up of his tea mug. Canny old scaffer. He's got it sussed. He probably comes in every day. Then on the panel, claiming for all his afflictions, the money never seeing further than the fifty-yard stretch from here past the bookie's to the offie. No that you can blame him but. If they want to top up his tea for free then it's no like he's going to stop them, is he? This is his patch; they know him here, and he is tolerated and fed titbits like a stray cat. How wouldn't you keep coming back?

Bread and eggs and biscuits and all this stuff they do their own brand of in the Co. Plus a bottle of whisky, for good measure. He's got himself a trolley, although he isn't intending filling it, see even if he wanted to he doesn't have enough cash on his tail. He last went to the cash machine just before Robbie and Jenna left, and he saw then that the account is pretty low getting. Which is how there's no choice but to phone in to work again when he gets back, and tell them he's coming in to sort out renting a car. Nay excuses this time.

It is quiet, this time of day. There's a calm atmosphere in the place, full of the steady sounds of overhead lights and fridges and a wee forklift chirring past with boxes of butter packs. Further down his aisle, there's a woman battling on with the messages as she tries to get her weans under control, pulling them out of freezers and fishing out rogue items from the trolley, crisps and cans of ginger and all these things that have found their way in there.

He stands watching his shopping move along the belt. It would have been an idea getting a vegetable or two. A bag of peas, or a nice big cabbage. Too late the now but. Next time maybe.

'Mick.'

He turns round. It is Mary. Pete is behind her.

She makes as if she's going to come toward him, but his trolley is in the way.

'How's it going?' Pete says.

'Okay, Pete, thanks.' The whisky bottle teeters as the belt jerks forward. He reaches for the divider, and his hand is shaking a little as he puts it behind his shopping. He keeps it held down a moment. 'Good time the day to come, this, eh?'

They are both looking at him.

'It is, aye,' Pete says. 'Quiet.'

The cashier is finished scanning his things. She's waiting for him to move forward, his items strewn now over the bagging area.

Mary is watching him. The cashier is watching him. They're bloody all watching him. His amount is showing on the screen, and it's more than he was expecting. He gets out the wallet, his hands still jittery and the whole thing turned by now into a self-conscious show of himself; nothing he can say or do that doesn't some way point at it, the dead wife. What's he doing for money now he's no been working? Is he gone on the broo? Or is he gone on the whisky, look?

There is enough money, and he pays. He gets bagging up as Pete and Mary's shopping starts coming down the belt. Chicken pieces, a *Still Game* DVD, a curry pack, wood varnish. That's the weekend lined up, well, chugging along. Suddenly a squeeze on his arm, and he looks into Mary's face, smiling at him. Here it comes, then.

'Mick, it's good to see you. We've no been thinking about anything else.'

Pete is looking on with a small pinched smile.

She takes her hand away. 'Call on us, please, Mick. Any time eh?'

'Thanks, Mary. I will.'

He picks up his bag and he sees that the cashier is at it now as well. All three of them smiling pityingly at him as he's about to leave; they look like relatives stood around a hospital bed.

He gets the kettle on, watching the sparrow outside pecking at bits of bread, and goes upstairs to wash his face. There'll be no more horrifying of waitresses in cafés, he has resolved. Then he comes down to drink the tea and watch a bit of television.

It is too hot in the house, so he gets up to open the windows – the one in the living room and then the kitchen back door. Let a bit of air pass through. And after that, a whisky? Why no? The afternoon's getting on now, and a couple of biscuits and a whisky could be just the thing. Calm the nerves. Get relaxed. Then when he's settled he can pick up the phone and ring in to work. No use sat about here all the time doing nothing, he's the better getting moving and keeping the brain occupied, and as well the whole social aspect, a bit of patter with the passengers; the other drivers. He gives a wee laugh. A bit of patter? And what about? Did ye see the game at the weekend, what a cracker, eh, and we were out after and ye'll never guess what happened, wait til ye hear this yin. Life goes on, Mick. What is it ye expect, eh, ye want us to stand about in silence because of what's happened, and it's no that we don't sympathize because we do, it's just life goes on, our lives they go on. Suddenly a loud bang jumps him, and a jet of whisky hits him in the face. He wheels round to look at the doorway, understanding: the draught, it must be. His hands are started going as he puts his glass down to go and fix it out.

It is. It's the draught. He closes up all the doors and windows and goes back to sit down and calm himself. Straight away it's hot again, but he'll have to live with it just, better that than a fucking heart attack.

Lynsey will have left the office by now; somebody else on the dispatch. Somehow, the thought of talking to her again, it unsettles him. Implications. All these bloody implications that there's no way around. Lynsey and the wee giggle they could always have, a flirt, you might call it even, but it's fine, it's fine because you get to an age and you're married and sex isn't in the equation when women are talking to you. You're no a threat, so you can have a laugh and a giggle because nobody's on the lookout for your physical needs and your desires – but now – see now those are all busted into the open and people are wary of you because that's exactly what they're looking out for.

He calls the office line. It keeps ringing, and he gets ready for what he's going to say on the answering machine, but mid-ring it gets picked up.

'Hello.'

He considers putting the phone down.

'Hello?'

'It's Mick. That you, Malc?'

'Aw, Mick, hi. How are ye? Ye're calling late, eh?'

'I didnae think ye'd be there still.'

'No, I got stuck here. I had paperwork to fix out and then the phone wouldnae stop.'

There is a pause.

'I'd like to come back in, that's how I'm ringing.'

He can hear Malcolm breathing on the other end.

'Thing is, Mick, we're no too busy the now. Mean, if ye want to take some more time, see the family, ye know, that'll be fine, it's no a problem.'

'No. I'd like to come in.'

He can smell the whisky returning off the receiver.

'Okay, well, that's fine. Ye sold the car, didn't ye?'

'I did.'

'Right, so we'll get ye one to rent again. Come in whenever and we'll find some shifts, okay?'

'Okay.'

'I'd best get leaving, Mick. We'll see you, then.'

'See you.'

He sits down, closing his eyes, trying to compose himself. It's done. Task completed. Now relax. But just then it occurs to him he hasn't checked the phone messages in a long while and there might have been a call. He goes back in the lobby to the phone. There's three new ones.

'Hello, Mick, it's Alan here, just to say we'll be with you late afternoon, it looks like. Depends how the traffic is. I imagine you might not have a lot in, food-wise, so we'll pick up some supplies on the way. See you in a short while, hopefully.'

What was that about no having a heart attack? Jesus. It takes him half the message before he realizes it's an old one and the Highlanders are not in fact about to arrive any moment. He replays it for the date anyway, just to be sure. Delete.

The next message is Robbie.

'Hi, Da, just calling to say we're back, and to see you're okay. Flight was a fucking nightmare in the end – not enough ground staff or something in Hong Kong so we were held up five hours, so we're both kinda whacked now. Jenna's asleep upstairs with Damien. Anyway, hopefully the Highlanders didn't hang around too long and you're doing okay. I'll speak to you soon, alright. Take care.'

The last is Robbie again.

'Hi, Da, I guess you might be working. Anyway, I'm just after seeing how you're getting on, is all. I'm back at work myself this last week, which has been good, you know, takes your mind off things a bit – Jenna's asking to tell you hi, Da, she sends her love – so, yeah, give me a call. Any time is fine, and I can ring you straight back. Okay, take care, speak soon, bye.'

End of messages.

Dark outside. He switches off the television. Pulls the bed covers and the pillow out from beside the settee, then goes upstairs and finds the camping mat. He drags everything together to the kitchen back door, and goes out into the garden.

It is cool outside, but pleasant enough, no wind, no noise either. He walks up to the shed and goes inside. There are boxes and a hammer on the floor, which he picks up and puts onto the cracked plastic table against the back wall. Then he takes the chairs and the rusted mower out to the back of the kitchen and returns to the shed with the bed covers, laying out the mat, the pillow, the blankets onto the floor. There is just enough space for it. A final check out the door that there's nobody spying over the fence, and he closes it behind him.

9

It is cold. There is a wind got up, and he lies with the covers pulled close, no able to sleep, listening to the glass clacking loosely in the window frame. He should have gave it a bit more thought, brought some blankets out. Good job he minded the whisky, well. He takes another mouthful, gulps, and feels it burning down his throat.

He turns over. Can't fucking sleep, man. Nay chance him going back in the house though. He'd rather go cold than stay the night in there: all the rooms, despite the clearout, still hoaching with nudgewinks, making him think about everything. No that he's faring the best out here either, in truth. We've no been thinking about anything else. We've no been thinking about anything else. Really, Mary? Ye sure about that? You've been thinking about what DVDs to watch and that your fence needs a varnish, but no, no, see what we've really been thinking about is Cathy and this terrible situation here. That's what's been on our minds the whole time. And have ye gave much thought, Mary, how it's Cathy copped her whack and it's no you? That's the question. Pete was in the yards the same amount of time – to the very day, in fact; they started the very same day – and you've shook the overalls out and washed them and vacuumed the carpets exactly the same as Cathy has. And why no Pete, for that matter? Or himself. Always the same question, coming back at him. How is it no himself? Him that was working with the stuff every day, brushing against the laggers and their buckets of monkey dung, walking under scaffold planks with great showers of it floating down like snowstorms. And the best question of all – ye ready for this, Big Man – how isn't it the brother-in-law? See if there's anybody deserves to cop their whack then it's him, surely, it's him and all the rest of they lying bastards, because they knew, they knew long before anybody else did what the dangers were, but they did nothing. Nothing. All the reports they must've had telling about the risks, and all of it sided off for the more important business of trying to keep up with the Japanese and the French and the Germans. How not the brother-in-law? But he was shut away, wasn't he, the door snibbed closed, pouring whisky down the throats of shipowners and insurance men. We've upheld our responsibilities and don't think we haven't. We've put the signs up – telling about ventilation and masks and dust checks and all these things that were never bothered with and nobody ever thought to ask for because you couldn't read the bloody sign even, it was that covered in fucking dust.

He presses himself into the crack between the ground and the wall, trying to stop the wind getting a run on him as it races through. The whole of him is aching. Hardly a surprise. It's pure ancient, this camping mat, worn down almost to nothing and if it wasn't already then it will be soon, all this tossing and turning he's doing. Another gulp of whisky. And another. Liars. Fucking liars – see what about all they poor bastards up at the asbestos factory actually making the stuff, hadn't they been lied to worse than anyone? You'd see them coming out with it pasted wet over them from head to toe from hosing the machines down. Each holding a newspaper to stick under the bahookie when they sat on the bus, trying no to piss the driver off. They'd been told it was only dangerous when it was dry. So they took it home, and then what happened – what do ye think bloody happened? – it dried again, didn't it, but that was fine, far as the powers that be were concerned, that wasn't a danger. Fucking lies, all of it. They deserved everything that was coming to them. And if it was him dying, then maybe he would go down that route. Secure a future for Cathy. But it wasn't; it was him brought the stuff in the house. And he should have known. Even if no at first, way back, then he certain could have done later on, when there was the warnings and the newspaper reports and he could have seen through all these lies and no been so blind to it. He'd even worked with somebody who thought they'd took a bad back. Actually known somebody die who'd thought that at first, but then when it was Cathy in the doctor's he didn't think to say anything about it, he fucking forgot.

Could ye have put it out at any time, anything ye can mind? Well, the vacuuming, maybe. See I had a wee twinge doing under the kitchen table no long back. And that was that. Decided. She'd took a bad back. All ye can do is rest it up a few weeks and do nothing – let the man of the house get acquainted with the vacuum for a while, eh? They'd all had a chuckle at that. And he did do as well: vacuuming, cleaning, ironing, with her sat laughing at him the whole month until they went back in when she couldn't stop coughing.

He can't shut the thoughts out now. He presses his forehead hard against the wood, as if to fight against them, but it's no use, it doesn't help. And see if he did put a claim in then the reminders would be there the whole time – for months, years, however long it took – and even that is still ignoring the main thing: why should *he* get a windfall? Him that brought it into the house and handed her the overalls to wash and here's two hundred grand, pal, take it, it's yours – you deserve it.

IO

The head is crawling. Stupit. He looks over at the bottle and not only has he wrecked his head, he's also wasted half the whisky rations. No very wise, but there you go, it's no the end of the world; which, in fact, isn't looking too bad this morning: the sun streaming in onto his legs through the small grubby window. He lies there awake a time, listening to the sound of things outside. Birds. A door closing. A distant radio. And all the while playing his toe around something soothingly cool and damp that it's probably no wise investigating what it is.

Anyway, up and at it. He goes to the kitchen, where he takes off his shirt and trousers and gives himself a wash from the sink. He dries himself with the one remaining teacloth, puts the clothes back on, and makes himself a pair of boiled eggs and a slice of toast for cutting into soldiers. Nothing like a boiled egg for a hangover. Except when he lops the heads off he finds he's done them too long and they are gone solid, so he scrapes them out with a teaspoon instead. He needs to go into work the day, get some shifts. It's unavoidable. The longer he leaves it the less they'll want him, and anyway he needs the money.

He stays sat in the kitchen a long time trying to force himself up. But he can't do it; he isn't ready. It feels too much – anyway he looks at it, it feels too much, even bloody getting there, christsake, even the prospect of that is bringing him out in a sweat. The morrow. He'll go the morrow. Rain or shine.

The nights are getting colder. He goes in the house and up the stair one afternoon for more blankets, a fresh shirt and trousers and a jumper, an action that proves a pure effort of will in itself even, just drumming up the balls to go into the bedroom. And the whisky is long finished too, which doesn't help matters.

After three stops, he starts to relax a little. Nobody is noticing him. They're on a different planet, these people, with their earphones plugged in, or just staring out the window. Even when Bertie the workshop mechanic gets on, it's fine, because he's stood in a spot near the back of the bus from where Bertie can't see him, two dozen armpits and raw razored faces in the way between. It's pure illogical but. He's going to have to see him soon enough, he knows. And Bertie's alright, anyway. He's a rare auld ticket in fact, always in there with a joke or a wee story to keep everybody amused. Mick watches him through the armpits. Even Bertie is away with the fairies this morning, it seems, dreaming up something or other, a funny tale to tell the drivers.

He lets Bertie get a way up the street ahead of him, and follows on behind. The stomach is something jittery getting when he turns onto the lane, but there's nobody about and so he goes straight in the office, a shabby small space set into one corner of the workshop, with a plywood divider on one side, and a computer desk and Lynsey in her headset on the other. She's typing something and doesn't notice him when he comes in. Her face concentrated on the screen, clabbered with make-up.

'Mick,' she says, looking up.

'Hello, Lynsey, how's it going?'

'Fine, Mick, fine.' She is uncomfortable seeing him, it is obvious enough. Doesn't know what to say. That makes two of them, well.

'I spoke to Malcolm. He said to come in.'

'Did he? He's no told me anything.' She looks at her screen a moment, then back at him. 'He's gone out just now, I don't know when he's due back. Will I give him a call on his mobile?'

'No, no, that's fine, Lynsey. I'll wait for him a while just, if that's okay?'

'Aye, if ye like.' She smiles, and he tightens up, ready for it, but then she says, 'There's Bertie about somewhere, and a couple of the drivers. Go have a wander. I'm sure they'd like to see you.'

He looks at the divider. The sound of an engine from in the shop.

'If it's alright I'll stay here for now, if I'm no disturbing you.'

'Naw, it's fine. Don't worry. Ye sure ye don't want me to give him a call but? See I don't know when he'll be back and he might be a while.'

'It's okay, thanks.'

There is a chair on the other side of the office, and he goes over to sit on it. He stays there a moment, looking around, noticing the gap beside the divider that looks into the shop. He gets up again, Lynsey glancing at him from her desk, and he walks over to a metal cabinet, on top of which is a paper. He stands reading it, or looking at it anyway. The corkboard on the wall beside him is pretty empty. Normally there would be a long list of accounts and pre-bookeds on there, but there's only a few names scribbled on, under the yellowing page-three girl who's been pinned on that board for over a decade.

'I might nick to the shops a moment actually, Lynsey, while I'm waiting.'

She keeps her eyes on the screen a few seconds before turning round.

'Whatever ye like, Mick, that's fine. I'll tell Malc ye've been by, will I?'

'Do, please, Lynsey. I'll be back in a wee while just.'

He leaves the office, giving a keek into the workshop as he turns toward the lane, where he can see Bertie, chatting with Steve and a young-looking guy that he can't see the face of.

Crapbag. He's a genuine crapbag and no other word for it.

He is in a bar near to work. He came in because it looked quiet through the window, and he was just wandering about, no sure where to take himself. Crapbag. These are his friends, christsake; well, if no exactly friends then his co-workers at least and that's something, sure that means something. Even now, it does. And no like they don't have their own problems to deal with. Steve, with the wee daughter's illness; Bertie, and his troublesome relations with the drink. Sure Bertie would be good for a patter; if there's one thing he's got still, it's his patter, even if he's lost the rest. Amazing to think now, how he used to be. The figure he was forty years back almost, during the work-in. A five-foot queerie with jug ears – no way anybody would ever have thought he could hold a crowd the way he did – but when he was stood up on his brazier with a hundred black squad around him, he'd have the whole yard in his spell. The high wheedling voice, beeling at the government, two hundred clatty ears hanging on his every word. The guy could go on for hours. It was the likes of Bertie that kept them going: even when the redundancies were announced, they stayed put inside the yard, kept building, didn't let the liquidators or any other of these bastards past the gateman; and all through that winter and into the next spring Bertie and the other shop stewards would still be there to hand them their wages. The campaign fund keeping strong; the wives and girlfriends bringing them their food parcels. Cathy and her piles of ham rolls wrapped in newspaper, passing them to him over the barrier.

Hard to believe, looking at it now – at Bertie, old and trembling – that they'd won.

He gets up and goes to the bar for a final drink.

'Half and a half,' he tells the barman, watching as he reaches up to the gantry for his whisky. Christ but the drink makes him maunderly. These will definitely be his last. A maunderly old crapbag, is what he is, and he grins to himself, the guy coming over with his beer and his whisky. He's a great beardie young fella, with small sore-looking eyes like a pair of arseholes, and an oversized T-shirt that says VAGITARIAN – one of they ones you only ever seem to see extra-large guys wearing. He puts the drinks on the bar top and Mick pays and goes back to his seat in the empty room. A cruel bastard, ye can be, Mr Little. A cruel auld bastard and ye know it. Aye, I do, I do, but see that's the drink to blame again, if the truth be told.

An unexpected turn of events: he has found himself in an electrics megastore. How he's ended up here it's hard to say, and given that the stumbliness of the drink is taking effect and that he isn't actually needing a new iPod the now, it probably isn't the most sensible destination. It's woke up the security guard though.

Nay chance he's going back into work now. That is obvious enough. No with the length of time he's been out for, and the smell of alcohol on him. He walks around at random, half aware of the guy watching him. There's golf on the televisions all down this aisle he's in, dozens of them all showing the same event: one of these sponsor's tournaments with a few pros playing round with rich men and celebrities – retired footballers and elderly film actors, that type of nonsense. Alan would love it. He's probably watching it the now even. Christ he's probably playing.

There is laughter somewhere. It's hard to tell where it's coming from, how far away it is, but it is a man and a woman. He has grown to recognize the voices from hearing them talking together sometimes if it's a warm day outside. They were arguing earlier the afternoon but now the sound is clearly of laughter, finding its way in under the door and through the cracks in the window frame.

He is cold. He has lain there with the covers pulled up all morning and there's nay chance he's tweaking the door open so he'll have to live with the smell just – the clinging stink of a fish supper he brought back a few days ago. A while later but he is too thirsty, and he does get up, leaving the shed to go for a drink of water from the kitchen. He is turning the tap when the phone starts ringing in the lobby. It startles him. He stays there, frozen, with the tap still running and his arm beginning to shake. It rings a long time. He waits for it to finish and he turns the tap off, putting the mug on the counter, and leaves straight out the house by the front door.

Maybe he'll take a walk down the water. Keep moving; he needs to keep moving.

He isn't too sure the time, or even what time is safest to come these days and what's best left alone, it's that long since he's been down. So he comes slowly up the path, scanning up the way ahead. There is a young couple he comes past, with their two tiny weans. One of them is in a pram, and the other running about, scampering between the headstones and her da trying to coax her back. She's got the right idea but. Why no run about the place, instead of teetering around the graves? They're dead, christsake, they're no bloody sleeping.

There's new flowers again. The ones Mick left himself are there next to them, gone dry and brown by now. He picks them off the plot and gets them slung over the palings. Strange Craig's left them there, although – no, see even that is probably done on purpose, as a reminder, a marker of the da's last visit. That's exactly the kind of thing he would do, in fact.

It's started drizzling, so he walks over by the palings and stands under a bit of tree. See what makes it the worse is it's hard no to pity the boy. The same useless fucking pity that everybody's so keen to stick on him, he's doing it too, when he imagines him up there in Yoker alone and angry, naybody to talk to. Or maybe he does. Who knows? There had been a girl he was seeing, Tina, was she called, but there's no way of telling if they're together still. Maybe not, in fact. It had seemed like something of a loose kind of arrangement, from what Cathy had said. He should ask him. He gives a short laugh at the idea. He's only once before been up to see him, and that was a few years ago. Into the dingy flat boufing with dirty plates and filled-up ashtrays, but no his place to say anything, so he didn't; and neither did Cathy even because, as she says, it's his life to do as he wants and see if he wants to make mistakes then he'll make mistakes, and he'll learn from them, same as the rest of us.

The family are on their way, ahead of him as he leaves along the path. The wee girl holding her father's hand, and him leaning over and giving the wife a kiss on the side of the head. You don't think, when you're that age, about all this that might happen – that is going to happen, actually, a pure certainty it is going to happen. You're too busy with getting the food on the table and clothes on the weans' backs and feeding the wife's bingo habit to start thinking about what like it might be when one of you is gone. And too right. Jesus. Too right. What a thing to think about.

There is a man outside the house. Mick has turned the corner into the street and is coming up the pavement when he sees him, standing at the front door. Mick turns straight around. Keeps moving. Gets back down the end of the street to the bus stop and spies through the glass. He's still there, just stood, waiting. From here, he can't see properly who it is, but he's sure he doesn't recognize him. He fights to get the breathing under control. Maybe it isn't his house, and he's mistaken, it's actually next door. It isn't but. It's definitely his house. The man is peering in the window now, cupping his hands around his face. He chaps the door. Now what? Wait, just wait. The man turns and starts inspecting the grass at his feet, as if he's looking for something, and then he's up to the window again, spying in. For a second, a strange hopeful thought hits him that maybe it's a robber, but just then the man turns and goes out the gate and he can see his face. It's nobody he recognizes, a big guy in a shirt and tie, who is getting now into a dark red car parked on the street outside. It's a while before he leaves but. The car stays there another few minutes before it starts pulling out from the kerb and swings round, moving off in the direction away from the bus stop.

Mick waits a moment longer, watching carefully. As he gets up and starts toward the house, there is laughter, and he spins around to see two teenage boys knotting themselves looking at him from one corner of the bus stop. He walks away quickly, checking around him, and gets in the gate and then the house, hurrying through it and out into the garden, snibbing the latch of the shed as he comes inside.

II

The cold. It is setting in. Keep the whisky flowing, my man, keep it flowing. He unscrews the cap and takes another bolt – a bottle he'd minded was in the kitchen, unopened, laid out on top of the cupboards. A present from Alan last Christmas. The usual gift from him, but no complaints, he's bloody grateful, serious. The bottle carefully chosen, you can tell: decent enough it's obvious he's spent some money, but never a single malt, never something that the average man, in the brother-in-law's opinion, should be drinking. But fine. Fuck it. Fine. Cheers then to the brother-in-law and to his charming wife, who haven't as it happens been down once to visit the grave since they left. Which tells you everything, really, everything. Still but you can't have it all ways, eh, and the better that he doesn't have to see them; plus as well of course, how does he know for sure that they haven't been? Maybe they have, see, maybe they have. No way. They haven't. There would be some display of flowers or something. They have not been. See if they come at all, they'll come when it suits them. When there's a film they want to see, or they need a new computer.

A stifty wind in under the door. He pulls the blankets close. Jesus, he's hungry. He drags the emptied tool box from under the table and feels about inside it for the end of a packet of biscuits, then gets eating a couple. It's nearly finished, the food store. A battle plan needed. Another problem for another day.

He has had a pure stroke of luck. He'd been one afternoon rummling about in the back of the shed for anything useful there might be, and he found the wee battery radio they used to put outside sometimes when they were sat or she was at the gardening. It's still working. A miracle. And it's good too, having it on, no bother that the reception is pretty fuzzy, it's better than nothing, especially these nights he's laid there just, with the brainbox going, no able to sleep.

He listens to the quiet voice of the nightwatchradioman. He's talking about this TV programme that he watched the day about assisted suicides and people going away for them, the legalities and all that. Mick's no hearing it all, but it's relaxing, the sound of the guy's voice. There is a call-in after, but they don't stick to the topic. People can ring in saying whatever's on their minds. What do ye think will be the score Saturday? Barry in Pollokshields predicts a thumping away victory for the Gers, and a hat-trick for the new boy. Here's hoping, Barry, here's hoping.

The food store is gone. It's fine but, it's okay; no like it has come out the blue. He's been intending the last few days to go the messages for one or two items. Bread. Biscuits. Cheap things that don't need going in the fridge and he can keep out here. Another bottle of whisky would be much appreciated too, but he's got to be careful watching the pennies, got to start thinking where's the money going to come from. He closes his eyes. Got to do this, got to mind to do that. It's too much to think about. Easier to shut the eyes just and go to sleep, no have to deal with anything just now.

12

Des is standing on the pavement out front of the Empress when he spots the distant figure of Mick approaching down the street. He drops his cigarette to the ground, picks up the broom that is propped against the wall, and gets sweeping the lunchtime dog-ends into the road. No that there's a great many. There'd only been a few in: the small group of staff from the recruitment agency round the corner, a couple of shopping-centre workers, and Pat, who is the only person left in the bar now, quietly drinking his Guinness over the racing odds.

He finishes clearing the pavement, and waits to say a hello to Mick if he isn't stopping in for a drink. Halfway down the street though, Mick crosses over and goes into the closemouth of a tenement on the other side, a blue carrier bag in his hand, and disappears. Des goes inside. He pours a refill for Pat, a Grouse for himself, then goes into the back for a sit down.

Maybe it had been someone else. Looked like Mick but. He sits back and lights a fag, keeping an eye through the bar to the lobby entrance. The family must have all gone by now: it's well over a month since Craig was coming by those nights, so he's obviously back up in Yoker. They might be on with a claim by now, from what Craig had been saying then. Awful fucking sad, what had happened. She was a great woman, Cathy, a cracker. Always had been. Back in the day, he used to have something of a crush on her. When he was a young guy first working the bar for his father, he'd look forward to her coming in with the other women during the work-in. There will be no bevvying, the shop stewards had told their men, so they were doing it for them, they'd joked. Just awful bloody sad. It could've been any of those women – still could be. The whole area is a timebomb. It could well be him next, or Pat, or any of the men that he'd stood and listened to from behind the bar, right from when there first started to be the rumblings, talking about it like it was something far off and no to do with them, even though they were sat there with the dust caked in their ears and their arseholes. A customer is coming into the lobby entrance. Des gets up, reluctantly wedges his fag in the ashtray, and goes through to the bar.

Mick comes back into the shed with a wee feeling of triumph and puts the items into the food store: bread and biscuits, a packet of cheese, tinned apricots and luncheon meat; even a paper for something to read and while away the hours. See all that stupit carry-on and then in the end it was fine. He's probably only been gone twenty minutes. He gave the Co a swerve, so all he did was get to the cash machine on the high street, draw out a note and ignore the fact the account is gone overdrawn, then dot in the minimarket on his way back for all these bits and pieces. Easy-oasy.

Now that it's done he steps out of the shed again and sets his sights on the house. He may as well get everything done in one go, collect more plates, a knife and a fork, and fill up the watering can with fresh water. Then he'll be set.

He stands outside the shed and looks down the line of back gardens, all empty; wet leaves and rubbish strewn about. Five minutes and he'll be done. Put the blinkers on, get in and get out. He starts toward the house. Grey pebble-dash; green back door. Strange but he doesn't recognize it, it's that unfamiliar somehow. If he'd been in the shed and he'd tried thinking what colour is the back door, what colour is the front door even, he wouldn't have been able to say, serious, he wouldn't. All they details: doors, carpets, furniture, they all merge into a general feeling you have, a habit, of being in the house. A place you return to at the end of the day after your toils, and relax. The familiar routines – putting your keys on the counter, sticking the kettle on, getting sat in your chair – it's natural just, you don't even think about it. All of it so far past the now. Gone. None of it fits.

The bulb is out in the kitchen. He goes to the cupboard for plates, working by the dim light coming in through the rain-smeared window. Grey shadows on the counter from the kettle and the toaster. He gets a cup, a knife, fork, then he rinses out the watering can; gets filling it with clean water. What would be a good idea as well is pulling the covers off Robbie's bed: the nights are too cold getting, even with the extra blankets he's brought out. He goes out of the kitchen and it's the speed of things, the combination of them all happening together, that undoes him. The light no turning on. The tide of envelopes by the door. A noise upstairs – a bump. It all happens in a second, before he can get registering any of it, and his heart banjos right up his fucking throat and he has to shove against the banister, pressing his back to it and craning to look up the stair. His breathing is heavy and snatched, he can't control it. It is gone silent up there. But then there's another bump somewhere above his head; he makes a dart for the living room door beside him. Quiet as he can, he crouches down behind the settee and gets lying in the narrow gap between it and the wall.

His leg is murdering underneath him, but he doesn't budge. Still nothing from up the stair. The blood in his ears is making it hard to listen, but he strains to hear, ready for any sound in the ceiling above him. Stupit. He is trapped, and whoever it is that's up there is just waiting, because they know it, or they've went, or they weren't even bloody there in the first place, Christ knows. So he stays put, the leg aching and his knees pressed into the back of the settee. From where he's lying, he can see part of the video player under the television, but the display clock is blank so he can't tell how long he's been there, maybe only a few minutes, or maybe hours, who knows?

Quietly, stiffly, he gets himself out from the settee. His ears are pure bursting, he's listening that hard as he edges out from the room and into the corridor, quickening his pace, coming into the kitchen and grabbing the things before getting out the back door. He clicks it softly shut behind him. A quick look at the upstairs window before he reaches the shed, but there's nothing.

He is sat in the straight-backed hospital chair with the plastic peeling off it and the foam poking out, while she stares out of the window. The white curtain is pulled shut in a horseshoe around them, and there's the peaceful hum of a dozen sleeping, snoring, dying women in the room outside. Through in the corridor, the faint hurrying patter of nurses' feet. And beyond the window, where she's staring, a gardener, whistling himself a tune as his pink head tots in and out of sight behind a hedge. After a while he comes round the near side of it, and he's got his shirt-sleeves rolled up, it's that sunny a day. The windows are open, and it's awful welcome, the freshness of the air outside coming in with his wee tune, pouring into the stale room. All of a sudden there is a fart somewhere outside the curtain – a loud, long, trumpety job – which causes him to chuckle and look at her, but she hasn't noticed it, she's still fixed on the gardener. She has been asleep all morning and she's lying restfully the now as he sits quietly watching her.

A nurse pops her head through the curtain at one point, gives him a smile and disappears again. She didn't signal she was coming in, it occurs to him when she's gone. But then what would be the point? She is the one that's changing her clothes, helping her go to the toilet. There's no need being discreet any more; it's past that. Maybe if he'd been sat there himself in the bare scuddy, his balls sticking to the seat, then maybe she'd start giving the signal. He grins. Aye, probably.

There is the gentle hushed sound of a relative talking. Outside, the gardener is lopping the heads off a line of finished flowers at the bottom of the hedge. Still the bright, tireless whistle. He looks at her. Is she listening? Can she hear it? He realizes then that he doesn't know if she can or not – if she's listening, if she can see him, or if she's just staring out at nothing. And that is when he understands. It's the precise moment, in fact. Maybe she can hear it, maybe she can't, but either way it doesn't make any difference because it's only time now, only time that is in the way. He stands up from the chair to move toward her, and her eyes shift to take him in. He smiles, and brushes the headscarf back to give her a wee kiss on the forehead; then he leaves out of the cubicle to go and get a coffee from the machine down the corridor.

13

The biscuits are gone stale. There is the dull snap of wet fibreboard about them now, and the cheese has broke out in green spots and a white frilly moss. He opens the door a nook, pushing against the sludge of wet leaves gathered against it, and slings out what's left for the birds. No use it going to waste.

The shed isn't best equipped for this rainy period that's come on. It gets in under the walls and the door, and drips down off the window. The blankets are pretty damp getting by now. Probably he'll come down with some horrendous illness and go the way of the cheese. The sparrows the first to find him, to notice he's copped his whack when they start pecking inside on the lookout for food.

Enough of that. Talk about maunderly. Jesus.

He is running out of shit pits. There's nay chance he's going back in the house, with its strange atmosphere and its lack of lights and its mysterious bumping noises up the stairs, so that just leaves the bucket at the back of the shed. He did consider using it before, when he stopped using the house toilet, until he came to his senses and realized that would be mental. Instead, he'd took a corner of the garden, the border on one side where Cathy used to plant her flowers, and used a trowel to dig a line of small pits, each with the mound of soil next to it to cover over after he's took a crap. But now the line is almost filled. And as well, he needs to get some toilet roll. All he's got left to use is torn out half-pages of the *Southside News*. A delicate operation, serious, though it doesn't make much difference how gently he does it – the backside is getting sorer, and blacker, pasted each day with new articles about tenement regenerations and Roma beatings.

There is a noise coming from outside. A faint, distant, rolling sound. He thinks at first it might be the wind, which is piping cold peashooters at his feet from under the door, but he understands after a while that it's Ibrox. There is a match on. He tunes in the radio, but the commentary isn't the clearest so he gives that up and listens outside just, waiting for the wind to blow him a favour. It does, and a few times he hears a muffled roar going up. Maybe the new boy is on form. Taken the league by storm this past couple of weeks and making mincemeat of opposition defences. Whatever the score is, it seems like they're winning, and the result is confirmed for him later, because there's car horns pamping in the night, together with what sounds like a brawl away on the high street.

14

Here they come, the wee chaps. He listens, enjoying the sound of it, as they begin skittering on the concrete outside the shed door. Something aye comforting about the noise of them pecking the ground, tapping, the odd time, on the side of the shed.

Until recently there'd just been the one – probably the same patient guy that's been coming all the while – but he's obvious gone and let dab to all his mates that they can come and eat here, and now there's a whole mob of them. Good for him, no keeping it all to himself. Obviously no an English bird. A genuine Southsider, that sparrow. It's mostly just bread he's buying now, each few days when he works himself up to leaving the shed, and he keeps a couple of slices from each loaf aside to put out for them. Sometimes, when he hears them arrive and gets open the door latch, he lays a short trail of crumbs from the outside, into the shed, to see if he can get any of them to come in. There's one time, he managed it. This tiny head, poking in the door and then following the line, unaware, or otherwise unbothered by the great hulking creature that was keeping still and watching him from the darkness under the table. Sometimes as well he tries to sneak a look outside at them, but each time he does they all fly off, and he has to wait a few minutes until the noise starts again: that small fluttery sound of them out there, getting beasted into their breakfast.

15

A dark red car is turning off the high street. It comes past the park and the cemetery, slowing a moment for a pair of old women to cross the road, then continues on until it pulls into a residential street, and a few seconds later parks up against the kerb. A short bald man gets out, followed by a larger, younger man in a pullover. They come through the gate to Mick's house and stop by the front door. The older man knocks firmly, while the other peers into the living room window. There is no response from inside the house so the older man hunkers down and looks through the letterbox. In a moment he stands up and pushes an envelope through the flap. Then the two men, without speaking, go back through the gate, get into the car and leave.

On the other side of the house, in the shed, Mick is sitting up close to the radio. It is almost out again, the sound distorting quietly like voices inside a hull. He needs batteries – all the ones that were in the house are used up; more bread as well; cash. For now he clicks the radio off and gets the few remaining pages of the paper over for another read, nothing else to occupy his mind now that the morning is by and the sparrows have finished their breakfast and left.

FIRST TENANTS MOVE IN TO NEW HOUSING ASSOCIATION DEVELOPMENT

SLOVAK ROMA COMMUNITY GIVES A HAND TO SOUTHSIDE CLEAN-UP

LOCAL LOLLIPOP MAN HAS REAL STAYING POWER

He gives a read of that one:

> Britain's top football juggler broke the record for keepy-uppies on Tuesday, when he kept a ball aloft for six hours at Debenhams in the St Enoch's city-centre shopping mall.
>
> Sadly, his effort was declared unofficial because there was no representative from the *Guinness Book of World Records* present at the event, although Graeme, 45, has still raised thousands for charity.
>
> Afterwards he said: 'I could have kept going but I had to stop because the store was closing.'

Mick gives a wee smile. Good on ye, pal. The thought of him there in the Debenhams, a crowd of skiving weans and confused old hens gathering round. 42,500 keepy-uppies. Fucksake. That's just mental. Interesting but, these stories that you hear. This other one he minds – about a restaurant owner with a rat problem: they're eating into his food stores and frightening the customers. See but these rats are too canny for the traps, and when they do eat the poison it isn't strong enough to kill them, so the guy decides he's going to leave his cat there the night in the hope the rats will start crapping it and scarper. So he locks the cat in the restaurant, and when he comes in the next morning he finds it out the back court, on top of the beer crates, devoured, only the poor creature's carcass left, and even then some of the bones are away.

Where'd he heard that story? Robbie, was it? Aye, it was – he'd been telling them while they were watching the TV, Lynn shifting about on the settee with a look on her like she'd just sat on a dod of crap, and Jenna elbowing at Robbie telling him it's no an appropriate story to be saying; but him carrying on anyway, nay doubt enjoying putting the mix in.

Probably he's been calling, Robbie. Likely he will have gave Craig a call too, asking him what's the story with the da.

He doesn't want to think about any of it though. It's more than he's up to the now; what he needs to concentrate on is this immediate situation in front of him. First things first, he needs cash, and that means bulling up to go into the bank to see about an overdraft.

He walks quickly, taking the back ways where he can until he has to come out onto the high street. He goes a short cut before the Empress, through a tenement close. There's nobody about. The door to a garbage cage is flapped open and the wheelie bins strewn all at angles inside it from the binmen coming collecting the morning. He comes down a side street and stops at the entrance to the high street, eyeing left and right. It's hoaching. It must be lunchtime: schoolweans outside the chip shop; traffic hurtling – and then, just his bloody luck, he keeks the woman from next door, pushing a pram on the far pavement. He retreats back into the side street, head down, observing the feet. Maybe she wouldn't recognize him even. There is some sort of oil smear down the one trouser leg, he notices, starting above the knee and staining all the way down to his shoes. Perfect. See there's him trying to keep the head down and remain unnoticed, but just look at the state of him – he's bloody bogging – he may as well be wheeling her along after him with a flashing light on top the coffin.

He looks up and watches the neighbour away down the pavement; the messages done, off back now to get on with the business of looking after the snapper, the husband no about, seemingly. And where is the husband? How come you never see him about? Easy to think the worst sometimes but maybe it's just that he's off on the rigs or something, you never know. Cathy would have known, sure enough, but otherwise you never know. There is a lull in the traffic and pedestrians, and he steps out onto the pavement.

When he gets there, the bank is queued out. He decides that he's best waiting until after lunch, and turns the other way down the street.

Which is how he finds himself in the library. It isn't what he intended, but he'd no been intending anything, and it looked quiet inside, so in he went.

She's very helpful, the girl at the desk. He can't have made himself awful clear when he came in, stood there staring just, not knowing if he needed a ticket or anything to go in.

'Can I help ye there?'

'No. Aye, well, see I'm just hoping to have a look round at the books.'

'Ye been here before?'

'No.'

'Come on well and I'll get ye up and running.'

She lifts the desk counter and he follows her as she gets showing him all the different sections while he shuffles behind picking books out at random, trying to seem like he's interested in them and he isn't just in there because he's too feart of everybloodywhere else. And it's good too, somebody being kindly that he doesn't know, who doesn't know him, who isn't sticking the whole pity routine on him. By the time she leaves him at it, he has a whole pile of books that he hasn't a clue what they are. He sits down and opens one of them, all the time looking about to see if anybody is watching him. No danger of that but. It's pretty empty in here. There is a guy that looks like he's a scaffer asleep with a newspaper spread out under his forehead, and three old hens at a table in the corner, each with a copy of the same book. Quite an animated conversation they're having.

'. . . he's clever, I think, he just doesnae get the credit, ye know. All these people that used to come on the show, and he could talk with any of them.'

'Aye, and he's awfy handsome too, say what ye want, but he is. Especially when ye look at the wife there next to him, she's that weary-looking.'

'Aw, come on, of course she's weary-looking – the man's a balloon!'

The three of them start chuckling.

'He is, Helen, he's a bloody balloon.'

The scaffer is woken up. He's got a pen and he's started ringing the classifieds, working down the column, putting a circle around every one. Fair play to him. I admire your confidence, my man. See really that's what he should be doing himself, having a look what jobs are going. If he can't deal with going into Muir's, then he'll have to think of something else, because he can't exactly live off nothing. What money they had, they used up while she was ill, and an overdraft is only going to last so long. A new job. Maybe move somewhere else. A different town. He turns the idea over for a moment. A wee flat somewhere he doesn't know anybody, with only a few simple things he needs in it – TV, kettle, heater – new, replaceable things.

The thought of Muir's, and seeing Lynsey again after he'd done the run-out last time. What they must be saying about him. His chest starts to tighten and he has to concentrate on his breathing, try to control the panic. Across the way, the guy is still going through the columns, ringing the lot, and he wonders if maybe he's some kind of headbanger. But then maybe he's just in here for the same reason he's in here himself. This is his place of refuge, where people leave him in peace and he doesn't have to worry about the outside and all the rub-ye-ups. That's him the now too. Another headbanger in the library. He stands up abruptly to leave, making sure to thank the lassie on the desk and picking up a copy of the *Southside News* as he goes out.

It is quiet in the bank, only a few people queuing up and two clerks on. Nobody he recognizes. He has to collect himself, get it done with, get it over, go back to the shed. The recorded voice calls him to a window. There is a young guy behind the glass. His neck is pinched and red, bulging out from his collar.

'I'm wanting to see about an overdraft.'

'Okay. Pass me your bankcard please.'

He takes it out of his pocket and drops it in the drawer. Across from him there is a dithering old guy stood at the next window – 'Ma what?' – and then the voice through the glass: 'Your statement, sir, I need to see the statement.'

'The account is in debit.' The clerk is looking at him.

'I know. That's how I'm wanting to see about an overdraft.'

He goes back to his screen, tapping away at the keyboard.

'See, I'm afraid there isn't the option of an overdraft on this type of account.'

'Okay, right.'

That's that well. He looks round and the old guy is still rummling shakily in his mac pocket for his statement, pulling out streams of tissue, coins, bus tickets. When he turns back to the window, the clerk is tapping at his keyboard still.

'It might be best, in your circumstances, looking into if you can get a new type of account. I could give you some information.'

So there it is, then, even the bank knows – it's there on his screen.

'I'll leave it the now, thanks.'

Hunger. No surprise there. He lays in the dark looking up out the window at the moon, big and bright the night. The food store is empty. Him and the sparrows finished the last of it for breakfast so now he's pure starving, and you'd think he would be feeling some kind of urgency about the situation but he's not – no a great deal anyway – it's in fact more a kind of relief now that he's no money left. Strange. Figure that one out. No money, no food, and no chance he's going cap in hand to anybody. The idea of that knots him up – obviously it isn't an option – but he allows himself for a moment to imagine it, some kind of odd pleasure from kicking his own head in. Going to Pete for a lend of some money. Anything we can do to help, Mick. Anything we can do. Except fucking for that, Jesus Christ, are ye cracked?

But of course the brother-in-law, that's a different story: he'd be pure delighted, guaranteed. A great song and dance over it, the ceremonious fetching of the chequebook, the smug showy putting on of the wee reading glasses. How much would you like, Mick? Really, it's not a problem. How much? And going on the broo is out the question too. The thought of that is almost as bad as the thought of going to those other two. Queuing up with the wine-moppers, filling out forms and forms and killing her over and over with each one. The same as it would be with the compensation. Deceased. Deceased. Deceased.

He'll be fine. He'll find a way. No like it's the first time he's found himself without any money, that's what he's got to mind, and this time as well it's just him, there isn't a whole family to support. Nothing could be as bad as the last time, when the job Alan had got him after Australia eventually fell to pieces. All they weeks and months of will theys, won't theys, and then the first wave of redundancies starting. Dozens of meetings with the shop stewards and the union men, and all that talk of refusing to give them an inch, don't forget the spirit of '72 and all that, but in the end it came to nothing. That's exactly what they got. Nothing. Alan and the Bowler Hats making their arrangements for theyselves, and all the rest of them left out to dry. See that was a worrying time. The severance cheque didn't solve anything, and the wife's job obvious wasn't going to keep the four of them for long. The arguments they had. So ye won't even consider it, well? It's the damned pride, is what it is, Mr Little. Ye know Don Paton is gone on the broo, so Sheila tells me, and no drama. I'm no saying it's easy, I'm no daft, see I'm only saying this frequenting of the Empress every afternoon and sitting about the house like a pound of mince isnae helping anybody.

She was right, obviously. And her taking on more hours at the store, it was hardly fair, plus on top of that having to come home knackered after work to him there on the settee, grumbling and drunk. Again. After she'd went through all this with him fifteen years before. Her working and him on the bevvy. Desmond the only person who was doing any the better out of it, his bar mobbed with black squad the whole time, drinking and shouting and scheming their plans of attack, convincing themselves that things could be got back how they were. That they knew what they stood for. I am a shipbuilder. That right, eh? So what are ye now that the shipyard has copped its whack and the job is away? I am a shipbuilder. Once a shipbuilder, always a shipbuilder, and all that tollie they'd told theyselves. No just the jobs that went, but the life. Ordinary life, it was gone; it had to be admitted. Himself a culprit. One of the worst. He wouldn't let go. Couldn't cope with the idea that things had changed.

He turns over stiffly and pulls the blankets up to his chin. The nights are too cold now to sleep all the way through. A rain is starting, pattering above his head. He needs to figure something out. He will but. He's managed before, and he'll manage again. Before he eventually got in with the private-hire driving he'd had to leave town to do it, disembark to Newcastle, the short-term contract at Swan Hunter. You battle on just. That's what he'd done then, even if he did spend most of that time lonely and drunk, and it had been against her wishes in the first place. She'd not wanted to be left on her own, looking after the weans, but he'd done it anyway, the same as he always did, the same as when they went to Australia – had that been a joint decision? Had it hell. He'd told her that was what they were doing and so they did it. The moon there out the window. A full one. The great yellowy cunt, bright as a bare arse. Always his idea. Pack your things, hen, leave your job, your friends, your home – we're off! That's how it had been. His idea.

16

'Ye have the item with you?'

'Aye, it's just here.'

'Can ye put it in the tray for me please?'

He takes off his watch and places it in. She inspects it a moment, turning it about in her fingers. She's pure laggered in jewellery: her fingers and thumbs, a gold necklace, and these wee pearly bullets in her ears. Must be she gets a discount.

'Give me a moment please.'

She swivels out from her chair and goes through a back door, and he stands waiting in the empty shop. It isn't like he expected. What was he expecting? Christ knows. Not this, anyway. There's nothing antiquey about the place, that's for sure, all bright lights and a blaze of yellow in the display windows. Sour red carpeting and security notices on the walls. It's like a bank. Actually, no, it's even worse than a bank. He goes over to the window to look at the pieces. Hundreds of rings and bracelets, each of them their own sorry story. In fact, see why don't ye just go and slit the wrists in the corner here – ye may as well if ye're in the mood, ye maunderly auld bastard, christsake. There is a dull chap on the security window as the woman returns.

'Twenty pound.'

'Serious?'

'It's quite worn.'

'No, mean, it's more than I thought.'

She smiles. 'Want it back, well?'

'No, no, it's okay, thanks.'

She is still smiling as she takes out the money and puts it in the tray.

A grey, dreich day outside, the tops of the multis merging into the clouds and the sound of car tyres hissing up water as they come past. Twenty quid. He should probably feel pleased but he's too bloody starving, on the approach now to a minimarket for a sandwich.

The watch was a fiftieth birthday present from the other drivers at Muir's. It must have been pretty expensive if he was getting twenty for it now. That birthday – him, Cathy and the boys, they'd went to a restaurant in the centre. He tries to picture her, but he can't. It was just before Robbie left for Australia because Craig was digging him up the whole time – gonnae send Kylie my love and all this – he wouldn't leave it alone. They'd sat at a table in the corner and she'd been next to him, the place full and noisy, the waitresses with these old-fashioned aprons on and Robbie awful cheeky getting with them, to Craig's annoyance. He can't see her though. He knows she's there sat right next to him but she's the only part of it that's a blank.

He gets his sandwich, and he walks over to the cemetery to go sit down on one of the benches and eat it.

Still a blank. The familiar tightening of his body coming on and he has to relax. He has to relax. Normally he can do that in here, that's aye how he comes, but he's no helping things rubbing himself up like this; he should just calm it down, eat his sandwich. Craig. Craig is here. He's going up the footpath. The first instinct is to duck the head. He's walked right past him, and now he's away up the path toward the grave. Did he see him? Impossible to know, he might've, he might, how could he not've – he's come right beside him. The heart going mental. His body rooted to the spot, but nothing he can do: he can't get up because that will obvious draw attention to himself so all he can do is stay put and hope he doesn't turn round. He gives a keek up. The back of Craig's jacket, a way up the footpath now. He watches as the boy passes through a line of trees to the next lawn and stops when he reaches the grave. He's got his work clothes on, by the look of it, although it's hard to tell from this distance. He's just standing there, looking down. Me and you, Maw, it's me and you against all the rest of them. He stands there a minute or two before he starts to bend and crouch down, and as he does so he turns his head. He is looking straight toward him. It's a bare instant just, a single second, then he turns back to the grave.

He flicks the light switch out of habit but of course it doesn't come on, but so what, he doesn't need to see any of it, the less he can see in fact, the better. As it is, he can still make things out in the half-dark. The mound of post at his feet; the bare, ripped ribbon dangling off the wall. This needs to be done quickly, or if not he's going to collapse in a heap no able to get up and that'll be that, never to be seen again. Except by the man up the stair, of course, that bastard – he needs to be calm, concentrate – no think about a man up the stair. He keeps it all blanked out as he goes through the kitchen, fetching a carrier, and then gets up the steps to the bedroom. He moves quickly inside. Ignores the dark heap on the bed. He pulls open her drawer and grabs a handful of jewellery, dropping it into the bag. His breath is snatching now, coming in jolts, but he's managing it, he's coping, taking another couple of handfuls to empty the drawer, and the truth is it feels good – there – so fucking what? What difference does it make anyway? She's dead. She's not going to wear it.

He'd be pure raging if he knew. But he doesn't, and he can get to fuck if he thinks he's got any more right to her than anybody else. He goes out of the room and back downstairs, where he gets his jacket and the small battered holdall from the lobby, and starts putting things into it: the carrier of jewellery, then out to the shed for his change of clothes and the newspaper. Then he's away. Gone. Goodfuckingbye.

'Ye back, then?'

'I've brought some more things.'

'Go on, well, let's see.'

He empties the carrier into the tray. She gives him a look but he ignores it, and he stares away toward the window while she inspects through it.

'Is it for loan or sale, this?'

'Sale.'

'Okay, well we buy gold and silver by the gram, so I'll need a wee while to price this lot up, that alright?'

'That's fine. I'll wait.'

She gives him £250 for all of it. It's worth a lot more, he knows, but no like he has much of a choice. There's a ring in there that used to be her grandmaw's, which must be worth a couple of hundred on its own, plus a few other things that were handed down to her when she was a wean in a big house in the Highlands and she hadn't yet disgraced and ruined herself with the dirty plater husband.

It's pishing it down when he gets outside. He could get on the subway, all this cash he's got on his tail now, but he needs to be careful saving it so he waits for a bus instead, standing a long time with the wind blowing in and water dripping off his nose. He gets the next one into the centre and gets off at the coach station. There is only a short queue at the ticket desk.

'When's the next coach to London?' he asks the guy.

17

There is a bronze statue by where the man waits. A life-size young couple greet each other, a bag on the floor beside them, and he is lifting her up, their lips about to meet, one hand sliding down over her bottom. The man smiles, looking at it. A couple of girls come past and notice the statue; they start giggling. His own bag is not much bigger than the bronze man's. In it, his few clothes, his work boots, a plastic wallet with his valuables and a little food for the journey. Already there is a large group waiting by the glass doors for the London coach, but he sits further off, on a plastic orange seat by the statue.

He goes inside his coat for his phone and makes a call.

'Yes?'

'Yes, my name is Juraj. I am arriving in London tonight.'

'Got an address?'

'Yes.'

'Passport?'

'Yes,' he lies.

'Right. You'll find details where to come in the morning. There will be a van waiting. Bring the passport, and the driver will need your expenses up front. He'll take you straight to the site.'

'Okay. Okay. The flat is not shared? My wife and son come here soon. The other man said it is not shared.'

'No, not shared. Polish?'

'No. I am from Slovakia.'

'Right, well. Plenty of Polish there. Slovak too probably. You come at six tomorrow. Details are in the flat.'

He puts the phone back in his coat and continues to wait for the coach. Things will not be easy once he arrives; he is not stupid. When the agency in Slovakia arranged for him to come to Glasgow, they told him the same thing. You will have your own room. It will be comfortable for your wife and child when they join you. And on the outside, the red brick building did look beautiful, if you ignored the – 'Govanhell' . . . 'Fuck off gypos' . . . 'Scum' – local poetry. He could not bring them to a place like this. Five cramped streets: no privacy, no heating, no landlord. White and Asian gangs. In London, at least, they will be hidden – Roma, Polish, Pakistani – nobody will care.

An old woman is standing in front of the statue. She looks at it for a moment, then moves away to where a line is forming in front of the glass doors. Back home, it is getting more dangerous: last month, his wife's brother was badly beaten and left in the tip next to where they live. There is no choice now but for them to come here; it is the right decision. The driver is opening the doors and climbing onto the coach. He stands, picks up his bag and goes to join the queue.

There are no empty pairs of seats left on the coach, so he sits down next to a man who is staring out of the window with his hands on top of his bag, clasping it to his lap. Past the man's head, he can still see the statue through the glass wall of the station, and he continues looking at it until the engine starts up and the coach rolls off. He grins. When my wife arrives here, he thinks, this is how I will touch her bottom.

A young guy with a shaved head is come and sat in next to him. It's okay but. He doesn't look like the type that's going to be chinning him all the way down for a conversation. Which is good, because it's a long-enough journey. More than nine hours. Arriving in London in the wee hours, when the pubs are shut and the cafes aren't yet open. He could've planned it better, serious. He could have planned it at all, in fact.

By the time they get leaving the city and the sudden leap of green at the end of the schemes, the gloaming is come on outside the window and he is falling asleep. When he wakes up the lights are turned off and it takes him a moment to mind that he's on a coach, people snoring around him, a dim strip of lighting along the aisle floor, fallen crisps and a crisp packet and legs stretched out. He looks out of the window into the rushing darkness. He doesn't feel jittery. He feels okay. He doesn't feel anything.

A while later and the neighbour is awake. Mick can hear him shuffling forward and unzipping a bag down by his feet. The sound of paper, or plastic, tearing. Then the smell of food, a sausage roll, which he brings up to his mouth and starts eating. Okay, well, a plan. The first thing when the coach gets in is to eat: probably he'll have to find a petrol station or a 24-hour minimarket and wait in the coach station until everywhere else starts opening up. Then onto the job hunt. For starters, this one he's seen in the *Southside News*.

The guy is looking across at him.

'You know where is King's Cross?' he asks, as if they've been pattering away all this time.

'I've no idea, pal, sorry. I've no been to London before.'

The man nods and carries on eating his sausage roll, then after a while he gets out his mobile phone and starts thumbing away. It's a pretty decent point – does it matter that he's never been there before? No, it doesn't. That's the best bloody thing about it. He needs to keep things simple. Keep away from any reminders. Go see about this job advertised in the paper and get on top of himself, fix things out. Englandshire. Nobody will guess that one. He's only been twice before: the six months in Newcastle was the last time, and way before that, when they weren't long married, a visit to Cathy's cousin and the husband in Northampton. Fucking terrible. There were a few of her relatives set up in England, and they'd spent a miserable week with these, himself going about the place trying no to spill and break things and none of her lot speaking with him unless it was to ask him stupit questions about the yards, that same way people use when they ask a wean how school is going. They didn't come to the funeral, that pair, as far as he can mind.

It is raining. He sits back and looks at the giant windscreen wipers going back and forth on the front window. Thinking about England. Newcastle. How he'd felt going down this very motorway, moving further away from home; the argument that him and Cathy had got into the night before he left, both of them shouting, Thatcher on the television in the background, bringing the poll tax to Scotland. See in truth he'd been lucky getting a job at all, because Swans had went the same way as everywhere else – privatized, shrunk – but he hadn't felt lucky; he'd felt fucking terrible. He'd rented a room in a house with quite a few Swans workers, young lads mainly, and a guy his own age from Southampton, he can't mind his name. They'd all go out together to the bars, come back and get the landlady raging. But the clearer memory is of the nights he'd spent alone in his room, drinking, wondering what in hell he was doing in this place. Sat there on his days off, the TV on, until it got too much and he'd go the long walk to the phone box a few streets away.

The neighbour is snoring. Mick turns toward the window, trying to shake the mood that has come over him. Remind himself it wasn't all bad. Because it wasn't. They were good men, for one thing. Mad for their football, anyway. There were always games down by the jetty after lunch; races up the bank by the young lads at the end of a shift; nicknames – Big Yin, they'd called him right from day one, because they knew Billy Connolly had worked on the yards. He never really felt part of it though. He couldn't, no with Cathy and the boys up in Glasgow. And it wasn't his yard; his river. He didn't belong there. Didn't get the same feeling from it: that sense of the river always being there, around him, inside him. The sheer thrill of a ship on its stocks, grown from just a few small pieces of metal, walking toward it each morning and seeing that it was bigger, looking like it was parked there at the end of the street, looming over the end tenement. He can mind exactly the feeling of it. The sound of the hooter. The gates opening and the mass of workers teeming through. Getting into the yard and seeing that the graffiti on the hull had been added to – jokes, patter, Proddy slogans – so that when the ship was near completion you'd look at her and the whole of her side would be a mess of chalk scrawlings. Comic pictures of the managers. Competitions of who could write the highest. Two-year-long conversations. And then, when she was built, it would all be painted over and there'd be no clue as to what was written underneath; except if you looked hard enough, the tiny scribbling along the waterline where the painters had wrote their nicknames.

The driver is pamping the horn to get everybody awake. Mick stands groggily, and presses into the line slowly moving down the aisle. As he steps off the coach, away into the terminal, it is the first chance he's had to see the other passengers. There's a fair number of East Europe types amongst them, it looks like. Something about the quiet way they get on with things, filing off to the exit and seeming to know exactly where it is they're headed – even the neighbour, striding off with his bag over his shoulder, King's Cross here I come.

There is a snack machine in the arrivals terminal and he gets himself a Mars bar, then sits down on one of the backless plastic seats, pulling his jacket tightly about him, and tries to get the brainbox working.

Somebody standing over him. A big fella with a meaty face.

'You okay there, mate?'

A sliver of belly poking out beneath the shirt.

'Do you know where you are?'

Mick chuckles. 'I've no got a clue, pal.' He notices then there's the half-eaten Mars in his lap.

'You can't stay here, I'm afraid.'

'It's fine, see I must've fallen asleep for a minute just. I'm looking for a cafe that's open, if ye know somewhere.'

'I do actually. There's one just round the corner, as it happens.'

He points Mick what direction it is and waits for him to get up and leave.

When he gets there it is open, like the man said. The pleasurable sound of chairs and plates and low conversation as he steps in and gets himself a table, reading the breakfasts off coloured sheets of card above the kitchen. A few coach-driver types drinking coffees. A street cleaner in a high-vis jacket, and he minds suddenly the incident with the parkie and the stolen flowers, but he shuts it out straight away as the guy comes over for his order. Bacon and eggs, and a tea. He's pretty friendly, the time of morning it is, humming himself a wee tune. Turkish, if the poster above the kitchen is anything to go by. Things have started well. A hot breakfast about to arrive, in a little wink-wink of a place that he's found, when instead he could easily be pounding about the streets right now for a petrol station.

When he's finished, he goes up the counter and asks the guy if he knows anywhere nearby he might get a room for what's left of the night.

'Hostel? B&B?'

'B&B, aye.'

He reaches for his order pad and pulls a pen from his trouser pocket, but then hesitates, deciding against it. He points an arm to his left.

'You see this street? You go down, you go left under the bridge, and there – there are many places. Ten minutes.'

Mick thanks him and picks up his bag to leave. No bad, eh, this London. No bad.

He can see the bridge up the way. It is a railway bridge, he can make out as he gets closer, walking alongside the high sooty walls that follow the road beneath. There is a narrow street just before the bridge and he turns onto it, past a builders' merchants and an MOT garage under the arches. A few minutes down and he spots a cracked white plastic sign: BED AND BREAKFAST: SINGLE £25, DOUBLE £40, FAMILIES £60. Fine. It will do. He just needs a bed for the night, it's no like he's choosy. He goes up the steps and there's no obvious buzzer so he tries the door, and it's open. He treads into a dimly lit corridor with a worn red carpet and the ribs of the floor-boards showing underneath. Yellow, chappit wallpaper. At the end there is a sign – RECEPTION – and an arrow pointing up the staircase.

He goes up to the first stairhead, where there is a door with a crumpled plastic file pinned on it. A piece of paper inside. *Back in 10 minutes*. It doesn't look likely. Probably it's too late the now to get somewhere, but just then a man appears on the stairs behind him, another Turk, by the looks of him.

'Have you lost your key?'

'No, I just, mean, I was hoping to get a room.'

The man leads him up the next flight of steps, fishing a bunch of keys from his pocket, and unsnibs a door.

'Single room?'

He nods.

'Single room is £25.' He stands there scrunching the keys down by his side. Ye reckon he wants the money up front, well? Mick gets out his wallet.

'Whereabouts is breakfast served?'

'No breakfast.'

'Eh? No breakfast? It says "Bed and Breakfast" on the sign outside.'

'No breakfast.' He takes his money and leaves.

No breakfast, then. Mick stands at the door and takes in his room. Poky, a stale clinging smell, the same peeling wallpaper as the corridors, and what looks like a giant shite-mark on the carpet. It's better than a shed though, so nay point complaining. There's no curtains, instead a grey veil pinned over the window with an orange glow coming in one side of it. He climbs onto the bed, which seems clean, and is that tightly tucked it looks vacuum-packed. He lies on top of the covers. He should be doing a stock-take of the situation, he knows, but his head is aching and it's hard to think clearly, so he lies there just, the eyes closed, vaguely aware of a streetlight buzzing outside, and at one point the rumble of a train going over the bridge.

Later the night he has to pee, the need for it building and building until it's too uncomfortable, and he gets up. He waits at the door a while, listening to make sure there's nobody about, then he comes out, and up the next flight of steps to a door marked BATHROOM. No that he wouldn't have telt it by the smell: sharp, sour, mixed in with bleach, the bottle of which is left out, sat on a ledge under the sink. When he's done he comes back in his room and snibs the lock.

Morning. He lies there a long time. His stomach is uneasy, and the whole of his body is aching like he's just come off a back shift. The streetlamp is turned off and daylight sifts dirtily through the window veil, exposing the room. That scunnery brown streak on the carpet, he can see now that it's a scorch mark. Christ. Ye dread to think.

A noise outside the door makes him jump. Somebody pounding down the staircase. Quietening down the next flight, quieter, then silence. His heart is racing at the suddenness of it. Just a noise. It was just a noise. Somebody running down the stair, it's nothing out the ordinary. But he is panicking and it's a struggle to get control of it as he presses the side of his head into the pillow, hearing the thump of blood in his ear. That's just the problem but – it *is* out the ordinary. No like he hasn't heard people running down stairs before, but no *here*, no in this place he hasn't.

Just a noise, just a noise.

But he's got nowhere to put it. A fucking noise, man – they've gone by now – but it's bouncing around inside him, unable to come to rest because everything else is jumbled up and bouncing around together, and he can't act or think normally because what *is* fucking normal? Answer that one. What is normal? There isn't a normal. He swings his legs over the bed and sits up. Everything racing and rushing. He is sucking for breath but it's no good, sitting up is making him feel boaky, so he lies back down again and gives up trying to stop it. Thoughts hurtling in, he can't keep them out. She is normal. That is what normal is. There, he's said it. But now everything is birling around and it's all to fuck because that's the thing he's been trying to steer clear of, thinking about the wife, and now he's let it in and there's no controlling it. *She* is ordinary life – she's as much a part of him as his legs or his stomach – and without her all the rest has lost the plot. The stomach fucking especially.

Cry, man. Just bloody cry. Nobody's watching. But he can't let himself – it's there, he can feel it in his throat like a furball, retching and stuck, but he's too feart to let himself. It'll just make him the worse. And then he definitely won't be able to stop, he'll be here the whole day bloody greeting.

There are voices in the room below. So what? He's staying in a Bed and Breakfast – well, a Bed – what do you expect, he'll have to deal with it just. He can't hear what they're saying but it sounds like there's a few of them, a family, because there's a baby shrieking or crying or making some kind of a racket. He gets up off the bed and pulls the table that's under the window over to wedge against the door. Then he gets back on the bed. No television, so no easy way to ward off the brain, except for sleep, closing the eyes and sleeping, he could sleep all day, he could sleep forever.

Later he goes down and gives another £25 to No Breakfast, who counts the money carefully and slides it in his pocket.

That night he sleeps fitfully, in and out, a lot of it just staring at the orange glow through the window.

The people down the stair are arguing. A woman shouting. It goes on for quite a long time and then there's a door shutting and it goes quiet. He needs to get some food. No easy thing going out into the day but. What he needs to do is just blank everything out, kid on that he isn't actually existing and do the zombie walk to wherever the shop is. Nobody knows him anyway. That's what he has to tell himself. Nobody knows him.

He finds a Costcutter after the bridge. There is a radio playing but he can't hear the words. He gets a damp pasty in a packet from the fridge, a couple of lager cans and a sandwich for later. He doesn't look up at the man as he pays. Another guy by the door as he goes out, sat behind a kiosk like some silent gremlin, selling phonecards.

The next few days he slips into a routine. Out to the shop in the morning, and forcing the food down when he gets back. Then sleeping and drinking and keeping the brain quiet until he has to go down and give No Breakfast his money. The wee patter between them: how's it going, pal? Oh, not too bad, thanks, business pretty steady at the moment thanks to you and as well the family downstairs. Good, good, I'm pleased. Clutching for a normal. It is some kind of an ordinary, however crap.

18

He opens the *Southside News* and gets to the page:

> Major hotel chain, UK airports: Glasgow, Birmingham, Manchester, London Heathrow. Staff wanted, all departments: Housekeepers, Food and Beverage Assistants, Breakfast Chefs, Kitchen Porters, Reservations Assistants. Live-in positions.

Work. Work is what he's came down here for, and work is what's going to get him back onto his feet. Spend too long without employment and what else are you going to do but occupy the whole time alone with yourself until the brain is turned to mince? That's another reason he'd never go on the broo. Work is busyness at least. So he needs to get off his bahookie and get some, get on the keel and give Robbie a call, because this keeping him in the dark cannot go on. And so what if he's never been a kitchen porter before? He can do it, he can lie if he has to, and it's perfect, really: something different from what he's done before, no reminders. Plus as well the money situation: he's running out.

He washes himself, or tries to anyway, with what little water he can bleed out of the shower head. Afterwards, a good examination of the face in the mirror. He could fine well do with a shave, but he doesn't have a razor. Still, it's long enough now that he has a decent beard on. A respectable beardie man, a Sean Connery type, that's the way he should look at it. Although being honest, respectable is probably up in the air when they get to looking at his clothes. He's got on the shirt and trousers that he had in his bag, but the problem is that both of them are crumpled as a toad's foreskin. See what he should do, he should probably give a phone down to room service and ask No Breakfast for a lend of the iron. He forces a smile at the idea of it. He feels okay. He feels fine. He is going to get on.

He packs his bag and leaves away into the street. What he needs is a good shovel of food, to keep him going the rest of the day, and where better to get it than at your man's down the way, the cheery Turk.

After eating, he gets negotiating the subway. Finding it is easy enough, although the actual thing itself is genuine a bit more complicated; a Rubik's Cube of colour-coded trickery compared to the one he's used to. He manages but. He is managing.

There is a young guy on the line of seats opposite him. He's got on a pair of tight blue trousers and pointed white shoes, his legs crossed over like a woman's. The pointy foot joggling in the air with the bumps of the track. He's reading a magazine with a cartoon drawing of two men on the front with comic stretched faces. He's about ages with Robbie and Craig. What would they make of him? Just then but the train comes to a halt and he has to concentrate to get hearing the driver, and he is able to stop the thought before it can develop. He needs to keep focused. The brain is a genuine minefield of all these thoughts that he's got to keep himself from thinking, for the moment at least, just for the moment, until he's got himself back on his feet. Then he can see where he's at.

The hotel is one of a fair number along a drag that he has to cross a great tangle of carriageways and multi-storey car parks to get to. It's huge – they're all huge – and ugly. A block of grey, stained concrete; the only colour is the massive lettering of the hotel's name above the doors. The woman that he speaks to on reception is friendly enough but.

'The operations manager is in a meeting until three,' she tells him after she's put in a call. 'Do you mind waiting?'

'No problem.'

The operations manager, it turns out, after he's waited a long while on a seat fixed to the table in an empty restaurant, surrounded by plastic plants, is a woman. She doesn't shake his hand. 'You're a kitchen porter,' she says, going behind the bar to make herself a coffee. 'You're not agency though?'

'No.'

'Do you have a CV?'

'No.' Great start. Bloody haddock. 'See, I was in the shipyards, and then my last job I was a cab driver. But when I was younger I used to work in kitchens. Hotels and that.' A pretty obvious lie. She is behind the bar still, looking at him as she stirs a sugar into her cup. It isn't the face of an impressed person.

'I saw the job advertised in a paper.'

She frowns. 'When?'

'A while back, actually.'

She comes out from the bar. 'Well, it's up to the chef anyway. Come this way.'

He follows her round a corner into a passageway where the carpet stops, and there is a pair of swing doors with small porthole windows. Blinding bright inside, mobbed with men in white jackets. She goes in and he waits outside, a tight feeling in his chest. Relax. Just relax. She is stood just inside the kitchen, and a tall man is coming over toward her. Behind him, at a gas range, one of the chefs is pouring a packet of something into a pan. The tall man keeks at him through the porthole.

'. . . is him,' he hears her say as the doors swing open. She walks off without looking round and the man is stood in front of him.

'You've not done KP before, then?' He is Irish. He's got baggy red and white checked trousers.

'No, mean, not for a while.'

'Scottish?'

'Aye, Glasgow.'

He folds his arms, narrowing the eyes and smiling.

'Here's the million-dollar question, then – Bhoy or Bluenose?'

Mick smiles. 'Bluenose.'

The chef gives himself a comic slap on the forehead. 'Fucking typical.' He grins. 'No, it's fine, it's fine, I don't give a shite. And you're the right colour anyway.'

He goes in the swing doors and Mick follows, keeping the head down and avoiding looking up at the other chefs. He reaches for a pen on top of a whiteboard by the door.

'What's your name?'

'Mick.'

He writes it down next to BREAKFAST: MICK WASH I.

'You've timed it well in fact – we had a guy left yesterday.'

They walk through the kitchen. He is staying calm. Heat, young men with shaved heads, the sound of a radio. They go past a heap of crates, and the kitchen throats into another room, smaller, dimmer than the main one. A very black man in dark green overalls is clattering a pile of frying pans into a sink.

'Eric, take this fella down to the staff rooms.' He turns to Mick. 'Take whatever one is free and get yourself settled in for today. Breakfast starts at six so get here just before and I'll sort you out some overalls,' he says, and leaves.

The black guy hasn't looked up from the sink, and Mick wonders a moment if he has understood. In a minute though he stretches off his rubber gloves and goes out through a fire door, the tap left running.

He follows behind him as they go down steps and through corridors, and it's becoming clear enough that your man here isn't going to speak, walking slowly ahead, the bare back of his neck shining under the fluorescent strips. At one point a stretch of tubing is out, and they walk on in near complete darkness until the next lit corridor, then down more steps, right into the bowels.

'Here,' the black man says, and goes back the way they came.

He is left in a long corridor with doors both sides. One of them is open, and he sees inside that it is a bathroom. He goes down the line of doors. Low music coming from one; snoring, another. Otherwise the place is silent. He stands there, wondering what is his next move. This is mental. Unreal. It's that far removed from reality in fact that it's hard to believe there's not some kind of chicanery going on, the auld brainbox playing tricks. But to these people it's just ordinary; he is ordinary even, that's the strangest thing. All of them – the manager, the chef, the kitchen porter – it's like they expected to see him here. He hasn't caused the barest ripple of an interruption. Go downstairs and go in your room and you're working at six the morrow, and everything just carries on as it was.

Somebody is coming out of a door down the way. A girl. She's in her pyjamas and barie feet. He stands there rooted as she comes toward him, and he's about to have to say something when she turns into the bathroom. She didn't seem to notice him even. What, are they on drugs, these people? He feels like he's totally lost his bearings, the quiet sounds of snoring and music and humming strip lights around him, a girl in her pyjamas, and he's losing track already if it's day or if it's night. The toilet is flushing. She comes out and starts walking back to her room.

'Excuse me,' he calls out. She doesn't hear him.

'Excuse me.'

She looks back blankly.

'Can ye tell me which of these is free, please?' He can see now that she's been asleep, the eyes half closed.

She shrugs her shoulders. 'I think maybe this one.' She points to a door by the bathroom, and pads off.

He pushes the door open slowly and the shapes inside become clearer as the light from the corridor filters through. The room is empty, the bed made. He finds the switch and the bulb takes a moment stammering on. It is like a compartment in a storage warehouse, threadbare and windowless; tiled drop ceiling. There is a sink and a chipped white Formica wardrobe, a waste bucket, a chair and a small table with an alarm clock, the hands pointing just the back of four. Unreality has hold of him now, carrying him numbly on as he arranges his few clothes in the wardrobe, takes off his shoes, puts them under the table and gets lying down on the bed. Careful. He needs to be careful. Too easy to get maunderly and think about things – the lack of daylight, for one, Christ – but actually what he should be thinking is good positive thoughts. He has found himself a job. He is on his feet. He has got himself what he was looking for. What was that, well? It was an anonymous room in a place with no reminders and no bastards to pity him or stick the boot on. The image of Craig in the cemetery comes suddenly to him, but he knows he has to shut it away, shut it right away. He looks about him. See if he gives the room a bit of a spruce up it might not be so bad. A mini television. Plants. Maybe he could knock a couple of plastic ones out the restaurant even – there ye go, now you're talking man, now you're bloody talking.

There is noise outside the door just before five: foreign voices, shouts, a woman laughing. Then it goes silent for half an hour, until all at once the noise returns and there's a few minutes of activity before it quiets down again. After that, there's just the occasional sound: doors shutting, a voice coming past, the flush of the toilet through the wall behind his head. Later the evening he leaves the room and finds his way eventually out of the hotel, making his way over to the terminal, where he gets a jacket tattie and a pint.

He doesn't sleep the best, so the early start isn't a problem. He is up at the kitchen for quarter to six, waiting in the potwash. Through in the cooking area he can hear the Irish chef instructing his shaven-headed team to get set up. After a few minutes he comes into the potwash holding a fryer smoking with bacon fat, and sees Mick standing by the machine.

'Shite, yes.'

He goes off a moment and returns with a pair of overalls. 'He'll show you, but it's easy enough. Wash 1 means you stand at this sink and scrub most of the crap off everything, then you stack it in these trays for him to put through the machine. And you clean the kitchen stuff.' He points at the bacon pan hissing in the sink.

There is nowhere to get changed so he puts the overalls on in there, on top of his clothes. And that is the first thing he learns: not to wear anything underneath. Within half an hour he is pure sweltering from his exertions and the heat of the machine. Wash 2 is fine but. He's got the right idea – just the bare black skin visible under his overalls whenever he bends down to stack something – he's genuine fine and breezy. No that he's said as much: he's hardly spoke a word since he came in. It isn't the same one as yesterday – he's taller, this guy, and he's fucking fast. It's hard work keeping up putting the plates and cups in the trays before he grabs and trammels them along the runners into the machine – the hoosh of steam as he pulls it down and sets it running. Thirty seconds and they come out dry, it seems, because he piles the lot straight up and takes it over to the racks. When he does speak, it's to tell Mick that he's doing it wrong – 'No. No' – and he'll stand in front of him and start stacking the trays himself. It's doable but. He is doing it. He is managing. First day on the job and he's on top of it.

It is a separate world but, the potwash. He'd've thought it would be different to this – all noise and shouting and Gordon Ramsay, waiters running about with their arses on fire – but it isn't. It's oddly quiet in there, cut off, just him and Wash 2 scrubbing and stacking, scrubbing and stacking. There is the clanging and jouncing of ovens and grills from in the kitchen, and each while a chef coming through, shouting, 'Hot pan,' but even through there, there's no noise, no patter. Strange. It's fine but. It suits him. Ye keep the head down, ye do your job. Scrub, stack; scrub, stack. The faces of waiters appearing at the hatch above the sink to dump the dirties on the ledge. You new, pal? What's your name? Good to meet you, how's it going? They don't speak. They don't see him even. Fine. That's fine. And there's something quite satisfying about the work as well – no exactly stimulating but it's mechanical, you get into a rhythm, repeating the actions, challenging yourself to get the pile down. The empty ledge. A wee pat-the-back moment of job satisfaction. See that, Wash 2? First shift but no messing, eh, no fucking messing about, look.

Of course but he's jumped the gun. There he is thinking he's such a big man for keeping his piles down, while there must be hardly anybody in the restaurant. It doesn't start coming properly until an hour in. Plate piles begin growing on the ledge, tall teetering columns of bowls and cups; the cutlery bucket swelling like a haemorrhoid; and the waiters finding their tongues at last, beefing that they've no space to put the dirties. He's not keeping up and he's soon enough sweating all over the place in a panic, desperate to get it down before the Paddy chef comes through and sees.

Wash 2 is fair agity getting with him by now, butting over to get the piles and stack them himself. And then, just when it's coming on the busiest, the baldies start barging in with all their pots and pans, fat-fryer baskets, chopping boards, long metal trays lined with burnt knickers of egg. His heart is racing. He gets rushing about, losing his scourer, piles increasing all around him. He trips on a heap of pans by his feet and near goes on his neck. Bracing his hands on the sink, he takes a couple of deep breaths, the black guy glaring over at him. Get beasted in just. Get the piles down before the chef sees, finish this shift – then he can put down a marker, then he'll know where he's at. He leans toward the machine, ignoring Wash 2, pulls over an empty tray and gets loading.

Toward the end of the service, as he's thinking it's started to quiet down, they begin coming with great long dishes and glass bowls in from the restaurant. He gets scraping them out, chucking leftover sausages and grapefruit segments into the bin, until one of the waiters starts going through him, saying he has to wait until they've cleared all the food themselves. It must get reused, he realizes. All of it, too, they clear the lot. Even the eggs, man, Christ.

By the time it's over he is pure wheezing, blowing for tugs. And that was breakfast – Christ knows what like the lunch service is, or dinner. Or if he has to work them all, either, that's another thing he's still in the dark about. Still but he got through it. His standards were up in the air quick enough, but he got through it – congealed crockery going straight in the tray and the scrub, stack of earlier turned into a dump, dump, dump. Fair unlikely that it was coming out the other side clean, but Wash 2 didn't seem too bothered, he just wanted to keep it moving through, the piles kept down, the waiters shut up. To keep their faces away from the hatch.

Wash 2 takes off his gloves and motions Mick to follow as he goes into the kitchen. The baldies are bent and kneeling, scrubbing inside the ovens. Wash 2 writes his hours on the board and hands him the pen when he's done.

'Dia, is it? Hello.' He holds out his hand. 'My name's Mick.'

It doesn't feel quite the right thing, a handshake, but the guy takes it, with a small nod of the head. 'Breakfast now,' he says.

Mick follows him into a bare, bright room with tables put together into two long rows. There is a queue of twenty or so staff getting food from a table in the middle. As soon as they go in he feels exposed, stood there in the bright room for everybody to look at. There is the noise of chairs scraping as people take their places and start eating. Dia is gone ahead into the queue, and Mick joins the end of it, one of the chefs getting in just before him. He stays close behind and shuffles forward. There is a great purple wart on the back of the guy's neck, his skin raw and pink around it where it's been catching his collar. Somebody behind him too now, he can hear him puffing his frustration at the queue. 'Come on, come on.' His eyes on Mick's back, taking him in. Chefs pushing in further up the queue; nobody saying anything.

Here are the eggs, then. By the time Mick gets to the table, eggs is mainly what's left, plus a few sausages, beans, fruit salads. He doesn't care. He just wants to get sat and get eaten, go back to his room.

Dia is on a table of black men, four of them sat together in green overalls. Mick goes to the other row, sitting himself at one end where the seats all around are empty. Further down there is a group of women, all dark haired, foreign-looking. One of them keeks over at him at one point, and he realizes he must be sat where their pals are about to sit. He eats up his breakfast quickly and at random. No that it's a meal you'd want to linger over. One sausage, a slice of bread, and a small clot of beans sharing juices with three pineapple slices. Nay wonder they're all so miserable.

Everyone's in their own group – the baldies at one table, the waiters another, the receptionists – all of them keeping in with themselves. It's like school. And it's so quiet, that's the strangest thing. Hardly anybody talking, just chowing their food down in silence, the only noise in the room the sound of knives and forks hitting plates. Most of them look foreign, maybe that's part of it, the lack of mixing. Still but, who's he to talk, the cloyed-up Scot there at the end of the row.

He is finishing off when the head chef comes in and walks over to him. He stands stooping opposite him, his hands pressed on the table.

'Go okay today?'

'Fine, aye, once I'd got the hang of it.'

Some of the women are looking over.

'You need to get your speed up, that's all.' He stands straight, looking off toward the door, then back at Mick. 'Next staff food is at five, and your late starts at half past, okay?' He pats once on the table and walks away.

He doesn't go to the next staff food. He holes up in his room, laid on the bed in his pants and his socks, done in, drifting in and out of sleep through the afternoon.

The late shift is longer, relentless, more types of crockery. At least but he is in the bare scuddy underneath the overalls, which is a pure blessed relief compared to earlier. And as well he manages to wrestle a few more words out of Dia, who is on with him again.

'Where are ye from?'

'Ghana.'

He realizes it's coming to a close when the waiters are only leaving tea and coffee cups, and these wee pots skinned with leftover mustard and ketchup.

When the kitchen start bringing all their pots and pans through, Dia gives him a hand scrubbing them clean, and afterward shows him where the mop is to follow where he's already swept. They are about done when one of the baldies comes through with a bottle of beer in his hand, sheer-legging over the wet floor to reach for his knife bag off one of the shelves. A beer. That would be pure fucking heaven right now. He doesn't say anything to Dia though, and they finish up, draining the machine and bringing out the rubbish bags before they leave, away back to the staff quarters.

He gets into his room and tummels onto the bed.

19

The next day is much the same; and the next. His body is feeling like it's took a kicking. By the time his day off comes, he's that exhausted it is all he can do to get out of bed in time for staff food, and he spends most of the rest of it asleep.

The rota is two shifts each day out of breakfast, lunch or dinner, and one day off a week. His mind is occupied, near enough, and then when he's no working he's too tired even to think. He gets kept on Wash 1 for the first week, either with Dia or with Eric. He doesn't try getting any patter out of them so it's aye quiet working, but no that it's frosty or anything, it's fine, it's just work. They two have their own reasons they don't yap on, the same as he does, and so they get on with it just, silently working as a team while the baldies flash in and out with hot pans and the waiters gurn through the hatch.

The afternoons, which are only a couple of hours if he's on a lunch, he rests up in his room, or he goes out the back fire exit to the terminal for a pint, or sometimes, if he can't stomach the idea of returning for the lunatic buffet, a sandwich.

The later staff food is harder going even than the breakfast. Usually there's a tray of mince, without tatties, and a tray of carrot omelette, or onion omelette, or sausage omelette. Then it might be chips, which are away in a second, and hard, chewy rice that gets stuck between your teeth. He sits at the correct table now. Takes his place with his African co-workers and chows away silently next to them. He asks the other two their names. Obi and Vincent. They wear the same green overalls, but they work in a different kitchen, he doesn't know where.

One day after the breakfast shift, the head chef comes in the potwash to tell him he needs to go up and see the operations manager: she has to get his details on the system.

He goes after staff food. Her office is on the same level as the kitchen, through a corridor with the same scuffed carpeting and bare walls as the rest of the staff side, but the occasional plastic plant and a wall clock with the hotel logo on it. A few shabby efforts at perking up the gloom – it's in fact no unlike the walk used to be up to Alan's office – which maybe explains how his stomach is feeling right now. Away, it's Mick! Good to see you. You're a kitchen porter now, I hear. Good for you, that's great.

He's about to chap the door, but he hears voices inside, what sounds like an argument, and he hangs back. Hard to make out what they're saying, but it's two women. Probably he should get leaving. But then there is movement inside, and he presses back against the wall as one of the housekeepers comes out, leaves the door open, and is away muttering down the corridor. The operations manager appears, sees him, scowls.

'I'm here to fix out my details.'

She turns away. 'Wait.'

The door shuts, and a few moments later she shouts him to come in.

She gives him a sheet of paper to fill in and ignores him, busy writing quickly onto a pad. She's rattled, clear enough. He can feel the movement in the desk as she writes. A great black printer between them with Post-it notes stuck on it: *Tronc adjustments. Gerry, Plane Food, 4 p.m.*

Scottish, he puts on the form, and Mick; the rest he makes up. He's filling this out on a need-to-know basis, is how it's going to go, and there's fine well certain things they don't need to know. Provan, he calls himself, after Dave Provan who played for Rangers when he was a wean. As he passes the form to her, he says that he doesn't have a bank account. She doesn't try hiding the scunnered expression that comes on her face, but it seems at least she believes him. They'll pay him in cash, she says, until he's got one. An envelope job. Nay problem. Nay problem at all.

When the first paypacket comes, handed to him by the head chef at the start of one dinner shift, he doesn't have any pockets to put the envelope in, so he tucks it in the top of his pants. When he's signed out and he gets back into his room to take a look, one side of the envelope is clabbered with sweat and it pulls apart easily. There is a wad of twenties. No a great lot of twenties, mind, for the hours he must have worked. He sticks it on the table, under the alarm clock. Next day off, he'll go buy a mini television. Christ knows where but. It isn't like there's shops around; or pubs, minimarkets, offies. The area around the hotel is a demented wasteland of concrete and car parks, carriageways and flyovers. The only place to go is the terminal. From what he can tell, none of the workers much leave the building. They keep to their rooms, or they lounder about the basement amongst their own squad. Mostly, though, they work. There's staff on twenty-four hours, and he's got accustomed by now to the comings and the goings during the night: the banging of doors and shuffling in the corridor; the toilet flushing and the noise of the pipes in the walls as the different groups come on and off shift.

Mainly it is KPs and housekeepers down there in the basement. The doormen as well, and the night porter, whose room is across the way from his and he hears getting in each morning just the back of six. Each squad is divided by continent, it seems, as if these are skills you're born into, the cleaning of saucepans and toilets. The KPs, apart from himself, are African; the housekeepers, South American; most of the chefs and the receptionists, East Europes; and the waiters, fuck knows.

That's what Dia has told him. The KPs are pretty much the only ones that ever talk in English. And they understand better than he'd thought, the times that he's had any conversation with them; which isn't a great lot, to be honest. Eric is still quiet with him while they work, although he has noticed that he's aye similar with the others when they're together. Dia is a wee bit more talkative getting with him though, telling him sometimes which of the waiters and the chefs he dislikes the most.

Outside of the potwash and the lunatic buffet, there aren't many places to go: there is a small staff room, round the dogleg at the bottom of the corridor, with a table and a few chairs, a battered oven, a kettle and a toaster, but Mick never goes in there, so the only place he sees anybody is in the laundry room. He goes in one afternoon, with a carrier of socks and pants, and Dia is at one of the machines taking out his clothes. Before he gets leaving, Mick chins him to ask about their pay. Dia smiles.

'It is not very much.'

'Aye, I've noticed.'

'You write down how many hours but it is always the same.'

'They take some off for the accommodation, then? They must do, eh?'

He grins. 'Oh, yes. They do. And food. We stay in a fine hotel. See?' He looks up and around at the drop ceiling. 'You are not with the agency?'

'No.'

'You are lucky. You are an Englishman. I am with the agency.'

'Careful, pal, I'm Scottish.'

Dia laughs. 'Yes, yes, sorry. Scottish. We are the same, then.'

Mick smiles. 'Aye, well, maybe.'

The next time he is on with Dia, they speak some more. Dia asks him about Scotland and Mick begins telling him about the yards, what like it was working in them. He quietens up soon enough though. Dia is obviously interested, but he doesn't press him. It's surprising, in fact, how much he knows already. He knows all about the big boats that were made on the Clyde, which probably goes to bloody show what dark part some of these ships they made had to play in people like Dia's history. Mick realizes he doesn't know if Ghana has a coastline even. Pretty bloody ignorant, really, but he doesn't ask. Dia tells him about his family. He has a wife and a baby, he says, at home in his country. He's going back soon to work as an accountant. That's what he studied, accountancy, christsake.

He is getting on. He's no maundering up in Glasgow with his head stuck to the freezer or rotting in the shed like a sack of potatoes; he is getting through the days and the already familiar pattern of work, sleep, work, sleep, work, day off, work. Over the next couple of weeks, he goes each few days into the terminal and gets a supply of four-packs for the bargain price of £6 each. One day off soon, he'll get out and onto the subway, buy the mini television, allow himself to think about giving Robbie a call. Even to see outside of the airport, that would be something.

He is dozing in his room one afternoon when he hears some kind of commotion down the corridor. He ignores it at first, but after a few minutes he gets up to have a hingie out the door at what's going on. It is coming from round the dogleg. He walks down the way, and keeks inside the staff room as he goes past. All the housekeepers are in there, it looks like, and as well he notices Dia and Eric inamongst. The women are talking in Spanish, but maybe those two understand anyway; it wouldn't come as a great surprise, in truth. He goes in the laundry for a moment, listening to the babble through the wall, then he leaves away back to his room.

He wakes up, sweating. The jittery sensation of knowing he's awake and the dream is by but the feeling of it staying with him. He sits up with the sheets resting damply on his stomach, the head muddled, the image still there. She is knelt down in front of him and he is looking at her from behind. A great dump of washing in front of her, and she is lifting a pair of overalls out of the pile. He closes his eyes and tries to keep the picture moving, to see the front of her, but his chest and then the whole of his body has started laddering, hardening. The yellow edge of light on top of the door and the dim shapes of the room coming into focus. Wardrobe. Table. Clothes left lying on the floor. He is in the hotel. A potwasher. On again the morning, a matter of hours just.

He gets up and perches on the end of the bed but it's impossible getting a hold on anything, it's all birling about the brainbox. He stands up and moves toward the bundle of clothes by the table, picks up the overalls and gets them under his arm. He claws a fistful of coins from the wardrobe drawer and leaves the room into the ever-lit light of the corridor.

His limbs are stiff as he walks and he's not feeling totally in the present, no at all in fact – he feels half asleep, the dream still pulling, like drag chains, behind him.

The laundry room is empty. He goes in and gets a punnet of powder from the dispenser, and puts the overalls into one of the washers.

He sits on a chair and watches them spin and flump through the glass; shuts his eyes and tries to see her.

The sound of a door opening and footsteps in the corridor. One of the housekeepers is at the doorway with her dressing gown wrapped about her, a pissed-off look on her face. She comes toward him and bends down, putting a hand on his shoulder.

'You should go to bed now, yes?' she says with a small sad smile, then she is away.

20

The butter bucket. Daft but you get fixed on it, studying how full it's getting, sat there on the ledge where the waiters scrape the butter dishes into it; a measure of how busy the service is. And then you start guessing what level it's going to get to, is it going to beat the record and all this. Daft. But it keeps the sanity. The busiest shifts, it's best taking a deep breath and getting stuck in, no a word between the two of you, each in your own worlds, the machine booming, the baldies shouting through for pan collections, and the ping of microwaves in the kitchen going ten the dozen like a sweet shop after school closing.

He gets put on Wash 2 now as well, which is pretty much the same story as Wash 1 except you get pish-wet through to boot. In the quieter moments, he talks to Dia, and a little bit to Eric now, who near knotted himself the morning he came in with his overalls a size snugger from drying them too quickly. 'Staff food is good, hey?' And he'd had a right chuckle at him. 'Must be, aye.'

One thing he's noticed: the lull before service starts, the waiters come past the hatch with a tray of teas and coffees for the kitchen. It's the same story with beers too, when the chefs go into the restaurant at the end of the night for a drink. There's times when he'll be pure murdering for a drink himself after a shift, but the other KPs don't seem bothered. Maybe a religious thing. Or maybe because it's normal just, it's the way it goes and they accept it. One shift he asks Dia about it, how they never get brought a tea in. Dia laughs. He pats the top of the machine.

'The machine does not drink tea,' he says. A strange way of putting it, but he gets the point.

Later the same shift, he tells Dia he saw the meeting in the staff room.

'It is terrible, terrible, they do this. These people' – and he chibs a handful of teaspoons toward the restaurant – 'we must not give them one inch, or they take the mile.' Mick can't help smiling at the phrase, but the head chef comes through that moment and they both quieten up. When he's gone, Dia tells him what the story is, with one eye watchful of the throat into the kitchen.

The housekeepers, he says, are wanting to go on strike because they aren't getting their correct pay. Some dirty chicanery it sounds like too. The hotel has started only clocking their hours for the time they actually spend in the rooms. So if any of the guests decide on a lie in or a lumber before breakfast, and don't vacate when they're supposed to, the housekeepers have to wait without being paid for the time.

'Serious?'

Dia nods slowly.

'How do they know? How they know the cleaners aren't in the rooms?'

'They spy.'

'Aw, that's terrible.' He pulls the machine down and starts a new cycle. 'And ye're joining in yourself, well, if they strike?'

'Yes. If they can do this to them, they will do this to us.'

The whole of the basement staff are in on it, he finds out soon enough. Too bloody right. Dia's no wrong, what he says. Give them an inch and all that. The next meeting is called one morning, wee nods and whispers after staff food, and he goes along to it. It's no exactly organized. The staff room is a fair rabble getting when he arrives, and for quite a long time nobody is looking too sure when it's supposed to start, until a few of them begin shushing their fingers and one of the women stands up on a chair. It's the one he saw in the manager's office. She speaks in Spanish, but he gets the gist. The finger jabbing away. She's good; she holds the room. A certain kind of magic that starts to happen when a person stands up like that and gives a voice to all these disgruntleds listening in.

After a few minutes, she starts saying it in English, 'No pay, no work,' and the KP boys are joined in with the clapping. Obi and Vincent are here as well. He claps with them. It feels good, being part of it. At the same time but, there's a sense of being cut off, all of them, cut off. They're clapping in a basement and there's nobody else here. It's hard no to think how small they are. When the work-in was starting and Bertie was climbing up on his brazier, everybody heard about it. That's how it succeeded. Everybody joining together to support them – the miners, the Dutch, the Beatles – there'd been eighty thousand on the march through Glasgow. Eighty thousand! And, as well, they were actually building something then, they weren't striking, they were actually keeping the work going, how could anybody argue with that? A strange kind of work-in it would be if they tried that here, scrubbing lavvies that haven't been sat on, plates that no food has touched. No the less, no the less. It is good, what they are doing. It is crucial.

He goes to the next meeting as well, a smaller affair with only a handful of the housekeepers and him and Dia. More of it is in English this time. A couple of the women get up and tell how much pay they've had nipped the week, or which rooms hadn't surfaced until the back of eleven. He keeps quiet, listening. Leaves when Dia leaves. When are they going to get doing something about it, is the question he's wanting to ask. If there's going to be a strike, who is behind them?

A day off. The thought of hauling himself up and out of the hotel, buying a mini television, making a phone call. Easier staying in his room, hidden, safe, a few cans left.

Without a window and any shifting of light, it's hard keeping track of the time. There is the alarm, obviously, but that only points what the hours and minutes are, it doesn't give a proper sense of the here and now, passing. It is marking time, but it's not his time that it's marking. A noise in the corridor. Voices coming past, gradually fading. Do terminal patients feel the time in a hospital, laid out on a ward? When the brain and the body are losing their functions, shutting down, sparked and lulled by drugs. Do they know how long they've been there, or do they stop feeling the hours – the long stretches between grapes and colostomy changeover speeding up as the mind slows down?

He gets up and dressed for staff food at five. They sit chewing in quiet. Occasional bits of conversation. He asks Dia and Eric if it's been busy and they tell him no, it's Thursday, always quieter on a Thursday. On the other row of tables, where the receptionists sit, he spots the woman he spoke to the day he arrived. It's the first time he's seen her – probably she only comes down for the lunatic when she's on a double, or maybe she brings her own food in usually, who knows? What does it matter? She is sat pattering with her co-workers. Smiling quite a lot as she talks. Probably that's how she stands out, the smiling, it's no exactly a common feature down here. Dia picks up his plate to get leaving, clapping Mick on the shoulder as he goes.

He stays and finishes his food, half listening to Obi and Vincent talking about an increase in their agency charge – Vincent hadn't noticed it, but Obi is saying he's seen it on his payslip – while across the way, she is the last of her group getting up. He waits for her to move over to the clearing table, and picks up his plate.

'How's it going?' he says, standing in next to her.

'Food could be better,' she laughs, scraping her plate.

'Look, see I was hoping to ask a favour, if it's okay.'

A wee look of surprise, or unease.

'Sure, what is it?'

'It's no a big one' – he tries a smile – 'it's just I'm wanting some paper. Mean, I want to write a letter.'

A look of relief. 'Of course, no problem. Tell you what, if you wait here a minute I'll go fetch some for you now.'

He sits down at a table, watching her go. The heart is clappering, he realizes. Stupit crapbag.

She is back quickly.

'This enough for you?'

He grins: he'd only wanted a couple of sheets but she's brought him the whole caboodle – a full pad of hotel writing paper, a pack of envelopes and a biro.

'Aye, that'll do it. Thank you.'

She gives him a smile. 'No problem. Let me know if you need anything else.'

Back in his room he sits down on the bed with the pad beside him. He tries to think. What is there to say but? There's nothing. There's everything of course but there's no way to put it without saying things he doesn't want to say. Without lying. See if Robbie knew the truth of it he'd be pure beeling. And no just with him either, with the whole family, Craig in particular. And then they'd all be drawn into it. They'd all know.

Dear Robbie,

I hope you and Jenna and Damien are well

is as far as he gets. He puts the pen down and stares about, trying to concentrate. Instead though he starts thinking about the receptionist. He doesn't know her name. He should've asked her. I ought to have written you sooner, I know, or gave you a call, but everything's went that fast I've lost track of how long it's been. Which is kind of true, but it's bullshit still. It isn't what he wants to say. The truth is he just hasn't called. He could have done, but he hasn't, simple as that. Nay excuses. The thought of her again. Being friendly with him, no pitying, friendly. Smiling.

An erection. Christ. He looks at it a while. Ye dirty auld bugger, eh. He pushes the pad aside and sits there staring at his dobber. After a moment he gets up and goes to the door to spy a look into the corridor. A voice, or a radio, sounding quietly down the way, but there is nobody about, all of them working, or asleep, or whatever else it is they do.

He sits on the edge of the bed, cleaning himself off. It is uncomfortable. Sore. He bundles up the toilet roll and drops it into the waste bucket. That's the letter writing by, well. No way he's doing it now. But as he goes to put the pad on top of the table, leaving it there with the pen, a scunnery feeling is started welling inside him. *Dear Robbie, I hope you and Jenna and Damien are well.* That's all he's got to say. And now this carry-on. He needs suddenly to sit down, close the eyes, screw them tight, fight back the waves of disgust that are convulsing in his stomach.

His chest begins heaving, erratic wet dribbles coming out of his nose, and then when he does start to greet it isn't in a great relieving burst like the other one he's just had the now, it is a jerky, tight, drivelling kind of greeting, which doesn't make anything the better because he knows as he's doing it that it isn't for her that he's bubbling; it's for himself. Self fucking pity. The desperate fucking emptiness of needing her there. Needing to tell her that he's sorry, but no for her sake, for his own. Selfishness. He gets off the bed, glancing down, as he goes over to his work clothes, at the stiff little pouch that is sat in the bottom of the waste bucket.

He stays on the chair and watches the machine foaming up. He has stopped greeting and his eyes and his throat feel parched and raw. His dobber, too, a similar sensation. The din of the machine as it starts spinning is reassuring, keeping out the mob of thoughts, but a moment later somebody comes in; he can see their feet out the corner of his eye. They turn around on finding him there and are immediately away. A door closing somewhere down the corridor. Out the blue he starts chuckling: Christ knows what they must say about him when they're all together.

21

She is up early, before the alarm goes off. By half nine, she has washed, dressed and dried her hair, and has a full hour before she needs to set off for the terminal. She switches on her laptop and draws open first the curtain, then the thin veil behind it. On doing so, she wonders if maybe they are better kept shut. It's not exactly the most appealing sight. Car parks upon car parks, an ugly trunk of ring-road, and, more immediately, a view into the corresponding room on the corresponding floor of the next hotel. Their curtains are still drawn, but the light is on. No doubt it looks pretty much the same in there as it does in her own room. The bright, speckled carpet and single chair; the watercolour print in wood-effect frame; the bedside ledge glued to the wall.

She checks in, then opens her inbox. There is a schedule attachment for the next ten days, which she should really have printed out earlier. It would have made life a lot simpler, and God knows what hoops she'd have to jump through to get it printed out in the hotel – it's not exactly the kind of place that has a business lounge – so she gets out a pen and paper to write it out. It's fine anyway. Gives her a chance to make some notes on one or two other things. When she's done as much preparation as she can be fussed with before getting on the plane, she clears her inbox: a few emails from the coordinator and the internal auditor in Zagreb, one from her brother, and an invite to a party that she will be away for. The chambermaid comes in at one point, a couple of quick knocks and then her face sheepishly looking round the door. The girl apologizes – 'sorry, sorry' – and leaves. Closing up the laptop, she stands and goes to switch on the TV.

The trouble with these places, even after you've got over the concrete and the carpets, is always the heating. The windows don't open to the outside so it's inevitably a choice between sweltering, or spending an hour with the baffling control panel and ending up freezing. She decides to swelter. It doesn't really matter; she'll be on her way soon. Certainly she's not going down for breakfast. She saw the restaurant on her way in last night. All plastic plants and unhappy Polish waitresses. Better to brave the airport prices and grab something in departures before she gets on the flight.

In the corridor outside the room, the housekeeper is knocking on another door. There is no sign around the doorknob, so, when no response comes from inside, she opens the door slightly for a look-in. A suitcase covered with clothes is visible on the floor by the wardrobe; she lets the door shut and goes back through the corridor. She has done all the rooms but two, and all but one on the floor above. With nothing else to do but hang about until they are vacated, she pushes the trolley into a lift and goes down to the laundry room. Inside, a few of the housekeepers are sitting and talking; another ironing bedsheets in the steam press. She takes a seat with the others, and waits.

He is lying awake one night when there is a quiet tap on the door. Before he can sit up, Dia pokes his head in.

'Mick, are you awake?'

A remote panic straight away upon him. 'Aye, what is it?'

'Come on. We are doing a raid.' Dia smiles broadly and steps out, letting the door close and the room go back to darkness. He gets up and pulls some clothes on. It occurs to him, amidst his confusion, that Dia knows which is his room.

In the corridor Dia is stood waiting with Eric, Obi and Vincent, all of them grinning and dressed in trackie bottoms. Christ knows what they're up to. He doesn't question it but. Dia puts a finger to his lips and Mick follows with them, away up the corridor toward the hotel. Who cares what it is, it's better than being awake in his room, anyway. He walks behind Eric, who keeps turning around smiling, a small rucksack on his back. He's never seen him so cheery. They are in their baries, all of them. Surprising how pink the soles of their feet are.

'Okay, wait.'

They are at the entrance to the potwash. Dia nudges the door open, looks inside, then turns round and motions for Mick to come in with him. Quickly, without speaking, Eric goes in before them; Obi and Vincent stay guarding the entrance. They've obviously planned it, then; or they've done it before.

It is dark in the potwash, and then in the kitchen, the blue light of the flytrap glinting off the microwaves. Eric waits behind in the throat and he follows Dia, who is taking a key out of his pocket; unsnibbing the padlock to the cold room.

It is big inside, and he feels the chill immediately as he goes in. There are shelves of food all around, cartons and packets everywhere. A whole wall lined with sausage boxes, bloody thousands of the bastards. Giant plastic sacks of chips humped on top of each other like mixing cement, or body bags. Dia clear knows what he's after: he's stood balancing on the chips with his hand feeling inside one of the top-shelf boxes. He looks down at Mick a moment. 'It is okay. The stocktake was yesterday,' he says, pulling out a handful of what looks like steaks, each tightly cauled in plastic.

The two of them are smiling as Dia hands him down five steaks, then gets ransacking another box off to the side. They are surprisingly squishy, the steaks, like tube feed-bags. Dia's got what he's looking for: mashed tatties. Even these are vacuum-packed. Fucksake, they no cook anything theyselves here? Dia gives the signal and they are away, quickly through the potwash and out to Eric and the others, who clock the steaks and start slapping him and Dia on the back.

Genuine a smooth operation. By the time they get back to the basement and go in the staff room, they haven't come across a single person. The door is closed and they start laughing. Eric gives him a no too brilliantly executed high five. And then, as Dia gets the steaks under the grill, Eric pulls out bottles of beer from the rucksack.

'How ye get the keys, Dia?' he asks as they drink.

Dia turns round from poking the mash with a spoon. 'The pastry chef, he is an idiot.'

The steaks are almost black, they're that well fired, and the mash is dry and powdery. Christsake it tastes good but. They eat without talking, like at the lunatic, but this time with satisfied nods and smiles and the sweet pure fucking magic of a stolen beer to go down with it. When they've finished, they clean away meticulously all the evidence and prop the door open as they leave, to clear the smoke. Firm gripped handshakes. Greasy smiles. Bloody genius.

Dear Robbie,

I hope you and Jenna and Damien are well. I'm sorry I haven't called or wrote to you sooner. I was meaning to call but for one reason or another I haven't been able to. It's no excuse, pal, I'm sorry. I'm in London now if you'll believe it. Don't know if I can myself actually. They let me go at Muir's and as well I just needed something different, you know, so when I saw this job advertised and they gave it me I decided I'd come down. I'm working in a hotel, believe it or not, in the kitchen. It's alright. I've got a decent place to stay and it's worked out okay. They are a good lot here, no the bosses of course but what can you expect? I'm getting on fine and I'm well so you don't need to worry. Food's not up to much but!

I didn't tell your brother I was coming down here. It all came about so quick to be honest but I will do when it's the right time, so you're no to put the mix in, okay? He's dealing with things in his own way and he's the better left alone until he's ready, so I'm waiting my time just before I tell him what's what. Same as I was with you, being honest, Robbie, I just needed to wait while I had things fixed out until contacting you. It's just it needs a bit longer with your brother.

I will write again soon, I promise. With where the hotel is, it's probably easier than calling, but when I've got my day off next I will go find a telephone and I'll call you.

Take care, son, love to the family,
Your da

He seals up the envelope and fishes the address out of his wallet. It's a fair pathetic effort but what else can he say? Whatever he puts it doesn't change anything, and as well if he'd been in contact with him sooner and given him the full run-down, Robbie would've been straight onto the plane, knowing what like he is. Nay point telling him it all the now. He is fine, that's all he needs to know. He'd thought about putting in about the stolen steaks or the housekeepers' dispute, but it didn't feel right; plus he wouldn't want him getting the wrong idea why he's got involved helping them.

He goes to the post office at the terminal on his next day off and gets the letter sent off there. Better that than seeing if the hotel's got its own service. You can fine well imagine the crafty bint up the stair, there with her envelope steamer, weeding out the radicals. So, the food's no good, then – that what you think, is it? We'll see about that, Scottie, we'll just have to see about that, won't we?

There is a meeting called for four o'clock one afternoon. By the time he and Eric get there after the lunch shift it is already under way, and they go and join Dia, beckoning them over at the back of the room by the oven. The ringleader is talking in English about a new development. The management, she says, have started putting out more spies on the floors, so what the housekeepers are doing is they've fixed out a system of lookouts, making sure there's always one of them keeping watch at the end of the corridors to signal when a bandit is on the approach. She tells this story that happened: a few days ago two of them are trying one of the doors with no reply, when they get the signal from the lookout and they hurry into the room, presuming it's empty. Inside but, there is a guy in the bare scuddy doing exercises in front of the TV. She does an impression of him, his face black-affronted, hands shooting down to cover himself.

They are all laughing at this story when the operations manager comes in the door.

She stands, looking at them.

'Every person in this room faces instant dismissal.'

She's no beating about the bush, then.

Silence. Confused faces. She's got the heavy team with her, two big fellas stood either side of the door, and another man in a suit beside her.

'Unauthorized meetings and organization of staff without consent is in breach of the terms of your employment, and is an immediately sackable offence.'

She stands there just, the arms folded, triumphant, the Iron fucking Lady there with her mince for brains bodyguards – Haggis 1 and Haggis 2. The terms of your employment? What are they, well? He certain hasn't seen them. Nobody moves. Not even the ringleader. She's still stood on her chair, looking exposed and daft like a schoolwean who's been caught goofing about by the teacher walking in. Everybody's waiting for who's going to do something, and it's clear enough the operations manager isn't in a hurry, the look on her face – she's enjoying it, you can tell. The guy in the suit next to her scanning about the room and marking onto a notepad – their names, obviously, however he knows what they are. Mick stays watching like the rest of them. It hasn't hit him that something real is happening.

There is a loud scurl from up on the chair and the ringleader steps down – she is marching toward the door and the haggismen side-step together, but then the operations manager moves forward and the two women come at eyeballs.

'It is not a meeting. How do you know it is meeting?'

The arms still folded. Smiling.

'You sack us, then you have no staff.'

She's pishing in the wind but, and the Milk Snatcher there knows it. 'You can let me worry about that.' She motions to the haggismen to unblock the door. 'Those of you who are supposed to be working tonight' – and she looks right at where Mick is stood with the KPs – 'you will not be required to complete your shifts. All of you can remain in the hotel for the night but you will be required to leave the premises in the morning by 9 o'clock.'

And that's that. Show over. They start filing out the room, slow, quiet, automatic, like at the lunatic. The haggismen itching for it to kick off, and the suit guy getting the final names down. There is the sound of the ringleader arguing behind them as they get into the corridor, and then, one by one, they each disappear into their rooms. With the staff room out, there isn't anywhere else to go.

He is laid on the bed and the brain is dreiched over. A chapping on the door. Dia. He comes in, calm as ever; cheery even. He perches on the table as Mick sits up on the edge of the bed.

'Don't suppose there's anything we can do, eh?'

Dia shakes his head slowly, tutting.

'Who's working now?' A stupit question. What does it matter? It doesn't.

'Vincent. Obi is in the café bar, so it is only him.' Dia grins. 'He will have a busy shift. They say they will leave as well but I tell them, no, stay. Why go? They were not at the meeting. Why go? So now they will stay.'

'What about you, Dia? What will you do?'

'I sign again with the agency. They find work easily because they take all the money.' He laughs. 'And the hotel, they go to the agency as well. Maybe they take me again, who knows?'

Mick smiles, and he realizes then this is probably the last he'll see of Dia. Unless he signs with the agency himself, of course, but even the brief thought of that starts curdling the stomach.

'And you? What will you do?'

There's no reason to lie to Dia but he feels instantly on the defensive. He hasn't let himself think about that.

'I'm fine. It's no a problem.' And then: 'There's someone I know telt me he's got a job going if I want it.'

Dia nods. 'That is good.' He stands up and steps forward with his hand held out.

'Good luck.'

'And yourself, Dia, good luck to you too.'

He must've slept a little, because it is morning, almost six, when he wakes up, still dressed. He goes to the wardrobe and gathers up the rest of his clothes into his bag, and that's him, offski. Nobody in the corridor, or up on the next level, as he leaves into the cold dim dawn outside the fire exit. Without much of a thought where he's headed, he goes toward the terminal.

22

'Well, ladies and gents, I'm still waiting for the signal at Hatton Cross. Should be any moment, I'm told, but that's what they said last time so your guess is probably as good as mine. Still time to sit back then, relax, read the paper, do your thing. I'll keep you posted.'

A funnyman, the driver. They're no laughing but. There is a business type sat opposite, shaking his head at the chummy patter that keeps crackling over the tannoy. So what, ye miserable cunts, we're no going anywhere, what difference does it make? See but if he had somewhere himself he was headed, maybe he'd be the same. Genuine a strange feeling. He does not know where he is headed. Unlike all these lot, late for their meetings and that – or maybe they aren't, who knows, maybe your man over there is just acting it, and actually all he's got in that briefcase he's finger-tapping on the now is a packet of sandwiches and a litre bottle of Buckfast.

'Okay, folks, looks like we're on the move, so mind the doors, please, and we'll be off.'

The train starts moving and he tries to think. Where is he going? Out of nowhere he laughs. He can't help it. It's actually funny, the situation. A few scunnery wee looks across the way. Probably they think it's something the driver said – Christ, what kind of headcase must that make him look? Serious but, what is he going to do? A good question, a good one, but still he can't drum up the effort to get thinking about it, and he is falling asleep by the time the train is slowing into the next station, mind the doors doors closing mind the doors please.

It is a decision of sorts, but one it doesn't seem he has made himself. A default. The easiest thing to do with no other brainwaves at the door; because even if No Breakfast is a crabbit bastard – which he is – he's a familiar crabbit bastard, and that feels easier the now than making the effort to think up anything else.

He isn't there though. Nobody is about. The *Back in 10 minutes* notice is up, so he goes back out and to the Costcutter for a sausage roll and a can of lager, and sits on a low wall under the bridge, sheltered from this Baltic wind that has got up.

When he comes back the sign is gone, but on chapping the door it is another man that opens.

'I'm, eh, sorry, I'm wanting a room. I was staying here a couple of months back.'

'Okay, sir, come this way.'

Here's a change, well.

He follows him up to the top floor. There are two rooms either side of the stairhead, and the guy opens one of them and lets him in. There is a television, he notices as he gets handing him the money.

'Okay?' He is younger than No Breakfast. A brother maybe.

'Fine, thanks.'

He must have been fair knackered, because when he wakes up the gloaming has came and went outside the window, and it is getting on for night. Okay, then. Nay use lying there just, composting on top of the bed, he needs to be up and about, decision-making. Better to keep the brain busy chasing after you, than you the one chasing trying to stop it. He gets up and goes over by the window. A plan needed, well. A decent plan. Firstly into the bag for a tenner from the money envelope, then out to the shop for what he needs.

He buys a pen, an A4 pad, a four-pack and a lamb samosa. Also, a free-ads paper, which, it turns out, isn't actually free but then what can you expect, this is London, pal. When he gets back in the room he realizes, seeing his bag, that he in fact already has these things – pen, paper – and the empty, aching sensation that the memory of it brings back causes a setback to proceedings, as he leans back against the wall behind the bed and takes a long drink, trying to quiet it down.

First up, the financials. He gets out the money envelope and counts what he's got, slowly, carefully, the first time, then a couple more times quickly just to be sure, the head of the English queen flashing like a flick book, the expression never changing, fish-lipped and disapproving. £497. Fine. Good. That gives him time. He doesn't have to rush into the first job he finds; he can make sure he gets the right one, a decent employer, no another bandit out to rob him. He opens another can and gets the TV on. Falls asleep in the chair.

The morning, and his back is sore, but he is straight up and about it, pulling open the paper and getting the jobs circled. There are quite a few minicab jobs, which being honest is probably where he should have tried last time, even though most of them are for registered-owner drivers. One or two but, that say they rent a car.

He begins with a place that looks like it's based nearby. He goes out and to a phone box to give the number a call. The familiar nervous feeling as he waits, watching his breath come in fits of mist, before a man answers and tells him to come over right now if he's able.

One thing he's noticed: the bus stops all have these wee maps in them, which makes it pretty easy finding the place. He is there twenty minutes later. There is a sign along the street and a steamed-up window with a light on.

Inside, a man behind the glass.

'Hello, I just spoke to somebody about the job.'

'Oh, right, that you was it?' He eyes him up and down.

'Like I say, I've plenty experience. I've been working private hire in Glasgow more than fifteen years.'

'Right. Do you have a reference?'

'Yes. See, I do, but I've no got it on me.'

'I'll need to have one.' He keeks down at his newspaper.

'What I can do, I can call ye with the number when I get home. I can't mind it off the top my head, is all.'

'Sure, fine. We'll hear from you, then,' and he walks off.

References. That's him screwed, well. Obviously he isn't putting a call in to Malcolm. They don't know he's here, even. That's how he came in the first place, christsake, to get away. Still, he has to crack on. He has to be positive. Not everywhere's going to want a reference – probably there's one or two need a new start straight away and they're okay seeing if he shapes up on the job just.

It is the same story at the next place though. Once he gets over there and he sits in a kind of waiting room – it's a chain place and it's a bit more proper – they give him an application form to fill out. There is nobody else in the room, so after he's tried at one or two of the boxes, he slips away. What's the point handing it in if half the boxes he can't put anything? Address. Telephone number.

References. It is only the back of eleven when he returns, but the day is finished. A quick dot to the shop and he's back in his room, the television on, a Plan B needed.

Plan B gets the swerve for the afternoon. He needs to gather the energies, build himself up to it again. He stays in front of the television; drinks a couple of cans. This programme about these famous people he's never heard of, a group of them going round each other's houses to see who can cook the best meal. Then over to the snooker. The picture is that bad it's near impossible to make out the colours of the balls, but it doesn't matter, he isn't paying too much attention; something comforting about it anyway, the silence, the clock-clunk of the balls and the gravelly patter of the commentators. He's always been quite fond of the snooker. They used to sit and have it on in the background sometimes, him flicking through the *Record* and the wife with her head in one of the Barbaras. Occasionally the both of them chuckling at something one of the commentators has said – double kisses and touching balls and all that – probably the same kind of things she's reading in her book there. The feeling of it is so familiar. He allows it to wash over him, a comfort, a dull, familiar comfort that is eased on by the drink, helping him to drift away just, stop to focus. It isn't the right thing to be doing. He knows that. But he doesn't stop himself, finishing off the cans and coasting further away from the here and now of things until the eyes are starting to close, and he falls asleep.

The one that isn't No Breakfast. He has been banging on the door. He wants his rent money. Mick opens up, rubbing his eyes awake as he goes over to his bag and crouches with his back blocking the guy's view, no wanting him to see as he takes the notes out of the envelope.

He gets onto the bed. The back is hurting. He's got to stop falling asleep in that chair. The television is still on but he leaves it, the volume turned down low as he gets under the sheets, the rest of the night to get through now, knowing he won't sleep.

The man gives him the once-over and says the ad shouldn't have gone in, they've already got somebody hired. A handyman job. There's a fair number of them in the building and trades listings and it's sensible thinking, because it's unlikely any of these places will need a reference and the money is decent, plus it's paid by the day, no the week. He tries the next one on his sheet: *General Handy-person, London W2, 50 hr per week, Mon–Fri, £6.50 per hour, temporary.* When he gets there but the guy asks him where he is living and he can't think quick enough what to say. He starts telling him he's in a B&B the now but he'll be looking for somewhere to stay as soon as he starts working. He gets told the same story: they've took on a guy already but come back next week in case he doesn't work out. He tries one more, who tell him on the phone they don't know about any job, and he decides to call it a day.

The trouble is, even if he does make up an address, probably they'd be able to check up on it these days. Even these yards that are just a mess of scrap metal and titty calendars, they'll still have some way of finding out on a computer if the address matches what you tell them, and then that's you screwed. He switches on the television. Maybe he's looking at all this the wrong way round. What he should be doing is fixing out a place to stay first. But no, that isn't right, he's thought through all this already: he doesn't have enough for the deposit; and even if he did, landlords will aye be wanting references as well. And he doesn't have those, that's for certain. He has to keep going but. Battle on. What is it they say – if ye get chucked in the Clyde, ye swim to the bank and haul yourself out, a fish in the one pocket for lunch, and one in the other for tea.

He isn't going back. That is the one thing he is sure about. Getting the coach up there with his tail between his legs and returning to that dark, silent house he can't even breathe inside, and everyone seeing that he's failed and pitying him. Everyone? Serious? Who's everyone? Nobody even knows that he went. And the house is up in the air by now anyway; someone else moved in, and the housing association after him for rent arrears.

He keeps to his room the next few days. The routine is set in. The shop in the morning, and the rest of the day he watches TV, drinking, dozing, the brain shackled. Zoning out like this, he can control it most of the time, keep his thoughts sluggish enough they can't get any speed up; although the torpor and the drink mean he is sleeping a lot, and that is when he can't control it. She is in his dreams, but out of reach, never clear. One afternoon he drops off and he has this vivid sense that he is in the house, in his chair, half asleep watching the football scores coming in on the vidiprinter. The house is quiet. There is a faint noise of chopping, coming through from the kitchen. He waits for the Rangers result, and when he's seen they've won, he gets himself up from the chair and goes out of the living room. The chopping noise is louder now, and as well the unmistakable sound of boys fighting upstairs. At the entrance to the kitchen he stops and looks at the back of her, chopping, away with herself humming and no noticing that he's stood behind her. Carrots. A stew. The pleasing sound of meat frying away on the hob. He is enjoying watching her – the quick hands scooping up carrot chunks and the smooth movement of her shoulders inside the pullover. 'Ye there?' she says, without turning round. He smiles, walking up to put his arms around her waist. 'Smells good, hen.' He leans forward and now she does turn around but it's no her, it's Mary, kissing him, and he stumbles back trying to grip hold of the counter, carrot tops getting knocked onto the floor, bouncing off the lino.

He wakes up hot and confused. Light outside, but he can't fix out what time of day it is. The racing sensation as his brain tries to make sense of where he is, whether he's awake or not. He is on the bed. Flakes of pastry on the pillow by his face. He flicks them onto the carpet and closes his eyes, everything spinning around.

Worse than these daytime dreams but is being awake the night. The darkness out the window seeming like it's going to go on forever and him hot and stiff on the bed, fragments of memories coming at him out the dark from nowhere. The drink helps. It pulls him under and he sleeps deeply for a few hours, but then always there is that point in the night when he wakes up and it is a long while until morning and he knows he's going to lie there just, a sore feeling behind the eyes, edgy at the slightest sound out the window or through the floorboards.

The daytimes when he is drowsing, he's in and out, on the border of dreams and memories. Not all about her, either; some of them good, wee things from the past. Another dream he has, that isn't so much a dream as a pure lifelike recollection of something that happened once at the yard. It comes into his head from nowhere. Charley Gordon. A great bear of a man, with a thick red neck and the half of his teeth missing out the big daftie smile. This when he was a plater's apprentice at John Brown's and Charley was his journeyman. A Catholic. One of the few, but Charley could handle himself, he aye enjoyed it even, the argle-bargle and the bigotry. All these stories he'd tell Mick of this or that wee nyaff that'd put the mix in and he'd had to sort him out. When he wasn't telling him these stories he was sending him off to the stores for whatever parts it was he needed. Mostly it was something simple and he'd go ask direct from the storewoman – flange nuts and mating screws, all these strange names that the things had – as he shuffled about and looked at his feet, too shy to talk to her. Other times there'd be a whole load of things that Charley would be wanting, and she'd let him in the stores to collect them up himself, up and down the sliding ladders to get them into his sack.

This one time Charley had gave him a long list of parts for a bevelling job he had to do, and Mick knew he'd expect him to be half an hour or so to fetch it all, but, cocky wee imp that he was, he reckoned he knew that store better than anybody, and so the idea comes to him that he'll chance legging it up the road to the pool hall for a quick game, before slaloming around those ladders and getting back in time. Course but when he does get in the store, he can't find half the parts, and by the time he's collected everything it is gone an hour and Charley is spitting teeth, they ones he's still got, anyway. He hardly speaks to him the rest the afternoon and he makes him work like a dog, ordering him everywhere to do all these tasks for him. It takes a few days until Charley's forgave him, and by then it's all a great joke: the tapping on the wrist and the big smile whenever Mick's back rushing in from the stores. So he thinks it's all forgot about, but then later the week Charley sends him off, and he's that wary of making any mistakes it doesn't even occur to him what he's doing as he goes up to the storewoman and asks her if she's got a pair of large red nipples. The slap she gave him, he could still feel it an hour later, stood at the countersinking machine with Charley chuckling away next to him.

Sometimes a memory like that, it appears from nowhere and it sets you wondering about things, like what happened to Charley? He still alive? Did he ever get himself that wee sailing boat and fuck off to the islands like he used to say he would? Who knows? Probably. Aye, probably. He didn't mess about, auld Charley.

No Breakfast is back again. Maunderly as ever. Sometimes it's him, and sometimes it's the friendly one, wanting to chin him for a conversation. He has a sense of floating most of the time now. He's outside of everything, outside of himself, giving the same attention to the world as he would to the TV on in the background – the handing over of his rent; the pamp of a car horn outside on the road; a street cleaner changing a bin, bits of newspaper and a banana skin falling onto the frosted pavement. He watches him absently from the window. A black guy. He's got himself a job, well. How did he do it? Probably he's qualified for something else, like Dia and Eric, washing dishes with a degree in the pocket. They get on with it but. They aren't too proud for any of it because they've got a purpose, is how, they've got a family to provide for and a house to build, so it doesn't matter how many times these English bastard employers stick the boot on, they'll always get back up and get on with it just.

It is night outside. He's not ate in a while but the truth is he can't be arsed dragging himself out to the shop. Hard to believe that no long back he was on the march across town looking for jobs, arranging interviews, speaking to people on the telephone. It takes him a long while getting up the energy to go out, and when he does, it is because he makes a deal with himself that he'll stock up with enough supplies that he can make them last.

He hooks the carriers on the window latch where they can hang outside in the cold. The food he wraps up in another carrier inside the bag, to keep it dry if it rains.

Apart from the rent visits down the stair, and the toilet, he doesn't leave his room for a couple of days at a stretch, each time moving only when he has to nick out for new supplies. The bathroom is on the floor below, and he waits listening through his door until he's sure the coast is clear before he comes out. One morning but, he gets caught out. He's about to go into the bathroom when a door opens to his side and a woman near walks into him.

'You going in there, mate?' She is young, wearing a baggy green sweater and tights.

'Aye, but you go – go on.'

'No, it's alright, I'll wait.'

He sees a sliver into the room as he walks past: clothes on the floor and a man having a hingie out of a window, smoking. Plants, a big poster on the wall. As if they are living there. He takes a pee and feels suddenly conscious that the woman will be coming in there after him. When he's finished, he takes a couple of pieces of toilet roll and wipes away the dark yellow spots that he's dripped on the rim.

The money envelope is getting thinner. As well, the last stores he bought in were badly got by the rain: the sandwiches are eatable, just, but they're too damp to last more than one meal. The cans are nice and cold but. See one thing that's for sure is that as soon as any employers start checking him up in their computers, they'll know straight away from the Employers' Federation or whatever that he's got something of a radical about him – with the work-in and the unions and that. Plus the episode with the hotel now as well, don't think they won't have that logged too, because they will.

There is a programme on. He watches it for a while. It's a good one. Interesting. It's about bears, grizzlies and polars, how global warming is forcing them to live closer together. The Arctic ice cap is melting that much each summer that the polar bears aren't always able to swim north to it like they used to, because it's too far away getting, so instead they're turning south toward the Canadian mainland. Which is where the grizzlies live. The inevitable sectarian battles resulting. But as well what's different is they've started mating with each other. The programme shows this photo of the first cross-breed bear, dead, killed by a hunter. Being honest, it looks to Mick pretty much like a polar bear, but apparently it's got a lot of the grizzly's features. In the photo, the guy that shot it is grinning away like a nutcase. He's got a massive army camouflage coat on, and is knelt down beside the bear with his hands splayed across its back. Stupit bastard. You have to wonder how that meeting went, when the hunter met the biologists: look, I've found you the world's rarest bear, a true wonder of nature, and I blasted it through the neck. The programme doesn't go into that but. Instead it shows all these polar bears loundering the streets of these freezing remote towns, bold as fuck, petrifying the locals outside the minimarket.

He drinks too much that night, finishing all his lager store. It's no a wise move, because instead of taking the edge off things it just makes him the more maunderly, and he lies on the bed unable to stop himself greeting. He is surprised – as if from outside of himself, observing somebody else – how long and loud he cries. The need to be with her coming on him so strongly that he can't stop it, and his whole body becoming tight and strained, searching for the feeling of being with her but no finding it, just a vacuum instead, falling and falling.

He is cold. It looks out the window like no the worst day – sunny, in fact, one of they bright, biting wintry mornings – but No Breakfast is scrimping on the heating and the room feels pure Baltic. He stays inside the bed. Some of the time sleeping, some of it with the eyes open, staring at the ceiling, the brain a blank except for occasional daft wee thoughts, like listening for the announcers between TV shows and counting how many programmes they do before somebody else comes on shift. Wondering what it is they do while the programme is on – do they have to sit there in their booth or whatever preparing for the start of the next show, or can they get up and wander about, get a cup of tea, go the newsagent's for a scratchcard? Daft wee thoughts. Daft wee thoughts that keep at arm's length the more important one of what the fuck is he going to do now that the money is almost run out.

When the time does come, he makes a decision. The twenty that he's got left, he will keep back for food and emergencies. It isn't enough to pay for another night anyway, and the most important thing is that he's got enough to feed himself; plus the emergencies, whatever they might be. Drink, probably, if the way he's craving for one the now is anything to go by. He packs up his things and goes for a wash of his face. Strange, but he has some energy about him now that there is no choice and he is on the move. He switches off the television and leaves the room.

He'd been hoping he wouldn't have to bump into anybody on the way out, but the reception door is open and the younger one sees him coming down. He must think he's paying another night, because he comes to the doorway, only then noticing the bag.

'You are going back to Scotland?'

'No.'

He nods his head. He's an alright type, even if he does stick the nose in too much.

'I'm done with the room but. Thanks.'

23

One thing is for sure: they don't like you sitting down in this city. He's been more than twenty minutes looking for somewhere to park down and eat his sandwich, but he hasn't passed a single bench yet. They don't want you staying put; they want you rushing about, horn-pamping, snatching the free newspaper. There are no people stood outside the pubs smoking. There aren't even any pubs that he's passed, christsake. He keeps on. He doesn't know where he is, and wanders at random, but it must be he does some kind of a loop or something, because after a while he is arrived back at the coach station.

It is hoaching inside, people milling about, queuing, sat waiting in the bays. That's fine but. The more people, the less obvious he feels, and as he walks through he wonders how many others in here are hiding, kidding on they're going somewhere but in fact just keeping out of the cold. He needs to pee. Another problem. A short search and he discovers that it's 30p for the pleasure of using the toilets. The money situation as it is, he'd rather not. See if he was needing a tollie then maybe that would be a proper use of the emergencies fund, but no a pish, nay chance.

There are a couple of carry-out coffee places near the station, but it's a while before he finds a pub. When he does, it is fortunate a busy one, and he has no problem sneaking in the toilet to take a fine long and satisfying widdle. The only problem, once he's done, is that now he's here he could genuine go a pint. No. First he needs to – well, fuck knows what he needs to do first, but definitely it isn't that, so he gets making his way back to the station instead. Finds himself a seat, lodged between a Muslim woman and a Chelsea supporter. There is a voice over the tannoy but he isn't hearing it. He is in the Birmingham bay, is the last thing he notices before he nods off.

When he wakes it is showing 17.44 on the information board. The bay is emptied and he is sat with empty seats all around him. He gets up and goes over to the newsagent's, looks at the price of sandwiches and gives them a bye, deciding on a chocolate bar instead. Then over to the nearest busy bay.

Outside, pulling into the slots a bit further on, the Glasgow coach. He watches uneasily as the passengers start to spill out. How long since he came here? It seems like forever ago but it's only a few months probably. He can't be sure. No the best few months, being honest. Very funny ye sarcastic bugger. The Weegies are started filing past the windows and he looks down. Hardly likely there'll be anybody that knows him, but so what, that doesn't mean it won't happen. It might. In fact it's a racing certainty the way things are going, so he keeps the head down, stares at his feet. His neck starting to strain. Waiting for it – a tap on the shoulder. Someone who recognizes him; someone who'll go back up to Glasgow and say that they've seen him, tell the Highlanders, tell Craig – and just for a split second he allows in the thought that maybe he's been looking for him, maybe actually it's him on the coach coming down on the search for him because how can you know? You can't, and all he does know is he has to get rid of the thought, get hold of it and get fucking shut.

'Hello. Are you okay?'

A young girl, sitting in beside him. He pulls back. Confusion and panic stiffening through him. 'Would you like something to eat?' He sits up and looks about to see if anybody's watching. The girl is sat turned toward him, smiling. She's got a wool cardigan with big wooden buttons; a woolly hat with these two bobble-danglers either side. He doesn't say anything and she starts going in her bag. He stands up. He has to be away. The heart is pounding. He moves down the bay; a man watching him over his newspaper, flicking the eyes back down as he hurries past.

A crawling, scunnery feeling follows him as he moves away down the road. Only one place he's headed the now; screw the rules.

He orders himself a pint. Three pound fifty pence, but no surprises there, he is in London. For some reason. For some reason he is in London. There is a game on the television. A few in watching it, but it's obvious no a football pub because they don't look too interested. The pint is calming him, settling the nerves. He stays and drinks it slowly. Takes his time before swallowing up to leave. Now what? Careful. Best no to think about the big picture right now, because it's just too bloody big, is how, and he's too close up to be able to see it properly. What he has to do is focus on one part at a time, stepping back until he can see the whole thing clearly and figure it out. Wee steps. He is cold, and he is hungry. He does his jacket up to the neck and sets off looking for something to eat.

He finds a kebab shop and goes inside, warmth and grease clinging about him as he joins the line of men at the counter intently giving the guy their sauce and salad directions. He feels comfortable in here. Warm. Unnoticed. The kebab man skilfully shaving strips of meat off the doner like a barber working at a throat. One thing's for sure, he could fine well go a kebab the now. Too expensive but. When it comes his turn he gets himself a bag of chips instead, and goes to sit at a stool in the window, biting them in halves and watching the steam lick out of the soft potato insides.

It is late. He steps out of the shop. This torpor all through him that he can't shake. He starts walking back the way he came; nay other suggestions rolling out the carpet for him. To get warm just. A wee nip of something, just to get warm, it's as far as he can think. Shortly before the pub he notices a side street, dark, too narrow for lampposts. Without much of a thought, he goes down it. It is cobbled, and a couple of cars are parked with the one tyre perched onto a pavement, and at the end there is just a wall, the back of another building. He steps onto a concrete lump and looks over the line of palings into a small rubbish yard at the back of the pub. Weeds and dog-ends and black wheelie bins.

There's only a few customers still in. The television is off, and he sits down at a table underneath it, slowly sipping at his whisky, feeling the warmth of it spread through him. He gets a second, and by the time he's near the end of it the barmaid has the mop out, doing behind the bar counter; she doesn't notice him leaving.

He drops the bag down and clambers messily over the palings, scraping the skin off the back of his leg. There is no lighting out here, but he can make out the push bars on the fire exit and, next to it, a stack of bottle crates. Further in, a large humming box like a generator, with gas cylinders propped against it. He puts his bag down behind the box, the other side from the fire exit, and sits down, hoping it might be giving off some warmth. Nay such luck. Here we are well. No an expected turn of events. He sits blankly for a time, more and more uncomfortable getting with the cold and the hard uneven ground knuckling into his arse through the bag.

After a while he gets up and goes on a search for anything that might improve the situation. And he's in luck, because lodged behind the wheelie bins is a whole load of flattened McCoy's crisps cardboard boxes. Okay. All it needs now is a bottle or two of beer left in one of these crates and he'll be laughing. He checks. There isn't.

The cardboard does improve things, laid out on the ground underneath him, but it's impossible to sleep still, no with this cold knifing at his body. Even with the whisky inside him he's pure frozen. And alert. Listening for the fire exit or anybody coming down the side street, propped rigid against the generator with his bag tucked behind him and the raw skin on the back of his leg stinging against his trousers.

24

He doesn't sleep, hardly at all, a few snatches just. The cold, and his back ridged against the generator, he's stiffened up and he can barely move. All of him is numb. A few times during the night he tells himself he needs to get up, keep moving, go find somewhere covered he can be warmer, but the effort of it is too much. The aching body will not budge. A pain that began in his feet and his hands, tightening over his frame until it has grip of every part of him starts, after a while, to lessen; the outside of him deadened, and the cold then working its way inside, into his nose and his throat, stopping the breath in his lungs and getting inside the brain, forcing it to press, paralysed, against his skull. Noise is increasing. Traffic on the main road. A bus braking. When he does move, he does it very slowly, muscle by muscle. It is dark still but there is a blue gloom to the sky. He gets out from behind the generator; stands up and perches his sore backside against it, looking at the dim yard. Dog-ends outside the fire exit. A cracked glass lampshade leant in a crate. A stack of rusted metal chairs lurching against the wall. He tries to pick up the cardboard and put it back behind the crates, but his fingers won't work so he shunts it behind the generator, then takes a few goes attempting to get his bag and his body to struggle over the palings.

Most the shops are closed. He keeps walking, the autopilot on; cold, still cold. The feet throbbing in his shoes. He finds himself headed for the coach station, as if the body is handling things on its own by now, no trusting enough of him to discuss such matters any more. Fine but. Fine. It's warmer in here, and he sits down in one of the bays. Quieter than yesterday, but it's early yet, and he looks over at the board – 06.53 – the whole day in front of him, unending. He pushes back into his seat with his bag on his lap and falls asleep.

He wakes from an uncomfortable and confusing dream with an immediate sense of alarm that goes twisting right into the stomach. He scans about him. There, again, is the cunt opposite, looking at him over his paper, tapping away with the foot. And there's others too, a whole line of them, watching him, just fucking sat there watching him. He stands up. He can't stay there, all these eyes, and no to mention either the ones in the roof – the cameras – sure they will have clocked him as well, sat two days in a row without getting onto a coach. He goes out of the station and stands by the entrance in a state of near-total unclearness. A man coming up to him jabbing a newspaper in his face and he tries to shake his head but the guy keeps sticking it to him.

'Fuck off.'

The man shrugs his shoulders and goes away, pointing it at a woman coming past.

He walks for a long time. Aimless. Trying just to shake the crawling panic that tenses inside him whenever he gets eyeballed, quickening past them, just keeping going, tired and sore but keeping on the move because he is too feart to stop. He is hungry, so when he comes to a minimarket he goes inside, picks up an egg sandwich and a four-pack and ignores the look on the auld bint's face as she passes it over the scanner.

He is walking and looking for somewhere quiet to sit and eat, when he comes upon the river. And right there on the opposite bank, the genuine shocking sight of a massive red brick power station, long since closed down by the looks of it. There is a bench free and he sits down. No many people about here. A few joggers. A man and a woman both in suits further up the way on another bench eating out of plastic punnets with wee plastic forks. He starts to feel more relaxed. A kind of peacefulness about things here, watching the river and the different boats coming past; the great bulk of the power station and its four giant white chimneys across the water. He snaps open a can. The better keeping out the way of things. Minding his own business and no having to worry about digging up any bastard reading their newspaper or poking it in his face. And if there's nobody about to look at him, then he doesn't have to get considering himself either – and what a fucking affront he is to them, the newspaper-reading types of this world, the young women wanting to foist their sandwiches on him. His bladder is filled up, so he waits until nobody is about and goes a short way down the pavement to pish through the fence.

Later, when the alcohol has took the edge off the cold and the panic, he takes a walk down the water. A good stretch of it, he keeps going for a long time, craps in a Burger King and ends up on a bridge with a beauty of a view over Big Ben, watching lights catch on the water ripples, staring at the strange image of people dancing in silent frenzy inside a boat that comes past.

The pub is closed when he gets back so he won't be paying them any rent the night. The cardboard boxes are where he left them, and he opens a couple out to put around himself like a tube. It is better, but no by much. He's still fucking freezing. He closes his eyes and he can't sleep, instead thinking about his big coat hung up in the lobby, how much warmer he'd be with it on than this jacket. The image of the house briefly staying with him, but fortunately the brain is too dumb with cold to imagine any further.

It is still dark when he leaves over the palings. His only thought: to get the body warm. He lounders along the pavements until the cafes are open, then goes into one for a cup of tea. The man is clear annoyed when he pays up, because he's been sat there that long with just the single mug, but so what, it's no like the place is mobbed with customers, so get to fuck, pal. A walk. The minimarket. Enough on his tail for an egg sandwich, but he gives the drink a bye, because that's the last of his money.

It isn't a bad sandwich in truth, for the price, anyway. No a bad spot by the water either, although as he approaches it now, he can see that somebody else has took it. A fat man in a suit, an empty sandwich case on his lap, just sat there. He walks past and keeps going along the pavement. Just a bench. It doesn't matter. There'll be plenty more down the water. But he can't help looking back, the fat cunt lounging there with his arm stretched over the top of the bench like he thinks he's got the invisible woman nestled in with him. Stupit, being angry about it. Pure ridiculous. But there you go. This guy has messed up his routine. And see as well he's probably got some warm office nearby that he's supposed to be in, with heaters and secretaries and the bloody whisky bottle stashed away in the drawer.

He is stood now, a way off, watching the man, who is fine well aware he's being looked at. He's kidding on he can't see him but. Sat defiant and unmoving, the arm stretched out. Go on, ye cunt, look at me. Think I give a fuck, eh? And now he is getting up, clearly displeased about the whole situation, the poor chap, giving him the ball bearings as he departs, but so what, serious, so what? He's glad. The wee battles you have to win. Good fucking to win one at last. He gets sat down and watches the man away down the pavement, the two great saddlebags shifting above his belt with each step.

A tugboat pulling into a wharf on the other side of the river. WASTE MANAGEMENT, one of the containers says on it. Twelve of them, he counts, full of what – binbags? Chemicals? Household tollies? Where does it all go, that's what you've got to wonder, where does it go to?

A man and a woman are stood in front of him. He has been asleep. The sky is gone darker, car headlights beading over a bridge, and he is hungry. They are talking. Smiling at him. He tries to get sat up, no the strength to move away, warn them off, and they are staying there, giving it this constant gentle patter to him – blankets . . . our Lord . . . sandwich table. He pulls his bag onto his lap. Food. They are talking about food. Cruel, cruel bastards. They know. It's all wired together somehow: the bank and the council and the electricity board and the auld bint in the minimarket. Now these pair. We have been informed as to your penniless situation and so are come the now to stick the boot on. The man is pointing down the road – see the big building there? It's the car park behind it. More smiles from both, and they are away. Nobody else about for miles. Where do they spring from? One minute you're asleep, and the next they've suddenly appeared from out the river and they're offering you sandwiches.

It is colder, and his left leg has got the shakes, a wee trembling that doesn't stop even when he presses down on it. Across the water, the power station is lit up. Something unearthly about it, holding him there, as if in a trance, unable to move, or think, or feel, until the stomach cramps and he is pulled back out of it.

There is a shooting pain in the trembly leg as he walks. He focuses on it, anticipating the short sharp jab each time he steps forward.

A passageway after the building, and through it, a car park. There is a minibus in the centre of it, with a trestle table pushed up against the open back doors. Bodies milling about. He stays in the passageway and watches. There is a group of four or five battered figures huddled on one side of the table. A short way off, a few others, all holding polystyrene cups. His blood is thumping; he steps back, against the wall of the passageway. An urge to bark out laughing moves through him, but it dies in his throat and he presses his palms hard against the wall, forcing them into the firm rough stone. He cannot do this. Better to starve than this, and he turns his face from the car park, starting out of the passageway and onto the street, back toward the river.

He keeps going, following the flow of the water. Now what? A pure aching need for a drink, but obviously that's out the question. The only option is to keep walking, or go back to the pub yard. He is actually that hungry the thought comes to him he could go through the bins. He stops. A car slowing down as it goes past him, coming to a halt at a traffic lights. He needs to eat. He needs to eat – it's that simple.

There are more of them arrived, stood in two groups further into the car park, but he keeps his gaze fixed on the table, steering toward it. He hurries on. A few people stood behind the table in big coats, one of them leaning forwards, smiling. He keeps his head down, doesn't look him in the face. There are cheese sandwiches on a plate, biscuits, crisps, fruit, a bowl of pasta. He clears his throat. 'A sandwich please.' The man puts one on a paper plate, then shakes a few crisps on the side, like a picnic. 'Would you like some soup?' Mick nods. He is handed a cup. 'Thanks,' he says, and moves round the other side of the minibus.

He wolfs the sandwich and crisps, although the soup is too hot to swallow down quickly. Why is he stood there anyway but? He could go. No like he's bloody beholden or anything, but still he stays put, staring into the side of the minibus, trying to get the soup finished and already it's too late, a woman coming round the side, approaching him. He watches her over the top of his cup, his shoulders tensing.

'Hello.' She stands there just, no saying anything, smiling. Obvious it's some kind of a ploy to make him talk. He stays quiet though, the cup held up to his mouth.

'Good soup?'

He nods his head.

'We always try to have a soup on. Especially nights like this.'

The roof of his mouth is scalding. Some noise on the other side of the minibus.

'Do you have somewhere to stay tonight?'

'No,' he says, mainly because he can't be bothered acting it.

She starts going in her coat pockets. 'Here.' Handing him a piece of paper. 'This has the address of one of our winter shelters which is open tonight. It's just off this main road, actually. Not far.' She smiles, and he takes a big gulp of soup, watching as she slips the hand into her pocket again.

'Do you have a faith?'

'No.'

She is unperturbed. 'Well, take one of these anyway. Something to read through, if nothing else.' And she holds out leaflets of what look like Bible scriptures. He doesn't take them, but she has turned round anyway, distracted by whatever's going on past the minibus. Some kind of scuffle is broke out. She starts toward it, and he moves forward as well, by instinct, looking what's going on. Some kind of argle-bargle between the two groups; facing off to each other, lots of shouting and birling about. One of the figures steps forward and there is a surge of excitement in the group behind him – 'Do the soup, do it, do the soup . . . go on, fuck off back to Warsaw' – and a soup cup is thrown, the liquid arching through the air. A melee starting, the Christians softfooting up to it, and he takes his opportunity to go; he puts his plate and cup on the ground and is away.

The cardboard was took out during the day and possibly he is going to die here, sat up against the iceberg generator. Both legs are shaking now, and his face is that frozen the teeth have gave up chattering. Instead, a random spasm of his jaw each few minutes, the two sets of teeth crashing together, so that by this point he's got toothache as well; no part of him wanting to miss out. He is past caring though. Nothing is real any more, even the pain. All that exists is the cold.

The street is dark and empty and he turns back a moment to check the name of it. It's the right one. Why shouldn't it be? What's he expecting: drunken, toothless scaffers spilling about over the road? A giant arrow – down and outs, this way? Further on there is a smaller street off the side, and down it, a church. He goes toward it in a kind of daze, without considering what he is doing; all he knows is that he's definitely way too fucking sober to be doing it. It is the cold that pushes him on, chibbing like a gun between the shoulder blades.

The great wooden door of the church is closed, no sign of anybody about, so he carries on round the side to a single-storey, modern kind of a building. A light through the ribbed glass above the door. He presses on the button, but nobody comes out, so he tries the handle and goes in. A small, dark foyer. Old books on a shelf; a poster on a noticeboard – Sunday service crèche club. Fucksake. What is he doing? Nay turning back now but, because a door is opening; the Hallelujahs are coming.

A tall man with close-shaved hair and glasses is looking at him from round the door.

'Hello. Can we help you?'

'I was told there's a bed.'

'Come in.'

He follows him through into a large hall, the lights turned out, but he can see well enough the humped shapes in bags across the floor. They go into some kind of office, and the man sits down at a table, motioning him to a chair opposite.

'Now, we require very little here by way of paperwork. We provide a place to sleep for the night, a hot evening meal and breakfast. All we ask is that you treat the church and the other guests with respect. That, really' – he smiles, holding up both hands in mock surrender – 'is as complicated as it gets.'

Guests. He serious?

'What is your name?'

He tries to think up something, but he isn't quick enough. 'Mick.'

'Hello, Mick. My name is Yann.' He is smiling again and Mick wonders if maybe this is the hallelujah bit coming. 'Whatever has brought you to us tonight, Mick, nobody here is going to judge you, and anything you tell us will be treated in confidence, as is the case with every one of our guests.'

'I'm no a homeless, just I'm in-between things, is all.'

Yann smiles. He isn't buying that one. 'That's alright.' He starts to get up. 'Let me get you a cup of tea. I'm afraid it's too late now for the evening meal. We don't generally allow admissions after eight, but we do have a space and I know how cold it is tonight.'

'I've already ate, thanks.'

'Good.' He goes to the door. 'Now, I need just to tell you, we don't allow any drugs, alcohol or weapons in here.' He smiles. 'We're pretty relaxed, otherwise.' He goes out the room. Drugs? Weapons? What does he look like to this guy?

A few moments later the Hallelujah comes back in. A small cup tinkling with a spoon and sugar lump on a saucer. He gives it to him and leans down to pick something up outside the doorway. A sleeping bag, and a rolled-up mat. He puts them on the table. 'Finish your tea, then I'll show you through.'

There is a couple dozen bodies. The room honks with feet and drink and urine. Cabbages. He is being shown to a space against the wall in between two humps, and all he can think is – no, he cannot do this. Leave, well. Remove yourself from the place and slam the door firmly shut behind – thank you, oh dear Lord, for no judging me and for the tea but that's me offski the night, goodbloodybye.

'Breakfast is at six thirty,' the voice is whispering, the mat getting laid out for him, 'and all guests are asked to vacate by seven.' Mick sits and takes off his shoes, a pure blessed relief, and even if the brain doesn't want him to be doing it, there's no chance the body is going to listen now as he slides into the warm bag. He will be up and out immediately as he's swallowed down some breakfast. Guests are asked to vacate by seven. What a fucking place. Hotel Hallelujah.

He is facing toward the wall. The bag pulled right over his head. Still but he can't shut out the sounds. Farts and wheezings all around him. Cabbages. He sleeps in fits. His chest cramping each time he wakes and then strains the bag tight about him, but the smell, that smell, it's inside the bag, inside him, right into the windpipe and the lungs, until he is pure desperate for some other smell that he knows, something familiar. But he can't mind any. Impossible to imagine that any other smell exists. It's just this.

A noise wakes him. A shout, somewhere in the room, followed

by a long wail. For a moment there is silence but then it comes again, a loud scurling sound. Like a fox; no something human. He closes his eyes, wanting to shut it out, but he can't, even in the quiet in-betweens, because he is braced, the heart tromboning, waiting for it to come again. He inches the bag down from his face and props up onto his elbow to try and see over the hill of whatever he's next to. There is no movement anywhere. Only the dim shapes of all these others, who don't seem to notice this desperate wailing noise, merging it instead into their own nightmares.

A hand on his shoulder. There is activity in the room, voices, light streaming in through the large, high windows. Somebody stood above him; walking away. He lies there rigid and watches as the cocoon next to him squeezes itself out. No a butterfly, that's for certain. He is old and scarred, the hair clotted, deep trenches in his face. Mick doesn't move, watching from inside his bag – all these hopeless creatures stooping and coughing, gathering up their beds. There is one pair that look young enough they could be schoolweans. Blacks too, Asians, the whole circus. Yann is there, chatting with a few of the other Hallelujahs, who bring out long tables and unfold them at one side of the hall. Women start appearing. Broken-looking women, worse gone even than the men. He sits there in a stupor taking it in. He's seen plenty enough scaffers before, in bookies, the park, on the street, but this is something different, seeing them all together in a room. Yann is coming over.

'How did you sleep, Mick? We have breakfast now, so if you want to queue up, they'll have it out in a moment.' A line is already forming by a table at the other side of the hall. 'Here.' He hunkers down beside him and hands him a leaflet. 'Each of these churches opens for a different night of the week. You can self-refer to any, but you'll need to book your place first.'

He half listens to the rest of Yann's spiel before joining the back of the queue, behind a woman with no socks on, her baries scarlet and bloated. None of it is registering properly. He sits down where there is nobody next to him. Staff food all over again. Except this is a better meal at least: scrambled egg, bacon, beans. Head down, he eats fast, ravenous and wanting to get out. Somebody is pulling in opposite him but. Mick keeks up, then back to his food. A man in a red woolly hat. His giant bawface blistered and shot, a drinker. If he can just get eaten up, leave this place, no talk to any of them. But this guy is staring at him.

'Ye don't always get the beans, know. Serious, ye don't.'

A bloody Weegie. Unfuckingbelievable. Mick doesn't look up. He resolves no to let a word slip out of his mouth.

'See the bacon is always – ye always get the bacon but the beans is hit and miss. Believe that? I'm telling them, get more beans. Beans is cheaper for them and it fills ye up the better.'

Mick nods, picking up his plate and standing.

He puts the plate and cutlery into the buckets on the table. How can somebody like that look at him and think – aye, there's a guy that's on my wavelength? No point dwelling on it but. Probably a headbanger. He goes warily over to his bag and then makes for the door, getting out the building before any other nutter can clamp onto him.

25

A man in a suit is sitting on a bench. A short way down the towpath, an elderly Mediterranean-looking woman in a huge fur coat is waiting for her small dog to finish shitting beside a tree. The man knows full well that she is not going to clear it up. He knows it, and it is irritating the hell out of him that he knows it, but still he cannot move his eyes away: the dog squeezes out the final pellet, and he watches in silent fury as the woman slowly wanders off in her enormous coat.

The man turns back to his lunch, but that just serves to annoy him further, so he looks up at Battersea Power Station instead – something reassuring about the size and solidness of it. He could kill for a sausage sandwich right now. That was his old routine: after the first couple of weeks last summer when all the new advisers would go together from the Department for Business building to the pub for lunch, he had taken to walking down to the river and buying a sausage sandwich en route. He looks down miserably now at his Boots meal deal: the juice drained in one go, sandwich vanished, colourful delights of the fruit salad still to come. The homeless man is there again. He is sat three benches further up, and there's little chance he could have seen him but even so the memory of yesterday returns, and he experiences for a moment the same sense of panic he had felt as the man had approached him, the crazed look on his face. He seems to be keeping to himself today, ignoring the passers-by and just glaring out at the river in what appears to be the same dirty brown jacket and torn trousers as he had on before.

He attempts the fruit salad. It is dry and soapy; he compresses a piece in his mouth but no moisture comes out. He knows that it is almost time to return to the office, but as soon as he thinks about leaving the bench he starts to become a little nauseous. There is a pre-meet at one to brief the Idiot for his afternoon meetings. No doubt the others will be prepared: they'll have been planning over lunch, devising a briefing strategy. They will have choreographed their spiel; and when, at the end of the brief, the Idiot turns to him and asks if he has any input, he will look every inch the pointless fat fool as he replies that he believes it's all been covered. In his whole time there so far, his single most significant contribution was the moment during a meeting with the Federation of Small Businesses when the Idiot passed him a squiggled note that read: *What is the minimum wage these days?* Remembering the stupid flush of pride that he had experienced on sliding back the answer causes the sick feeling in his stomach to increase now, as he rises from the bench.

A runner comes past in a gold-coloured pair of lycra trousers, his large muscular buttocks seizing as he pounds down the towpath. The man starts back toward Westminster, but immediately as he does so the strange, horrifying image enters his head of himself in the same pair of trousers, entering the building and suddenly everybody looking at him – the security guards suppressing their mirth as he passes through the scanners – and the sight of his fat golden arse repeated all around him in the unending glass and mirrors and polished flooring. Suddenly he stops right there on the towpath, looking round to check nobody is nearby, and, with the fruit salad punnet, he scoops up the four small nuggets of dog shit from beside the tree. He ties up the Boots carrier bag around it, continuing alongside the river, and drops the package into the next dustbin he passes.

Further down the water, Mick is viewing across the way to the power station. One thing that must be admitted: it's bloody big. When did they close it? Who cares, what does it matter? It doesn't. Probably the Milk Snatcher but. We don't want power stations, what we want instead is more apartment buildings – these ones you can see here all along past the bridge, curving swirls of bright blue and green.

He pulls out the leaflet and turns it over. One thing that's obvious, looking at the map: these churches are spread miles apart. And, on top of that, the Monday one is the other side of the map from Tuesday, which does not neighbour Wednesday, and so on, and so on. Obvious it's done on purpose. To make things difficult, for whatever reason. The absurdity of it all. An absurd situation, would ye no agree, Mr Jogger, in your – and let's be honest here – pretty daft leggings? Fucksake, he needs a drink. The pub just a little way down the road but him sat here with no money on his tail. Cruel. Very cruel.

It takes him two hours to walk there, and he arrives while it is still light. Maybe that's how they keep them so far apart. To give the scaffers something to do. Pass the time. The Hallelujah that comes to the door isn't as friendly as the other one. He's in fact quite annoyed that Mick's turned up out the blue without booking his place. He's not supposed to arrive before seven. He should have phoned ahead. A good one, that. See the thing is I was going to call ahead on the mobile phone but then I was that busy on the line with clients and contractors and all that, I forgot. He doesn't bother arguing with the guy. No the energy or the pride, so he keeps quiet and the man agrees to book him in, only he has to go away the now and no come back until seven o'clock. He leaves, walks about, wondering how he's supposed to know when seven o'clock is.

Shepherd's pie and a spoon of boiled vegetables. The set-up is different here – it's a bigger place, and there are small round tables to sit at, but he manages to find one where he's on his own. He recognizes one or two of the faces. The beans guy is here, sat over the way at a full table, laying it off to some poor ancient scaffer about something or other.

The Hallelujahs wait until everybody has got food, then they fix out plates for themselves and sit down inamongst the tramps. Mick stares down at his plate, eating quickly, but nobody comes. Afterwards he gets a sleeping bag and finds a space, then sits against the wall next to it, making sure he doesn't catch eyes with anybody. Some of the scaffers stand together in dirty clusters, talking. Others keep with themselves, avoiding the groups, like he is doing. No. As long as he remains outside of it, eating the food just and accepting the shelter for now, and no talking to any scaffers or any Hallelujahs, then he will stay afloat. Only if he accepts that he is part of this, that he belongs here, will he be done for. Because if he does that, then there'll be no control over it, and he may as well throw in the towel. Game over.

A dribbly day, but no too cold. He takes a free paper from a stall he passes, to lay down on the bench. Irrational, maybe, no the sensible man's choice, but he goes the trek to his usual spot. The night's church is in the other direction but it doesn't matter, better anyway to use up the day by walking. He is sat staring at the power station when a young lad, looks like a student, comes and sits in next to him. It isn't long before he turns and starts talking. Mick keeps quiet, hoping he'll get the message. He doesn't. Incredible sight, he is saying, wet day, and all this. Go bloody sit inside well if it's too wet for you. He has started fiddling about in his rucksack.

'Would you like a muffin?'

Mick ignores him.

'It's okay. It's spare.' He is holding his muffin out to him. 'Well, I'll just leave it here in case you change your mind.'

The boy stays sitting there. He keeps looking over, Mick can see him doing it out the corner of his eye. After a while, he turns toward the lad, the muffin still there on the bench between them.

'I've ate already. I'd take a pound but, get myself a cup of tea.'

The boy obvious isn't too sure about this and he delays a moment, nay doubt thinking – how do I know he isn't going straight the offie with this? Which is exactly where he intends going with it, but the lad is by now getting out his wallet, and he hands him £1.50.

He uses the money smartly. £1.29 buys him a decent-size bottle of Polish lager and he saves the rest to call ahead to the church. It runs out after about five seconds, but the guy rings him back.

The journey is much more pleasurable with a drink inside him. No bevvied, but warmer, more relaxed. In such a state it is easier to ignore all the rub-ye-ups bustling past and eyeballing him along the pavement. Away home to their evenings of curry dinner and telly watching, argle-bargling with the wife. Plenty of scaffers about too: alone in doorways; stood in wee groups; blocking the thoroughfares selling their magazines. He is coming into a more posh area. There are wine drinkers inside a giant café window, flower stalls, well-to-do clothes shops. This one that he passes. A naked mannequin in the window, bald and bare, with the one hand on her hip. The sudden temptation to run in and steal her. Run off down the street with the baldy woman tucked under the arm. How far would he get? How many yards down the pavement before the heavy mob catch up, huckling him down some back alley to put the boot on?

No that there are many back alleys this part of town. Nay chance. It's all boulevards and butchers round here, they Italian ones with cured meats hanging in the display above the olive oils and the giant cheese wheels.

It is a Catholic church this night, and the space is a side room off the church building itself, the walls above the sleeping mats covered with ornate lanterns and candles, lifelike statues of nuns holding crosses and looking out with serious faces at the scaffers. There are less staying than the previous two nights, but still one or two of the regulars, they ones that know they're onto a good thing and have got themselves in with the bricks. He ignores them, managing to keep to himself. Eats his food. Drinks his tea. There is a prayer session after dinner, but the Hallelujahs don't force it. Quite a few take part though, going through with the Bead Rattler, who has been walking about the place in his robes and his rings, for a wee patter with the Big Man. Hard to know how they're asking him for anything.

He rolls out his mat and his bag and gets lying down. How quick you get used to things. Settle into a rhythm.

In the morning after breakfast, one of the Hallelujahs, a woman, approaches him.

'Sleep okay?'

'Fine, thanks.'

She stands by the tea table while Mick is fixing up his tea and his orange juice. How is it people are always wanting to put the nose in and can't leave him be?

'It's Mick, isn't it? I haven't met you before. My name's Jenny.'

'Pleased to meet ye, Jenny,' and he starts to turn and get leaving back to his place at the table.

'I was wondering – have you had a chance to use the daytime centre at all?'

'I have, aye, thanks.'

'Oh, right. Good. And you know we have caseworkers too, who can help you with accessing services.' The beans guy is arrived at the table making a tea, listening, a wee smile on him.

'Thanks, Jenny, I'll bear it in mind.'

'Right, okay.' She smiles and starts to move off. 'Have a nice day, Mick.'

Oh, aye, it's going to be a belter: away down the boulevard for a new suit, then off to a restaurant with the baldy woman for Guinness and oysters.

'How's it going?' Beans is looking at him, still the wee grin. The red woolly hat pulled right down to his eyes.

'Good.'

'Ye from Glasgow, well?'

No use kidding on now he's been rumbled.

'I am.'

'Whereabout?'

'Clydebank.'

'That where ye were born?'

'Aye, Clydebank.'

He gives a wide smile. One side of his top lip is chappit and bleeding. 'I'm from Paisley.' He holds out a giant purple hand. 'Keith. Ye're no a religious case, eh?'

'No.'

Beans turns his eyes for an instant up to the roofbeams. There is a large dark gouge in the stubble under his chin. 'Thank Christ for that, then. Enough of them about, no think?'

'The Hallelujahs.'

He lets out a loud lunatic laugh, which makes Jenny and the woman she's with look round a moment. 'Aye, the Hallelujahs, you said it, pal, fucking right.'

He is still chuckling with himself as Mick gets leaving.

Where do they go to? There's aye the ones that are sat in the doorways and selling the magazines, but what about the rest of them, where do they go? The women? You never see the women. The nights at the churches, there's been quite a few of them put up. They get a separate room, or if it's one of the smaller places they get a plastic barricade wheeled up in between to keep the men off them. The tollie tugboat is on the approach, docking up with its cargo of shite. He watches it turn around on the water, coiling slowly into the wharf. No great mystery but. It's pretty obvious where most of them go, the men anyway, the male scaffers. They ones that aren't sat next to a carry-out cup, tapping pedestrians for the price of a bottle, are down the broo office signing on. See but how is he any different? Sponging off the Christians for food and orange juice. Fucksake he eats more than anybody there!

He doesn't stop going. He's there each night for his free meal and his free entertainment, listening to the night terrors erupting through the hall. He has a shapeless awareness that he needs to be doing something, but it's getting more difficult to hold the thought and do anything with it. The brain is unable to deal with it. The Hallelujahs aren't but. They keep going on at him about it. Especially the guy Yann. Does he know there's a laundry and showers at the daytime centre? Has he had any thoughts what he's going to do when the shelters close at the end of February? He's going up to Glasgow, he tells him. Going back to see the family. Yann is delighted. That's good, Mick. That's very good.

What will happen to all this lot then? Where will they go? They're that settled into the routine, some of them. Maybe they are actually in fact secret bloody millionaires and when this all packs up they're away in their jets to their lochside mansions, and that's how they're all so unbothered about it, who knows? Because that's what they are. Unbothered. It's true. Rare there is an incident. Sometimes but. Nothing much. The odd squabble a couple of times, arguments over who's took whose sleeping space, but that's usually it. It is a while before he sees anything like a proper fight, and when he does, it's two women. The one of them starts screaming at the other that she's stole her gloves, and when she denies it and starts walking away, the accuser jumps her from behind and gets clawing at her face. The Hallelujahs are straight in there, breaking them up, wheeling out an extra divider the night.

Beans reckons he knows the whole back story. He is sat down at the same dinner table laying it off to him.

'She's had they gloves for years, see. She was gave them as a present by somebody, so ye can see how she's angry. I'd be angry, somebody lifted my hat. I'd be fucking beeling.' Mick sits drinking his tea. 'Know what I think?' Beans continues. 'I think it's no about the gloves. Probably there never was a pair of gloves even. Sometimes it's like that, know what I mean? Christmas is aye the worst. This place is eggshells then. Depends what like is the family situation, course, but most of these lot are biting the carpets.'

Christmas. He's not even noticed that it has came and went. He must have been at the hotel. He tries to mind when it would have been, if there'd been any sign of it, but he can't think; the whole thing is a fog. Plus as well this great bampot right in his face.

'See me, I'm no staying around much longer.' He is looking intently across the table at Mick.

'How's that?'

'Mean, I know this place, close, quite close, beds, kitchens, comfy, ye know, no like this.' He turns and looks about behind him a moment. 'All I want is to go for a crap in peace.'

He is grinning at his joke. Mick notices there are bits of dandruff on the outside of his hat.

'See how I'm telling ye is because you should go there too, we should both of us go there. Ye can't stay here.'

Mick looks away over to where the tables are getting folded back up for the night. The first of the sleeping mats being rolled out onto the floor. He's right, obviously. The memory then of the pub backyard, the cold humming generator. At least this guy has got something going on upstairs, unlike himself. He's thinking, at least. Even the headbangers have the march on him these days.

It rains a couple of days solid. Quiet down by the river during this time, the fast-flowing water foaming and stinking with the downpour. The occasional determined jogger dragging past. It is too wet to stay there. He'll be sat thinking it isn't so bad because the bench is partly covered over by a tree, but then a branch will give up under the gathering weight and dump a bucket onto his head. He goes up the coach station. He sits in the bays, drookit and shivering, frightening the passengers. Pneumonia but, it's good for the handouts. Both days, he taps a pitying face for the price of a can and goes to drink it under the railway bridge, or on the walk over to the night's church.

Beans is sat near the end of a long table, on his own. Mick goes over and sits in opposite him.

'Alright?'

Beans is away with it though, staring down at his untouched chicken and chips.

'What ye said before, mean, I think I might take ye up on the offer.'

Beans looks up slowly. 'Offer.'

'Aye, what ye said, this other place.'

Beans doesn't say anything. He stares off now to the side, at nothing, at the wall. Maybe he's bevvied. He doesn't smell but; no of drink, anyway.

'Well, I thought I'd let ye know, okay.'

He doesn't push it after that, and carries on eating his food while Beans sits there, vacant, until after a while he pushes his chair out and walks off, leaving his food where it is.

Mick watches him, over on the far side of the room, sitting down with his back against the wall. A new one, this. He's never seen him when he hasn't been bouncing off the ceilings and chewing everybody's ear off. He continues staying there, alone, while the tea comes out and then the chairs and tables are cleared away, and he's still there, unmoving, while Mick and the others are getting into their sleeping bags for the night. A Hallelujah goes over to him eventually and he gets up slowly, moving over to his pitch.

The next evening though Beans comes up to him in the car park where Mick is stood waiting for the church doors to open. He does mind the conversation. And no just the first one either, but the no-conversation last night as well.

'So what I thought was Sunday.' There is a scaffer sat smoking on the steps who tilts his head up to listen, and Beans pulls Mick off to the side. 'See the thing is Sunday's a good day to try cause there's always chuck-outs the weekend, after people have been on the batter.'

'I'm no sure, mean it's –'

'Nay worries, I'll sort it, I'll sort it. I know the place, see, I know how to play it.' He grins. 'A bed, man. A fucking bed, eh.'

Hard to know what to think, and hard to think at all anyway, so he doesn't. He sits near Beans at tea and half observes him rattling on ten the dozen to anybody that goes near him. They eat. Go to sleep. Up the next morning and he's out again into the cold, away the long stiff journey to the shelter of the coach station. His feet are pretty swollen getting. The walking, or the temperature, or his socks, which cling now like a second skin. One moment to the next. That is all he can do. One moment to the next. Avoid the Hallelujahs and sit quietly as he gets his ear chewed off by this strange creature that is smiling at him now. 'Come on, then.' Plates getting cleared away. 'Ye ready?'

26

'See, what I'm saying is never let them think that ye've hit the scrape because if they do then that's you screwed, man, terrible, fucking terrible. They'll never leave ye alone. Plus as well they'll give ye the worst of everything – room, bed, fire alarm, giro, the whole bag all to shite.'

Mick looks down at the pavement. It is dark. Cold. Their breath fluming in front of them as they walk. Actually, no – Beans's breath fluming in front of them – because he never shuts up. Since they left the church it's been non-stop: benefits, religion, piles, the population of birds. He needs to rest but he's too tired to think about doing anything but trail along with this guy through the dark streets, stumbling into busyness where the pavements are hoaching at bus stops and crossings; down deserted side roads, past closed shops, pubs, a girl with her arms tightly folded, smoking in a doorway. The problem with birds, he is saying, is that they're all dying because the farmers are greedy arabs and they've torn down all the hedgerows, the same as they tear down the tenements and now there's nothing, everything is bare just. Mick is trying no to listen. This place they are going to was supposed to be close by, but they've been walking Christ knows how long and he doesn't recognize any more where they are. To close the eyes just. Close the eyes. Sleep. No have to think. No have to listen.

'Where d'ye say it is, this place?'

'Naw, don't worry, don't worry. It's near here. I know where it is.'

'Ye've stayed before, well?'

Beans halts abruptly on the spot, jolts his body upright. 'Have I stayed before? *Course* I've stayed before. *Course* I have.' And he starts walking again, chuckling to himself. Has he been bevvying? It's hard to tell. He's a mighty queer ticket, whichever way. There is a period of quiet. They keep on. No a slow pace either – the guy walks with these great loundering strides, the shoulders stooped over and hunching, bunching, as he steps. It had came as a surprise, during the lunatic moment back there, how tall he actually is when he stands straight. A big man, and this large army-type overcoat that he wears, making him look even bigger. Impossible but to tell how old he is. The hair, when he's took off the woolly hat to sleep, is a full coverage – dark, straggling below his ears and greasy as drag-chains. His face though, lined and scarred; purple. Whatever it is he's been doing with himself, it looks like he's been doing it a long while.

He is trying now to hoick his tattered Ikea bag higher onto his shoulder. Mick is conscious of his own faded holdall, smart in comparison, and as well his clothes, which if maybe they aren't the cleanest, they are normal clothes, they are his clothes. He isn't going around in an army greatcoat and a pair of silver running trainers with the soles flapping off them. Beans is hammering away again: the weather, how it's freezing but it isnae wet and that's the important thing because it's blashie weather that's the worst. Jesus, he could do with a drink.

'See, look, this is what I'm telling ye. Here.'

They are outside a grey concrete building at one end of a street. A woman's voice on an intercom by a heavy, unmarked door and they are getting buzzed in. A corridor; straight ahead a staircase and two doors off either side. Bare walls and grey carpet tiles. The strong smell of bleach. Beans doesn't seem too sure where to go and he hesitates a moment, a quick neb in the one door, then back out, and he tries the other one; goes inside. Mick follows him in.

It looks like a doctor's waiting room: plastic chairs backed against the walls and a single battered settee, a small television that is turned off, and a low table sprawled with mangled, thick magazines. An Asian woman is sat at a computer on the other side of a small security hatch. Beans goes straight up and puts his hands onto the counter. They look massive in the stark lighting, veined like cabbages.

'We've booked a place the night. I was in earlier.'

Mick sits down on the settee. Comfort flooding his legs. He could go to sleep right here, close the eyes, go to sleep.

'No, see, I came in Sunday but there was no rooms so I was told come back the day and they told me earlier there was places for us, that's what I'm saying.'

The woman's voice is hushed, barely audible past his huge back. He is arguing with her; the protective shutter above the hatch about to roll down any moment. Beans turns then and comes toward the settee. He dumps down and Mick near slides onto his lap.

'Says we've got to wait for the hostel manager. She's no too sure we're booked in but that's pure crap – I was here the morning and I spoke to the guy, I telt him we were coming. Fucking *indirect* access, ye ask me.' He keeps speaking, but Mick sits in a kind of a daze, wanting to let the brainbox go to rest. Hostel. He is in a hostel. He tries no to think about what is happening; trying no to think about any of it, least of all this blowhard sat here next to him, staring now at the underwear models in a worn-out clothing catalogue. An agitated old black man noses in at one point, his trouser bottoms rolled up unevenly to show dirty yellow walking socks. He glances toward the television a moment, then backs out.

Mick is falling asleep, Beans quietly looking at the magazines, and another man coming in, younger, smarter, a trimmed beard. Beans is stood up, talking to him. The man goes away, through a locked door into the room with the woman; returning with sheets of paper. He gives some to Beans, then he's looking down at Mick, handing him the papers and saying something – he can't hear it properly, it's quiet like a radio with the batteries going – benefits, it is something about benefits. He tries to sit up. The man is talking to Beans again. No visitors. No alcohol. No drugs. He repeats it. Beans nodding his head. Grinning. He looks demented.

The room is small. A cubicle. Three beds with high plastic sides, lined up like cots. He puts his bag down at the foot of one of them and looks out the small window at a brightly lit car park. Lies down on the bed. He can hear Beans outside, laying it off to the man because the room isn't big enough. He stares up at the ceiling. The same smell of bleach; sanitizer. Strange but he is glad of Beans being there. The ceiling is starting to swim. He shuts the eyes. So tired it feels his breathing is about to give out.

A shout wakes him. He sits up. His clothes are on and it is dark apart from some lights outside a window. A hollow racing sensation as he gets his bearings. There is another shout; it is in the corridor – *Go on!*

it sounds like. Then feet pounding and a tremor in the floor as they come past his room. *Go on!* More than one person. Three or four. Men's voices. A moment later it is quiet again, but the tight panicked feeling does not leave him and he lies there rigid, exhausted but no able to get back to sleep.

When he wakes up again it is getting light outside. The room is empty. Tummelled sheets on one of the beds. He is hungry, but he doesn't know if there is a breakfast in this place. He doesn't know what or where the place is either, for another thing. After a while he gets up and listens through the door, and goes out.

The kitchen along the corridor is empty. Plates and pans are heaped in the sink and there are blackened scratchings of food littered on top of an electric hob cooker. Something in the room which is boufing. Doesn't smell much like food but, and he realizes as he gets closer that it is the bin. He moves away from it and toward the fridge. Inside, a bundled-up Tesco carrier and a snipped-open packet of pasta sauce inside the door. That's the lot. A stank of yellowish liquid pooled at the bottom. Second inspections but, and he undoes the carrier to find a plastic tub of cocktail sausages. No like they're going to miss a couple, and no like he's fussy either, so he puts one in his mouth; but there is something wrong about the taste of it, and he gets standing up, shuts the fridge door, awful, fucking awful. Posters on a noticeboard. Needle exchange. Substance-use worker. His stomach lurches and he bends over the sink, about to boak, but he doesn't – he stays there, poised, with the stomach spasming but nothing coming up, just this thin dribble hanging off his lip. He sticks the tap on and swills his mouth. The rush of water splashing against the plates and pans and wetting his front. Where is he? He wants suddenly to laugh. Where in fuck is he? He turns off the tap and goes out, back to the empty room, and into the bed.

Beans is stood at the foot of the bed, looking at him.

'Fancy getting some breakfast eh?'

Mick gets up automatically, without thinking. Starts putting his shoes on. Beans is over by the window, his hands clasped behind his back, calmly gazing out as if it's a loch view.

Once outside, they are straight away on the march. No the worst day. Warm on those parts of the pavement that the sun is shining, although pretty snappy still in the shaded areas, past offices and residential blocks, under a bridge, past a line of parked buses. They go by a small scrub of a square and a mob of scaffers around the benches on one side. Seven or eight of them, women in the mix, sitting and standing about, drinking. Beans slows down, watching them. For a moment Mick is feart he is wanting to go over, but they carry on past, although Beans still has his attention turned to the group. They continue up the way. Truth is, he's glad to be out of the hostel. Away from that room. Probably most of that group back there are staying in the place too. The thought of it, of being in there with them, himself in a room alongside, it doesn't make sense. He can't reckon with it. Better outside in the open, away from it, even if that means being with your man here. They are stopped outside a cafe. A large scratched sticker on the window – a fat chef holding up a steaming forked sausage. Beans is going in, but Mick hesitates outside.

'Ye coming in?'

'Aye.' But he stays where he is, looking in past the fat chef.

Beans grins. 'It's on me, pal, it's on me, don't worry.'

'No. It's no the game,' but Beans is off inside already, and he follows him in.

They go up the counter and Beans immediately orders two breakfasts and two teas, then they get themselves sat at a table by a wall, away from the busy middle of the room. Pathetic. He knows it is. Somehow but he can't feel it. He's that hungry, and weak – that's what it is, a weakness – that he can't bring himself to say no. The breakfasts come and Beans is beasted right in, mushrooms flying about, ketchup and brown sauce and mustard all mixed together on his plate like a mental sunset. Every bastard in the place probably looking at them. The odd couple in the corner. It's a good breakfast though. A buttery stack of toast, the warm mush of the sausage. Suddenly the thought that maybe Beans doesn't have the money to pay for it either, and he's going to do a run-out. The scunnered faces of the other customers and the cafe owner on the phone to the polis.

He does have the money, it turns out. A ten-pound note comes out the pocket, calm as anything, no chicanery, no hystericals. He walks up the counter just, pays, and they leave.

It is bright out still. They walk for quite a while, Beans talking – they aren't allowed back into the hostel while evening, he is saying – until they arrive, suddenly, at the river. A stretch he doesn't recognize. Beans is saying he wants to show him something, and they go through a gate with a broken padlock – *Permits required to access this property for the purpose of nature conservation or fishing* – into a small wooded, weeded area. Down a sloping thicket and thorns path, long grass and random rubbish – empty cement bags, a broken office chair on its side – to a sprawling bush, which they crawl under, emerging onto a patch of open ground that looks out on the water.

'The veranda,' he declares. They sit down, legs dangling over the banking. He likes to sit here and watch the boats and that come past, he says. And to drink too, judging by all the cans lying about. There is a swan who stays under the scrub off to one side where the banking stops, Beans tells him, only she's no there the now because she's out and about getting her nest together. It's hard to believe him – anything he says – but then Mick sees the nest, lower down, sticking out from under the scrub, all these twigs twined into a great bowl on the wet ground amongst plastic bottles and lager cans. Bold as ye like. He gives a smile at the sight of it. These swans that he minds, who made their nests by the fitting-out berths, their feathers clatty with oil, but who'd come and go like they were boating on Loch Lomond.

At one point during the afternoon Beans goes off for a while, and returns with a couple of four-packs. They sit in the sun drinking, and Mick tells him what type are a couple of the boats that come by, Beans listening as if it's the most fascinating thing he's ever heard.

It is only when it gets evening and they are on the approach to the hostel that it starts to loom over him again. The bare room. Bogging of bleach. Surrounded by homeless. They walk past a bar and he almost asks Beans if he fancies going a pint, but obviously it's impossible because of the money situation. It's bad enough he's tapped him already for his breakfast, plus now the cans. So they go in, Beans away into the reception to chin the staff and leaving Mick to go up on his own.

He is on the stairhead about to turn onto the corridor, but there is noise up the way. Voices. He waits round the corner, the heart going mental already. Hard to hear what they are saying, but it sounds like there's a few of them, and this other noise as well that sounds like somebody thumping rhythmically against the wall. He is that fixed on what's ahead of him, he doesn't notice the group coming up the stair behind.

One of them laughs.

'You alright there, mate?'

He spins round. There are three of them. Young lads. They stand there grinning and leering at him.

'Fine, aye,' and he moves on down the corridor, the others up ahead turning to watch him, and these behind following him, one of them making a tootling noise, like a trumpet. He gets into the room, closes the door and pushes one of the cots up against it.

The sun straining a thin light through the curtain. Beans asleep in his clothes. Noises coming and going outside, keeping him awake, on edge.

It is dark. He has been dreaming. Christmas. Christmases, all jumbled together. The first one he is sat in the living room and the boys and the Highlanders are there sat in their positions, a wee plastic Christmas tree behind the television, Lynn sat on the settee next to Alan with her crabbit face on, like it's the last place in the world she wants to be the now, this craphole, with its stained carpets and cramped corridors, and the wobbling banister as he goes up the stair and into the bedroom. Robbie and Craig sat on the kitchen chairs with plates of Christmas dinner on their laps, looking toward the shape in the bed. Craig cutting up the turkey breast into tiny pieces; quartering the Brussels sprouts.

He is awake. The mind out of its box, spinning, all over the place. A few minutes and he's managed to calm himself a little, lying awake until he is able to sleep again.

Another Christmas. Australia. He is sat at the table waiting for her to come in from the kitchen. The cracker hat clamming to his forehead and the full works there on the plate in front of him – turkey, roast tatties and parsnips, bread pudding, cranberry sauce – and outside, all of the gardens down the road are empty because the whole of the Tartan Terrace is at the same game: the only weekend of the summer nobody's got the barbecue out.

Morning, and he's lying in the bed, the body aching, sticking. Beans suddenly in through the door and frowning. He looks at him a moment. 'Breakfast?'

They sit at the same table, the same positions. The only difference is that Beans isn't as rosy this morning: his back is up from something that's happened in the hostel, and it's making him mutter and scratch fork points through his swirly sauce sunsets.

'See the problem is with these people, they've no respect for a person's privacy, know? Mean, it's no better than the clink, serious, and I'm expecting a bit of privacy myself. That's the least I'm expecting.'

'What happened?'

The eyes widen, far enough to expose the white outsider parts that are normally sheltered under the lids. 'What happened? That bastard the manager, that's what. He says to me, the magazines are supposed to stay in the reception, they're no for taking out. Believe that? He's no even asked me. He's telt me I've got them but he's no even asked me first, that's how I'm beeling about it.'

He cloys up then and they don't talk any more about it. They finish eating and Beans pays.

It is colder, blowier, the day, and after a walkabout they go into a train station, park themselves on some seats by a pasty shop. There is a scaffer hanging about the ticket machines and Beans is watching him, the bristles up, like a dog. The smell of pasties wafting; a rare moment of enjoyment. He thinks for a moment how the shame of leeching like this should be making him the more desperate to get doing something, but it's not, it's the opposite – he doesn't think, doesn't care; he is into the routine. They are walking again. Fine but. Fine. Keeping on the move. A stop at the offie on the way to the veranda, and it is okay once they are sat down because the wind is mainly kept off by the bush all afternoon. As soon as they get leaving though, the familiar feeling starts to kick in, the nerves already on edge.

Fortunately but Beans doesn't go in the reception, he's wiped his hands with them, he says, and there is nobody about as they go up the stair and into the corridor. Open the door and go inside the room.

'Aw, Christ.'

It has been turned over. All the bedding is thrown on the floor and the drawers under the one small table are wrenched open. Their two bags have been taken. He sits down heavily on the bed, his breath constricting. Beans is away out the door. 'Fucksake, man. Fucking hell.' He puts his head down on the mattress. Stares out the window. A wean is kicking a ball against the car park wall. He lies listening to it beat repeatedly on the brick.

'She says there's nothing they can do, we should've locked the door. Bastards. Probably them that did it. Serious. It probably was. Ye okay, pal?' A hand is on his shoulder. 'Look, nay worries. No like we had much anyway eh? First thing we'll do the morning, we'll get out of this place. Okay?' He is hauling one of the cots up against the door. 'The better on our own, serious, nay cunts nebbing about.'

27

The group have been there all morning. At any one time there are between four and eight of them: sometimes a pair will wander off toward the street, or a new arrival will come into the square and for a few minutes the silence is broken as the others get on their feet, talking, shouting. One of the women keeps herself slightly removed, on the end bench. If one of the men approaches where she is, starts saying something to her, she ignores him, and eventually he returns to the others. The air of the group is edgy, quiet, getting worse as the morning goes on. Nothing to drink. She feels cold and nervous, sober, aware of the staring line of people at the bus stop.

Shortly before midday, three men arrive, two of them each holding a heavy plastic bottle of cider. The mood changes straight away. There is laughter and movement, the first of the bottles getting opened and passed around. She stays where she is on the bench, and before long another woman comes and sits next to her, passing her the second bottle. This other woman is grinning, looking at her coat. 'Jesus, Anna, alright for some.'

From the first swallow she is elsewhere. Her fear leaving; warmth spreading from deep inside her; the people at the bus stop disappearing. There is a burst of laughter from the group, one of the men saying something that she cannot hear, and the other woman resting her head now against the arm of her coat, closing her eyes. The woman's hair is thin, and she can see there is a rash on part of her scalp, and on the very top of her head, a large dark blue scab.

A fight has broken out. It came out of nowhere – she didn't see what started it – but two of the men are stalking stiffly around each other, and suddenly one of them crumples to the ground as he is struck by something from behind. In an instant the square is filled with shouting, the others in the group rushing in to join the scuffle.

She lifts the woman's head from her arm, lowers it gently to the bench slats and hurries away.

She breathes thinly as she moves down the street, past a line of parked buses and under a bridge, before slowing, her legs aching and frozen. At least her top half is warm. The coat is expensive and new, with a soft lining, and she pulls it tightly around her, making sure that the top is buttoned up to the neck. She needs to pee, but it is quite a way still to where she's headed, so she takes a detour to a public toilet by the river. When she gets there though, she finds it has been boarded up. Fuckers. She is reminded of the stupid drunk dickheads fighting up at the square and she vows not to return there later in the day, whatever happens.

There is a pub on her way and she goes into it. On entering through the heavy swing doors she is immediately watched by the bar girl, and by the time she has gone down the narrow spiral staircase into a dingy basement corridor, there is a large man in chef trousers standing in front of the toilet entrance. He is slowly shaking his head. She turns, avoiding looking at his face, and goes back up the spiral staircase. She walks through the bar; the girl looking at her from behind the counter. Her limbs are heavy and she thinks for a moment that the swing door is not going to open. She desperately needs to pee. With a painful heave the door pushes open, and she turns her head back as she steps through it.

'Fucking bitch.'

There is at least ten minutes left of the journey and she feels like she is about to piss herself. She comes to a side street leading toward a train station and goes down it, crouching behind one of the cars parked next to a high metal fence. Before she has finished, a man, and then a woman with a young teenage girl, come out of the train station exit and start walking along the pavement on the other side of the street. The woman and the girl are talking and do not see her, but the man crosses the street a short way ahead and must see the urine dribbling into the road, because he looks now through the car window at her and for an instant his mouth opens and he mutters something before hurrying away.

When she arrives at the house her mouth feels dry and her arms and legs are faintly shaking as she reaches for the buzzer. She waits in the doorway, until a moment later a man's voice answers, and there is a click as the door unlocks and she lets herself in.

On the veranda, looking out. A yacht coming past, sails blustering in the wind. A woman's face in a porthole. Away to the Med, says Beans. Champagne and Charlie. Only watch out for the Bay of Biscay or ye'll be boaking it all up into the sea. Anyone's guess how he thinks he knows these things. Maybe he does. The money is finished, he says then, but it's nay worry. He's got a plan. He is kneeling up and lifting the bush to get out. Okay? Okay?

There is a noise up on the pavement. A woman's voice, and, quieter, a man's. He tries to listen, no able to pick out the words, but they are getting closer. A gust of wind or something and suddenly he can hear them coming toward him and he scrapes deep into the bush, lying flat underneath it. He cannot let them see him; he pulls his jacket over his head. But they keep coming – they are onto the path now, and he can see the crabbit face, irritated at all these roots and thorns snarling about her ankles. They spot him then, laid out under the bush. She's pure scunnered at the sight of it, but he has a wee smile on him, unsurprised, keeking down now at the cans by his feet.

It is colder when Beans returns, the river turned black and treacly. He has a dark blue ski-jacket-type overcoat under his arm, and a carrier that he starts pulling things out from: a loaf of bread, an open tin of beans, a stack of beers. He sits down next to him. 'Here,' he says, and lobs the coat over. 'Put this over your jacket. Keep ye warmer.'

They make cold beans pieces out of the first few bread slices, and start on the cans. He has been drinking already, it seems. He isn't out the game, but he's talking loudly, laughing, and he makes them clink cans every couple of minutes – plus, each time, an extra one for the swan. 'Thanks,' Mick says, after one of these toasts, 'the coat and that.'

'Aw, you're welcome.' Beans puts on a panloaf English accent.

'You're very welcome.' He takes a long gulp. 'This fella I know, I called in a favour. He's alright, no a bad guy. He's a cunt, ye know, but he's alright.' They are laughing. A warm enclosed feeling from the beer.

'It because I'm from Glasgow, how ye're helping me out?'

'What!' He sits bolt upright and gets standing stumbling to his feet. 'Ye're from Glasgow? Serious? I'd have gave ye the swerve if I'd known,' and he collapses to the ground again, cackling to himself.

In a moment, Beans kneels up. He gets scrabbling feet first under the bush, thorns pulling at his coat and revealing his back, pale and mealy as a white pudding. His head appears over the top of the bush. 'Come on, I'll show ye.'

They go at an angle from the path, through the weeds and the undergrowth, until Beans stops beside some wire netting. An orange sign on it he can't read in the dark. Some kind of a tunnel underneath the road. Beans peels the wiring back and squeezes himself in behind, the wire springing back to its original position. 'Come on.' He steps forward. An old trainer shoe by his feet.

He gets in behind the wiring and it is dark. A smell of stagnant water. Beans is dragging a piece of matting along the ground. 'Here, lie down.' Bits of rock poking at him, their two backs pressed together, shuffling; warm but, where they are touching. The echoing sound of traffic above their heads and the matting no big enough for both their bodies, part of his leg and his arm sticking out and pressing into stones, rubble. The drink but, it is keeping him outside of it, no fully aware, helping him fall to sleep.

Light. The head pounding. His throat dry, chappit, and his legs and his body senseless, except for a jabbing in the small of his back where Beans's elbow is sticking into him. He tries to go back to sleep, but it is too cold and he can't, so he sits up and looks about him. On one side, through the wire, weeds and trees; a glimpse of the dark straining river. There are bits of wood and breezeblocks in the gloom of the tunnel. Dark water pooled into a stank, a Sprite bottle floating on top. On the other side, more wiring, and past it, a construction site – a great hole in the ground, scaffolding, a mini JCB. Beans is sat up now too. Silent. They stay the both of them like that, sitting, for quite a while, and he wonders if maybe Beans is hungover, that's how he's no talking. But he keeps quiet and to himself into the morning, as they go and sit out on the veranda, cold, shivering, until eventually Beans gets up just, no a word, and leaves.

There is a key ring in one of the coat pockets. *London*, it says on it. A pair of palace guardsmen with their daftie hats on. He turns it about in his fingers. No key. Course not. Why would there be? There must have been once but. Or at least somebody's bought it that had one. A car owner. House owner. Seems unlikely Beans knows a person like that. More likely the coat's been lifted. Nay fucking chance he's taking it off though. He is shaking with the cold now. A bit of a wind and a spray coming off the river. An agity feeling is building, uncertain if Beans is going to bring any drink back this time. He can't bring himself to think about how it will be if he doesn't. A whole day and a night to get through in the cold, time not moving on, clotting around him. He finds a few loose pieces of chinex in the other pocket, puts one in his mouth and chews away.

It is dark when Beans returns. Another half-loaf with him. No beers but. Mick doesn't say anything, and they get eating the bread. He's still in the same mood, Beans, keeping cloyed up, and Mick starts feeling an irritation build inside him that he is behaving like this. He doesn't say anything though. He lets it stay there, choking any words he might get saying, watching Beans chuck the empty loaf packet out onto the water. Sleep is impossible the night. The temperature feels like it's dipped even further. The only warmth, Beans's back sweating against his. He wants to get up and walk away somewhere, just walk, but he can't, he can't move.

Afternoon. The dull anxiety waiting for if there's beer or if there's no beer. There is. A big plastic bottle of superlager. Beans in a good mood too. They get stuck in and numbness starts to flood through him. A distant laugh, which he realizes is Beans. How is he getting it? He'd said the money was gone. He can't be bothered maundering on it but – so what, just drink, just fucking drink it down. He starts laughing. He's like a wee bird. That's what he is. A wee chick, a wee sparrow chick staying put in the nest all day while Beans goes back and forth, getting him food and drink, coming back onto the veranda and regurgitating it up for him. Every day. How many? How many days? Fuck knows, and he is laughing again. He turns round and Beans is laughing too, anybody's guess what at. Strange how the time goes. There it is, stretching out in front of you – only the river, boats, the sound of traffic, and the thought mob raring to stick the boot on.

28

Beans's voice up the path, coming back, talking to himself. The heart starts going, in anticipation, or panic, or habit just, fuck knows. He turns round and looks through the bush, and Beans is there with another man. Panic tightens through him. They are crawling under the bush. 'See here's the guy I'm telling ye about.' The man is nodding at him, sitting himself down on the veranda. He is younger, the hair closely cut, his sweater and his jeans pretty clean-looking. A bottle of superlager is being passed between Beans and the guy, who takes a long pull, gulping twice. Then they pass it to him. The two of them talking. 'They're taking all the old spots, is the problem.' He is English. 'Come over for the building jobs and all that but then they get here and they've already filled all the fucking jobs, so they're out on their arse but they can't afford the fucking fare home.' Beans laughs with him, passing the drink. Then the guy sees the swan and he's off down the banking. A big stick suddenly in his hand and he is laughing, poking it at the nest. The swan is hissing and it's looking like she's going to up and stiffen him any minute, until Beans gets in there first. He jumps on the guy's back and the pair of them start tummelling about in the wet scrub by the nest. Beans on top now, pounding him. Seconds later the guy gets scrabbling up onto the banking and he's away under the bush. 'Fuck are you doing? It's a joke, Jesus, it's a fucking joke.'

He opens his eyes. Daylight. He is outside, and he is freezing. Beans is sat staring out, eating. Mick sits up and he gets handed a sandwich out of a carrier.

He looks at it a moment. 'There's a bite mark in this.'

Beans turns, frowning. 'Aye, so what?'

'Just, mean, there's more teeth marks in it than you've got teeth,' he grins, and Beans creases over, knotting himself.

Later, and Beans is stood above him, giving him these wee kicks in the thigh. 'Come on. We need to go the messages. I told ye.'

Onto the road, the pavements. Odd. Like he's there but he's in fact no there. They are looking at him, but from somewhere else, another consciousness, another world. Like being bevvied. Operating in your own space and everybody else fogging up around the edges of it. No that he's drunk but. The soreness all over his body is sure enough sign of that. 'This is the best time. Ye have to wait the last minute, when the fella's there with his gun, stickering all the stuff up.' True enough, there he is. Fridges. Shopping trolleys. 'Discreet, right. We need to be discreet.' But Mick is started laughing. Discreet! No likely. They look like a pair of cartoon characters, stalking behind tailing the guy as he is going about putting on the stickers. Into the baking aisle. The comforting smell of it. A wean stood staring while his maw chooses between the brown breads. He doesn't know what to make of the pair of them, his mouth in a wee study, slightly open, then he's darting off with his mammy, holding the hand. Beans has a stick of bread, and a piled handful of tinned salmon – *Reduced to clear.*

Outside, in the car park at the back of the building, there is a gap through to where the warehouse bit is. The shutters are closed but up against them there is a stack of red plastic crates. 'Here.' Beans passes him a couple. They are shallow but long and wide, and they have to hold them with arms stretched out, leaving quickly away down the road, taking up half the pavement between them.

'Bread crates,' he says. 'Good mattresses. Plenty of give, see, and they keep ye off the ground.' He's right too. They work well, slotted together with the matting laid out on top, and he is much more comfortable the night, no forgetting as well the bottle of superlager they got from the offie on the way back. He is able to sleep, even though he wakes up often. Each time he does, the tunnel boufing with a rank smell. The sour stankwater – but then there is a hiss of air from behind him, tickling the backs of his legs. The salmon.

Rain. They keep to the tunnel but it is filling up with water, so thank Christ for the bread crates. They stay sat or lying on top of them all night and all day as the blashie weather continues; his body aching, disintegrating, but always auld Beans there, trusty as ever with the bottle. The sun appearing. Beautiful spring sunshine. Daffodils. Bloody daffodils, where they come from? We have received a number of complaints. Sat throwing chuckies into the river, aiming at a can caught up in the yellow foam. Beans is a fair aim. A man of surprises, ye are. Aw, fuck off, pal, I used to play cricket for Scotland, ye know. The pair of them falling about pishing themselves. They are just stood there looking. A few residents have made complaints. Residents? Ye kidding? Who's that, well, the fucking swan? She's fine, man, she knows the score, she's no a bastard like yous. But they aren't finding it so funny, they're just stood there in their high-vis jackets and their fishermen's wading boots. If you don't move, we will have to get the police. Eh, what? Who are yous, then, if you're no the polis? They are laughing again and started throwing the chuckies at these three but the game's over. Up in the air. Suddenly the polis, the protectors of the residents, are arrived and they are being pulled about and corkscrewed up the path – bloody hell, says the one of them, as he keeks the drinks cabinet. They let go of their arms a way up the pavement, and it looks a banker they're about to get slung in the meat wagon, but no – get walking, they are told. The polis following at a short distance behind. Onto the roads and they keep going, miles and miles, turning round one point and the polis are gone, Beans muttering to himself, grumbling, chapping now on a door. After a while an Asian guy opening. No, he says, and he shuts it again.

They are going up a stairwell and his legs give out. He slumps down on the step and Beans is dragging at him until he gets up and labours on. Another door.

'You.'

'Me, aye.'

They are being let in and they follow the backs of a man's legs up a staircase. Who's he? My pal, that's who. A small room and a TV going. He is sitting down on a settee and Beans and the man have went into another room. A plate on the floor with the remains of a jacket tattie, just the well-fired parts of the shell left over. Beans and the man appear in the doorway, grim-faced.

Cans coming out; he gets handed one. The man's eyes are large and swollen, the top lids delicately folded scrotums. The air clung with smoke as he gets through his pack of fags, Beans smoking as well, dog-ends on the floor, a shoe, some bundled sheets. He doesn't say much, your mate, through the smoke. He's fine, he's fine. Darkness, and he wakes, alarmed and shaking. Beans on the settee, one cadaver leg hanging off the edge. He is lying on the floor. The stink of smoke in the carpet. The tattie still there; he crawls over and starts into it, tearing at the boot leather skin.

Always with Beans he's on the march somewhere, some plan or other he's got in his head and he isn't stopping until he gets there. They arrive at a small car park behind a low, flat-roofed building. There is a fence all round with a neat bed of green shoots in front. BUTTERFIELD MEDICAL PRACTICE, on a sign plugged into the soil. Alarm seizes suddenly in his stomach, working up into his throat until he is almost breathless, choking, needing to sit down on the path by the flower bed. Beans slapping him on the back. A pure desperate urge to drink now has hold of him as Beans makes him stand up, and they get walking, away again onto the street.

They come to a park – no a park but more a patch in between a couple of road crossings, with a square of grass and a rubber-matted play area big enough for about three weans a time to go on. A see-saw. A wee elephant slide with a trunk for a chute. There is a bin beside a bench, which Beans has a neb through before going in his pocket and handing Mick a five-pound note. 'Gonnae go the offie while I find us something to eat?'

The man in the offie is a bastard, but what can you do? Mick thumps the two bottles of superlager onto the counter and the guy doesn't say a word, he gives this wee look just, but he's made himself fine well clear enough. I, the seller of refreshments, know that you, the scaffer, are going to get yourself paralytic, and if it so happens that you kill yourself falling into the road, or you kill somebody else falling into the road, then it's no my fault, and I'll stand here with my face to vinegar just to show who is the better out of the two of us. Nay problem. Fine. Just hand over the beer, pal.

29

A woman, coming toward them.

'Excuse me.'

Beans straightening up, the eyes alert suddenly.

'Nay bother, madam. Ye haven't interrupted anything.'

Her hands on her hips.

'You can't drink here. There's kids playing.'

How old is she? Thirty? Forty? Her weans over on the see-saw, and another woman there too, nervous wee looks up the way. Beans is giggling, saying something, impossible to tell what. The woman stood with her arms folded. 'Excuse me.' She is looking at him now. 'Can you understand me?' The weans are stopped playing, lined up on the rubber play area watching. He has a dim sense of wanting her to stay there, a sort of longing, but Beans is acting it still, muttering on, and she is gone, angrily gathering up bags and weans and marching out of the park to go fetch the heavy team, or the polis, or the council – wading boots on, lads, the residents arenae happy.

There is only one bench in the park, so they take turns, a night each, to sleep on it. The nights it isn't their turn they lie out on the grass aside or underneath it. One time but Beans gives a try sleeping on the slide, although it's obvious no big enough, and Mick finds him in the morning crumpled at the bottom of the chute, looking like something the elephant's boaked up during the night.

He wakes. The sour taste of alcohol in his mouth. Against his face is an empty creased bottle that he'd put there as a pillow. The sun is up, and warm already, but he has got the shakes. No just the arms, or the legs, but the whole of him: head, chest, elbows and hips, all the way down to his toes. Shuddering. He caulks the eyes shut but they pinball in the sockets until they are pure throbbing and he can no longer stop this fear that is rising up him, overwhelming him, a genuine terror made all the worse because there is nothing to fix it to, no reason, it is there just. He presses his forehead hard against the slats of the bench, pushing against the ache. Slitting the eyes open. Beans isn't there. The sudden thought but of getting up to look for him – it's impossible, even the thought is impossible and makes his stomach start to heave and his throat retch, even sitting up, even opening his eyes fully, impossible, impossible. Easier to lie there just, shivering and sweating. The sun no helping matters either – sapping him and making him the more nauseous. He hasn't the energy to take off his coat though. The smallest things. Impossible. But through it all he is craving for a drink. An urging of the body; a pure physical need for it, just to stop all this, drive away again the ache and the fear.

It is getting darker and he is cold. Beans has gone for a crap in the bushes beyond the play area. Away on the road, a streetlamp flickering on. Then another. All along the side of the park they are coming on at random intervals, and he realizes that it's the ones in the darkest spots where the smaller trees are coming to leaf which are turning on first. Interesting. The wee things you notice.

Beans is shaking him on the shoulder.

'Come on, gonnae wake up?'

'What?'

'Breakfast.' The familiar grin. His breakfast grin. 'I've been researching.'

He gets himself up off the ground. It is drizzling and his back is soaked, some of it sweat probably, although he doesn't feel too bad this morning. Their money has ran out, so they haven't drunk the full bucket the last couple of days. They get walking through the rain until a short while later they arrive at a building that looks at first like an office block, but when they go through the glass doors and bare lobby it opens into a large hall, full of scaffers. Bright overhead lights, tables, din. Beans turns to him: 'Ye okay? Check the food, eh. No bad.' He can't see any food. The place is hoaching with scaffers, shuffling about, yapping, staring. 'Ye coming?' Beans is gone ahead and he hurries after him, clinging behind like a wean, he's that dependent. See what if Beans leaves him? Gets so sick of him laggered onto his back like some diseased lump that he gives him the slip? The possibility of it makes him start to panic as he follows on to a trestle table with large pots of food on it. He waits in behind Beans, copies how he gets his meal and moves to the next area for a tea. They sit down at an empty table and eat hungrily. Toast. Scrambled eggs. 'Pretty good, eh? I should've minded this place earlier. It's one of the best. Only open a couple of hours but, so ye have to be quick.'

A young guy is watching them. He is sat at another table with a couple of others, forking egg into his mouth but clear enough looking over. Beans doesn't seem to notice, or else he's ignoring it. Mick keeks away. He wants to be out of here. Beans has other ideas though: 'Finish this and we'll go the showers, okay?'

In another room there are washing and drying machines, and cardboard boxes full of clothes. Beans is off through a doorway and he is left stood there unsure what to do. An old woman with a name badge hung around her neck comes up and tells him to help himself to some of the clothes, so he rummles through and pulls out a faded black pair of trackie bottoms and a grey shirt with a dark smudge on the collar.

In the next room, through a door marked MEN, there is a queue for showers, and Beans is further up the way already. They aren't communal, thank Christ: there's five or six separate ones, each with a curtain, though a couple of the men at the front are down to their pants already. Fucking terrible, the state of them. Scars and veins and jaundice.

He waits until he is inside a cubicle before he starts to undress. Even removing his coat feels odd. He's no took it off since Beans gave it him. Then he peels off the rest, all of it damp and rotten, clabbered to his skin, and he gets in the shower. It's been that long since he's seen himself in the scuddy that he doesn't recognize himself. As if the body isn't his; it belongs to another time when nakedness was something that had to be dealt with on a daily basis, and now he doesn't own it – he's removed himself from his body like he has from everything else. The only clue that it's there the now: that it hurts. There are bruises on his legs, down his front, his hips, fucking everywhere. His forearm skin is turned loose and chickeny; he pulls on it, the spring gone. The penis down there. Genuine difficult to believe that is his. He puts a hand around it, tries to mind what it means, the having of a penis. Nothing's doing but. His dobber's no sure about it either, and the two of them dither there for a while, waiting for something to happen, a connection. There is none. Or maybe it's just that neither of them are too comfortable about the line of half-naked scaffers queuing outside, which is in fact fair enough, being honest.

He gives himself a good wash, using the soap from the dispenser to rub over his head and his body, and special attention to the feet, which are started looking like a couple of raw beef kidneys. It feels good. The force of the water. Cleaning. Paying attention to all these parts that he's forgot about. The belly button. Armpits. Nipples, christsake.

When he comes out, he goes in the toilets and takes a very satisfying crap. The first time in a long while he's no had to sneak into a pub for one, or go in the park with a stolen toilet roll.

He puts his dirty clothes in a washer. Pretty pleased as well with these new ones. The shirt is a decent fit, and the trousers comfy enough around the waist, even if they are a wee bit on the short side. No the less, see even if his socks are on show, he definitely doesn't look half as daft as Beans does. He clocks him out in the hall and goes toward him, chuckling.

'Jesus. Check you.'

He is wearing a pair of black jeans and a white denim jacket, the both of them a fair few sizes too small for him. Beans grins. 'Gallus, eh?' Then he holds a finger in the air and spins around slowly, showing the back: ATLANTA HAWKS.

'If you say so, pal. If you say so.'

Beans goes back to the clothing room, saying that he forgot to look for another pair of socks, and Mick moves over to the juice table. There are plenty of name-badge people milling about, topping up cups, handing out leaflets, chatting. They don't seem like Hallelujahs. Any case, there isn't anything religious on the walls, only posters everywhere – chiropodist, walk-in clinic, housing advice – things he should be finding out about, probably, but the awareness of it only makes him feel the more sluggish. Through in the clothes room he can see Beans talking to somebody. He is pointing a thumb at his jacket, showing it off, but suddenly a hand shoots out from behind the door frame and grabs him by the collar, pulling him forwards. Beans stumbling, out of sight. There is too much noise in the hall to hear what is going on. He moves quickly toward the room, a few looking in now.

It is the young guy that had been staring. He is stood right up to Beans, putting the face on him.

'Fucking give it me.'

Another guy as well, behind him, eyeballing Beans, who is rocking on his feet, confused. 'Look, see I got it out the box, that's what I –' but he is getting shoved again, the veins on the guy's neck standing out and Beans falling to the floor, straight onto his arse. Mick rushes forward, standing in front of him before the guy can stick the boot on. 'Leave it, come on. What ye doing? Leave it.' The young guy is looking at him, this odd smile, like he knows him.

'The jacket's mine.'

Name-badge men are coming in the door. Beans behind him, getting up. The situation as it is, he looks even more ridiculous right now in the tight denims. The guy's pal is pulling on his shoulder – 'Come on, let's go' – but he's a fair solid build and he's no budging, and it's pretty obvious that the jacket cannot be his because it's way too small for him. In an instant the two men are barging out the room, pushing past the name badges, and it is over, just like that. Beans looks shook up. He is fairly shook up himself; but, through it, a small feeling of elation.

Nobody is moving, and it's Beans who is the first to speak, looking out the door through the bodies. 'Psychies,' he says, going over to the box and starting to root about, still after his socks.

On the way back to the park, carrying a new blanket and their cleaned clothes in carriers, Beans doesn't talk about what has just went on. He patters on as normal, like nothing's happened, telling him instead about the holidays he went on as a wean. Mick has the incident on his mind but. Wondering if Beans noticed his part in it even. 'Fair Fortnight, ye mind it? We'd go to Rothesay. Always there, nay discussions. One time my maw says let's go someplace different this year, maybe go see her cousins and that in Irvine, but the da he tells her we're going to Rothesay and that's that.'

Mick smiles. 'That's where we went, ye know, Rothesay.'

Beans stops in his tracks and a man on his mobile phone almost walks into him.

'Fuck off, serious?'

'We did, aye. Every Fair, mostly.'

Beans is still rooted to the pavement, amazed. Residents diverting past them. 'Mind that station the Friday morning? The platform mobbed with all these Fair Invaders packing in and the conductors playing hell with ye if ye got too close the edge – but what could ye do, eh? There was nowhere else to go!' He starts chuckling. 'Who ye go with, the parents, brothersisters?'

'No. Mean, my da died when I was wee, so it was me and my maw just. These other guys she was with sometimes, but mostly it was just us.'

They walk on in quiet for a while. If the two of them are in fact ages, then it's actually possible they would have been there at the same time. He is tempted asking him what years he used to go, but he stops himself. Something about Beans, this sense that he doesn't want pinning down and it's the better no to push him on things. Who's he to talk but? He who bloody cloys up at the barest mention of anything that might make him have to remember.

Beans is still on at it as they get back into the park. Ye mind the fiddle player on the Wemyss Bay ferry? Ye go the Punch and Judies? The pleasure boats? The tackle shop and dangle your line through the cracks in the pier? Mick is listening, but he's trying as well to figure out how they are going to make up the price of a bottle and get through the rest of the day.

'Once or twice we stayed in a caravan but most times my maw would be thumbing it through the small ads for one of they rooms that families rented out for the holidays. And see my da, he was a bevvy-merchant, right, and he was always away to the whisky booths or else he was there drinking in the room. But this landlady I mind we had, she knew what like the score was, and I don't know if it was cause it was her weans' room normally or what it was, but she starts into him this time – "Ye can't bring your drink in here, this is my house, a terrible man ye are" – and all this, and me and my maw and my wee sister are sitting there like three pounds of mince, thinking he's gonnae belt her, a pure certainty that he will. But he doesnae. He gets up just and he lets himself out the door, away to the whisky booth, and the three of us and the landlady staring at each other with nay clue what to do next.'

He is sitting on the bench, laughing, as if it's a happy memory he's just recalled.

'Amazing, eh, you going to Rothesay, no think?'

Without the money for a drink, it leaves a hole in the afternoon, so they decide what they'll do is go up the river and pay the swan a visit.

The gate has a new padlock on it. 'Bastards.' Beans strains over the palings, then is off scootling down the path. The swan is out. Or maybe she's been evicted too. The nest is still there, but the whole area has been cleaned up: the cans and the rest of the rubbish gone, and new wiring over the tunnel entrance. They sit down on the veranda and throw chuckies at the floaters, Beans starting up about the Fair again. It is all there in what he's saying – the Winter Gardens, the beach, Italian ice creams – but for some reason there is something queer about how he's telling it, as if it's no true somehow. Like he's heard all this off somebody else but he thinks it's his own memories. Or he's making it up. Maybe it's just himself but, trying to find holes in it. Maybe he doesn't want to believe it's true.

Later, they have a walk down the water. Beans tries it on, tapping passers-by for a few coins, but without much luck. They don't have any change on them; or they don't speak. Head down. Eyes to the tarmac. No a total disaster though. Eventually they come past a young pair kisscanoodling, who give him a two-pound coin.

The gloaming is come on when they return to the park. They drink the single can that they've each got, and take their positions, Mick on the ground with the blanket, Beans up on the bench. Without much superlager inside to numb him up, it is impossible to get to sleep. The cold nipping, and this unsettling feeling going through him in waves that is related he knows to the bringing up of old memories. He must doze off at some point though, because he is dreaming about a paddleboat and a boy fallen off the side when he is suddenly woken up – noise, heat, and a great blaze of fire above him that he realizes, through the flames, is Beans.

He is stumbling, flapping about, his chest and arms ablaze. Mick blunders to his knees, the fire crackling, a smell of petrol. 'Keith,' he shouts, uselessly, pushing him onto the ground and only then clocking the group of men stood on the play area. Watching; walking over. The guy from earlier, a can in his hand, laughing. Beans is thumping his hands on the grass and Mick tries to roll him, this kind of growling noise coming out of his throat, and his face damp, pieces of skin peeling off his neck. The hat – if it caught fire – and he scrabbles to pull it off him, Beans's eyes pleading, crapping it he's going to die. And Mick is thinking it too but he knows, in that instant, rocking the body on the grass, that his own fear is for himself. The men are stood over them. One of them puts an arm out and lager is pouring down, hissing on the dying flames. He is powerless, he just keeps rocking the great charred mass back and forth, burning his hands, until the fire is almost out, and he tries then to take the jacket off but it is too tight – more laughter – so he tears at it and it comes apart in pieces. One of the men suddenly puts the boot on, kicking Beans in his side. Then another of them catches Mick in the stomach and he is keeling over, bent double on the hot grass, no able to breathe.

They are away, running down the path, jumping the gate. 'Keith. Ye alright, pal?' Stupit question. He's alive but. The lips are quivering in his raw bleeding bawface; wet, red patches on his chin and cheeks. Mick pulls off the shreds of his jacket and his shirt, trying no to look at the body, then he takes off his own coat and rests it on top, lying down beside him, his hands stinging, too done in the now to move or think about getting somewhere safe.

30

Beans is sat up on the bench, quiet. He's got the coat draped over him like a blanket, but underneath it's possible to see what's left of his clothes, stuck to him in black tatterings on his chest and belly, patches of red wincing flesh, skin bubbles.

'Ye're well fired, then.'

No the right thing to say. He isn't amused. Just sat there, staring ahead. He's got his woolly hat back on, turned now a darker shade of red. Below it, one of his bug-ladders is burnt off, a few blackened stems of hair poking out from the blistered skin, and the bottom of his ear is yellow and gluey with pus, like an upturned clam.

'Want something to eat?'

Beans shrugs his shoulders just. Gives a kind of snort. Clear enough what he's meaning: who's going to get it, well? Mick stands up and goes to the bin. It hasn't been emptied yet from yesterday and it's overflowing: a magazine and an empty Lucozade bottle sticking out the top. The best he can find though is a bit of brown banana left in its skin and a few crisps in a bag. He takes them over to lay beside Beans on the bench, but he doesn't even turn his head. All the life is went out of him.

He sits again on the bench, the crisps and banana between them.

'I've seen a guy on fire before,' he says then, just to be saying something. 'A welder. Just pure unfortunate, really, cause he was doing this job that he had his mask on for and as well one of these flame-retardant suits, but see that was the problem. He starts jigging about and nobody knows what he's up to at first, they think he's dicking around, but actually a spark is got inside the suit and nobody can see that his clothes is on fire cause, like I say, the suit's flame-retardant.'

Beans isn't listening. His head is sunk down, looking at the grass. There is a scorched patch in front of where they are sitting.

'Anyway, so by the time his mate's clocked what's going on the poor guy is almost fried, and when he comes back from the hospital he's got third-degree burns and everyone's telling him he should go the courts but he says he's no gonnae because it was his own fault for no doing the neck studs up.'

'This supposed to be cheery?'

Mick turns round, relieved. 'Right, sorry.' He smiles. 'Sorry. See what I mean is it could've been worse.' Beans is looking now at the banana and crisps, not moving. His lips are swollen and bluish. 'Worse,' he says, in a quiet voice.

There is the problem of food and also, now, the problem of where to stay. They don't discuss it but it's clear enough they need to move from the park. As well, Beans is in blatant need of some medical attention. When Mick says they should go the hospital, however, he just gives a wee laugh. It's the only thing he responds to all afternoon. The rest of the time he just sits there in silence, pulling the coat around him and covering his wounds, but Mick can see well enough what like the state he is in: his face and neck hugely swollen by now, and the top of the coat soaked with whatever it is that's running out of his sores.

Later, Mick gets up and tells him he's going off to find some food. He starts down the road, looking in the bins. A few people watching him as he gets grubbing inside them but he's too hungry to care, pulling and digging at all this stuff that the residents have decided isn't fit for them any longer: magazines, a bunch of flowers, newspapers with this picture of a politician type on the front. There is food too, plenty of it. Sandwich cartons, some with just the crust left, but a couple that there's actually an entire half-piece in there. Unfuckingbelievable, really. In another bin he finds a Japanese roll left in one box and two more with these pink pickled frillies on the side. He gets it all into a pair of sandwich cartons and leaves back to the park.

He lays it all out on the bench. Beans nods his head slightly – one eye is half closed, the lid above it pink and inflamed – then he stares off again without touching the food, back into whatever it is he's thinking.

They wait it out the afternoon until the light starts to change and Mick gets them on the move. Beans doesn't argue. He doesn't do anything, just keeps cloyed up, loundering slowly behind as they go down the road. They come again to the doctor's practice. He leads Beans down a path to the back of the building. All the lights are turned off and the car park is empty, so he lays the blanket down under an archway by the back door. He sits Beans up against the wall and sets off for more food.

Strange but it's gave him something of a punt up, what's happened. Fucking terrible, of course, he's a terrible bastard to think it but it's true. He feels more of a purpose about him. It's down to himself the now. Showing Beans that he's no just some leech that can't get by on his own. He can be useful. He is being useful. After a long walk he finds a full bin round by a kebab shop. A few looks but so what? Go fuck yourselves. On the way back, it starts to rain. He gets a hurry on, clutching the warm carton of collected chips and doner meat under his jacket.

Beans has moved. The blanket is laid out still, an empty carrier beside it. The rain tearing out from a gutter, hammering onto the concrete.

He eats half the food. Watches the yellow flowers over in the bed, nodding, drooping. Puddles growing in the car park. Which gives him an idea, and he gets up to go on another bin search, eventually finding an empty Coke bottle. Nobody on the street but. When he returns to the pitch he props the bottle with a stone out in the rain.

With the damp, and no overcoat, he sleeps fitfully the night, waking frequently with the same familiar sense of alarm. The blanket bare next to him. By morning, the rain has stopped, and the bottle is filled up quite a bit, stood there in the half-light of the glistening car park. Beans is gone still. He stays there, awake, the sun coming up and the sound of traffic increasing on the road, until eventually there's no choice but to move on before anyone arrives.

He sits on top of a wall across the road, watching the entrance to the car park. The cleaner arrives. He watches the dim shadow of him through a window, slowing passing the mop. Doctors. Patients. A woman with a screaming snapper in a pram, halting and shouting at it to get shut up.

There is curtain-twitching going on behind him. He can see the movement in the corner of his eye when he turns his head to look down the road. Next thing the meat wagon will be blaring up the way, nay doubt. Well, get to fuck, then, he isn't doing anything; he's just sat there. But then what happens, it's no the polis, it's the man of the house opening the door and coming out. 'Excuse me.' The wife in the doorway behind, in her dressing gown. He's got a T-shirt on – DUBLIN MARATHON *FINISHER* – and he means business: it's his wall, get the fuck off it. 'Excuse me, can I help you?' Mick starts to laugh. The residents don't know what to make of that though, they're exchanging glances, wondering what's their next move. Aw, sod off, and he hops down from the wall, gets walking away down the pavement. That's him, then. No use waiting there any longer, so he decides to go to the river and check the veranda.

No sign of him. A hundred places he could be.

He spends the night at the doctor's. Cold, shaking. Panic sticking the boot on at every turn and keeping him from sleep.

The familiar places: the river, the park – he even starts toward the day centre one morning, but then as he's on the approach he turns about. An ache is growing inside him, taking over the whole of his body. Hunger, for one thing. Something else but. Too big. It's too big. A sense that is inseparable as well from needing a drink – a pure desperate fucking need for one. So he starts going up the coach station again. It takes him a long while to walk there, using the wee bus stop maps and getting lost all the time but so what? Kills the time. Can ye spare any change, madam? Spare any change, sir? They can't. Or some of them can, but most of them give him turned shoulders and the silent treatment. He doesn't care. He needs a drink, simple as that, and everything else – it's all a great blank space above the clouds, himself lying there on top with the hands behind the head and the blanket underneath him, slipping and floating across like he's on a magic carpet. Any change, sir? Ye don't? Nay danger, don't worry, don't worry. An auld hen, her hands tucked together, that way auld ladies do, fingering in her bag. God bless ye, madam. A man gives him his apple and he goes over to Newcastle to eat it, hid inamongst the legs and dragged suitcases as the driver appears with his cup of coffee, climbing onto the coach and getting the doors open. A few moments of noise and bustle. Singsong voices. A wee man walking past, joking with his mate. Somebody he minds him of. Who? Sure there's somebody, and then he does mind – Ken – and he smiles at the memory. A great guy. About four foot two in his work boots, and a smile like a shopping trolley pulled out the river. One of the platers at Swan Hunter. This great singing voice he had on him, always belting out something or other – 'You ain't seen nothing like the Mighty Quinn' – that was one he was always giving it, because Newcastle had this striker at the time that was banging in thirty goals a season.

The bay is thinning out now, a line of people forming outside on the coach park.

The other thing about Ken, most people never guessed until it was too late, he was a serious hardman. He'd bring in his own pieces every day, which the wife had made for him in these neat paper bags. Ham and pease pudding. Every day. He was aye particular about it. What sandwiches you brought today, Ken? And it was funny because he never knew you were kidding, he was that proud of the wife's pieces. So one day this plater's helper called Tommy Lambton thinks it'll be a great joke to take the pieces from under his work bench and hide them while he isn't looking. Come lunch break and Ken's raging. Which of you's took em, then? And suddenly he's got the whole plating squad lined up, blank-faced, because in fact nobody does know where they are, until eventually young Tommy can't hold it in any more and he starts knotting himself – they're here, Ken, and he hands the sandwiches back, fair squashed and grubby by now. That's the end of it, as far as anybody thinks. But later the lunch break Tommy is in the canteen sat down eating, yapping about the great trick he's pulled, when in steps Ken, who comes toward the table and, calm as a waiter, picks up Tommy's plate and walks off with it. Then they're all following him through the yard like he's the Pied Piper, Tommy included, quiet as a mouse now and with this black-affronted look on him, as Ken goes up to the launching berth and tips the food into the water. Then he hands the empty plate back to Tommy and leaves, all the rest of them watching this pie case slowly floating down the Tyne. One guy joking that it just goes to show how much filling they put in those bloody pies.

He laughs at the memory of it. A woman reading her magazine

in the next bay, frowning at him. Chichester, she's going to. Course she fucking is. He gets up and leaves her to it; resumes with his collecting.

There is enough for a couple of cans and a sausage roll. He goes up the river, the old spot, looking out over the power station and the tollie tug. He doesn't stay long though. Even with the drink, he can't get relaxed. Not on his own. The panicky feeling is there, the heart going, some part of him always on the alert now it's only him to keep lookout, and as well nothing to distract him, nobody in his ear giving it the problem with bird-murdering farmers and all the rest.

The park is empty. No weans, or mothers, nothing. It's a pretty dreich day but. The patch of charred grass is still there, less black than it was, but just as dead. He moves on. Down the road he nicks into a pub to go for a pish, but it's dead inside and the landlord cops onto him before he can get in the toilets. Another pub opposite but, and he slips in unnoticed. He washes his face, and nabs a toilet roll from one of the cubicles.

Further on there is a subway station, and he sits down by the cash machines without too much of a thought but that he needs to sit down, so he may as well do it here and tap some money into the bargain. Pure murder on the arse after a while though, even with the blanket and his carrier of clothes underneath him. Thickets of legs, coming in waves, up the stair from the subway. He doesn't look at them. No up at their faces. He keeps his eyes on their ankles and their shoes instead. Without the body and the face on top, the feet take on a life of their own, like it's the feet themselves that are wanting to get a hurry on, them that are annoyed at having to swerve around him. That's fine but. Fine. Feet, he can deal with.

The first afternoon, he makes 87p. The next day, the weather is better and he gets there earlier. Somebody drops him a baseball cap, which he puts on to shield his face from the sun. Another gives him a cup of tea, and when he's finished it he leaves the empty cup on the ground next to him. His earnings almost double. Chink. In it goes. Like pressing a button. He spends his nights in the usual spot behind the doctor's, awake already and away early the morning. Sandwich, superlager; easy enough, the routine, and it gathers around him like a fog, guiding him and protecting him. Inside it but, thoughts and memories appear suddenly like figures out of the mist – he tries to lose them, give them the body swerve; always the same race between the reminders and the drink.

He's slept right through and they are come to move him, the light up and a crowd of blue jackets moving through the car park, one of them picking up an empty bottle of superlager, Beans not there, these rub-ye-ups grabbing at his legs – come on, come on – a man craning down toward him, his face tight with disgust.

The buses. A much better idea. Good and bad points but, obviously. Good and bad. There is a stretch of road with four or five bars knuckled together, and he learns after a couple of tries elsewhere that this is the best place to get on, wait while they're closing and the stops are birling with drunkens trying to cram and heave through the doors. Once on, up the stair and to the front is the best spot, a bit of extra space for the legs and the pilot's view out the window. The smell of chips and vinegar. Kebabs. Listening to the songmakers away at the back. It's only when the front's been took and he has to sit further down that people start putting the mix in. A lassie on her mobile phone sat next to him with her face turned to the window, speaking in a quiet voice and no realizing or caring that he can hear what she's saying. Another time, he falls asleep right in the thick of all these posh, clammering English boys, and wakes up to them laughing, the aisle full of legs and the one sat next to him wearing his baseball cap. The rest of them in knots about it. He sees Mick awake and turns toward him, grinning, takes the cap off slowly and puts it back on Mick's head. He closes his eyes. Too tired to do anything. 'Fuck off.' But that just sets them going again.

When the bus gets further out of the city and it starts to empty, is when he can sleep. Sometimes he'll have a carrier with some cans and he'll drink them up against the seat in front until he's knocked himself out and he sits slumped against the window, eventually the lights shuddering and turning off. Then shuddering on again. The bus starting to move, back toward the city; tired-looking African and East Europe types getting on, staring silently ahead, keeping to themselves.

No uncommon that a fight will break out. He tries to keep out the way, but one night there is one that kicks off across the aisle from him, a proper frontpager. Two pale lads laughing and shouting, going at the staring matches with anybody that looks over. One of them lights up a fag, the smell of it drifting through the bus. Right in front of them, this great belly man in a rock music T-shirt and a kind of perm haircut tumbling over the back of his seat, and the two lads start pishing about, kidding on they're going to set the perm alight. Then the smoker starts blowing smoke past his ear, leaning in so close it looks like he's about to kiss him on the neck. The big guy is getting irritated, tapping the foot and muttering away in a language that's no English. The whole thing kicks off the instant one of them touches the back of his head, and he jumps up and turns around, suddenly clambering onto the seat and standing on it. The two lads totally blindsided, sat staring up at him.

'You wanna see my poothy?'

Giggling from somewhere up the front of the bus.

'You wanna see my poothy, hey?'

The lads don't know what to do; they're sat watching, rigid and seething, and then suddenly the big guy starts into a lap dance, practically in the one boy's face. 'You wanna see my poothy?' And it's more than the boy can take, leaping up and getting the hands around his neck, pushing him back over the next seat and exposing the giant belly from under the T-shirt. Men jumping in now, a young guy in front of Mick standing up but his girlfriend pulling at his arm trying to stop him. There's four or five of them holding the lad back, his mate one of them, but the boy's beeling still, desperate to get at the lapdancer, who is walking away down the aisle by now. The veins standing out on his forehead and the whole face looking like it's going to explode from the skin – eyeballs, teeth, the lot. And then it does. A couple of girls in front screaming as his nose busts, wee red missiles flying everywhere.

31

'Tell you what, I'll give you a call after I speak to Kenny . . . He's coming on straight from college, I think . . . He won't have, but I'll ask him. Okay, got to go.'

The boy puts his phone into his jeans pocket and waits. The woman in front of him is literally taking forever. He glares at her back. When finally she does take her card out he steps forward, but she's not moving, she is staying by the machine, and now she is actually putting the card back in. Unbelievable.

When the woman at last shuffles off and it is his turn, he hesitates a second by the machine, unsure how much money to get – whether or not the plan is to get some food before they go in. He takes out thirty, turning away from the tramp on the pavement, and slips it into his wallet before he moves into the crowd of people streaming toward the tube station.

It is easier in the daytime. Mostly he can sit there for hours and hours without thinking about anything, watching the feet just and then sometimes, chink, and he'll look up at them walking away, a back of the legs and a backside, disappearing down into the subway. He never drinks in front of them. Common sense, that's all. He saves the bevvying for the end of the day when he leaves, and he always spends up whatever he's got, meaning the good days usually are followed by bad ones. Sat there the morning, turning green on the pavement. The sweats. The shudders. Shivering against the wall trying no to move his eyes, and the heart torn and flapping from the paranoia that is rising up inside him that any moment one of these pairs of feet coming out the subway are going to belong to somebody he knows. A total conviction building that Robbie is on the approach. He tries to fight against it but it's hopeless, hopeless, he hasn't the strength, he just wants to sleep, to sleep, to forget and let the brain go numb but he's too fucking sober and his breath is dying each time Robbie's haircut emerges up the stairs. He closes his eyes but it's impossible to stop the sense of him coming toward where he's sat; and then he has to look up – but he's gone, lost into the crowd.

The middle of nowhere. A bus depot. Quiet streets and closed shops. A car showroom; a cemetery; a golf driving range that it is easy enough getting round the back of and into one of the alcoves. It's actually quite comfy there on the spongy green felt with the wooden roof over his head, looking out over the field with its distance markers and a tractor perched at the side.

Screw the buses. There is an office block close to the subway, a big concrete one with dark, morning make-up streaks down the side of it. It is set back from the road, and there's a large, covered doorway at the top of some steps, in front of a revolving door. The lights kept on the night, so it's no the darkest, but see maybe that's in fact a good thing, because even if he is visible, so as well is any other cunt that wants to come along and get acquainted. He huddles in against the doors and gets drinking. Big, frequent gulps, anxious to be bevvied quickly, obliterate the memory. Through in the reception there is a grand flower display, an empty desk, and on the wall beside it a black-and-white TV screen flicking between images of the building: vacant corridors; an office floor; the bare insides of a lift. Nobody anywhere. It looks like the nuclear bomb has gone off. Fucking Trident, man, crank up the engines, float her up the Clyde. But then, the queerie shot of himself, bundled in the doorway. The only survivor. He gives a wave and sees his arm moving. Just him, then. The rest of the world is finally went away. Cheers. The head swimming now. Cheers to that, well.

The cleaners come when the clock in the reception is showing just the back of six, and he has to get up and move on. They are alright about it, being fair, but it's obvious that staying put isn't an option. It is cold, that time the morning, and he is stiff and sore from the ground and the drink, so he walks around for a couple of hours to get the blood going before making his way to the subway. A giant bruise is looming all down his side. He hitches up his shirt and jacket and he can see that the whole area is raw – no a great purple job, but kind of flamed and scarlet, like a rash. Maybe it is a rash, actually. Either way but. He isn't keen on investigating.

The streetlights are still on, and the pavements almost deserted. A few unchancy types. A damp, pink jogger labouring by. He comes after a while to a high street, and there is more action: shutters ratcheting up; a delivery van reversing; the soaked front patch outside a newsagent's. He is a ghost. Nobody seeing him. He walks on down the pavement. An Asian man in a butcher's coat is opening out a board by his shop window: *Star Buy – medium fresh chicken. £2.50 kg.* He starts chuckling. Medium fresh chicken. Good luck with that one, pal. And then he sees that the guy is an exact Asian John Virgo, serious, he is, and that just makes him laugh the more. The delivery van is parked outside. The back doors are open, and two more Asian men are handling what looks like a skinned sheep, hung over the one guy's shoulder as he goes into the butcher's, dark stains all down his coat. The limbs on the animal joggling lifelessly, like a tired wean over a da's shoulders. As Mick walks on past the van, he sees the second guy stood inside it, twisting another carcass out of a pile and lobbing it toward the back doors, where it falls on the wooden boards with a wet thump.

Up the way, a charity shop is open already. A business type stood outside, fingering through a row of books on a trolley. He steps up and stands in beside him, pulling a book off the trolley and starting to give a flick through the pages. A sideways glance from your man, but so what, serious? He slots the book back in and gets reading the spines, and halfway along the row his gaze is checked.

He reaches to take the book but his hand is shaking. A noise coming up his throat but he is only dimly aware of it, the man looking at him, walking away. *Remember*, by Barbara Taylor Bradford – 'An Unforgettable Tale of Passion and Suspense'. He looks up. Through the window, a woman is bent over, rummling inside a plastic bag, and he slips the book under his jacket and moves away.

Somebody brushes against his arm and his body stiffens, the whole of him suddenly turned cold. He doesn't know where he is but there are crowds pouring down the street and he is searching through them, stupit, stupit, but he can't stop himself, desperately trying to mind her face, but he can't.

32

There is somebody coming toward him. A man. He's on the approach from the road, coming up the steps, a carrier in his hand, and Mick is started to tighten, the bevvy no taken hold yet and this cunt in front of him all too fucking real.

'Would you like a sandwich?'

He is holding one out toward him, like a bone.

'It's fine, take it. There were some left we didn't sell.'

He looks at the sandwich in the guy's hand, tightly wrapped in cling film.

'What type is it?'

He brings it to his face, inspecting the filling.

'Not sure. Prawn, I think.' He holds it out again.

'Ye have any beef?'

The man gives a wee laugh and pauses, then gets rustling about in the bag.

'No. He brings out another. 'Tuna?'

Mick shakes his head. 'I'm alright.'

He is staring at him. 'You don't want any of these sandwiches?'

'No.'

A wee lift of the eyebrows.

'Okay, then. Fair enough.' And away he goes. The Master of Sandwiches. Fuck you, pal. Who's he getting annoyed a person doesn't want to take his leftovers? He doesn't like fish sandwiches. That simple. The smell of them. One of the only things he can mind about his da, he used to eat these tins of pilchards, and the stink when they were opened, it was honking.

Sandwiches. Always fucking sandwiches. They never come and offer you a bloody bottle, do they?

*

He is sat on the blanket staring at the book, the sun gone behind the clouds. He takes his cap off and looks out at the pavement. An empty can rattling along the fence with the wind.

'Fuck me. A man of riches.'

He looks up. It is Beans. Stood over him, grinning, peering into the cup. He bends down and sits against the wall next to him. His neck and the side of his face are red and leathery, his ear a great black scab.

'Check you – in the money, eh?' He points at the cup. There is the rumble of a train underneath the ground. He is stretching himself out, sticking his legs onto the pavement. Mick closes his eyes. Tries to make sense of things. It's too much an effort but, and he opens them again, looking across. Beans has got a blue jumper on, a tear down the side of it, his head turned away toward the cash machines; a big peel of skin coming off behind his ear. A moment later and he is lumbering to his feet.

'Come on. Ye hungry?'

Mick doesn't move. The eyes fixed on him from under the dirty red hat.

'No. I'm sticking it out here.'

'Aw, right.' He stays there, dawdling, pedestrians trying to get past. 'I'll see ye, well.'

The rest the afternoon is sunny and he gets quite a few drops. He doesn't feel relieved, or angry, or anything, about Beans. As if he wasn't really there, he imagined him just.

He is real enough though. He appears again as Mick is about to get leaving, a carrier of lagers with him. Mick gets up his things and they are away up the road together to find somewhere to drink it. Simple as that. Back into the routine without so much as a word about all this time that's passed. Easier just carrying along with it. And immediately he is feeling safer. Which is stupit, obviously, seeing as all the unchancy situations he's been in it's because Beans has put him in them. He's got the beers in but. The one thing he can always be relied on for. They sit on a bench in a drab concrete square and get drinking.

'See me, I wouldnae beg. Mean, begging's fine – I've done it myself.' He is scratching at his throat. 'But thing is ye're a sitting duck. I'd rather go on the broo. And see, if ye do well then they move ye on just. They don't want you making more money than they are making, know?' He chuckles, beer bubbling between his lips. 'Plus piles as well. Fucking piles, man, it's a killer on the arse.' Mick lifts the can to his mouth. The superlager is already kicking in. Drowning it all out.

Beans approves of the office block. Good and sheltery, is his verdict. And he likes being able to see himself in the television screen too. He spends most of the evening until he collapses watching himself in it, waving, dancing, mooning. Mick sits and watches him. The guy is a pure marvel, serious. And no for the first time, he finds himself wondering: who is he? How long has he been living like this? No that you could ever get a straight answer out of him. Impossible. The truth is but, it's difficult to imagine him any other way, to imagine him as a young man, a wean. No watching him the now, anyway, blootered on the superlager, pulling bits of skin off his face.

'Where is it ye went, then?'

Beans straightens up a moment, the eyes narrowing, like he is trying to remember.

'No, see I didnae go anywhere.' He starts laughing. 'I was on my holidays. Rothesay. That's where I was.' He is falling about laughing, and that's the last either of them say about it.

They settle into a pattern. The square, the office block, and then going their ways until Beans comes to pick him up at the end of the afternoon. One night, a couple of people come up to them at the office block. Hard to tell if they're Hallelujahs, or sandwich brigade, or what they are, but Beans soon enough scares them off, great drunken guard dog that he is.

Asleep. Dreaming. The image hits him like a scud in the ribs, repeatedly, no going away. Her hair draggling wet over the tops of her breasts and the bathwater seeping into the pages of her book. Turning the pages over with damp fingers. But the picture is wrong, it doesn't fit. She is too young. She is the girl in the ship-launch photograph; before they were married. He can't stop looking at her.

33

They stop at the lights alongside a heaving pub. There are men packed in the doorways; smoking on the pavements. A row of bum cracks along a window seat.

'Champions League,' Martin says, putting the van into gear and moving on through the lights. The roads are not busy, and they make quick progress, turning onto a high street and scanning shop signs for the Superdrug. Martin is keeping fairly quiet. There is nothing awkward about it though, and she sips her coffee, eyes peeled out of the window.

When they do find the Superdrug, it is deserted. They park up outside and she looks at the sheet to check it's the right location. It is. They get out and have a scout around. The doorway is wet, clean and freezing. 'Bastards,' Martin says, and they separate to search down the street in opposite directions.

'Anything?' she says when they reconvene at the van.

'Nope.'

They set off again. Past another busy bar with steamed-up windows.

'Big match?'

Martin smiles. 'Quarter-final.'

'You should have changed your shift.'

He turns to look at her for a moment, then they both go silent as the van cuts through an empty street market, past bare stalls and tumbled stacks of cardboard boxes by the rubbish bins.

They have better luck at the next site. In the arcing entrance of a shopping centre, a young man is sat up amongst blankets and a large red sleeping bag. He recognizes them as they approach. Danny. This is the fourth contact with him, and on their previous visit he had told them that he would be happy for the team to make a referral. He seems quite bright tonight, smiling as they hunker beside him and explain that they have arranged a visit to a hostel, for him to get a look at the place and do an initial interview. He is pleased at the news. They organize a time that they will come and collect him, and he laughs. 'I've not got many plans going anywhere,' he says.

Danny, they learned on the second contact, is from Hartlepool. His mother died when he was sixteen, after which he went to live with his sister. The sister, though, had her own family and Danny moved out, feeling he was in the way, and, because he thought there was nothing for him to do in Hartlepool, he came down to London. There were a couple of people he knew that had moved down there, but after a short time of sleeping on the sofa of one friend, and not being able to find the other, he ended up without a place to stay, and has been moving from pitch to pitch for the last six months.

Buoyed by this development, they are both feeling quite cheerful as they get back into the van. They stop again on the high street so she can nip out and get them another coffee. Martin watches her through the entrance of the shop. As she turns to leave, she sees him, and he looks away while she comes back with the drinks.

Their next stop is behind a budget hotel, in a small complex of office buildings. There are a pair of men staying in the main office doorway, who they first visited a couple of weeks ago after a phone call from one of the hotel workers. That first time, the pair had been too drunk to talk with properly, but the next contacts had gone slightly better. They have come down from Glasgow, possibly together, although it has been quite difficult to build a clear picture. One of the men, Mick, keeps very quiet while the other, Keith, is obviously the one that does the talking for them both. They have no plans, and nowhere to go, that much is clear. As they come up the steps to the doorway now, the two men appear fairly sober, although they don't seem to recognize who they are. When Martin reminds them, Keith stands up and exaggeratedly shakes both their hands. He has severe burn marks on his face and neck, although he won't be drawn on how he got them. A fight, is the most he will say clearly.

The following week, when they meet the two men again, they have begun drinking, but Mick especially is becoming more comfortable with their presence. They learn as well that both men had been staying in a night shelter before they came here, but left when their belongings were stolen and there was some kind of argument with the management.

One night, they are sat in the parked van, eating doughnuts. Martin has sugar on his shirt-sleeve and on an impulse she reaches forward to brush it off, but he withdraws. A few moments later he restarts the engine, and they carry on with their round.

The police have notified them of an elderly man sleeping outside the underground station. They find him, and he is awake, but disorientated, and he backs away, shouting, as they approach from the van. He carries on shouting as they stand at a distance attempting to talk to him, and after a minute or two of this he picks up a shoe and throws it at them. They decide to leave him in peace and try again on another visit. The next time they come to the underground station, though, he has gone, and it is the last they see of him.

Danny, too, has moved off. There was no sign of him at his pitch when they came to take him to the hostel, and he does not reappear on any of the next few visits. The office call around outreach teams in neighbouring boroughs, but nobody knows anything. There is, however, some movement on Keith and Mick. After a couple more successful contacts, a referral is put in to a nearby hostel. The two men are brought over for an initial visit, and they are placed on a waiting list. Although Mick is at first reluctant to move, he seems to draw confidence from Keith, who, although unpredictable, has declared that he is very keen to move into the hostel.

One week, Mick has a bruise on the side of his face where, Keith tells them, he was kicked sitting outside the underground station. It has clearly caused him some distress, and she and Martin are growing concerned, especially given the experience of their previous accommodation, that the connection might break before their places become available. For the next couple of weeks, however, they remain where they are, and when the time does come to move them on there is not in the end too much difficulty getting them into the van, and inside the hostel.

Once there, both men become somewhat agitated, and it is not possible to complete the induction that night. It is agreed that the forms can be completed the following day, to give a clear night for the men to settle, and orientate themselves in their new surroundings.

It is a good result, and they leave the hostel relieved, walking quietly together back to the van.

34

He sits now on the edge of the bed, torpid, brainless. He was awake most of the night, listening, and has slept through the morning. Everything in the room is white: the walls and floor, the curtains, the wardrobe, even the bedside table, which is pushed now up against the door. It's like a hospital. A mental institution. He is hungry, but he's no even thinking about food the now because he isn't moving, he is not leaving this room; his eyeballs staying alert on the locked door in front of him.

At the end of the room there is another door, and through it, a small bathroom. En suite, bloody believe that? There's even towels and toiletries inside. A few times he gets up for a pish, but otherwise he stays on the bed. The room is silent. No sounds through the thick door, or the double-glazed window which looks out onto a road. Cars queuing. Shops. A sign on the second floor of the building opposite – *Mumtaz Carpets*.

Earlier the morning, somebody came for him. Renuka, she said through the door. He had missed his appointment with her. It is very important they speak before the end of the day. He presses his head into the pillow; keeps quiet. The heart careering for a long while after she's gone.

Sudden moments of clarity keep interrupting him, in which he knows what he is going to do: he's going to wait it out until dark and give Beans a knock, tell him he's for the off and going back to the pitch. But he doesn't know what room Beans is in. He doesn't know where they are either, for that matter – *Mumtaz Carpets* the only clue. And then all his energy for the escape idea will disappear immediately, the brain dreiching over again. He has the thought a couple of times, until, as if accepting defeat, he takes off his jacket and goes to sleep.

He doesn't wake until late the afternoon. The small clock on the bedside table, its wire stretched taut along the wall to the door, is the only decoration apart from a mirror and a plywood TV stand at the end of the bed. He stares a long while at the clock, then at the imaginary television. What now, well? He needs a drink, but the possibility of taking out his bits of smash and going on the hunt for an offie – it's too much of an adventure. Even in the silence, the locked door with the furniture pushed against it, he feels exposed. Defenceless. As if at any moment that door is going to open and some terrible calamity awaits him. He gets up and goes to the door hook for his jacket, puts it back on and immediately feels more at ease, a snail with his shell returned.

A chapping on the door and he opens his eyes.

'Mick.'

He hunkers down pretending to be asleep, suddenly feart she is able to see through the peephole.

'Mick, it's really important we have our meeting. Mick. We need to get your claims put in, or we won't be able to hold your place for you.'

He can see the shadows of her feet under the door. They stay there a minute or two, then she goes away.

She is back again the next morning though. From the sound of the shoe squeaks she is not alone this time, and she knocks more fiercely, her voice sterner.

'I'm going to have to unlock it if you don't respond.'

He sits up, breathing heavily. A few seconds later he can hear the key in the lock, and the door starts shifting and butting against the bedside table.

'Mick, you're going to have to stop obstructing this door.'

He gets up slowly, and pulls the table aside. The door opening, and he stands there stupidly in front of her. She is alone. Small, Asian. Annoyed.

They go through the empty corridor, and into another room on the same floor. She is his key worker, she tells him. She motions him to sit down at the desk and then she starts laying it off about his licence agreement and how he has to begin cooperating. He sits there silently trying to listen, or at least act like he's listening. When she is finished, they go out of the room for a tour of the other floors, him keeping the head lowered as they come past other people and she gets showing him inside all these doors he needs to know about: the canteen, the day room, the computer room. Through the window to the art room, a line of wonky clay pots humped on a window ledge.

She leaves him back at his room, and arranges a time for their next meeting. When she's gone, he gets warily down the staircase and through the reception, out of the hostel. On the busy road outside, he finds a minimarket and uses up what he has on a loaf of bread, a packet of ham and a four-pack.

Beans finds him the next day. He bangs on the door, calling his name; Mick squinting through the peephole at the giant, scarred bawface. He opens the door, half expecting the familiar grin – 'Breakfast?' – but instead Beans just walks straight in and sits on the bed.

'How's it going?' He is looking out the window. 'Decent view, that.'

'Okay. Yourself?'

'Fine. Fine. Only this cunt in the door next me, plays his stereo the whole time. Quiet in here but.' He looks about the room, then up at Mick. 'Been the canteen?'

'No.'

'Come on, well, let's go.'

He hesitates a moment but Beans is already out the door, summoning him away.

He stays close as they go down a floor and into the canteen. A few people milling about. Hard to tell which of them are the homeless. One or two obvious candidates but. A pale, thin girl talking to an older woman; a ramshackle beardie man in a wild assortment of clothing. They go up the glass counter and tell the guy what they're wanting. Both of them take the full works: scrambled eggs, sausage, fried tatties and beans, then they get sat at one of the small round tables, away from where the other people are clustered together.

'Who pays for this, well?'

Beans grins. 'You do, pal, so get beasted in.'

They don't talk as they eat. A murmur of quiet patter in the room. The pale girl comes past their table and looks at them, but he puts the head down, ignores her. Strange, but he feels easier with Beans. He keeps the world away, somehow. Mick looks over at him, eating and scratching away at his face and neck, something he keeps doing the whole time they are sat there. He's still got the woolly hat on, pulled down over his ears. No the less, it's visible enough that one of them is a write-off, the lobe dark and shrivelled into a wee currant.

Beans finishes his plate quickly, clattering the knife and fork down.

'How ye finding it, then?'

He shrugs. 'Okay. I've no really left the room.'

Beans nods. 'I know, I know. Seems – well, it's pretty comfy, eh? Still got to keep the edge but. Don't trust anybody.' And as he is saying it, he gets glaring past Mick's shoulder at two young men who are going up the counter.

'That's him.'

'Who?'

'The neighbour.'

The two men are laughing at something with the guy behind the counter.

'Which one?'

'Him there, that skinny one with a face like underneath a fridge-freezer.' He starts to get up. 'Come on. Ye got any money?'

'No, I've –'

'It's fine, I do, come on.'

They go down another flight to Beans's room on the ground floor. It is pretty much identical to his own. Beans goes into the bottom of the wardrobe and pulls out a couple of cans, hands one to Mick, and they sit down on the bed.

The hostel is not far from where they were. There is a large map of the borough on a wall in the reception, and he has a study of it one morning when there isn't much traffic passing through, only the woman on the desk, occupied at her computer.

He walks there the first time, getting sat in the old spot by the cash machines. Coming back that afternoon, he figures out there is a bus he can get that goes right down the road the hostel is on, and it's one of these bendy ones you can skip the fare onto. A bonus. Plus as well, thanks to the en suite bathroom, he's no boufing like he was, so his takings are on the increase.

Rare there are many people about on the corridors or in the reception. He has little difficulty keeping out the way. There are four floors, sandwiching the men and the women. Probably about fifty people in total, he calculates, but the only place he sees them usually is the canteen. A few looks but that's all. It's different here to the other places they've been. The scaffers don't all look like scaffers, for a kick-off. A lot of them are clean and normal-looking. Decent clothes. Even one black guy that goes around in a suit and tie the whole time, the hair gelled into a side-shed and his shoes polished as steel. There are groups, obviously. Wee cabals. He steers clear of them, even though there's none he's seen yet that look like they might be trouble. Quite a few of the men and the women mix together, in fact, and the atmosphere is pretty calm, orderly.

He copies Beans's idea of storing his lagers in the wardrobe. It's allowed, it says in his agreement, but the better to be careful. And nay chance he's leaving them in the fridge in the corridor kitchen, which he comes past on the way to his room, keeking inside at men from his floor, cooking, talking.

He meets with Renuka each Thursday in the small, cramped office that she shares – if the scattered papers and flyers are anything to go by – with Daniel Katongo, Complex Needs Worker. There is a shelving unit built into the whole of one wall, packed with box files labelled things like: Risk Assessments, Overdose, HEP / TB, Serious Incidents. They talk about his benefit claims, and where is his family, do they know where he is? No exactly his favourite subjects, so he usually cloys up and stares at the files or at the photos on the walls. One of a woman in a skirt suit shaking the hand of a bemused-looking old guy inside the hostel entrance; another of Renuka stood amongst a line of people in yellow T-shirts, their arms around each other's shoulders, smiling.

On their second meeting she had asked him if he's using drugs. No. He isn't. Alcohol? Sometimes, maybe – who doesn't? No like he keeps a bucket of electric soup by the bed. Does he drink in his room? He tells her he doesn't. Time to time, maybe. She's alright but, is Renuka, she doesn't put the boot on. She is helping him get a bank account and sort out his claims, arranging his interviews for housing and broo money. The first time he goes up the jobcentre is a pretty fucking dreadful experience. A cheery enough black woman with dreadlocks that deals with him but he's just too bloody shamefaced hardly to speak to her. He is leeching again. Him that once was pure sickened by the very idea of it, who watched others going down the broo office while he was too proud even to get off his bar stool, and now this. Moved from Beans to the broo. An unchancy pair, that's for sure.

Beans isn't having things so easy with his own key worker. Or, more likely, the key worker isn't. He's no comfortable sitting in they type of rooms, he tells Mick; he needs to get up and move around. Which is the first thing this guy Robin is in his ear about. Plus he hasn't been too forthcoming himself about the drink. He's told Robin he's teetotal. Robin says he isn't helping himself with this attitude, that there's services in the hostel he could start making use of – but once he's said that, Beans digs the heels in just and starts into the usual chicanery.

As well, there's been some argle-bargle with the neighbour. The skinny guy has been putting the mix in, or Beans has been putting the mix in with him, it's hard to tell from Beans's account of it. Either way, this guy, even though he's quite young, he's obvious in with the bricks and he's pretty testy about what's his plate and what's his fridge shelf and all this. Something to do with the fridge getting flooded that started it off and now the two of them are at each other's throats at the flick of a switch. He fancies he's some kind of hardman, according to Beans, even though he's no but a scrawny wee fuck, and a couple of times the neighbour's tried to hang one on him, the last of which ended with Beans sat on his head. Robin is very unpleased about it all. They've got the zero-tolerance rules to aggression here, and if he carries on like this then he's out on his arse.

A slow, heavy sadness is weighing on him. He feels lost – adrift. Now that he isn't distracted by the need to keep warm, keep safe, keep fed, it's as though a layer of something protective is went away and now he's floating in space with nothing to shield him from his thoughts. Fragments of conversations, images, keep coming at him and he is powerless to block them out. Robbie. Craig. He lies on the bed or sits on the pavement with his eyes tight shut and waits for them to pass, but then all he's left with is this great unmoving solidness inside him. The drink no helping either; making it worse. Nothing to do. There is nothing to do. Sleep, that's all there is, but even that is become totally random now: sometimes he won't get more than two minutes at a time, awake for long stretches through the night, then other days he'll hit the pillow and sleep for fifteen hours straight. He needs something to keep the mind occupied. To get him off the bed. There is the day room, which has a TV and a pool table in it, and sometimes he thinks about asking Beans if he fancies going a game, but then he'll convince himself it's a bad idea – nay doubt the skinny guy will be there and it'll turn into a bloodbath. He could go up there on his own and watch a match, a film, but the idea of it straight away makes him uneasy, the thought of the room hoaching with people, eyes, noise.

He is lying on the bed one afternoon when it occurs to him that he's got the book. The Barbara. He gets up and takes it out from the bottom of the wardrobe, then sits with it on his lap for a while, looking at it. Trying to work out if he recognizes the cover. Maybe. Hard to tell. They were all pretty similar, from what he can mind, always these good-looking women on the move in expensive dresses. He turns it over and reads the back:

> Television war correspondent Nicky Wells is a media superstar. Courageous, beautiful and renowned for her hard-hitting reports from the world's most dangerous trouble spots, her life is shattered when she loses the only man she ever truly loved – dashing English aristocrat, Charles Devereaux.

He chuckles. No Dickens, is it, hen? He flicks it open though, and gets reading the first couple of pages. By the time he puts it down to go the canteen and meet Beans, he's already a fair chunk into it.

The battle with the skinny guy shows no signs of stopping, but his own neighbours are fine. One side doesn't come out of his room much, and when he does he doesn't say a great lot. Mick passes him sometimes on the corridor, or in the kitchen if he's getting a cup of tea – quite long grey hair tied in a ponytail, and always the same green tracksuit on. They nod the head at each other, and get back into their rooms. The other side but is a different story. It's almost a month before they cross each other's path, but when they do it's immediately obvious that the guy is a yap. They are both going into their rooms when he stops in his doorway and turns to ask Mick if he's got a shelf in the fridge, before delivering pretty much his entire life story right there in the corridor as if Mick has just asked for it, which he hasn't, he's hardly said a word.

'I've been here a year, myself. I'm supposed to've got my flat but I was behind with my service charge and now they won't move me on, even though they know I'm good for it. I am. I was in the army. Infantryman, but I got injured, see.' He lifts up his jeans to show a dark scar on his ankle running all the way up to the knee. He looks at Mick; no clear if he's expecting a challenge, or for him to be impressed.

'Where were ye stationed?'

'Cyprus. But then I got injured, right, so I went and lived with my brother in Stockport. He's long distance with the lorries, so it worked out sound because I usually had the place to myself. You know those lorry parks? In Calais and wherever. Pretty much just brothels, honest to God, all these girls that work between the lorries. And the beds fold down off the sides so him and his mate are practically sleeping on top of each other. So what happens is, my brother, he's always got a cob on when he comes back from a run, he doesn't want me around, and eventually we have this big fight and he chucks me out.'

Mick stays quiet. Hard to put an age on him. He could be anywhere from twenty to forty. Behind him there is the sound of a television and a faint bogging smell coming through the open door, the walls covered in posters and magazine pages. He didn't know you were allowed to do that. Maybe you aren't.

'That's why I came down to London, because I had a friend I knew I could stay with. I knew him before I went in the army and he's always been pretty sound. His mates are an alright lot too.

There was always these parties. You wouldn't believe it, just wild, man, like the wildest parties you've ever been to. There was this roof, and you weren't supposed to go on it but everyone did, and you'd go up and there'd be the whole building out there on the lash. I remember one time somebody had got a pig – and like I'm talking a whole pig – fuck knows where they'd got it, but it takes about a dozen of us to drag it up there because it's as heavy as a car, I swear. Then once we'd done it, somebody goes, hey, let's chuck it off, so we get it to the edge and then' – he does a pushing motion with his hands – 'it hits the road and it must've exploded or something because it just sounded like this massive wet fart. And then this car pulls up in front of it, and a bloke gets out and stands there scratching his head, not a fucking clue what's going on – he thinks he's just knocked over a pig – and he never looks up but we're there on the roof absolutely fucking pissing ourselves.' Mick is started edging into his room, no sure when is the end to this story. 'What I didn't know though is that this lad, my mate, he's stealing from me. Fucking stealing, right in front of my face, honest to God. I come in one day and he's there going through my bag. Says he's looking for fags but he's lying and that's it, man, I'm fucking gone.'

The neighbour's name is Paul, he tells him before Mick's managed getting back into his room. He's okay. He's a yap but he's okay. They have the same conversation a couple of times. No too clear if Paul can mind he's told him already, or if he's honing the details just. They aye change anyway, the details. The next time he sees him, Paul is washing up a load of mugs in the kitchen, and it isn't Cyprus where he was deployed, it was Afghanistan. So what though? Even if it's made up, what does it matter? No like he's writing the guy's biography, and if he wants to keep talking about himself then that's fine, it's better than him asking questions.

A half-hour walk from the hostel, there is a park. No a scratty job either, but a big green one with ponds and boulevards and sunbathers. He takes to going up early each afternoon, to be doing something just, no just sitting in his room festering. There is a bench at the top of a large sloping lawn, in front of a rose garden, a bit out of the way. A view of the tennis courts, off to one side; and, in the distance, a group of homeless that he has to walk past on his way to the bench, who sit drinking by a plantation of young trees. East Europes, they sound like. Strange, it occurs to him as he's sat there on the bench, how there's none in the hostel.

He keeps on with the book. It's quite gripping, actually. This woman, Nicky, she meets an old photographer friend while she's reporting on the Tiananmen Square protests, and the two of them start getting increasingly friendly on each other, but she's still haunted by the death of the dashing English aristocrat. No the less, the photographer's got a farmhouse in Provence and there's the inevitable steamy lovemaking when she goes to visit. The relationship going from strength to strength, until she gets watching the news one day and she sees the dashing English aristocrat in a crowd. Not drowned, as it turns out, and so she sets off across Europe in search of him.

He finds himself sat up in the bed with the cup of tea and the plate of biscuits reading it. Sometimes it's no a tea, but there ye go, such is life. The book is a genuine doorstop and it takes him a few weeks to finish it. A strange mood that comes on him afterwards. A sense, which dogs at him and he doesn't try blocking out, of emptiness now that the book is gone.

35

A lot of the time now, he is having thoughts about the boys. Unsettling ones, which make him want to shut himself away in his room and go to sleep. The smallest thing can set them off. He'll be sat quietly drinking on the bench with nothing rattling about in the brainbox, the dull distant thwock of tennis balls over on the courts, when a toddler comes tottering toward him, falling onto her hands and lying there with the head up, silently looking at him until her maw is along to scoop her up and away. And then the thoughts will kick off. They don't know where he is. He is sat here on a bench in the sunshine and nobody knows it but himself; and a great wave of self-pity will come over him, the sense again that he is abandoned. No. No, he isn't and don't fucking try acting it any different, because if there's any abandoning went on then it's him the one that's done it. That is the fact of the matter, fucking go deal with it.

Renuka brings it up sometimes during their meetings. Does he have any feelings of blame, or guilt, toward his family? No, he tells her. And then he'll go silent while she moves on to talking about activities and employment and housing solutions.

Beans has joined the art class. Mick laughs when he tells him this, in the canteen while they're eating a watery chicken curry.

'No, see it's alright, serious. And it's good for the points too. That guy Robin is always on at me to join this or that group and get exercising the auld grey matter, so I thought, fuck it, why no?'

'What do ye do, paint?'

'Aye, paint, draw, all that. I've only been twice. Ye should come.'

The next time it's on but he gives it a bye, deciding instead to stay in his room and batter his head against the walls.

It's no until the following week, after a fair while of Beans protesting, that he steels himself and goes.

It is a bright room with a few large school tables put together into a square. He sits on one side, next to Beans. There are four others – two men and two women, who have obvious all been coming for a while, because they're giving it the patter with the teacher, Chris, an Englishman, twenty stone, white curly hair and glasses. An okay guy, it turns out. Friendly. He asks Mick his name and tells him to help himself to the tea and biscuits. As he's getting the kettle on, he looks over the room. They are all busy with paintings that they've started a previous week. The suit and tie man is here. He is humming away to the radio, each now and then quietly muttering something to himself.

Beans has got a lot of paint onto his paper. There's parts of it where he's went over a dried bit from earlier and the paint has formed into a kind of ledge. It isn't clear what he's painting exactly. The sea, maybe. A sunset.

'It's me on fire,' he says when Mick asks him.

'Aw, right. It's good, aye.'

There is nothing himself he can think of to paint, so he sits there a while, drinking his tea and observing the others. The two women stick close together, talking, occasionally a wee joke with the suit and tie man. One of them is quite a bit older than the other, and it's clear enough the young one looks up to her, leans on her. A mother and daughter? No, how could that work? Maybe but. How does any of it work? Fucked if he knows. The teacher is coming over again. He asks if he's struggling for ideas, and then he says why doesn't he try and think of something that he knows really well. Then he moves on to Beans, and Beans is looking at him intently as the guy examines his painting. It's good, he tells him. Maybe be a bit lighter with the brush though. And away he goes to the other side of the table to speak to the women.

He starts painting the *QE2*. It's quite a good likeness, actually, except for he's done the mooring line too thick and it looks a bit like there's a tail behind it. It's relaxing but, painting. Quietly getting on with it, the mumble of the radio and the suit and tie man in the background.

The next session he keeps going on the ship. Paul is there, sat with him and Beans, they two yapping away while Mick paints and listens. Both of them are agreed when he's finished it that it's a decent painting. So too are the others, at the end of the session when the big fella asks them all to show the group what they've done. Detailed, the two women say about it. The young one has done a sunflower, and the other woman has done a picture of her daughter, who from the looks of it is black, so that rules out the young one unless she's had a mix-up with the paint.

They are allowed to keep what they've done, so he takes his painting to his room and puts it up on the wall. He has spruced things up a little with his giro payments and the room now contains: a collection of mugs, a mini television that he saved up quite a time for, a mat, a kettle, and as well two more Barbaras and a potted plant on the windowsill.

Something he thinks about quite a lot these days: what would she think if she knew? He is staying in a homeless hostel and the family is disintegrated. Of all the guilts putting the boot on, it's this which is aye the worst. This feeling that goes with it, crawing at him, that it's too late. That things are too far gone the now ever to be put back.

Each while, Beans goes into one of his maunderly phases. He'll cloy up and keep to his room or stay outside all day, until the point comes when he'll disappear, for days, sometimes for weeks. His key worker tearing the hair out wanting to find out from Mick where he's went to, but he genuine has nay clue either. Usually a fair bet the skinny neighbour and his squad have something to do with it though. One night, Beans is asleep in his room and a mob of them are outside in the corridor, digging him up, banging on his door every few minutes. The next night it's the same story, and the next, until eventually Beans snaps and he charges out the room with a wine bottle. A mighty scrap in the corridor, one guy's face getting ripped, then the polis arriving and the whole pile of them away in the meat wagon to the station.

Soon afterwards, Beans does the disappearing act. No sight or sound of him for two whole weeks until one evening he's suddenly there in the canteen, cheerily queuing up for shepherd's pie. No word about where he's been. The usual performance. Everything back to normal. After they've eaten they go up the day room for a game of pool, and Beans is once again full of the usual patter.

At one point, he is bent down about to take his shot, when suddenly he straightens up and starts into a life history of Chris the art teacher.

'Know he used to be a serious artist? Ten, twenty years ago. He was selling paintings and he was a proper somebody, mean, he was known in the art world. See but he liked a wee refreshment. A bevvy-merchant. So what happens, he's been to this party, an artist party, and he's driving himself home totally out the game, and he knocks into another car, a young couple on their way back from holiday. Dead. Instantaneous. Your man gets put away for a good long stretch, and when he comes out the clink he's totally hit the scrape. Too drunk to paint, and even if he could, the art world has gave him the swerve because of what's happened. So he's going about staying on people's couches, bedsits and that. Ten years, a total wipeout. Now he doesn't paint any more, but he does this class because he used to stay here one time. And he does them in the prisons as well. A decent guy, serious. Just the bottle, man, know what I mean, it ruins ye.'

He leans down, finally, and takes his shot.

Mick stands looking at him.

'How ye find out these things?'

Beans shrugs the shoulders just. 'Don't know. I keep my ears about the place.'

Both of them keep going to the art class. Most weeks it's painting – oils, watercolours – but sometimes they do other things as well, like pottery, T-shirt printing. Renuka is pleased that he's stuck with it. It helps with his move-on. Activities, jobseeking, reduced bevvying, it all counts toward it. They last two maybe haven't been quite so successful as the activities, but such is the way of things. Renuka seems happy anyway. He's been a couple of times to this room in the hostel where they've got some kind of link with the jobcentre and they try fixing you up on these volunteer schemes, training programmes and the like. Although to be honest, fuck that. Trainee. Him employed twenty years in the shipyards and now to get working for nothing. Even these jobs that he keeps applying for, the main reason he's doing it is there's no choice: they want to see work-related activity, as they call it, if he's to get his giro.

Strange to feel that way about it, when normally work has always been the answer. And he knows as well that he does need to get doing something, to get out of the building, get out of his room; but he's just no got the will for it. Back in the day, at least he knew it was going somewhere, the money. He needed it. There was a family to support and he went into work and could aye see what he was working toward because it was bloody right there in front of him: eighty thousand tons of it, sat on the water. But why apply for all these crappity jobs that you can't get anyway because apparently you're no good enough? And then even if you did get them you've still nay chance earning your rent, so you're never going to see any of the income because all you're doing is trying to tread water with the benefit money.

It goes up and down, how busy the art class is. Some weeks it's just him, Beans and the two women, but other times there might be nine or ten turn up. Some who are pretty decent at the artmaking; others who come just to sneak a mug of sugar under the coat and leave. One or two who spend the whole time in your ear giving it the life story, or – like Beans – everybody's life story but their own; and as well the ones who sit and barely speak a word. Probably there's a lot more of the quiet types staying in the hostel, just they keep themselves hidden. The yaps are about all the time, in the canteen and the day room, or hanging about the reception biting the receptionist's ear off, but the silent ones stay in their rooms. Mostly they're only likely to come out if there's a fire alarm – which actually is about three times a day – everybody gathering outside in the car park in their bedclothes and their baries; keeping to themselves, or pattering with the firemen that stand in groups waiting for the all clear.

He is outside Renuka's office for the weekly meeting. She is running five minutes late, she tells him round the door, and he waits in the corridor until she's ready for him. When he comes in she asks if he'd like a cup of tea, as is the routine, and he gets sat silently while the kettle boils and she finishes off tidying some papers away.

'So,' she says, sitting down and looking at him across the desk. 'How are you feeling?'

'Fine. Okay.'

'Good. That's good.'

She is looking right at him, like she's testing if he's telling the truth.

'I've received a letter, Mick, that I need to show you.' She reaches for a piece of folded paper from her in-tray. 'It's been forwarded to me from the Missing People charity – and I should just say right now that whatever happens from here is entirely up to you.'

Confusion. The brainbox jumbling.

'I know this must seem quite out of the blue, but you were registered as missing in February. Obviously the charity will have been making efforts to locate you, but the letter simply asks if you would like to get in touch with them to decide on a course of action.'

His head is spinning. He steadies his mug on the desk and fastens the hands tightly around it.

'Robbie?'

'The letter doesn't say.'

'How they find me?'

'It doesn't say that either. Here, would you like to see it?'

She passes the paper across.

He takes a moment and tries to read it. They would like him to contact them. They never disclose information about people's whereabouts without the missing person's permission. Missing person. He is a missing person. Course he fucking is, what else is he: a holidaymaker?

'It's up to you, Mick. There's a number of options.' She is looking at his hands on the mug. 'You don't have to do anything, would be one. Or, I could write back to them and say that you would like to initiate contact. But if you don't want to do that, or you don't feel ready yet, we could ask them simply to let your family know that you are safe and well, without saying where you are.'

He feels sick. Renuka is smiling faintly at him. The side of her computer that he can see flicks now to a picture of a wean by a swimming pool, and it's actually funny, the absurd pointedness of it, he could in fact laugh out loud only he's feart he might boak up onto her desk. She is still smiling, and he realizes what a massive cunt she must think he is. He has abandoned his family. He has abandoned his family and now he is sat there at her desk and if he doesn't feel ready he may pass on a message to inform them he is safe and well. But if they want to know where he is then get to fuck, they can't.

They leave it at that. He is to have a think about it. He takes the letter and stands up to return to his room.

He barely sleeps that night. Or the next. He sticks the television on and keeps it quietly going in the background. The letter on the windowsill, weighted under the plant. How is it his decision? That's what he can't understand. How is he in charge of the situation, and they've no say in it? They. Is it? Is it they, or is it Robbie, or maybe is the whole of Glasgow out the now looking for him? The not knowing about any of it is what's chibbing at him. He keeps to his room, gets his own food in. Misses the next art class. The wardrobe stocked again with superlager, no that it does any good: it's lost the ability now to numb the brain. In fact it's bloody turbocharging it. February. They declared him missing in February. Which means he must have been gone a few months before they notified anybody. So what? What difference does it make how long it took or who did it or if Alan's involved, or if Robbie's had to keep coming back from Australia, or any of it, because it doesn't; what matters is what he has done, what he is going to do. The idea of making contact. Hello, it's your da, how's it going? Unthinkable. Totally unthinkable.

36

A girl is sprinting down a path through the park, her bandy legs looking like they are about to knock each other over at any moment. She passes the rose garden and begins to slow down, out of breath. A group of her friends are sitting in a circle in the middle of a wide, open area of grass, and she goes to join them.

It is hot, and she rolls up the bottom of her T-shirt, then she lies down and rests her can of Coke on her belly, the way the others are doing. For the last few days, the man on the bench has been there the whole time they have, and they've had to move further away from the rose garden. He never does anything though. He just sits there being drunk or falling asleep. They think he is probably mental. Sometimes he starts talking to himself, not loudly, like the mad woman who is always in the bus stop, but anyway you can see his mouth moving even though there isn't anybody next to him or anywhere near him.

There are quite a lot of drunk and mental people in the park. Further down the path, there is a group of Polish homeless men who lie on the grass by the little trees and get drunk. Sometimes they stand up and chase each other about, and once they came over to where her and her friends were and started shouting something in Polish, so they ran away and that's when they started sitting up by the rose garden instead. And, as well, there is a pub near the entrance on the other side of the park, where the drinkers come over the road to lie on the grass and take their shirts off to drink with their big red bellies out.

Most of the time since they broke up they come and sit and listen to music or talk or usually just lie in the sun. She is going on holiday to Spain in a couple of weeks with her family. They went last year as well, but it's not too bad, it could be worse. At least she's not going to stay in a caravan like Carolyn with her mum and brother and Shitface Anthony.

The days when it's not sunny she stays at home or sometimes Carolyn comes round and they watch TV, but usually it's hot so they go to the park. One time the hobo has a friend in a woolly hat that comes and joins him, and he is properly mental. Whenever anybody walks near them he starts shouting or laughing, but you can't understand anything he says because he is drunk too. Nisha saw him weeing into the rose garden, just standing on the grass and doing it over the little fence onto the flowers. Most days though the man that talks to himself is on his own. His face is all red and sunburnt. Even on really hot days he never takes his jacket off. If he is asleep and you get quite close when you walk past, you can see that the knees of his trousers are all muddy and his fingernails have got loads of dirt under them.

The last day before she goes on holiday is the hottest day all summer. No point going to Spain, really. When she leaves, the others are just lying on the grass passed out, and pretty much that's where they'll be when she gets back so it's not like she's missing out on anything. On her way back to help her mum pack their things, she stops and watches the tennis players for a minute, and then, because she is on her own, she takes the path to the other side of the park from where she lives, so she doesn't have to walk past the Polish men.

37

He tells Renuka to write back to Missing People. He is safe and well. He will get in touch with them when he is able. Pathetic. It makes it sound like he's been fucking kidnapped.

Beans is back heavy on the drink, and they are returned now to the old routine. Away up the park and into the superlager. A few times Beans puts the mix in with the East Europes by the trees – for some reason he's decided that's where he wants to be sitting, and what right do they lot have taking the best spot? A couple of shouting matches but Mick is able to pull him away and get over the other side of the park before they both get skelped. One night, they have been drinking all afternoon, the both of them totally away for oil, and they don't make it back to the hostel. They find a line of bushes along a path and collapse into it. The night is warm and still, and he lies there awake with the familiar warm weight of Beans pressed up against him. Safe and well. Blootered in a bush next to a madman, his head blaring with drink and sunburn, but he is safe and well, thank Christ for that.

When he is not up the park, he stays in his room with the television on, staring at it, or out the window. Thoughts about the wife, the family, hovering around him the whole time now. He doesn't try to hold them back, there's nay point, and sometimes it builds and builds until he feels like getting up and putting his fist through the window – but instead he just lies there on the bed, staring or greeting. That is another thing he's doing a lot of the now, greeting. It comes on him out of nowhere: sat absently watching a cookery programme and suddenly he's bubbling up and it will go on uncontrollably for a long while, until his face is as hard and sticky as if he's just woke up under a tree. He lets himself do it; he encourages it even, searching for how many ways he's failed her, trying and no being able to get a sense of her, and then blaming himself for that as well.

A chapping at the door. He ignores it. A few minutes later and it's there again. He tries to blank it out, but the heart is going and he knows that much more of this and his nerves will be that ripped he'll have no choice but jumping to his bloody death on the pavement below. He gets up and looks through the peephole. It is Paul. 'You alright in there, mate? Mick? Everything okay, mate?' He stays as still as he can and tries to control his breathing. After a while, Paul goes away. The sound of his door closing.

Renuka has been informed he's stopped going to the art classes and has missed his benefits interviews. She is concerned about him. His eyes and his face and the general honk of him nay doubt pointing to the drink. Is the letter still troubling him? Does he want to think about a different course of action? Aye, I think we should get the whole family down here for a visit, have a tour round the place; then wipe the slate clean, let bygones be bygones.

Paul comes in the kitchen one evening while he is waiting for a plate of food in the microwave.

'How's it going?'

'Okay, thanks.'

'Not seen you at the art class for a while.' He pulls a packet of ready-grated cheese out of the fridge. 'Fancy a knock on the pool table later?'

'Think I'll give it a bye the night, thanks.'

'No worries, no worries. If you do – just give me a knock, right.'

More and more, he is going over the time when she was ill. He tries to mind it, what like it was, what happened, how much of it he was there for. He hadn't finished working until a few months from the end – he couldn't, even after he sold the car, they couldn't afford otherwise – but he can't stop the thought of her alone in the house, in the bed, knowing she was going to die. See if they knew she wasn't going to live, why was he working? Who was he working for? The rent, bills, food, keeping things going, how could any of that have been for her? The smell of the house when he came in off a shift. Going up the stair and seeing her, alone, asleep. Or with Craig. There at the bedside with her. All the wee details, he strains to mind them. Who had called round the house; what had he cooked for her; when did it first come up, the talk of putting in a compensation claim?

As well, an image he keeps recalling. She is picking up the front door mat, taking it outside and shaking it. He recalls it over and over, screwing the eyes trying to make her turn round, see her face, but it is always the same picture: him looking from the doorway, watching her beat the mat on the gate and a cloud of white dust puffing out with each clout. He dreams about this scene and when he is awake he finds himself searching for it, until he doesn't know any more if it is actually a memory, or if he's made it up.

38

His benefits have been cut, and they are threatening to withdraw them on account of the missed interviews. As a result he has no money and he is got behind with his service charge. He keeps to his room. Reads a lot. A new Barbara he's picked up, about this successful businesswoman that owns a string of international inns. She is preparing for her daughter's wedding when she finds out she's suffering from this strange illness that nobody can diagnose, and the only way she can find out what's wrong with her is to go round the world uncovering all these secrets from her past.

All day and all night, even if he's no directly thinking about it, he has an awareness of the family out there, somewhere. Searching for him. Fine well clear enough, the message he's sent out, that he doesn't want to be near them. Pure torture, thinking about it, but that's what he's engaged in – here's my brain, my body, let them fucking stiffen each other. He isn't interested in deadening himself with the drink any more; the torture is more relieving. No that he's gave the drink the go-by but. He still gets to the offie with what little he has on his tail. It's too instinctive not to.

An anxiousness is welling inside him that he cannot leave them hanging like this; himself, hanging. To keep them thinking that he doesn't want to see them. Because he does; he does want to see them. Not all of them, obviously. But the boys – the pull of seeing them, it's undeniable, and it wrests and knots at him because no matter how strong it gets, that pull, it's never as strong as the one that is wanting to keep them away, to keep them from seeing him here.

Up until the letter he had been doing well, at least they seemed to think so, going the classes and up the broo office. He tells Renuka that he's going to start again with the activities, that he's cut out the drink. He goes to the next art class. Everybody says it is good to see him. Maybe they've been talking. Possible they know the score.

Unlikely but, seeing as he hasn't told anybody about the letter, even Beans, who has been going through his own dark patch of late. They have been doing clay objects, bowls, ash trays and that. He makes a small pot, and digs up some soil and a wee flower in the park to put in it; sticks it on the windowsill next to the other one. It dies a couple of weeks later, and he washes out the pot to use as a mug for tea and superlager.

To have something to focus on, something to do, it is good for the nerves. Paul is going to the art classes too and he takes him up on the game of pool. Mick cuffs him. No that Paul seems to mind. He's happy just being up there in the day room, it seems, talking. Amazing, all these things he says he's got up to. One story he tells him. Each fortnight when he gets his giro, he draws a twenty out the cash machine and goes straight up the supermarket. The security guards are always on his tail whenever he's there, so what he does, he tries to look as unchancy as he can, jinking in and out of the aisles, giving these shifty wee glances at the guards – then he grabs a bottle of champagne and something else expensive, a steak, or a pack of smoked salmon, and he slips them under his coat and legs it to the tills. Just as the heavy team are sweating and shouting up the aisle, he sticks them on the belt and pulls out the twenty, all calm and swaggersome, and the meatheads are left standing there just, panting and stupit. He's okay, is Paul. He's been on a script the last six months, he tells him, and he's trying to sort himself out. There is a woman that comes round quite often to visit him: his girlfriend, Monica, who he knows from when he lived up north. She's friendly too. A couple of times she comes in the day room and chats with them while they're playing pool.

Renuka and him talk about whether he feels ready to start with the move-on process. Yes. A pure certainty he is. She explains to him that he needs to get his service charge on track, and then she lays out how it works: that they get given a quota each year to put on the housing register; that it's no a very big quota; that it might take some time. Fine. Whatever it takes. He is compliant.

Posters go up around the hostel for an outing to an open-air theatre production in the park. Beans and Paul are dead set on going, so he puts his name down. A sunny day, when it arrives, and the play is in fact quite enjoyable. It's about this young Asian girl who is supposed to marry a guy she's never met, but she's fell in love instead with a white lad that works on the market. Racial differences. Arglebargling families. Eventually the pair try to escape and there's a tragic ending in a cash-and-carry car park. Pretty interesting, parts of it, although you'd think it's actually the ten of them from the hostel who are the real show, the way the residents stare at them from their blankets. Beans, at least, enjoys the attention – laughing loudly at all the jokes and getting up each while to walk a circle around the back of the audience, his hands clasped behind him, smiling and pattering away.

He meets Renuka in the computer room and she shows him how to go the internet and get looking at properties. Incredible, really, all that just there at the fingertips. She has to demonstrate a few times, the same patient way she explains everything else, writing notes on a piece of paper so he can mind for next time. They put in his bidding number and look together through the vacant flats. A few decent ones; a few genuine shitholes. She does another session with him, and he puts a couple of bids in. If he prefers, she can do all this for him, she says, but he tells her no, he's fine doing it himself. He wants to do it himself.

There's never many in the computer room. Sometimes one or two with the giant headphones on, listening to music; and usually as well the young woman from the art class, sat quietly getting on with her own things. He doesn't mind coming in here, especially now the weather is on the turn and the park is cooler and blowier getting. At least he is out of his room doing something. As well, there's the anticipation through each week of seeing if your bid's come in, followed by the inevitable finding out that you've went down again. One day he is getting up to leave, the same time as the woman is for the off, and they go out the door together. She slows down in the corridor, turning to speak to him.

'You're bidding for a council house, aren't you?'

'Aye. Ye doing the same?'

'Yes – four months.'

'Serious? Nothing?'

'Nope. Well, I went to look at one a couple of weeks ago that was just a dump. Everyone ahead of me had obviously turned it down.'

He's no heard her say this much before. Surprising how well spoken she is.

'You on the Clearing House?'

'The – mean, I don't know.'

'Well, maybe better not to be anyway.' They are come to the reception. 'Good luck with it.' She smiles, and goes toward the main entrance.

The longer goes on, the more restless getting he is. Nearly eight months is by now since they notified the charity that he'd fucked off and left them. To get on his feet just, be in a flat. Then he could face them. Face the music. Could he? See that's what he's been telling himself – that's what's been driving him through – but, if it comes to it, is he actually going to be able to look at them and no just wither in a heap at their feet? And as well, who's to say that they do want to see him? Consider that one a moment. There is a hollow feeling he gets when he starts thinking like this. Hard to stave off the drink but he's trying. A loneliness that circles about itself, because then he'll start thinking about Cathy, searching for her, this sense that she is there but out of his grasp; and it leaves him empty, longing.

He speaks to Renuka about the housing situation. The lack of a housing situation. She makes him a tea and puts her doctor's face on. The problem with the letting scheme, she says, is there's crap-all housing stock left in the borough. He can keep on as he is, and points-wise at least he's no badly stacked, but there's no guarantees anything will happen soon. Or, he can try for a private-rented tenancy. More likely he'll get something that way, but more likely as well that it'll be expensive and temporary and the landlord will be a bastard. No quite her words, but he gets the picture.

He asks her to stick him forward for it. At the same time though, he carries on with his internet bidding. The art class girl, Terri, is in the same boat and the pair of them are in there each week, talking about have you seen this house or that house. As well, Beans has got himself involved. No that they're letting him think about getting his own flat – Robin is still doing his box in at how he carries on – but he can't resist getting in the mix, telling Mick which flats he should and shouldn't go for. Amazing, but he's pretty good at working the computers. When he gets bored of looking at the properties, he turns to his own screen and starts pulling up TV shows, news, underwear models. Anybody's guess how he's learnt to do it. In other hostels maybe. Nay point asking him. Sometimes it's easier leaving off the questions and just marvelling at the guy.

His benefits have been mostly restored and he is working at paying his service charge arrears. Still applying for the jobs that he's even less of a sniff of now after the missing period, and starting on something of an economy drive: less bevvying, more of the Barbaras. He is reading one about another female reporter, in Kosovo, whose colleague gets shot and she leaves the war behind to do celebrity photo shoots. This playboy artist she meets and falls for, but everything that's happened in the past continuing to plague her at every turn.

He keeps up with the art classes, and goes a couple of times to a film club that gets run in the day room by a chuckling retired Welshman called Peter. Sometimes as well there'll be an event going on in the hostel. One day, a visit from a member of the English royalty, or the aristocracy, or Christ knows who he is, but Mick comes down to the thing for the same reason everybody else does: because there's a free lunch going. It is an old guy with gold jewellery draped off his blazer, so maybe he's the Lord Provost or something. He shakes the hands, keeps the stiff smile on his face, eats a polite amount of sandwich triangles and mini sausage rolls. The weeks continuing to go by. The outside colder and colder getting and the heating turned up to blasting so that everybody starts wandering about the place in vests and shorts. Occasionally new people being admitted, led numb and shivery through the reception.

His art collection grows to include a fruit bowl with no fruit in it, a painting of a tree and another of Ibrox, a papier-mâché swan and a T-shirt with *Bluenose* stencilled on it. He is passing time, waiting, but when one morning Renuka knocks him up with the news that a private-rented flat is become available, he feels, at the same instant as relief, a sense of foreboding; unsure suddenly if this is what he wants, if it wouldn't in fact be easier staying put where he is.

39

There's no great ceremony about it, thank Christ. No staff lined up to pat him on the back and give him advice. Nobody at the door to collect and drive him away. He packs up his things into a large hold-all he bought in a charity shop and goes down to the reception, where Renuka hands him his new set of keys. She is arranging their meeting for later the week when Beans comes loundering in with a frying pan.

'That you, well?'

'That's me.'

'Good. Great.' He shuffles about a bit, and holds up the fryer. 'Here.'

'Ye got me a frying pan?'

Beans nods.

'Cheers.' He takes it, smiling. The coating is worn off the inside rim and it's quite possible he's lifted it – the skinny neighbour, more than likely – but no the less, no the less, and he stands there looking at Beans as a lump of gratefulness and fear together lands in his stomach.

Beans is grinning. 'Off ye go, well. Flatman.'

The bus goes past another parade of shops and he tries to recognize where he is. To mind which is his stop. No yet. He keeps the eyes trained for the boarded-up pub which is where he has to get out. Nobody is noticing him. Strange, that he's thinking they might, that all of them know the score somehow, when actually they don't even see him. There's the occasional wee keek over from a teenage lad across the aisle, but he realized a while back that he's just looking at the frying pan and papier-mâché swan which are rested on his lap.

He gets off and walks round the corner past the boarded-up pub, acting it that everything is normal and okay as he approaches the building and punches the code in. There is nobody about. He gives the lift a swerve and gets walking up the stair, his feet echoing against the grey painted steps. A couple of floors up, he stops on the stairhead and looks out through a narrow cracked window at the surrounding roads and buildings. Nowhere he recognizes. All of it alien, and he carries on up to his own floor.

It is a room and kitchen type of affair. The main room with a bed against one wall and a small shiny brown settee against the other. A plastic table with two chairs in the middle. When he first came to see it, the landlord said he should feel free to change things around however he wants, and him and Renuka had a wee chuckle about it afterwards. Bed this side, mini settee the other? Or mini settee this side, bed the other – what do you reckon? There is a doorless opening into the kitchen that he goes through now: toaster, microwave and a kettle, which he fills and flicks on. He puts the swan on top of the microwave and the fryer into the empty sink cupboard, then goes to sit down in the other room, listening as the kettle starts to boil.

No tea. Obviously. Or milk. Crap. He goes for a lie down on the bed instead. Closes the eyes, a heavy tiredness now come over him. A no unfamiliar situation. Careful. Just fucking be careful, my man.

He goes out later and finds a chip shop along the main road. Brings back a fish supper. Pretty decent, it turns out.

After sitting the mini television onto the table and fiddling about with it for a bit, he manages to get it up and running, and settles in to watch it. He should have minded to get napkins from the chip shop, because he's put grease marks over the settee, and he makes a note to wipe them off later. Nothing on the tellybox. Crap just. He gets up and goes to the window, looks out again at the city. It is still light outside, and he notices there's no blind. Another thing that will need sorting. Tomorrow, he can make a list or something. In that moment, the great grey expanse of the city stretching out in front of him, it feels all of it too much, and he leans forward to rest his head against the glass. He imagines Robbie and Craig stood there in the bare room, scrutinizing it. All of it, too much.

Ye battle on but. Ye battle on.

He keeps in and about the flat over the next couple of days. Staying busy. Going the messages for bread, milk, ham, beans, washing powder, loo roll. Normal things; normal people things. Then as well the wee chores: washing the clothes, getting them hung on the radiator and the back of the settee, cooking, washing up, pinning the pillowcase over the window. The evenings, he watches the television, eats, drinks a few cans.

On the third day, Beans comes round, the loudness of the entry buzzer surprising him as he's brushing his teeth, causing him to jab himself in the gums. He's at the bottom, the voice comes through the speaker, he needs pressing in. A surprise as well, Mick considers as he waits for him to come up the building, that he has minded the number.

He comes in and looks the place over from the doorway.

'How much is it, this?'

'Hundred and fifty.'

'Fucksake. Terrible.'

He goes up to the window and fingers with the pillowcase a moment, nods his head, then turns about. 'I'd go a cuppa.'

That day, and the next, they go up and down the high street spending his resettlement grant on bits and pieces for the flat. A broom, radio, hammer, nails, wire wool, a blind, bleach. He isn't too sure about the five packs of wire wool, but Beans is adamant it's an essential – keeps the mice out – so he gives in and buys it. He's keeping interested in all this, Beans, longer than he does most things. Possible that he is wanting to prove himself, let Robin see that he's no just some useless troublemaker. Mick is in the main room, investigating for gaps in the skirting boards, when there is the sound of something heavy scraping through in the kitchen. A moment later and Beans steps out, hands on hips.

'Place needs a paint, no think?'

The painting project begins the next day. Probably it isn't allowed in his contract, but so what, screw the landlord, no like he's going to do it himself, is it? Straight away, the place starts looking brighter. The radio on and a cold draught coming through the window, he starts in the main room while Beans gets stuck into the kitchen, his eyes red and squinting with concentration, specks of paint all over his hat and onto the kitchen counter. Mick grins, finishing round the window frame, at the idea of Beans as a neighbour. Knocking him up because he's run out of loo roll, giving it his wild stories, ear-biting him down the pub. No the worst thought, being honest.

It is Beans anyway that gets him acquainted with one of his own neighbours. They are coming out the lift on their way back into the flat, and there is a woman on the stairhead with a baby in a pram and a dog tied to one of the handles. Beans goes straight up to the dog.

'How's it going, big man, eh? How's it going?' He is bent down, patting the dog on the neck. 'He a Staff?'

'Yeh.' She snatches a look into the waiting lift.

Beans is pulling the dog's cheeks back roughly, no that it seems to mind.

'I had a Staff myself, a long while, I had him. He was a great dog. Walter. Like a fucking radiator, man – oh, pardon me.' He looks into the pram. 'True but. See that's how I called him Walter. Walter water bottle.'

She gives a smile, and presses the button as the lift doors close. Beans is moved onto the baby now though, waving at him with the big cabbage hands. 'Gonnae give me a smile, pal? Gonnae, eh?' It isn't looking likely. The baby is transfixed staring at the big red beardie face, trying to work him out, wondering if something frightening has happened to Santa Claus. The doors open again and she gets moving the pram inside.

'Nice to meet you,' Mick says, and she smiles briefly before the doors slide closed.

Awake, asleep, the awareness of Robbie and Craig presses on him all the time. What he would say to them. How their faces would look if they knew where he's been, where he is the now, that he is on benefits. One moment he is saying to himself: fuck it, I'm fixing this out, but then the next moment the whole weight of everything will be holding him powerless on the bed. Even if he was being offered jobs – and each week he goes up the jobcentre it is looking the more likely that it's never going to happen – how would he earn enough to pay the rent even? He wouldn't. And that's for a craphole like this. It would take years saving up for somewhere better. Just thinking about it makes him feel tired as hell, but he makes a deal with himself only to think about it when he's outside, on the move, and no when he's alone in the flat. Plus as well there's only one radiator in the place and it's pure nipping. So, when Beans isn't about, he spends whole afternoons taking these long walks, getting familiar with the local streets and grassy areas, turning it all over in his head.

How can you attack things full pelt when it's enough already just getting through the day-by-days? The way things have been, even the most wee things feel like an achievement, like he's winning. Shaving. Going the messages. Putting a blind up. They're effort enough as it is that the idea of getting those done and then saying – right, well, that's they sorted, now let's crack on for that warehouse job I've been passed over for five times already – it saps all the energy from him.

It's one of the things Renuka talks to him about when he sees her next. He takes a bus to meet her in a cafe for a chat about how he's getting on. She tells him he is at a contemplative stage of his Cycle of Change. A good thing, apparently. Important that he acts on it. Crucial. The next stage looming all the time over him. Does he feel ready? Almost, he tells her, his stomach dropping through his arse onto the bits of lasagne on the floor by his feet. Almost.

It is afternoon and him and Beans are sat in the flat watching television. Beans hasn't spoke in a while, and he is staring now at the adverts, scratching the backs of his hands, his eyes bloodshot, unreadable.

'Ye crabbit, eh?'

Beans ignores him.

'Hey, you,' Mick grins, digging him in the leg. 'Ye crabbit or something?'

He stands up suddenly. 'This is keech, let's go the pub, eh?'

'Sure. Okay.'

The nearest pub is a walk. Beans seems to know well enough where he's headed, and they walk on past the high street, down a couple of quiet residentials.

'I'm on the bell,' Beans says when they arrive, going up to the bar while Mick gets sat at a corner table. The place is quiet. A couple of men playing pool in a small room on the far side, and four regulars on barstools who eye Beans silently as he counts the smash in his hands and asks the barman what the pool table takes.

Mick watches as he goes and puts his coin on the table, the pool players exchanging glances as he does it.

They drink quietly for a bit, Mick staring at the slumped backs of the regulars and the tattered silver Christmas decorations drooping off the gantry. After a bit, he turns toward Beans.

'Know that dog ye were talking about – Walter – when was it ye had him?'

'Jesus, cannae mind.'

Mick takes a drink.

'What was it recent, like?'

'Eh?'

'The dog, was it a long while ago or was it recent?'

'Christ, a long while.' He stretches his neck round to look behind him. 'Fucksake, they no done yet?'

One of the pool players is walking back to the room with a couple of pints.

'What happened to him?'

'Copped his whack, didn't he.'

'Sorry, I didnae mean –'

'Fine. Fine. He was old, he'd done his stretch. I was in this place anyway, I had to give him up, they wouldnae allow dogs.' He turns round again. 'See that? Fucking kidding me?' He pushes his chair back and gets marching toward the pool room, where the two men are racking up for a new game. Mick sits watching, as if through a haze, a dream, the two men standing close together with their pool cues propped on the floor, Beans shouting, he can't make out what over the Christmas pop music. This song, he minds the video, the English comedian and the blonde lassie, what was her name? A line of angled heads at the bar, and Beans bent over the pool table, scattering the balls. Kim Wilde. That's her. Whatever happened to Kim Wilde? Beans away now out the pub doors. The barstool men slowly turning to look at him instead . . . *the Christmas tree, have a happy holiday. Everyone dancing merrily* . . . no these fuckers, serious, look at them. Jesus. He stands up. Gets gone.

Beans is already off down the pavement.

'Hey, wait up. Wait up a moment.'

But he's away. On the march. A cloud of breath above his head. Mick hurries behind, calling out, all the way to the high street. A bus pulling up – Beans makes a run toward it and hops on.

For the next couple of weeks Beans is even more unpredictable with his visits. He comes round twice, briefly, without any announcement, but then over Christmas he is there almost every day. They buy a chicken. Sprouts, tatties, superlager. They fix up a proper feast for Christmas day and fall asleep blootered in front of the television.

He makes Renuka a tea while she sits at the table and looks about the room.

'It looks good in here,' she says when he comes through with the mugs.

'Better, eh? Keith has been helping me get the place fixed out.'

'Good. Actually, that's something I was hoping to ask you about. Keith's key worker wanted to know if he's been round at all. His depression has been quite bad of late, and he's been absent from the hostel a few times. How has he seemed to you?'

'Fine, fine. Normal. He's been a great help, being honest.' He decides no to tell her about the business in the pub.

'Okay, good, I'll let Robin know.' She clasps her hands around her mug. 'So, you said last time that you'd been thinking about us being in touch with Missing People. Have you given any more thought to it?'

He takes a drink of tea and rests the mug on the table.

'Ye might say that, aye.'

40

He is there early, even with the traffic. Time enough for a wee settler before he arrives. It is a big place, pretty empty the now in the quiet after lunchtime. One of these bright-lit chain affairs, low leather settees around low tables. He gets sat on one of the few normal table and chairs, near the middle of the room, facing the entrance. A couple of business types in suits are stood at the bar, drinking lagers and talking loudly. Mick takes a sip of his half. His giro isn't due until tomorrow, and he's spent almost the last of his money on new shoes and trousers. He didn't consider it. The thought then of Robbie having to buy the drinks. Alarm starting to race through him again and it's a few minutes before he can get it under control.

He continues to drink slowly. A pure battle no to neck the thing but he manages to keep nursing it, while the businessmen move onto the spirits and the bar staff have a short argument what music to put on, and so he isn't anywhere near as well on as he'd want to be when, early himself, Robbie walks in.

He hasn't seen him. He's gone straight to the bar, standing in next to the businessmen and saying something to the barmaid. Mick stays sat. He looks the other way, toward a television screen with no sound because all you can hear is the music that is playing over the speakers. He cannot move; his whole body is turned to mince. On the screen there is a wee video of footballers on a training field and the rolling news underneath – the big story from the English League One is that the Carlisle United manager is for the chop and another guy is lined up already for the hot seat. He turns around. Robbie is coming toward him. A pint in his hand, approaching the table.

'Robbie.' He tries to get standing up but he is rooted.

Robbie stands on the other side of the table, looking at him. His face – he sits down and Mick cannot look at it so he fixes his gaze on his hands instead, resting flat on the table. How steady they are, his son's hands.

'How are ye, Rob?'

He knots his own hands together around his pint, and they look like an ale jug, one of they old-fashioned type of ale jugs. A stupit thought to have the now. Stupit. Will he no speak? Is he going to sit there without speaking for the whole duration, however long that will be, the duration, perhaps a fucking lifetime? Mick glances up at him. He is greeting. No bucketfuls, but his face is tightened and the eyes are welled up, and Mick has to look away – will Rafael Nadal overcome his knee injury in time for the Australian Open? At the moment, his chances aren't looking too rosy.

'I don't know what to say to you.'

'Ye don't have to say anything, son.'

The two businessmen are away, one of them laughing and putting the arm around the other's shoulders a moment, then withdrawing it, clapping the hands together. Off blottoed back to the office for an afternoon's work. He looks at Robbie, who is watching them leave.

'I'm sorry, Rob.'

There is silence as they take a moment to consider each from their own side of the table how pathetic it sounds.

Robbie turns back toward him.

'What, were you homeless, Da?'

'If that's the word.'

'What else is the word?'

'No, well, it's that one, aye.'

'Mean, you were on the street?'

'Some of the time.'

'Jesus.' He is staring now at the table. 'Didn't you think I would've helped you?'

'I know ye would, son. I know.'

Robbie is screwing his eyes, scowling. 'We didn't know if you were alive. Most of them thought you were dead.'

He hasn't drunk any of his pint.

'I sent a letter.'

'Oh, yeh, your letter. Suddenly I get this letter and me and Alan are come to stay in fucking Heathrow for a month but nobody there knows where you are either, only that you were calling yourself Mick Provan and you got the sack.'

The barmaid is coming toward them. She is carrying a large black drinks tray which she sets down on the edge of their table, and picks up Mick's empty glass to put on it. She hovers by them for an instant, looking like she's about to say something, until she seems to clock that the atmosphere's no the best and she walks away.

'Alan was with you, then?'

Robbie shakes his head slowly. 'Fuck off, Da. He's been bloody great. Do you know it's him that was paying the rent arrears after you abandoned the house?'

He closes his eyes, or the elastic has went. His insides are turned to liquid, the bones alone holding himself on the chair, somehow. How is that? How are they holding him on the chair still? He was fixing things out. He was out the hostel and into a flat and he was fixing things out. He opens his eyes; sits upright in the seat. The thought comes to him suddenly that he is glad he hasn't shat himself.

He tries to say something but no words come.

'Do you understand what I'm saying? Craig's there telling him to –'

'Robbie,' he interrupts him, 'look, I'm sorry but, mean I don't think I can hear all this the now. I'm sorry.'

'What? What is it not a good time or something?' Robbie stands up. 'You're right.' His voice is shaking. 'You're right.'

He steps out from the table and tucks his chair back under. Then he turns, and starts to walk away.

He stays there, sitting. The bar is empty. After a few minutes the music is turned up loud, no paying customers left for the bar staff to worry about, only one old guy on his own sat staring at the sports news.

41

The rest of the afternoon is a wipeout. The door locked; television on. Renuka and Beans no calling round, or if they do he doesn't notice.

He is in and out of sleep the night, the television on in the background, an educational programme he tries to get listening to, occupy the mind – how does the criminal justice system work? – it's boring enough but it doesn't knock him out, and he lies there gazing at the spasm of blue light on the ceiling.

The next morning he is stood in the kitchen waiting for the toaster to finish when the entry buzzer goes. It is Renuka.

She comes in and sits with him at the table.

'I spoke to Robbie yesterday evening. I gather things were difficult.'

'They were.'

'It isn't going to be easy, obviously, as we said before.'

He nods.

'He's quite keen though, your son, to keep trying.'

'Ye think?'

'Well, yes – he's sat in a cafe down the road waiting for me to call him. He wanted to come straight here, but I told him I needed to speak to you first.'

She is smiling but he turns his face away from her. Out the window, it is started snowing.

'What did he say?'

'He just said that you both need to keep trying.'

He looks round at the tiny room: the unmade bed and the childlike paintings on the wall above it.

'I don't know I'm ready, Renuka.'

She is nodding. 'I know. The thing is though, if you leave it like this, things will only be more difficult the next time.'

She is right. They will. Plus as well the boy lives on the other side the world, so nay doubt he'll need to be going back anytime soon; and he is reminded again with a crawing of the stomach that he has come away from his family for this, for ten minutes in a chain bar and the da to tell him he's no wanting to see him still.

'The stupit thing is, I was that bloody terrified going there, I just needed to see him the more.'

She is nodding again. Patient as ever. Plotting where all this puts him on his Cycle of Change; or thinking he's a bastard just, who knows?

He comes in the flat with Renuka and stands in the doorway looking at him.

'Robbie. Come in. Want a cup of tea? Renuka?'

Robbie and Renuka wipe the slush off their feet and go in the main room while he takes the kettle over to the sink to fill it up. He can hear him treading through in the other room, inspecting, judging. Renuka telling him that it's his father that's fixed the place up, with the blinds, the paint job, and Robbie keeping quiet; whatever he's doing in there he's no saying anything about it.

He moves the television onto the floor and they sit down all three of them around the table. Get drinking their teas.

'So,' says Renuka, 'I can be here, or not be here – just tell me which you'd prefer.'

'No,' Robbie says, 'stay. It's fine. Yes?'

He nods.

'Look, Da, yesterday – I didn't mean to be difficult. Just there's things I don't understand.'

'Aye, course.'

'I don't know where to start.'

'No, me neither.'

Robbie is looking at the art work on the wall above the bed.

'You an alcoholic, Da?'

'No.'

Renuka is keeping quiet. It would look better, he realizes, if there weren't the empty cans of superlager on the floor by the bin.

'Just I don't understand how it's happened. If I'd known how things were, I would've stayed. Course I fucking would. Why didn't you say anything? I've felt that fucking guilty.'

'Christ, it's no your fault, Robbie, I didnae know any of this would happen. I should've answered your calls, you're right. Things got on top of me just.'

'Know you've lost the tenancy now? Alan couldn't keep paying it forever.'

He is glaring at him. Challenging him. Mick keeks down at his tea. The mug is chipped already. Pound-shop tollie, what do ye expect?

'I'm no going back, son, if that's what ye mean.'

A long period of silence. Much tea drinking. Renuka glancing from one to the other of them, weighing up when is the right time to step in.

'That's another thing I don't understand,' Robbie says finally.

He waits for him to go on, but he is gone quiet, looking at the table.

'What's that? What ye no understand?'

'That's where she is.'

He looks up, but the face isn't angry, he just looks horrendously fucking sad, which of course sticks the boot on a hundred times worse; and, together with it, he is seized with a feeling of desperate closeness to the boy, of wanting to be close to him.

'That's how I couldnae be there, Robbie.'

There is another stretch of quiet, broken again by Robbie. 'See, even if I can get understanding it, I can tell you for sure, Craig won't.'

Renuka is giving him a pitying look and it seems at that moment like she's about to put her hand on his. He withdraws it, gets it under the table.

'He knows he didn't act right, Da. Neither of you did. When I was staying with him, he said that. But then when you didn't come back, it – he – it was too much for him, I think.'

'Yous two come to blows?'

Robbie gives a wee smile. 'You might say that.'

There is obviously more but Robbie has cloyed up, gazing out the damp window.

'Either of you go another cup of tea?'

Robbie shakes his head. 'No. Thanks. I think we should call it a day for now, okay?'

'Right.'

They all stand up.

'Where ye staying?'

'I'm in a hotel in King's Cross. My flight's booked for next week. I can't leave them any longer.'

Renuka stays in the main room as he steps with Robbie to the door.

'I am glad to see you, you know,' Robbie says, and moves to put his arms about him. Mick comes forward uneasily. It is awkward and odd, being touched, and he stiffens up immediately. He can feel Robbie's chin on his shoulder. After a few seconds, they pull back, and Mick is about to say that he is sorry but he stops himself. He worries how he smells.

'I'll call round again tomorrow, okay? You should get a phone.'

He comes early the next afternoon. They sit on the tiny settee drinking coffee with the television on in the background. There is too much that needs saying to be able to say a lot, so they keep fairly quiet. He does anyway. Robbie is more conversational, if that's the word for it – more an interrogation, which it seems at times he's trying to hold himself back from but he can't; all these questions that he needs answers for. Why didn't he tell anybody he was leaving? Why did he go to London? What happened at the hotel? Why did he write the letter and then not make contact again, even when he was homeless?

If there were straight answers that he could give, then it would be easier. Why *did* he go to London? Why did he do any of it? Christ knows. He needs to be fair but, to be open, so he attempts to tell him at least some of what he's asking, even if he is light on the details.

Later on they try again going for a pint. They give a bye to the bearpit up the way, and walk a while longer in the other direction until they come to a decent-looking place next to a private gardens that is white with a covering of untouched snow. His giro is come and he's able to get the round in. Robbie of course is quick enough asking him how he's living, so he tells him. Whatever he thinks about it, he keeps it to himself. A few others in. A couple of old English boys in ties and blazers. There are things that Robbie wants to tell him: how it's been, all this time without knowing where he was. He was staying with Craig at first, he says, but then it got too much and he rented a temporary place for himself. Eventually he had to go back to Australia. His job. The family. Mick is wanting to ask him about Jenna and Damien, but he can't bring himself to. Before he returned, Robbie tells him, he went down to Newcastle, wondering if maybe that's where he'd went. Trying to dig out anybody he might have worked with; persuading landlords and bookies to let him put up these posters that the charity had printed. The rare time he did find anybody that minded him – how he had to explain the whole story to them about what had happened.

He doesn't want to hear any of this but he knows he has to let him say it. He certainly doesn't ask who it was Robbie found that used to know him. The thought of his mugshot up in a string of pub lobbies, there for every bevvy-merchant to have a gawp at – it's no exactly something he wants to get thinking about.

That evening, when they come back from the pub, he overhears Robbie in the kitchen, talking on his mobile phone. The tap is on while he washes up the plates from their curry carry-out, and Mick is through in the main room with the television on, but he can hear well enough.

'. . . he's got this flat, he's . . . Yeh, I know, I know, but I want to . . . No, it's fine . . . No, he's on benefits.'

The tap is turned off then and Robbie is saying goodbye. He turns the television up louder. Afterward, when Robbie has left, he wonders if he had meant him to hear.

The following morning, Robbie comes round with a new telephone in a cardboard box. As they get opening it, Robbie says that he's spoke to Alan. He wants to come down and see him. Mick keeps quiet and concentrates on the box as he is told this.

'Don't worry. I told him it's too soon. He can wait, but you're going to have to see him sometime, with all he's done.'

'Aye, I know,' he says, even though there's absolutely nay fucking chance in hell he's ever going to let that meeting happen. 'And Craig?'

'I've spoken to him, yes.'

'Doesn't want to see me, eh?'

'He's relieved we've found you, Da.'

'Right.'

'He is.' He puts down a handful of phone entrails. 'He's going to find it difficult that you don't want to be in Glasgow, like I said.'

They get on with taking wires and parts out of the box, arranging them on the floor, and they let the subject go quiet. One thing's for sure: these telephone manufacturers don't like making life simple. Even the phone isn't a phone yet: it's in blocks of plastic that need fitting together. Robbie gets reading through the instructions leaflet, and Mick is started on screwing the handset together, when the buzzer goes. He gets up and answers it. Beans. For a split second he considers telling him it's no a good time, but then the great cargo of guilt that he's carrying everywhere is straight away weighing upon him, and he changes his mind.

This is the first he's seen him in a while. A nervousness builds as he waits for him to come up the lift that he won't be sober, that his clothes will be clatty. He has told Robbie that there is a guy he's known, who helped him when he was on the street, but the most he's said when Robbie's asked what like he is, is that he's from Paisley and he's something of a queer ticket.

Beans is puzzled at first that there is somebody else in the flat.

'This is my son, Robbie.'

'Yer son? Oh, right. How's it going?' He puts a hand out, and Robbie shakes it. 'Keith. Ye come to stay?'

Robbie glances over at Mick, understanding then that Beans obvious isn't up to speed with the situation.

'I'm here visiting for the next couple of days. I'm stopped in a hotel in King's Cross.'

Beans is giving him a quizzical look.

'Where ye from? You an islander?'

Robbie grins. 'Naw. Govan.'

Beans doesn't look convinced. 'That's a strange accent ye've got. I'm no being rude.'

Mick stands in the kitchen doorway, observing the pair of them.

'No, don't worry, my wife tells me the same. I've been living in Australia for ten years, that's how I sound like this.'

Beans laughs. 'I knew it. I knew there was something strange about you. What's all this?' He has spotted the dismembered phone next to its box and is going toward it. 'See me, I'm good with telephones.'

He gets immediately trying to put the thing together. With no little success either. Making Robbie see him over the different coloured wires and screwdriver heads, demonstrating how it's done. Robbie is clear intrigued by the guy. Right from the kick-off there is an easiness between them, which in fact shouldn't be too surprising: he's pretty straight down the line like that, Robbie, takes people as he finds them.

The phone is fixed out in no time. Robbie gives it a call off his mobile phone to check it works. It does. He is connected. He is attainable 24/7 and nay excuses. Robbie notices then that he has a message from Jenna and he goes in the kitchen to make them a cup of tea and get reading it.

'Who's Jenna?' Beans asks when he's gone out the room.

'His wife. They've a wean too, a toddler.'

Beans goes quiet a moment, thinking.

'He come over to see your flat, then?'

'No exactly.' He may as well tell him the score. 'Turns out I've been on this missing persons list for quite a while. They were looking for me.'

Beans is nodding slowly. 'That's good. They've found ye. That's very good.'

The last two days of Robbie's stay pass quickly. The temperature is dipped to freezing but he's bought a new two-bar heater and they keep most of the time to the flat, or the pub, Beans joining them for a pint but keeping on pretty good behaviour. The last afternoon, when Beans goes off, they get wrapped up and go on a long walk, at one point passing the subway station, Mick keeping quiet as they move by. It is good, being around him; he enjoys his company, always has. Strange how you forget. No that it's perfect but.

Obviously. There's moments when he can feel Robbie is gone quiet and he knows that he's thinking about things, withdrawing from him. Fair enough but. Fair enough. Robbie doesn't bring it up but he knows that he is missing the family, and from what he can tell when he's talking to Jenna in the kitchen, she's feeling the same way.

The morning of his flight, they sit in a cafe along the high street eating ham, egg and chips. Robbie says he wants him to come over to Australia for Easter.

'I've talked to Jenna about it. It was her idea, actually.'

Mick looks up at him without speaking. Robbie's got that face on him that says he's ready for a fight if one is needed.

'That's kind of you, son. See but –'

'I'm paying for your flight.'

He shakes his head. 'It'll cost a fortune.'

'I know. Tell me about it. But you can't afford it and I'd be paying the fare to come over here anyway. And this way you'll see Jenna and Damien.'

Hard to argue with that, but he tries.

'See, I'm no long in the flat yet, is the thing. I don't know if I'm allowed.'

'I've spoken to your key worker and she says it's fine.'

He winces at Robbie using the word.

'Fucking hell. Da, I'm only talking about a couple of weeks, it's not like I'm asking you to come out and live with us.'

'No, course, I know that. Just it's a big thing, is all. I'll need to think about it.'

It is decided but, and he knows it.

The next few days he is thinking about it constantly, sitting in the flat or on one of the afternoon walks, worrying. Guilt, money, the whole caboodle. An agity excitement that breaks through but when he imagines being there. Seeing the grandwean – although of course he understands well enough that part of that is because Damien is too young to understand any of what's happened. Unlike his maw. He is nervous about the thought of seeing her, what she must think, all this time that Robbie has been gone from them because of him. If he could be employed by then, it would be easier. Obviously he couldn't afford the flight still, but maybe he wouldn't feel like such a bloody leech – he'd be able to pay for things when he's out there. It isn't looking too rosy though, the job search. It's enough of a struggle convincing them that he is a reliable, time-keeping, non-bevvied type of individual, let alone that he's qualified for anything. He goes into the office and sits waiting for his turn, never with the least expectation any more that anything will come of it.

One afternoon when he is returned from a hailstorm, there is a flashing red light on the telephone. It takes him a while retrieving the message, but when he has, it is Robbie, saying that he's wanting to speak to him so he'll call back later the evening.

When he rings again, Mick is in the middle of cooking tea. He turns the grill down and wipes the grease off his hands before going through to answer.

'Craig is coming,' Robbie says.

'Eh?'

'Craig. He's coming over here for Easter.'

There is silence on the line.

Jenna probably in behind, listening.

'Da? You hear what I said?'

'He know I'm coming?'

'He does. He needed a bit of arm-bending, but he's coming.'

. . .

'Da, it'll be fine.'

'The Highlanders as well?'

He can hear Robbie chuckling. 'No. It'll just be us.'

He goes on to explain the arrangements: where he'll be staying, the food they're going to eat, the trip down the coast they've got planned with Jenna's sister and her own baby. He doesn't take much of it in. Robbie says that he'll call again next week when he's booked the flights. He puts the phone down and goes back through the kitchen to get the grill turned off. The tops of his hash browns are burnt, but he plates them up as they are, with sausages, beans, and goes to sit down at the table and eat, as the hail starts up again outside, tapping and scratching against the window.

42

He is on the bus, the top deck, looking out for any signs of a toy shop. He'd tried down the high street but with no luck, so he decided instead to get a bus into the centre. Even now though, it's no looking likely. He gets down the stair and steps off. Wanders up a busy shopping street for a long time – clothes stores, fried-chicken shops, pharmacies, junk stalls – nothing. In the end, without any particular thought, he goes into a sports superstore.

It is a massive warehouse-type shop floor, mobbed out with swivel rails of trackie bottoms and luminous shirts. There isn't much of an order about it, and he has quite a difficulty getting through, squeezing between the huge bulging roundabouts of all this noticeably unsporty-looking clothing.

In one corner, where football and rugby boots are displayed on a wall, he finds a giant basket full of mini footballs. He rummles about through them on the off chance there's a Rangers one, but course it's all Chelsea and Tottenham and Man United, although he does eventually find a plain one, no team markings on it. Probably it isn't the best present for a toddler, but it's no bad. No bad at all. He decides he'll get it, and looks up the way, trying to plot a route through to wherever it is he has to pay. Radio station music playing loudly through giant corner speakers. A shop-assistant boy bent over, bundling up fallen heaps of shirts from the floor. Snooker cues, mounted on the wall like rifles. He snakes his way through, moving past the shop assistant. The clink of metal hangers going onto the rail – and an image comes into his head, distinct, vivid, the wife shopping. Out of nowhere. He puts a hand out to hold the rail, disorientated, needing to sit down. A buffit-step type thing by the wall, next to three cardboard cut-out snooker players with their arms folded, serious looks on their faces. He parks down on it and closes his eyes. Tries to hold on to the image. He can see it clearly. She is fingering through a line of tops, swivelling the rail around.

Her face. It is a study of concentration, looking down with a frown, a wee double chin pressing against her throat. Pulling out and discarding the tops back into the wrong place on the rail. He has started greeting. The suddenness of it. An overwhelming feeling of emptiness that he lets come over him, and he stays sat there a long time, minutes, hours maybe, fuck knows.

He opens his eyes. The cardboard snooker players stood around him and the shop assistant looking over, a grimace of confusion on his face. Probably he doesn't even know he's doing it. He gets up and wipes the eyes, gives the boy a wee smile. 'Don't worry, pal, I'm away the now.' And he gets walking off, squeezing hard on the mini football, to see if there's any tills through this bloody jungle.

It is going to be another hot day. Already there are people putting up parasols and windbreakers on the beach, arranging cool boxes and pulling down trousers. There is not much wind yet, but the light breeze that comes off the sea is welcome as he jogs along the uncrowded promenade, past hot-dog vans and ice-cream stalls whose shutters are now being opened and awnings stretched out.

Where the promenade angles toward the town, he turns away onto the beach. He wipes his forehead, looking out over the sea: small still boats moored in the harbour, gently flapping banners mounted on buoys to advertise sea trips, hotels, the amusement arcade. The pleasing crunch of pebbles under his trainers. He continues down the beach, enjoying the stillness of the early morning. Seagulls. Waves sucking back through the shingle. A circle of pensioners doing knee lifts. Further on, along the base of the high wall – above which a line of bars and clubs looks out onto the sea – there is plenty of evidence of the previous night: broken pint glasses, cigarettes, fish-and-chip wrappings, a belt. He smiles, stepping up his pace as the beach arcs round and a long stretch of coastline comes into view – the pier jutting into the ocean, and, in the distance where the beach has ended, miles and miles of rocks and landslips and high, windswept farmland.

He has a sweat on now, continuing along the base of the town wall. He approaches a part of the beach where the pebbles thin out to reveal small patches of sand. On one of these, a short way ahead of him, there is a body reclined against the wall. He begins to swerve around it, keeping the same speed, until he is almost alongside, at which point he slows, turning to look at the man. Something unnatural about the way his body is positioned. Bent double; unmoving. It is fairly common on his Sunday-morning runs to see late-night revellers passed out on the beach, but this man is clearly homeless; that much is obvious from the state of his clothes. He is wearing no shoes or socks and his feet are hugely swollen and purple, a dirty red woollen hat pulled down over his face, which is bruised and blood-shot, a pink scar running down his cheek and neck and under his coat. He stops, just for a moment, and then begins again into a jog, following the brief wet curve of sand over a stream before it turns again to pebbles, and he continues on towards the pier, where the dim drone and convulsing lights of the amusement arcade have already started up.

Acknowledgements

I would like to thank Mary Mount and Peter Straus, my editor and my agent, for making it easy, even the difficult bits. Also to Joe Pickering, Jenny Hewson, and everybody else at Penguin and RCW, all of whom I feel very fortunate to work with.

For his early advice on the book that I thought this would be, thank you to Paul Chambers, and for what it did become, to Corin Pilling at the Cardinal Hume Centre, and Simon Hughes, together with all the staff and residents at St Mungo's Mare Street.

I am grateful to Bruce Biddulph for all that you shared with me, and to John Dolan and Jim Moohan of GMB for your willingness to help with my research. Furthermore, and especially, to Jimmy Cloughley and all at Clydebank Asbestos Group, whose aid and advice continue to support so many of the victims of asbestos and their families.

To my family, and the Tiptons; to David Vann (who had the idea for the title); and, more than anybody else, to Tips. Some of this book comes, however indirectly, from you. And thank you for helping me to make it better, even down to the bloody acknowledgements.

About the author

About the book

Read on

Insights,
Interviews
& More . . .

A Conversation with Ross Raisin

© Angus Muir

Ross Raisin's first novel, *Out Backward*, was nominated for eleven awards, including the *Guardian* First Book Award, the John Llewellyn Rhys Prize, and the IMPAC, and was awarded the *Sunday Times* Young Writer of the Year Award and the Betty Trask Award. He is an occasional contributor to the *Guardian* and holds an MFA from Goldsmiths College in London, where he resides.

Describe your childhood.

As a child, you would most likely find me walking on a hill in oversized grey clothing, which may sound idyllic to some, but when you're thirteen you'd probably disagree. I think because I was always quite skinny, my parents tried to dress me in large shirts as a disguise, and they thought I didn't like bright colors, so these clothes were usually grey. I am today wearing a medium-size purple jumper.

Your name, tell us about your name.

My full name is Ross Radford Raisin, which never fails to amuse people. I hope I'm not giving a bad impression of my mum and dad here. I should just say that they are wonderful, supportive people with a sense of humor, hence the name, which I have always liked. I'm not sure where Raisin comes from, though, as I don't know much about my dad's side of the family. I know more about my mum's: they come partly from Argentina, and my great-grandmother was forced to marry her uncle, so she escaped to Turkey and had an affair with a fighter pilot.

When did you first take to writing?

I'm not sure that I have yet. I find writing difficult and slow.

What were you reading in your teens?

Horror—James Herbert, Dean R. Koontz, Stephen King, Ben Elton, and Graham Greene.

Which football team do you root for?

Root. Well, I root for Bradford City. I begin every day by looking at the club website for news (our reserves just lost to Huddersfield, our local rivals, who, even though a division above us, average much smaller crowds). You might not know much about Bradford City—they are in the bottom division of the English League—so here is a potted recent history:

1995: Mid-table in the third division, a not-so-local, fat, rasping businessman takes over the club. His name is Geoffrey. He promises us a future beyond our wildest dreams. We are a snowball rolling down ▶

the hill, he tells us. He invests money into the club, lots of money. He argues with the Huddersfield chairman in a live radio discussion. We love him.

1996: We are promoted to the second division.

1997–1999: More and more money invested in the club. We start to dream of the Premiership. We don't think much about where the money is coming from. We are a snowball rolling down the hill.

1999: We are promoted to the Premiership, captained by our star player, our hero, Stuart McCall.

2000–2001: We enjoy a magical time in the top division; we go to Manchester United (and lose 4–0); we buy expensive, celebrated, glorious players, who come from places like Italy, not because we are paying them £20,000 a week, but because they love the cold, windy, ex-industrial feel of the city.

2001: We are relegated. Our manager leaves. There are allegations that Geoffrey has been trying to pick the team. We begin to realize that the money has been borrowed, at high interest rates. Our snowball is at the bottom of the hill, thawing, unpleasant things it picked up on the way sticking out from it.

2002–2007: Geoffrey leaves, a rich man (allegedly, allegedly). We are relegated (twice), close to bankruptcy, crowds down 300 percent, the banks want their money back, we have no money or, at some points, it seems, players.

2007: In the bottom division, it is the end. But then Stuart McCall (the hero) comes back as our manager. A local businessman takes over as chairman and clears the club's debts with his own money (allegedly). There is a surge in ticket sales, we begin the season well, previously disgruntled supporters feel fresh hope and start looking at the club Web site every morning. We are a snowball rolling down the hill . . . I look forward with interest to seeing how much of this gets edited, and how much of it is libelous.

Describe the objects on your desk right now.

Let's see. To answer this I will need to go over to the desk, which I don't work at because it is an impenetrable jungle. It is too small, really, with the computer behind it balanced on a fold-out camp bed covered with a piece of cloth. There is: a Bradford City mug containing pens; three manuscripts of *God's Own Country* (the novel's title in England); tissue paper, looks used, not mine; two horse chestnuts; a booklet of new menu descriptions; a Bradford City paperweight; a cutout "win a holiday" competition page from a magazine; books; files; and,

I suspect, somewhere, the pile of CVs that my girlfriend has been this morning stamping about trying to find.

Does music play any part in your writing process?

None. I struggle unless everything around me is completely silent.

What is your favorite word in the English language?

At the moment: crop-dusting. It is a word Australian waiters use to describe when they fart at one end of the restaurant and walk the smell through to the other side.

Name your pastimes.

Pubs; theatre; playing squash; camping (I've only done it once, but I really liked it); Bradford City.

What has been your fondest experience on a train?

A lady in Anne's dad's village, who has a season ticket to London, very kindly gave us a booklet of the complimentary tickets she receives. So now, whenever we go to Yorkshire (Anne is from Yorkshire too) we go in the first-class carriage, which is brilliant, because you get as much free tea as you like, they keep filling your cup up. My least fond experience on a train was when I was coming back from holiday and a Frenchman stole all of my underpants.

What are you reading these days?

Illywhacker, by Peter Carey; *Herzog*, by Saul Bellow; *So He Takes the Dog*, by Jonathan Buckley.

Can fiction save the world?

Only if you are posh. This is Anne's answer, but I kind of agree with her.

What must you do before you die?

Write past page two of my new novel.

From the Moors to the Banks of the Clyde

Novelist Opens a New Chapter

Courtesy of the Yorkshire Post. *This article originally appeared in the* Yorkshire Post, *Wednesday July 6 2011. By Chris Bond.*

A TRENDY CAFÉ in London's colorful Soho on a sweltering summer's afternoon is perhaps an unlikely place to meet the author of *Out Backward*, a widely acclaimed debut novel set against the sparse, untamed backdrop of the North York Moors.

But the capital has been Ross Raisin's home for the past few years, during which time he has gone from being a humble waiter to one of the most lauded young novelists of recent times, winning the *Sunday Times* Young Writer of the Year award in 2009 and heralded as one of the most exciting literary talents to emerge from these shores since Martin Amis.

This week sees the release of the thirty-one-year-old's much-anticipated follow-up, *Waterline*, the moving story of an ordinary man who, stricken by grief following the death of his wife, struggles to come to terms with the hard, unrelenting edges of modern life. The story revolves around Mick Little, a former Glasgow shipbuilder, and takes the reader on a journey from the banks of the River Clyde to crowded streets of London.

"I wanted to write about the journey of a homeless man and the most clichéd shell of a homeless person I could think of was the rough-sleeping Glaswegian alcoholic, an often mocked and decried figure in TV and writing. I wanted to think about that stereotype as a real person and how he became this character," explains Raisin, a former Bradford Grammar School pupil.

"It's not really a plot-twister and part of the idea from the beginning was there would be a sense of inevitability about it which I wanted to plant in the reader's head. I was also interested in a sense of place and industry and what happens when the industry leaves it and what this does to the people who live there, because shipbuilding is a totemic industry in west Scotland and the Clyde was the biggest shipbuilding center in the world at one time."

In *Out Backward*, he wrote in Yorkshire dialect, and Raisin adopts a similar style in *Waterline*, this time using the Glaswegian vernacular. As well as spending time in Glasgow researching the city's shipbuilding heritage, he spent months studying local dictionaries and working with a voice coach to get the dialect right. "The closeness of the narrative to the main character's voice in both books meant to not use their language would have struck an odd note."

Raisin spent three years writing *Waterline*, about the same length of time it took to complete *Out Backward*. But given the success of his debut did that create added pressure? "There was a certain amount of acclaim for my first book, but even now it seems silly and a bit odd, welcome and pleasant as it has been. But I don't think I've ever taken it seriously although I did have struggles with *Waterline* and it would be untrue to say none of that was to do with pressure from the first one. I wrote *Out Backward* off my own back; nobody else wanted it or expected it, whereas with this one I'd been paid to write it so there is greater expectation."

He admits there were times that he hit a brick wall. "You can't just sit down and reel off page after perfect page; you have to ▸

From the Moors to the Banks of the Clyde *(continued)*

work at it, and what I am still learning is that a lot of the process isn't enjoyable. There is a lot of struggle and there are times when you feel insecure but that's part of it."

When it comes to writing, as any author worth their salt will tell you, there is no secret formula other than practice. "It's never a eureka moment where you suddenly think 'that's the idea' and you sit down and write the story," says Raisin. "It's usually more subtle and painful than that. It's about finding the idea for a particular novel and finding a style that suits the idea and when you've got that you have the voice of that particular novel. When I finished *Waterline* I was happy with what I had produced and I do feel it's a lot stronger than my first book; it's more relevant and complex."

Despite being feted by the publishing world and literary critics, up until a year ago Raisin still worked as a waiter at John Torode's restaurant, Smiths of Smithfield. He says he misses the camaraderie and bustle of working in a busy restaurant. "There's something about working a really busy shift and managing your tables that is very enjoyable. But also if I'd been writing nine to five and it had not gone well and I was feeling a bit low I would forget it instantly when I went to work. I miss working in a team and having a bit of a laugh."

He worked on the restaurant's top floor, which housed the fine dining area and provided the perfect opportunity to indulge in a spot of social observation. "There's a certain social awkwardness about being in a restaurant that brings people out a little bit and makes them more interesting, especially when they're drinking. It can make some people much less socially awkward or just very unpleasant sometimes, particularly if you're working with the City boys," he says.

"If you have a table of businessmen who are maybe with clients, they unthinkingly feel they have to make themselves feel bigger. Quite often they like to show they're a man of the people by having a bit of banter with the waiter and most of the time it's absolutely fine and enjoyable. But one of the worst instances I ever had was when there was a group in and they asked me where I was from and when I said 'near Bradford' one of the businessmen said something flippant about the Bradford City fire disaster which was horrible and I immediately told him he was out of order and the other men at the table didn't realize what was going on and it changed the atmosphere completely."

Although Raisin has lived in London on and off for the past thirteen years, he grew up in Silsden Moor, near Ilkley. "I used to read quite a bit; I liked horror novels, people like James Herbert, Dean Koontz, and

Stephen King started me off and then I got into Thomas Hardy and Graham Greene. One of my favorite books is *The Return of the Native*; the moor in the book is very dark; there's nothing wishy-washy about it and it has a presence throughout the novel, which I liked."

Despite this interest in books there was no burning desire to be a novelist from an early age. "I never had that thought 'I want to be a writer' and I still don't think I have. I've wanted to write a particular book and then wanted to write another one." After finishing university and deciding he wanted to write a book he enrolled on a creative writing course at Goldsmith's College.

With *Out Backward*, his first attempt at a full-blown novel, he hit the ground running, securing a lucrative two-book deal and bypassing the usual pile of rejection letters that often greet even the most gifted fledgling novelists.

Although he's not lived in Yorkshire since he was eighteen, he still has a fondness for the place. "My wife's from Northallerton and even though we don't have plans to move back at the moment, I'd see us going back there at some point; I certainly hope so."

Despite all the critical acclaim, Raisin is wary of the pitfalls of believing your own hype. "I think it's better to do things step by step than have this big, pressurizing career in front of you where you have to write X number of books and each one has to be brilliant and better than the last."

In fact, he doesn't even like to call himself a writer. "I still feel reticent to call myself that because it feels a bit naff. I think a lot of writers, not all, use it to try and sound impressive and I don't feel that. Maybe there's a certain part of me that thinks if you talk about it too much then you might chase it away. I can't really do it now, but in the past I would usually say I'm a waiter when people asked what I did, because it was true."

He's recently started writing short stories and is enjoying the challenge of doing something a little different, not that he takes it for granted.

"There's always that nagging feeling that you won't be able to do it again. I never sit down and think 'yes, I've nailed it, I know exactly what I'm doing.' I always have to work for it and when I finish a book there's no sense of tub-thumping euphoria, it's more a sigh of relief."

Have You Read?
More by Ross Raisin

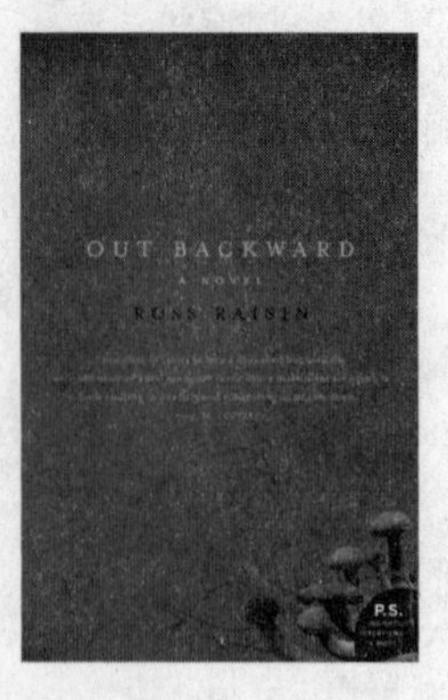

OUT BACKWARD

Sam Marsdyke is a lonely young man, dogged by an incident in his past and forced to work his family farm instead of attending school in his Yorkshire village. He methodically fills his life with daily routines and adheres to strict boundaries that keep him at a remove from the townspeople. But one day he spies Josephine, his new neighbor from London. From that moment on, Sam's carefully constructed protections begin to crumble—and what starts off as a harmless friendship between an isolated loner and a defiant teenage girl takes a most disturbing turn.

"Ross Raisin's story of how a disturbed but basically well-intentioned rural youngster turns into a malevolent sociopath is both chilling in its effect and convincing in its execution." —J. M. Coetzee

"The lush language in this debut novel has some fine literary ears (Colm Toibin, Stewart O'Nan, Mary Karr) in awe. . . . Your heart goes out to Sam, creature of the moors. There's an ancient Celtic strain in Raisin's writing, all but unspoken: the idea that monsters are the embodiments of our darkest selves, pushed to the edges of normal life, straining on the outskirts."
—Susan Salter Reynolds, *Los Angeles Times*

"*Out Backward* more [than *A Clockwork Orange*] convincingly registers the internal logic of unredeemable delinquency, a dangerous subjectivity that perverts compassion and sees everything as an extension of itself."

—*Washington Post Book World*

"Undeniably he's made a new world. . . . Utterly frightening and electrifying."

—Joshua Ferris, author of *The Unnamed* and *Then We Came to the End*